University Libraries and Scholarly Communication

A Study Prepared for
The Andrew W. Mellon Foundation

by
Anthony M. Cummings, Marcia L. Witte,
William G. Bowen, Laura O. Lazarus,
and Richard H. Ekman

Published by The Association of Research Libraries
for The Andrew W. Mellon Foundation

November 1992

Library of Congress Cataloging-in-Publication Data

University libraries and scholarly communication: study prepared for
the Andrew W. Mellon Foundation / by Anthony M. Cummings ... [et al.]
p. cm.
"November 1992."
Includes bibliographical references.
ISBN 0-918006-22-8
1. Academic libraries—Collection development—United States.
2. Scholarly publishing—United States. I. Cummings, Anthony M.
II. Andrew W. Mellon Foundation.
Z675.U5U5477 1992
025.2'1877'0973—dc20   92-44941
                                              CIP

∞ The paper used in this publication meets the minimum requirements of the American
National Standard for Information Sciences—Permanence of Paper for Printed Library Materials,
ANSI Z39.48-1984

Contents

iii

List of Figures and Tables

TABLES

APPENDIX TABLES

Foreword

This report has had an extended and complex history. Its origins date to the spring of 1989, when Neil Rudenstine, then executive vice president of The Andrew W. Mellon Foundation and now president of Harvard University, and I decided that the Foundation should undertake a study of the economics of research libraries. Both of us had long been interested in research libraries, initially as users and then as university administrators. We were convinced not only of the great importance of these institutions but also that, in certain respects at least, they were at risk of becoming an endangered species. Rapidly rising costs of both library materials and space were one evident source of pressure; the proliferation of journals and other library materials was a second pressure point; and it was also far from clear how these libraries were to be affected by, and were to respond to, the rapidly developing electronic technologies.

Support of research libraries has been one of the continuing interests of The Andrew W. Mellon Foundation,[1] and so our personal interests were merged with a strong institutional interest. The trustees and staff of the Foundation have been committed to continuing to support the evolution of research libraries, but, in company with almost everyone else, have been unsure how best to address what are clearly systemic questions. There was a pressing need, in our view, for a careful analysis of trends in such key variables as the volume of acquisitions, the worldwide pool of publications from which acquisitions were made, prices of monographs and journals, and library expenditures—seen both in absolute terms and as a percentage of overall university expenditures. We were also interested in knowing more about trends in the composition of library expenditures and, even more particularly, about experience with automation and its costs.

Thus, a principal objective of this research has been to describe the library landscape as it appears today, in its collecting, operating, financial, and electronic dimensions. The picture that emerges is by no means definitive, but we believe that it does provide a basis for exploring new directions in a more thoughtful way than we could have done otherwise. In company with other research projects that have been conducted by the staff of the Foundation,[2] this study was intended to inform our subsequent activities, including grant making. We are making the report generally available in the hope that it will be of interest to others concerned with these same issues—not only librarians, who will already be familiar with much of the material presented here, but also college and university administrators, publish-

---

[1]My predecessor as president of the Foundation, John E. Sawyer, played a major role in stimulating support from many foundations for the work of the Research Libraries Group. More generally, he played a leadership role in thinking about the future of libraries and especially of ways in which more collaboration might be possible. It is significant—and fitting—that the library at Williams College, where Mr. Sawyer served with distinction as president, is named in his honor.

[2]In particular, studies of the outlook for employment of faculty (William G. Bowen and Julie Ann Sosa, *Prospects for Faculty in the Arts and Sciences*, Princeton, N.J.: Princeton University Press, 1989) and of the effectiveness of doctoral education (William G. Bowen and Neil L. Rudenstine, *In Pursuit of the Ph.D.*, Princeton, N.J.: Princeton University Press, 1992).

ers, scholars, and all others involved in the process of creating and using scholarly materials.

As is explained in Chapter 1 (the Introduction), much more work could have been done—and, we hope, will be done by others interested in pursuing in more detail questions that we have only highlighted. We do not anticipate, however, that the general findings reported here will contain a great many surprises, especially to members of the library profession. Rather, the report will be more useful, we believe, to other members of the scholarly community, all of whom have a major stake in the future of the research library.

This has been a truly collaborative effort, a "many hands" project. That characteristic has been a source of strength, thanks to the presence of a number of complementary perspectives, but it has also been, we have to say, a source of complications. Participants in the study have come and gone, and the project now faces a new reality in that the person who has worked longest and hardest on the study, Anthony M. Cummings, and his chief collaborator, Marcia L. Witte, have both left the Foundation this summer to pursue other interests. They have made heroic efforts to complete their analysis before leaving, and, recognizing that a project of this kind is never really finished in any case, we have concluded that it is better to release the document as it stands now rather than to seek to add to it.

The fact that the entire field of scholarly communication is, we believe, about to undergo even more profound changes than those that it has experienced in recent years—with implications that are far from fully understood—reinforces our sense that we should make the report in its present form available without further delay. The timeliness of the subject, the rapidity of new developments (especially in the area of technology), and the tendency for commentaries to become dated so quickly all combine to encourage prompt publication.

This Foundation intends to continue to pursue aggressively a number of the issues raised in the report but not resolved. Specifically, we are examining the possibility of evaluating systematically some of the "natural experiments" in new modes of electronic publication and dissemination now going on, and we might simultaneously encourage the development of some carefully structured experiments designed to address some of the open questions of quality, means of access to materials, convenience, and costs.

One of our concerns is that fascination with technology per se may interfere with or detract from attention to the quality of content—to the value of what is "published" or otherwise made available. Also, it is far from clear how different kinds of libraries, different categories of scholars, and different groups of potential authors may be affected by prospective developments. While it is relatively easy to speculate about future developments, it is much harder to know what their effects will be on readers and users, authors, publishing entities, libraries themselves, and other institutional participants in the process of scholarly communication. At issue are not only substantive questions of the quality and quantity of scholarship and of access to it, but also mundane but vitally important ancillary issues such as pricing, costs, and financial returns. The Foundation will continue to seek ways to stimulate thoughtful explorations of these fascinating—and complex—issues.

THE BROADER ROLE OF THE LIBRARY

Before identifying the participants in this study more fully and thanking others who have helped with this research, I wish to add a more personal comment concerning the broader role of libraries. I want to recall aspects of libraries that transcend, for me at least, information processing. There is a danger that current and prospective developments will exalt the technocratic and the impersonal over subtle characteristics and qualities that need to be preserved if libraries are to continue to serve their full educational function. At their best, libraries are warm and welcoming places that speak to some of the most fundamental values of the academy and of the society at large.

It has been said often that all of us are autobiographical when it comes to education, and I would not deny the proposition as it relates to my own experiences with libraries. I have a stronger recollection of days (and nights) spent in Doane Library at Denison University than of any other aspect of my undergraduate education. To this day I remember vividly the arrangement of the stacks, the location of the most comfortable working spaces, the faces and names of librarians, and the inscription that I passed each time I entered the building:

> Books are the treasured wealth of the world
> The fit inheritance of generations and nations.
>   —Thoreau

Then, at Princeton, my life as a graduate student and as a faculty member revolved around Firestone Library. My carrel is still "my" carrel, and I was fortunate to have my first faculty office right in the library. The department reading room, seminar room, and lounge on A Floor of Firestone Library were the locations of many of my most educational experiences. And the privilege of browsing through the stacks, finding books that had been checked out by faculty members such as Jacob Viner, was just that—a privilege.

Why do great libraries have such a hold on so many of us? In part, I think, because of their ambience, the sense they give of the power of ideas and the luxury of being stimulated and encouraged to think for one's self. Libraries are humbling places, because they remind us of the vast store of knowledge which we can approach but never really control. They are humanizing places, because we are brought into contact with so many lives lived in the past as well as in the present. They are symbols of the continuity of learning. They stand for such basic principles as freedom of expression, the need to recognize and respect a diversity of views, and the obligation finally to come to one's own conclusions—and then to be held accountable for what one has written.

I do not believe that new technologies will, should, need to, or can supplant the pleasures of holding a book in one's hand and turning its pages. Somehow, someway, we have to take fullest advantage of the power of high-speed processing and communication without losing sight of the larger purposes of the enterprise. It is true that the library is under significant pressure not only to change but also to accelerate its rate of change. It is no less true that the processes of change must respect all the functions and attributes of the library if it is remain a vital center of learning in the broadest sense.

The Participants in The Study

When we first began this study, we were fortunate to obtain the part-time services of an exceedingly able person, Laura O. Lazarus, who devoted countless hours to assembling the raw data from the invaluable historical files maintained by the Association of Research Libraries. In addition to entering the data for our four library composites[3] on spreadsheets, Ms. Lazarus did a considerable amount of statistical analysis, including estimating trends by means of least-square regressions. In short, she did most of the spade work for what became Part 1 of this study.

In the summer of 1990, the project acquired a new leader. Anthony M. Cummings, a musicologist who has just become dean of the College of Arts and Sciences at Tulane University, returned from a sabbatical at Villa I Tatti in Florence and agreed to take primary responsibility for completing this study. While Mr. Cummings has worked hard on all aspects of the project, he played a particularly critical role in drafting all of Part 2, which is concerned with the implications of the new electronic technologies for research libraries.

Marcia L. Witte, a research associate in the Foundation's New York office, has also been a critically important participant in this project. After working on the library project sporadically (while doing a number of other things), she worked essentially full-time on it for the six months following January 1992. Ms. Witte has reworked all the figures and tables in Part 1, which is concerned with historical trends in acquisitions, expenditures, publications, and the prices of publications, and she and I have collaborated on the text of these chapters.

The last of our principal collaborators, Richard H. Ekman, has reviewed the entire manuscript, made any number of revisions and additions (especially in Part 2), and seen the final report through to publication. Mr. Ekman, as secretary and a senior program officer of the Foundation, is also responsible for leading the further efforts in this field that the Foundation is now developing.

The Foundation's vice president, Harriet Zuckerman, also made valuable editorial contributions, especially to Part 2 of the study.

This brief summary of the roles played by a shifting constellation of staff members is intended to document the collaborative nature of this study and to assign some measure of credit—and responsibility. The Foundation is indebted to all these individuals for their hard work on this project.

Acknowledgments

A very large number of people and organizations gave generously of their time and advice in the course of our work on this project. Some are identified in the pages that follow. A few should be given special mention here. The Association of Research Libraries, and particularly Duane Webster, Ann Okerson, and Jaia Barrett, assisted us at many stages. We are indebted to Ann Okerson especially for her helpful synopsis of the report, which has been enhanced by her own extensive knowledge of this field. A near-final draft of this document benefited from readings by Richard De Gennaro and Jerry Green of Harvard University, Kendon Stubbs of

---

[3]These are sets of libraries with similar characteristics. See Chapter 1 for a full discussion of these composites and of the underlying data.

the University of Virginia, and David Penniman of the Council on Library Resources. Patricia Battin of the Commission on Preservation and Access, James Coleman and John Haeger of the Research Libraries Group, Donald Koepp and Ira Fuchs of Princeton University, Scott Bennett of Johns Hopkins University, and William Y. Arms of Carnegie Mellon University were also helpful to us at critical times in the life of the project. Our colleagues at The Andrew W. Mellon Foundation were patient and supportive while we were in the throes of this study, and Alvin Kernan, the Foundation's senior advisor in the humanities, gave us fresh perspective at important junctures. There are literally hundreds of other individuals with whom each of us had instructive conversations along the way, and we apologize to each of them for not including specific expressions of our gratitude here. The views expressed in the following pages are solely those of the authors, and we take full responsibility for any errors of fact or interpretation.

William G. Bowen
November 1992

Synopsis

Libraries are and will remain central to the management of scholarly communication for the foreseeable future. Out of concern for the well being of institutions vital to scholarship and science, The Andrew W. Mellon Foundation set out to address two main issues in this study.

- The explosion in the quantity of desirable published material and a rapid escalation of unit prices for those items *jeopardizes the traditional research library mission* of creating and maintaining large self-sufficient collections for their users. Issues of pricing, acquisition, and collection are the focus of the study's sustained statistical analysis, which brings together kinds of information not often, sometimes not ever, gathered in one place before.

- The rapid emergence and development of electronic information technologies make it possible to *envision radically different ways of organizing collections and services* the library has traditionally provided. Insofar as the finances of collection development approach a crisis, the new technologies offer possible mitigation and perhaps a revolution in ways of knowing.

This study is distinctive in taking the long view. Moreover, its purpose is not to project the near future, but to propose and consider the issues raised by a better understanding of the past and present. It relates current concerns to the fundamental principles of scholarly communication and to the role of the research library in facilitating that communication.

We have lived for many generations with a world in which the technology of publication meant that access *required* ownership, in other words, that scholarly information was usable only if it were gathered in a large, site-specific, self-sufficient collection. The pressures libraries now feel have already driven them to various forms of resource-sharing, notably interlibrary loan, that begin to provide alternative models. New electronic technologies allow the possibility of uncoupling ownership from access, the material object from its intellectual content. This possibility is revolutionary, perhaps dramatically so.

As one reads this report, some related concerns remain open: Is access to scholarly information narrowing as libraries respond less comprehensively to general trends in book production (that is, as they purchase less printed output)? Does contraction in acquisitions expectations mean that libraries sacrifice some of their individual aims in favor of pursuing goals that they share with other libraries? Is distinctiveness lost, and worse, overall richness of collections nationally, as libraries are chastened to more modest collecting ambitions? Can we say with confidence what rate of acquisition is optimal? In any event, might the greater restraint of the larger institutions in the 1970s have reflected a sense that they could afford the contraction without damage to their mission, while the smaller institutions may have felt they simply had no alternative but to keep up their buying levels? What is the viability of the traditional model of the library as a single-site comprehensive collection of printed materials?

METHODOLOGY

The study concentrates on research libraries. It uses as its database the experience of twenty-four major United States research libraries, chosen for their range of size and mission and for the availability of high-quality information over a substantial period of years. The Association of Research Libraries' (ARL) database of library statistics is the main source, from which this study selects 24 libraries for closer examination. In some cases, data are reported for all 24 or for the twelve grouped below as Private 1 and Public 1 (especially for the period before 1963, when data tend to be thinner), but in most they are described under four sub-groupings based on institutional character (public/private) on the one hand and size and age on the other. The groupings are: Private 1—larger private institutions (Chicago, Columbia, Cornell, Princeton, Stanford, Yale); Public 1—larger public institutions (Berkeley, Iowa, Michigan, North Carolina, Virginia, Wisconsin); Private 2—smaller private institutions (Boston U., Georgetown, NYU, Northwestern, USC, and Washington U. in St. Louis); and Public 2—smaller public institutions (Florida, Iowa State, Maryland, Michigan State, Rutgers, and Washington State). *In general, it should be noted that the same trends tend to be found within all four composites.*

Data on overall university expenditures were obtained from the Higher Education General Information Survey (HEGIS), which was administered annually by the National Center for Education Statistics (NCES) and is available up to 1985–86. Data for expenditures after that year come from the Integrated Postsecondary Education Data System (IPEDS).

Data on domestic book production come from the R.R. Bowker Company (compiler of, for example, such reports as *Books in Print* and the *Bowker Annual of Library and Book Trade Information*) and the Association of American University Presses; international production is tracked through data from UNESCO. Data on periodical production in selected fields come from the Modern Language Association (MLA) and the Institute for Scientific Information (ISI), while data on prices of books and periodicals come from R.R. Bowker and various issues of the *Library Journal* and *Publishers Weekly*. Note, finally, that for more recent years, chronological data sets were constructed for the periods 1963–70, 1970–82, and 1982–91. (See the "Glossary" for some definitions of special terminology.)

PART 1 OF THE STUDY: THE STATE OF RESEARCH LIBRARIES TODAY

The broad patterns of development this study reveals are unsurprisingly congruent with the recent history of higher education in this country. The 1960s saw an unprecedented boom in library acquisitions; then the 1970s and early to mid-1980s saw a sharp slowdown in the rates of increase of acquisitions expenditures in the face of rapidly inflated costs, thus a drop in the purchasing power of the acquisitions dollar. As a result, the rate of increase in number of volumes added to collections slowed considerably and at many institutions was actually negative—i.e., in a given year fewer books would be purchased than in the year before.

From 1912 to 1991, the major libraries grew steadily and rapidly. Annual growth rates peaked in the mid- to late 1960s and then fell slowly throughout the 1970s. One of the closest correlations with other academic trends is with the number of doctorates conferred, for research libraries and doctoral programs tend to grow hand in hand. But when the 1970s saw contraction in the number of doctoral degrees conferred, library acquisitions were reined in less sharply. Acquisitions decisions are, after all, investment decisions affecting the long term, while degrees conferred reflect year-to-year production decisions taken with an eye on many variables. Furthermore, during the 1970s caution seems to have set in, so that when a modest recovery in the number of doctorates granted came, it was matched by an even more modest recovery in the annual number of "volumes added gross."

The boom of the 1960s affected the private universities on the whole more than the public; and the recovery since the mid-1980s has also been more pronounced in the private institutions, while there is little if any evidence of persistent recovery in acquisitions at the Public 1 institutions. But the most vigorous performers in the 1960s boom were the Public 2 institutions: at that period, for the most part, these were the smaller institutions with more rapid expansion plans, especially in their graduate programs, than those of corresponding more senior public institutions.

The patterns of growth, contraction, and modest recovery are nationwide and do not reflect specific stages in growth or maturity of institutions. Indeed, though smaller libraries might attempt to "catch up" in boom times, larger libraries showed in the 1960s that they could still stay well ahead of smaller ones as all parties showed enthusiastic growth figures. It was in the contraction of the 1970s, in fact, that the gap between larger and smaller libraries narrowed most, as the largest libraries showed the sharpest contraction.

It is difficult to select the most accurate measure of library expenditures over time, but however expressed, the increases are substantial and do not show signs of being closely tied to the GNP deflator (a form of general price index). The study's analyses further confirm that the boom years of the 1960s were anomalous and that a longer-term view shows a more consistent pattern. In fact, analysis of the years after the 1960s shows that library expenditure increases have been much more modest than might have been expected.

With that background, principal findings or observations of the Mellon study are numbered and highlighted:

1. **Libraries have not taken a larger percentage of the university budget; their percentage has shrunk.**

Contrary to the conventional wisdom, library budgets have tended to increase less rapidly than other university expenditures. The library's percentage of total expenditures has tended to decline. It may well be that as old ambitions became impossible of realization, newer, rather more modest aims gave ground for a more restrained growth in expenditures. The developments affecting library budgets in the last twenty years have, in fact, led to institutional adjustments in fundamental assumptions as to what was both desirable and sustainable.

When measured against U.S. Department of Education figures for educational and general expenditures (E&G) by universities, budgets (of the libraries studied) took an increasingly large share of the pie through the 1960s, leveled out through the 1970s, and have actually declined through the 1980s to the point where they have lost almost all the ground gained in the last thirty years. These institutions' library budgets may now have stopped dropping, as some evidence suggests a plateau over the past very few years. When measured against instructional and departmental research expenditures (I&DR), the decline in library share of university expenditures over the last twenty years is slightly less pronounced than by some other measures, but the pattern is still clear.

Analogously, limited assessment of the comparative situation in college libraries shows that in these smaller institutions, the library characteristically looms significantly larger as a percentage of overall expenditures. The same broad trends described above appear in small college library budgets over the last decades, though it must be observed that the growth in library budgets of the last ten years has been much less pronounced in the colleges than in the universities.

Having considered overall expenditures (termed "total library expenditures" or TLE by the ARL), the study then analyzes the TLE's chief components. In the ARL statistical reports, these are: "materials and binding" (combined until 1963; two separate categories thereafter); "salaries and wages;" and "other operating expenditures." Materials and binding is subdivided into "non-serials" (largely though not entirely books and monographs, and hereinafter so called) and "serials" (heavily but not entirely journals).

2. **Materials and binding: these acquisitions-related expenditures have remained a remarkably constant percentage of TLE as a whole, but mask a significant reallocation between books and serials.**

In the 24 libraries studied, the total materials and binding component of TLE ranges between 33 and 35 percent of the whole—in other words, a similar percentage of the budget has bought books and serials over the years. Nonetheless, though that share has increased in dollar value, fewer book and serial titles can be bought for that money.

An essential comparison matches "volumes added gross" (a rough surrogate for acquisitions) with expenditures. The curves first began to diverge in the late 1950s and then diverged sharply beginning about 1970. From about that time, measured in real terms, expenditures on *materials and binding continued to rise at the same time that the rate of volumes purchased actually declined.*

Furthermore, the overall stability in the share of the TLE that has been devoted to expenditures on materials and binding conceals a pronounced internal shift in allocations: a far higher proportion of the materials and binding budget is now being spent on serials. Serials hold an important place in the budget: Research 2 institutions, smaller and working harder to maintain their standing, spent through the 1970s and 1980s approximately 10 percent more of their materials budgets on serials than did Research 1 institutions.

3. **Books (non-serials): in the 1970s and 1980s, the rate of increase in volumes added at university research libraries virtually halted, while domestic and international publishing continued to produce greater and greater numbers of new titles each year.**

The growth of collections is measured against the trends in the numbers of books and periodicals published. In its broadest terms, book publication can be said to reflect general economic conditions. The boom in publication that began moderately in the 1950s and took off in the 1960s has slowed only slightly. Library acquisitions in the 1960s showed a growth that ran ahead of the increase in book publishing, but in the years since 1970 volumes added gross have remained roughly flat, while the figures for all domestic titles published have continued to rise at a steady rate. Comparison of publishing output to library collecting is difficult, and the questions must be asked several different ways in order to reach comparable approximations of the truth. Subjective issues arise easily, such as whether abundant production of scholarly information reflects a decline in its quality or is merely a function of the growth in the community producing such material, with the per capita output remaining close to what it was in the past. One probable influence is that the decline in the academic job market in the 1970s and 1980s increased competitiveness, one measure of which has become quantity of publication. All other things being equal, per capita scholarly production might be more likely to increase in bad times than in good.

Changes in the relative popularity of specific subjects of publishing have an important influence as well. Literature/Poetry/Drama as a category, for example, has fallen from a 17.2 percent share of the total national output in 1970 to 9.1 percent in 1988. On the other hand, the fields with some of the greatest increases in their share of the total output have been precisely those with the highest average per-volume hardcover prices: business, law, medicine, and technology. (Science has the highest average prices and remained at a more or less constant and significant market share of about 9.5 percent.) Library acquisitions reflect shifts in curriculum and research interests, and so may be presumed to reflect heavy purchasing in precisely the fields with the greatest price increases and the greatest increases in share of total titles published.

Among book prices, scientific/technical titles have diverged significantly from the other categories since the mid-1980s and are now being joined at the leading edge by medical books, while titles in arts and humanities, social sciences, and business have stayed with rates of increase close to the GNP deflator. As the most expensive fields have been the ones with the highest percentage increases in recent years, book prices are now showing some of the price-increasing tendencies characteristic of serials—not an encouraging sign for those who must be concerned about library budgets.

Examination of U.S. university press output also provides a measure of the adequacy of library acquisitions. Since 1974, it is clear that university press output has far outstripped library acquisitions increase rates.

International publishing production has also increased, ahead of the rates of increase of libraries' acquisitions for the period 1950-88. From 1950 to 1970, U.S. libraries actually increased their buying faster than the European publishers increased their production, but the two curves began to converge after 1970 and actually crossed around 1980, with the publishers' output now advancing at a rate steadily ahead of that of U.S. libraries' acquisitions. European book publishing indeed has grown at a rate substantially ahead of United States publishing, so that the six most productive European countries (Switzerland, Italy, France, Germany, U.K., Netherlands), which in 1971 produced about 1.5 times as many titles as American publishers did, now produce almost twice as many titles as the American industry.

To add to the difficulties, the sovereign position of the dollar through the boom years for libraries was lost when the dollar was allowed to float in 1971, and at various times during the period of study the dollar's low value has exacerbated the consequences for library buying of all materials. In one hapless interval from 1985 to 1988, the dollar fell against western European currencies by about 60 percent. (West) Germany has been the most productive publishing country in Europe and the least favorable exchange-rate partner since the early 1970s.

In sum, then, the number of volumes added yearly (books and serials) within the group of 24 libraries decreased between 1970 and 1982 at an annual rate of –1.4 percent, while the number of titles published, domestically and internationally, was increasing at a rate of greater than 2 percent per year. Over this period, libraries have been able to purchase less comprehensively in response to output in the publishing industry than at any time in this century.

4. **Serials: many speak of a "serials crisis" at the heart of library difficulties today, and it is prices, and in particular science journal prices, that drive the crisis.**

Because of the high rates of serials price increases, the forces creating the gap between volumes added and publishing title output have been principally external rather than internal to universities, and individual institutions have been unable to respond proportionately. It would not be an exaggeration to say that of the various factors in the constellation affecting university libraries in recent years, the rapidly rising prices of periodicals have in many respects been the most important. Subscriptions encumber the materials budget, and serials prices help explain the widening gap between volumes added gross and book titles published. Library budgets have been steadily redeployed towards serials as the primary way of dealing with the pressure of rising serials prices.

In particular, the study makes the following findings regarding serials prices:
- Serials prices have run consistently ahead of the GNP deflator, even in the years 1963-70, with scientific and technical journals consistently leading the rises.
- Within similar groups of fields (e.g., among humanities fields as disparate as history, philosophy, and literature, or among the sciences in chemistry/physics, mathematics, and engineering) remarkable consistency is noted: subject area is a powerful determining force.
- The most expensive serials show the largest *relative* price increases. The highest rates of increase are sustained by the journals whose prices are largest in absolute terms.

Serials expenditures have increased rapidly for the entire period since 1976, but 1981-86 saw moderating increases, while 1986 to 1991 showed the most rapid increase (an overall annual rate from 1986 to 1990 of over 11 percent). Some institutional data suggest science journals account for approximately 29 percent of the total number of serials but 65 percent of the serials budget.

Comparing book and serial prices, the study shows that average prices increased at comparable rates between 1963 and 1970, but about 1970 the pattern changed profoundly. Book prices remained close to the GNP deflator in their rate of increase until about 1978, when the periodicals index began to rise sharply. The proliferation of journal titles presumably created more specialized journals with shorter subscription lists and higher unit prices. For the whole period from 1963 to 1990, serial prices have increased at 11.3 percent per year, against 7.2 percent per year for book prices, and the GNP deflator lagged at an increase of about 6.1 percent per year (average).

Serial prices for scientific and technical journals from 1970 to 1990 have increased at an average rate of 13.5 percent per year. In so doing they lead a serials price surge in which virtually all science/technology fields run well ahead of the GNP deflator. In 1970, the typical U.S. journal in chemistry/physics cost $33; in 1982 it cost $178;

in history, the average journal cost $7 in 1970 and $20 in 1982. To reduce such increases too quickly to measurement by constant dollars would be a mistake; it is useful to remember that many of the factors driving the national inflationary spiral (e.g., energy prices) have little effect on serials pricing and thus the nominal numbers are important in their own right.

Several factors correlate with high serials prices:

- Scientific and technical journals can be more expensive to produce than others, and journals with specific higher costs of production for pages per issue, issues per year, and the presence of art work are more expensive.
- Journals published by commercial publishers are more expensive (not least because a fuller range of their costs are passed on to subscribers, unlike those managed by nonprofit publishers, with hidden and not-so-hidden subsidies contributed against the costs of production).
- Journals with smaller subscription bases are more expensive.
- Specialization plays an important role. New journals tend to be more specialized than older ones, and hence have a smaller subscription base and higher prices.
- Demand for periodicals is less elastic than that for monographs: journals are perceived to be important vehicles for scholarly communication, and continuity of series is a powerful factor in discouraging cutbacks.
- Discriminatory pricing has been a factor. It would appear that in the early 1980s, foreign publishers began charging differential rates to compensate for a relatively strong dollar, but made no compensatory decreases when the dollar later weakened.
- Concentration of science journals within a few publishing houses has had some impact. Three European commercial publishers (Elsevier, Pergamon, and Springer—the first two of which merged in 1991, further concentrating control of pricing decisions) accounted for 43 percent of the increase in serials expenditures at one university between 1986 and 1987.
- Additionally, journals that accept advertising can have lower prices.

Measuring production of serial titles is fraught with its own difficulties. What constitutes a serial, and what within that group constitutes a "scholarly journal," is not easily measured. How many journals are published? Estimates range from less than 5,000 per year to upwards of 100,000. One standard guide is *Ulrich's International Periodicals Directory*, and on that measure, libraries have lagged. From 1972 to 1988, total serials listed in *Ulrich's* have grown by over 50 percent, while serials acquired by the twenty-four libraries under study have increased by only about 25 percent. Measures that look at date of founding of journals show a corresponding proliferation in the 1960s and especially through the 1970s, with some tapering off in the 1980s, but those numbers are hard to assess because there is no count of numbers of journals ceasing to do business during the same period. Some say that in recent years cessations may in fact be running ahead of current inceptions. One study of language and literature journals finds that over half the titles currently available were first published sometime since 1970.

In sum, then, in view of the increasing size of the periodicals universe (and increasing specialization of journals), the relatively fixed materials and binding budgets at libraries have resulted in decreasing numbers of subscriptions per title. Prices per title increase further, and a vicious cycle begins and continues. A similar dynamic, as suggested above, is even beginning to affect monograph publishing: one representative academic press confesses to a decline in average print runs between 1976 and 1986, from 1200-1500 to fewer than 1000. Of course, university libraries constitute a significant part of the market for university press titles, and the pressures on library budgets, for example, as they shift resources from monographs to serials, are an important contributing factor to this cycle as well.

In the face of this pricing crisis, libraries have responded essentially by redistributing their resources, a mode of response that cannot go on indefinitely. Instead there is a growing realization that no research institution can hope to sustain a self-sufficient collection into the indefinite future. Even before the "crisis," libraries were actively collaborating and sharing resources. Under the circumstances described in the study, and even absent new technologies, libraries would have been led to pursue "without walls" philosophies energetically. With technological hopes rising, possible contributions to mitigation of the "crisis" can come from a combination of:

- modification of the academic reward system that drives proliferation of publication.
- possible reduction of first-copy costs by publishers' application of technological advances.
- savings through use of electronic technologies in distributing and storing information.
- accelerated resource sharing.
- perhaps even alterations in the law of intellectual property governing "published" material.

5. **Salaries as a percentage of total library expenditures have declined over the last two decades, while "other operating expenditures" (heavily reflecting computerization) have risen markedly.**

Salaries in the composite libraries consistently constitute more than 50 percent of the average library budget. Staffing has increased since 1912, but at a rate somewhat less than that of collection size, so the number of books held per employee has risen to the highest level ever. The number of volumes added gross per staff member has declined, however, reflecting not staffing so much as the even greater effect of recent negative forces on acquisitions.

Between 1960 and 1970, average staff size in the Research 1 libraries nearly doubled. In the next fifteen years, the *total* increase in staff size was a little less than 7 percent; and from 1985 to 1991, a total increase of almost 6 percent showed a modest recovery. There can be no doubt, however, that drastic constraints were placed on staffing size around 1970 and that the easing in recent years has been modest in comparison.

Other operating expenditures have taken a larger share of the library budget over the last twenty years, apparently largely to reflect computerization of internal operations: circulation, cataloging, and acquisitions. The share of library budgets taken by salaries, meanwhile, has declined from around 62 percent in 1963 to 52 percent in 1991. That decline has been offset by increases in other operating expenditures, up from 6 percent in 1963 to 14 percent in 1991. That the decline in the staff share began in the 1960s probably reflects the shift in the age distribution toward younger employees as the staff size increased—rapid increases in staffing are often accompanied by less rapid increases in payroll costs because of the growing fraction of staff earning entry-level salaries. Post-1970, the decline in share taken by salaries reflects the sharp curtailment in recruitment, while other operating expenditures grew across the four sample groups of libraries chosen.

PART 2 OF THE STUDY: ELECTRONIC POSSIBILITIES

6. **The pressures described in the first part of this report will need to be addressed in many ways, but the possibilities of a significant increase in the role of electronic text distribution, maintenance, and use have the potential for being the most dramatic.**

The technology of print turned information into a material commodity. Recorded usually in linear form on sheets of paper and distributed in multiple identical (or almost identical) copies, printed works have a relatively high cost for production of the first copy and relatively low cost for subsequent copies. The physical objects—the books—contain a fixed, immutable text with which the reader is permitted to interact only in limited ways. Aids to non-linear access (e.g., tables of contents and indexes) are relatively limited and supplied largely at the author's discretion. The study keeps its eye on a few trends closely affecting traditional arrangements. Large changes in conceptions of property and association may very well accompany adoption of new electronic information technologies on a wide scale. (As a historical analogy, consider that few are likely to have guessed in 1470 what the printing press, or in 1910 what the automobile, would bring.)

Currently, both publishers and libraries inhabit a world in which their standard practices require them to anticipate demand: the publisher must predict the market and the library must know its users in order for all the economic transactions to be carried out with the greatest efficiency. There are backups in place to adjust to unexpected demand (e.g., interlibrary loan, currently a rapidly growing activity in libraries), but so far those makeshifts have been considerably less satisfactory than successful anticipation of demand and providential provision of suitable materials. This "just-in-case," local-ownership model is one with familiar costs and benefits—including such bonuses as the creation of large, intricate collections of information that lend themselves to serendipitous, potentially interesting discoveries made by searchers on another trail or merely by browsers.

In particular, technological advances support suggestions that management of scholarly communication can now begin to separate access from ownership and concentrate on assuring access to scholarship and research, with questions of physical location of materials becoming secondary.

7. **Until very recently, automation in libraries had addressed itself to existing internal functions (circulation, cataloging, and acquisitions), but the range of uses is becoming much broader.**

Now electronic technologies have been conceptualized to provide secondary bibliographical resources (catalogs, information about information, access to other institutions' holdings, periodical indexes, etc.). And increasingly, the technologies are beginning to be applied to problems of assembling and ordering the primary information itself. The "virtual library" with all the world's published riches at one's fingertips is largely a vision at this point, but a potent one.

Large-scale projects that provide computerized bibliographical information are under way. The two most notable national organizations in this area are the OCLC (the Online Computer Library Center) and the RLG (the Research Libraries Group). Both of these organizations are experimenting with ways to make their very large databases, reporting the holdings of member libraries, more accessible and useful to scholars. Of particular interest are RLG's efforts in improving the quality and availability of bibliographic information on what might be called "non-traditional" materials: everything from musical compositions to unpublished archival sources. In addition to the national services, many individual libraries make their catalogs available on the Internet. The utility of such online catalogs is limited when retrospective conversion of the card catalog is not yet substantially complete, but more than half of ARL member libraries report that they have already converted 90 percent or more of their card catalogs to machine-readable form.

Unlike books, serial literature is regularly indexed not by the libraries but by independent, often commercial, services. One caution is that because many of these services are provided outside the not-for-profit institutional environment, costs of access have been and can be substantial to individual users. When institutions purchase or utilize such indexing and abstracting services online, they try to contain costs by having their own trained personnel conducting the search. Yet the ideal of allowing individual access remains strong.

The next step beyond obtaining information about information is to share the texts themselves, as has been done traditionally by interlibrary loan (ILL). As emphasis shifts from ownership to access, models of information provision and electronic text availability permits, in principle, a degree of resource sharing among institutions far greater than that allowed by traditional ILL. As transmission improves, availability of resources outside the home institution will increasingly affect local collection development. Already the RLG Conspectus project attempts to help libraries make better informed choices about their acquisitions.

A newer model of resource sharing is document delivery. Document delivery services recently developed include the Colorado Alliance of Research Libraries' (CARL) UnCover service, which supplies abundant bibliographical data on articles, and UnCover2, which provides rapid delivery service for full texts, via mail or fax with Internet delivery planned. A copyright royalty fee is collected and paid through the Copyright Clearance Center for each transaction. RLG's Ariel system allows any printed material to be scanned directly as a page image, then stored, transmitted over the Internet, and received for printing at the target site. Among commercial for-profit services, Faxon Research Services, Inc., in a program called Faxon Finder (for bibliographic information) and Faxon Xpress (for document delivery), looks promising. Only fuller experience with such experiments will enable institutions to make the necessary careful analyses of contrasting cost implications, balancing collection development with resource sharing.

8. At the present time, electronic publishing comprises many different kinds of information dissemination.

The study's discussion to this point assumes that the primary text is printed and that the electronic technologies are used to facilitate access and delivery. But, when the primary artifact is itself electronic, the real revolution will begin. The changes such electronic publishing will bring, for example in the relationship between interpretive works and the underlying data or primary texts on which they are based, are the subject of much thoughtful speculation. Over time, for example, printing costs have worked against the thorough presentation of data: in electronic media, the possibility re-emerges of substantially complete publication of *all* the data on which research is based, and better still, publication in a form that others can continue to manipulate and enhance. It may soon be possible to think of producing shorter, less-expensive print products that contain little or no documentation.

What remains to be seen is how far new *forms* of publication will emerge, ones that that can *only* be displayed in an electronic environment, using sophisticated "hypertext" functions or offering three-dimensional, graphic, moving simulations, for example. Electronic texts can remove the limitations of print on paper. They can be dynamic, mutable, and are potentially eminently interactive. They may allow the producer and the user to uncouple the material object from the intellectual content.

Electronic texts have one signal advantage over print: they are far easier to transmit for purposes of resource sharing. There are experiments under way in this area, for instance, where textbooks are created on demand out of available online materials and distributed for a fee.

The transition to alternative forms of scholarly communication will not be easy. A particular technology, of whatever type, is joined to a set of economic and legal arrangements appropriate to it. So, one must not underestimate the difficulties involved in anticipating a reconfiguration, nor the important role traditional print media are likely to retain far into the future. For many applications, print products retain considerable advantages over electronic ones. There will be no near-term, wholesale replacement of print with electronic media (the way the vinyl platter was overwhelmed by the CD-ROM for music reproduction). The electronic media add a dimension to what we already have, but for the foreseeable future, the old media will be with us as well.

And it is impossible to be sure how far the technological possibilities will go. A wide range of predicted futures has been arrayed by thoughtful observers, and at some future point the changes may be *considerably* more far-reaching, affecting every aspect of our institutions and the communications on which they thrive. The library, the publisher, the printed book, the monograph, the learned journal, the process of peer review, copyright practices: all these and other familiar elements of the current system are at least somewhat at risk in the face of the new technologies. The following list suggests some areas in which difficult issues will have to be faced.

9. **Scholarly publishing is closely tied to academic prestige, a link that exercises a conservative force on new arrangements.**

The reward system for scholars and scientists depends for now on traditional publication as a defining criterion for rank and status, with the real compensation for publication coming not from sales of the material itself but from the advancement in rank, salary, and prestige that publication makes possible. Any new system will have to satisfy scholarly and institutional leaders that it is adequately peer reviewed and reliable before new types of publications can be rewarded. Until assurances of such rewards are in place, faculty will be reluctant to put their best work in new forms.

10. Options for distribution of electronic texts are numerous and their costs at the present time uncertain.

Options for electronic text distribution are many, and no one can predict which will prevail, where, or how. Individual institutions might choose to maintain local electronic repositories of frequently-used titles; on the other hand, some publishers might choose to retain their texts themselves at central sites and distribute them on a fee-for-use basis; collaborative arrangements between repositories of various kinds in various places may emerge in which a consortium of libraries, say, may together hold a full set of resources, without each institution having to pay the full cost of housing such a set.

Cost factors may well force the determining choices on institutions irrespective of technological possibilities. Some say that electronic scholarly communication will be more affordable than print-on-paper. To determine with any precision what cost savings, if any, might emerge from any new methods of distribution is difficult, and there will undoubtedly be reallocation of costs within the university system. Who will pay and how much are vital, but still unanswerable, questions. Consider the development of the serial/journal in a new environment. The very concept of an "issue" of a journal is challenged: individual items can be distributed separately, as they very often are in the experimental e-journals now operating. This calls for different subscription and pricing policies, both for individuals and institutions.

11. Campus computing and telecommunications infrastructures will need to be upgraded to make the new technologies possible.

Some of these upgrades are necessary in any event, but they carry real costs. Proponents of the new National Research and Education Network system (NREN) estimate that for every dollar appropriated for this system by the federal government, five to ten dollars will have to come from state and local governments and private institutions.

The full realization of the potential model of electronic scholarly communication described here depends, finally, upon the development of an adequate national telecommunications infrastructure, capable of moving vast quantities of text and data at very high speeds. The final chapter of the study provides a brief history of the emergence of the national scientific and academic networks now in existence and describes the upgraded, harmonized network that is, or will be, the NREN. The three-tier structure (a national backbone, then regional networks, then campus or local networks) puts heavy responsibility on individual institutions to maintain a significant share of the national network. But the improvements to service will be astonishing: a roughly 600-fold increase in speed of transmission as rapid as a billion bits a second will move texts with blinding speed and almost make possible acceptable speeds for the more data-intensive forms of information such as high-resolution graphics, moving pictures, and multi-media formats.

12. Traditional roles in the publishing process will undergo transformation.

Libraries and publishers already play multiple roles. Libraries and publishers as we now know them are institutions created in and for the technology of the printed, or at least the written, word, depending on information to be produced, distributed, and possessed as a collection of material objects. But it is also critical to realize that both libraries and publishers play other parts as well. Publishers, for example, function as gate-keepers to the world of scholarly communication in managing scholars' and researchers' peer review, which in turn determines what is printed and what is not. Libraries, in turn, have collection development and management functions, but they also serve as indexers and pathfinders for information they do not own. Already such a model departs from the "just-in-case" approach to acquisition and approaches a "just-in-time" model, where material is acquired as it is needed. There may be some blurring in the distinctions among the historical roles of publishers as producers, vendors as intermediaries, and librarians as archivists. The electronic revolution may provide the potential for developing university publishing enterprises through scholarly networks supported either by individual institutions or consortia.

Peer review, editing, and composition will all remain important parts of the preparation of scholarly material for distribution. How much of this remains as the role of current publishers and how much is taken on by other participants in the process remains to be seen.

13. Consistency of standards and of protocols has not yet been found.

Existing heterogeneity of access and retrieval protocols poses a real problem in the short to medium term; here the solution is in the first instance technical, but various interest groups will have to negotiate their way to the suitable solution. What are called "expert systems" should further ease translation among computer formats.

14. Adaptation of current copyright practices to the new electronic environments poses numerous difficulties.

The ease with which electronic material can be duplicated and retransmitted means that whatever controls the publisher places and seeks to enforce on users, whether by copyright or licensing agreements, can be circumvented with ease. If revenue depends on "sales" of the retail product, the retransmission represents a potentially threatening black market that could undermine publishers' ability to recoup their costs. The need to control will compete with the demand for wide and easy access to material. There are implications also for information accuracy and integrity.

The most critical issues are those that arise from the challenges to the law of copyright implicitly posed by the new technologies. Copyright in the United States is based in the Constitution and confirmed by statute. The original intent of the constitutional protection was to encourage intellectual productivity by securing rights to the authors. In scholarly practice today, rights are commonly assigned to publishers, in return for the substantial contribution they make to scholarly communication, while the rewards expected by the scholars themselves are those of prestige, rank, and institutional compensation mentioned above.

The U.S. copyright law's doctrine of "fair use" defines the way reproduction of copyrighted materials may be carried out. Some copyright scholars maintain that a key factor affecting determination of fair use appears increasingly to be the effect of that use on the potential market for the work, and it is on economic grounds that publishers scrutinize practices carefully for possible violation. Current litigation continues to define more precisely the scope of this doctrine.

The point at which resource sharing runs the risk of violating copyright can be a delicate matter. Eventual development of fee structures and payment mechanisms is one way to respect current copyright privileges. Licensing agreements freely entered into by purchasers of information are already used somewhat and offer another resolution for some of the issues raised.

Alternatives to current copyright management can be imagined. For example, universities could claim joint ownership of scholarly writings with the faculty they pay to produce them, then prohibit unconditional assignment to third parties, thus becoming important players in the publishing business themselves. Or universities could request that faculty members first submit manuscripts to publishers whose pricing policies are more consonant with larger educational objectives. Another possibility is that university-negotiated licenses could grant unlimited copying to libraries and individual scholars and specify such permission in the copyright statement. All these proposals are extensions of the broader idea under current discussion, that universities should reclaim some responsibility for disseminating the results of faculty scholarship.

15. In the end, larger social issues will need to be addressed.

Many concerns about management of the networks that distribute this material are already being articulated. Who has access, who pays, who worries about integrity of texts and privacy, who monitors ownership and legitimate use? Academic institutions, individual scholars, and their commercial partners in the transactions to come will all have their own agendas, and they must learn to work in an atmosphere of mutual respect and cooperation.

CONCLUSION

The heart of the scholarly enterprise is the exchange of ideas. University campuses offer myriad informal loci for dialogue, but the formal locus par excellence is in the dialogue between scholarly writer and scholarly reader that has been mediated for half a millennium now by the printed page. One scholar is quoted in the study and summarizes well the sense of responsibility that accompanies that dialogue:

> In *Notes on Virginia*, Jefferson described the process: 'A patient pursuit of facts, and cautious combination and comparison of them, is the drudgery to which man is subjected. . . if he wishes to attain sure knowledge.' Jefferson is still right about the patient pursuit of facts . . . . We have, however, taken much of the drudgery out of the process and made it easier to find sources, but we still have to read carefully—probably more carefully than ever—and we still have to think. The difference is that searching no longer takes much time and energy from the scholarship of thought.

The optimism of that passage is specific to the dawn of the computer age, but similar optimism has been expressed at each historical moment when the advance of technology has brought new riches closer to readers.

The indispensable mediator in the dialogue between writer and reader has been, for more centuries than even the printed book has been around, the institutional library. The study addresses the present and future of scholarly communication with particular reference to the research libraries that bear so much of the responsibility for making that communication possible, with particular focus on the research university library, whose special purpose is to support advanced scholarship and scholarly communication.

Ann Okerson
November 1992

CHAPTER ONE

Introduction

For centuries the library has been a repository of the written record and a powerful symbol of human intellectual achievement, but today, as perhaps never before, fundamental questions are being raised concerning its nature as an institution.

Libraries of different types serve different communities, of course, and it is important to say immediately that this study is concerned primarily with only one type: the research university library, whose special purpose is to support advanced scholarship and scholarly communication and the research activities of faculty members and doctoral students at Ph.D.-granting institutions. Undergraduates also make heavy use of these libraries, but the provision of services to undergraduates is not the distinctive purpose of the research library. (Chapter 3 contains a discussion of the differences in library expenditures at universities and at liberal arts colleges.)

The forces affecting research libraries are numerous and complex, and they are not easily described and calibrated. As indicated in the Foreword, this is in no sense a definitive study. Rather, this report is best seen as an initial examination of some of the relevant trends, intended to improve our understanding of the issues and choices that are emerging so rapidly. In the main, it is an attempt to collect in one place a considerable amount of both statistical data and information on technological changes affecting libraries. We have tried to assemble these materials in a way that draws together parts of the library puzzle that are often considered separately.

ORGANIZATION OF THE STUDY AND PRINCIPAL PROPOSITIONS

It may be helpful to think of the principal challenges facing research libraries today as falling under two broad headings, which correspond to the two parts of this study.

- First, libraries must continue to acquire the books and periodicals necessary to maintain and strengthen collections in the face of both (a) a rapidly proliferating universe of published material that it seems desirable to collect and (b) rapidly escalating unit prices, especially for some journals. In almost all cases, university budget constraints have compelled research libraries to acquire an ever smaller share of the universe of materials from which they are accustomed to make selections. Part 1 of the study documents trends in the sizes of collections, rates of acquisitions, levels and categories of expenditures, publications of monographs and serials, and prices of these publications.

- Second, libraries must determine how to respond to the rapid emergence and development of electronic information technologies that permit one to envision radically different ways of organizing the services the library has traditionally provided. As currently configured, the library is a print institution whose essential characteristics have been determined by the technology of printing. That technology in turn entails a particular set of legal, economic, and cultural relationships among scholars, their universities, publishers, academic book vendors, libraries, and other participants in the process of print-based communication. A new technology with different characteristics will almost inevitably entail different arrangements among these participants—with far-reaching implications for scholarship, graduate education, and the economics of creating, publishing, disseminating, and using scholarly information. Part 2 of the study deals with these topics.

The analysis in Part 1 parallels in certain respects the study of trends in doctoral education sponsored recently by the Foundation.[1] The library has traditionally been the most important of the university facilities supporting advanced scholarship, at least in the humanities and related social sciences, and its continued vitality has been seen as critically important to the vitality of Ph.D. programs in those subjects and to the ability of institutions to support distinguished programs.

Because of this close association, it is not surprising that the data documenting historical trends in the growth of library collections resemble closely certain trends in doctoral education.

- The number of volumes added to library collections increased rapidly during the 1960s, when university enrollments were expanding, new doctoral programs were being established, and considerable funding was available from external sources. The increase in the number of titles acquired was both a stimulus to and a consequence of the expansion of graduate education: a larger library collection supported the research activities of larger faculties and graduate student cohorts; larger numbers of active scholars, in turn, produced more scholarly works that research libraries then acquired.

- The widespread financial and programmatic retrenchments of the 1970s and the early to mid-1980s are similarly reflected in the library data studied here: rates of increase in expenditures for acquisitions were much slower in the 1970s and early 1980s than during the previous decade, and the inflationary trends of the period are reflected in the prices of library materials, which rose still more rapidly; the purchasing power of acquisitions expenditures was therefore diminished. The rate of increase in the number of volumes added slowed considerably and at many institutions was actually negative—that is, the number of volumes added in any particular year was lower than the number added in the preceding year. The moderately improved financial situation of the late 1980s permitted some recovery, though not to levels characteristic of earlier decades.

One perhaps surprising finding in Part 1 of this analysis is that library expenditures have *not* tended to increase more rapidly than other university expenditures over recent decades. On the contrary, the library's share of total expenditures has tended to decline in spite of the rapid increases in the prices of materials, especially serials. We suspect that this shifting relationship between library expenditures and total expenditures, which is remarkably consistent across various kinds of libraries and universities, reflects a judgment that there was simply no way in which constrained university budgets could accommodate the increases in spending on

---

[1]William G. Bowen and Neil L. Rudenstine, *In Pursuit of the Ph.D.*, Princeton, N.J.: Princeton University Press, 1992.

acquisitions that would have been required to maintain past rates of increase in acquisitions. The conclusion may well have been that, if it simply was impossible to keep up, it made sense to accept this reality and restrain the growth in expenditures for acquisitions in keeping with limits on the growth of overall university resources.

Although many of the challenges described here are universal and affect libraries of many different types, the ever-expanding size of the universe of published materials and the rapidly increasing prices of these materials are especially troubling to research libraries. Such libraries have traditionally aimed to be as comprehensive as possible in their acquisitions practices, to provide faculty members and graduate students with access to as much of the entire professional literature as can be acquired. The fact that university libraries, with few or no exceptions, are now able to respond less comprehensively than ever before to general trends in book production is widely regarded with anxiety, in that access to scholarly information may be narrowing.

A related concern is that pressure on acquisitions budgets will cause various research libraries to look more and more alike over time, as each ceases to purchase as many of the more esoteric publications and chooses rather to be sure that essential volumes are acquired. The consequence could be a decline in the richness of collections overall, not merely a decline in the range of holdings of any one library.

These broad trends raise deep questions concerning the viability of the traditional model of the library. The rapidly rising prices of materials, the continued increase in the number of items available for purchase, the fact that university libraries seem to be acquiring a declining share of the world's output, the impracticality of continuing to build large, costly, warehouse-type structures to shelve printed materials, thus replicating collections that exist elsewhere—these and other developments cause one to ask whether established practices, which are already eroding, can be continued for very much longer.

Part 2 of the study suggests that electronic technologies may permit different assumptions and practices to characterize scholarly communication in the future. In a sense, the technology of print demands that individual institutions build self-sufficient, comprehensive collections, in anticipation of user demand. There is no other way to ensure prompt local access to scholarly information, given that printing results in the production of material objects that must be purchased, shipped, classified, and shelved. Electronic technologies, in contrast, permit different practices; in principle, information in electronic form can be disseminated much more rapidly, and its storage is altogether different in kind.

Such characteristics have led many observers to suggest that the process of scholarly communication can now be based on a principle of access rather than ownership. More than ever before, libraries, or the institutions that may succeed them as they undergo redefinition, can envision building collections in collaboration with other institutions, specializing locally in certain kinds of materials and distributing resources among the members of a consortium. The ability to share materials readily in electronic form obviates the need for each institution to attempt to build a comprehensive collection, with all of the costly redundancies that such a model entails. These new technologies also have major implications for the allocation of expenditures among library functions and activities (see Chapter 4) and certainly for the space requirements of libraries.

We hasten to emphasize that the transition to any such alternative model will not be easy, for the reasons mentioned earlier: a particular technology, of whatever type, is joined to a set of economic and legal arrangements appropriate to it. As we discuss in Part 2, the technology of print fits hand-in-glove with copyright practices as they have evolved to the present day; moreover, the current model is sustained by a set of complex economic relationships among publishers, vendors, and libraries that have been carefully worked out over decades. New technologies, in contrast, will result in new sorts of relationships yet to be defined and agreed upon; it will not be easy to reach agreement on such matters.

Some observers believe that the new electronic technologies will have considerably more far-reaching effects, that their emergence signals the beginning of a fundamental shift in accepted practices governing the dissemination of ideas and even their development. According to that view, the institutions, practices, and forms of a print culture will undergo complete transformation or in some instances disappear altogether. The self-sufficient research library, the scholarly publisher, the printed book, the monograph, the learned journal, the process of peer review, and copyright practices—these and other familiar elements of the current system are all implicitly challenged by electronic technologies.

Electronic methods of disseminating information are at least as different in kind from print as print is from manual copying and may be much more so. We are not yet far enough along in the transition to a fully electronic environment to be certain of what new forms and institutions may ultimately emerge; but we may be certain, we would argue, that they will be *very* different.

DATA SETS, LIBRARY COMPOSITES, AND OTHER SOURCES OF INFORMATION

For the first part of the study, data pertaining to internal library developments were obtained primarily from the Association of Research Libraries (ARL), an organization founded in 1932 and presently located in Washington, D.C. For the academic years 1907–08 through 1937–38, the data were collected by James Gerould, who was university librarian first at the University of Minnesota and then at Princeton University. Following his retirement in 1938, members of the library staff at Princeton continued to collect the data through 1961-62, when ARL assumed direct responsibility.

The data are derived from an annual questionnaire. The version used in 1990-91 with accompanying instructions is reproduced in Appendix A. Despite minor inconsistencies, the ARL database is a highly reliable source and the only longitudinal data set of this scale in the library field. We have chosen to emphasize categories that reflect broad changes in the collections and patterns of expenditures over time. These categories also are presented in Appendix A.

Of the 107 university libraries that are current members of ARL, we have chosen 24—at twelve private and twelve public institutions—for intensive analysis. These 24 universities were chosen to reflect the experiences of four broad sets (or composites) of libraries, which we call Private 1, Public 1, Private 2, and Public 2. Composite values of relevant variables were obtained for each set by calculating an unweighted average of the values for each component institution. The resulting values are intended to describe the experience of the "typical" library within each set.

These 24 libraries have been chosen to permit systematic analysis of broad developments over time within different sets of well-established research libraries. They are not meant to be representative of the universe of ARL libraries. For example, they include a disproportionately larger number of private universities and libraries that have been long-time members of ARL. We selected particular universities based on the consistency of their data over time, similarities to one another in terms of academic strengths, and our general knowledge of individual institutions. For our purposes it was especially important to have a fixed set of institutions, so that comparisons over time would not be distorted by the addition (or subtraction) of a particular library from the database. This is why trends in summary measures for the entire universe of ARL libraries are so difficult to interpret.

The universities included in the Private 1 and Public 1 composites are the older and for the most part larger of the ARL libraries (all were charter members of ARL).

- Private 1 universities are the University of Chicago, Columbia University, Cornell University, Princeton University, Stanford University, and Yale University.[2]
- Public 1 universities are the University of California at Berkeley, University of Iowa, University of Michigan at Ann Arbor, University of North Carolina at Chapel Hill, University of Virginia, and University of Wisconsin at Madison.

The libraries included in the Private 2 and Public 2 composites tend to be smaller, and many are more recent members of ARL.

- Private 2 universities are Boston University, Georgetown University, New York University, Northwestern University, University of Southern California, and Washington University in St. Louis.
- Public 2 universities are University of Florida, Iowa State University, University of Maryland, Michigan State University, Rutgers University, and Washington State University.

At some points in the analysis we found it useful to group the Private 1 and Public 1 universities into a larger composite called Research 1. And in much of the discussion, we group all institutions into a single composite called All 24 Universities.

Complete data were not available for every institution for the entire time period that we discuss (1912 through 1991). Discussion of trends prior to 1963 focuses primarily on the Research 1 universities. Discussion of developments after 1963 makes use of the full data set. In general, we discuss broad trends for All 24 Universities and then note any significant differences by sector.

One finding of this study, which can be generalized from the previous discussion of the relationship between library expenditures and total expenditures, is that the same trends tend to be found within all four composites. This suggests that the forces affecting libraries have been quite general, with the same waves washing over

---

[2]An obvious omission is Harvard University. We did not include Harvard in the Private 1 composite because it is in a class of its own with respect to scale and would skew the averages for the composite. In 1989–90, for example, Harvard reported a total of 11,874,148 volumes held, while most of the universities in our Private 1 composite reported volumes held in the general range of 5 to 6 million (with Yale at the top of this list with holdings of nearly 9 million volumes).

all these institutions. While idiosyncratic patterns of course exist (with some libraries, for example, almost surely operating more efficiently than others), these individual variations do not seem so pronounced as to obscure general trends—especially when it is possible, as it has been in this study, to work with averages for sets of libraries.

Data pertaining to university expenditures in general were obtained from the Higher Education General Information Survey (HEGIS), which is administered annually by the National Center for Education Statistics (NCES). These data were available for the period up to 1985–86. The data on expenditures after that year were obtained from the Integrated Postsecondary Education Data System (IPEDS). The data showing expenditures for college libraries, in relation to other expenditures by the same colleges, were obtained ultimately from this same source.[3] The definitions of the categories we used from these questionnaires can be found in Appendix A.

Internal developments—trends in collection growth and expenditures, described in Chapters 2 through 4—are then related in Chapters 5 and 6 to a series of important external developments: trends in book and periodical production, both domestic and international, and in the prices of library materials.

Data on domestic book production, which have important limitations described in detail at the appropriate point in the discussion, were obtained from two sources, the R. R. Bowker Company and the Association of American University Presses; data on international production were obtained from the United Nations Educational, Scientific and Cultural Organization. In each instance, subsets of the total were defined in an effort to confine the data to a more relevant set of fields. Data on periodical production in some representative disciplines were obtained from the Modern Language Association and the Institute for Scientific Information. Data on the prices of books and periodicals were obtained from the R. R. Bowker Company and various issues of the *Library Journal* and *Publishers Weekly*.

For the years since 1963 the longitudinal data sets were often subdivided into shorter time periods: 1963–70, 1970–82, and 1982–91. In this way we were able to pinpoint with reasonable precision exactly when various trends began to emerge and to document the "boom and bust" syndrome that characterized so much of the experience of institutions of higher education (including their libraries) during the 1960s, 1970s, and 1980s.

The second part of the study is very different in kind from the first. We shift from a quantitative mode of analysis to a synthetic one. Our objective in Part 2 was to summarize some of the more important statements concerning the alternative model of scholarly communication proposed by many observers and offer as clear a description as possible of some of the principal elements: the availability of bibliographic records in electronic form that provide scholars with information about the professional literature and collections housed elsewhere; the potential applications of electronic technologies to scholarly publishing; the possibility of the kinds of collaborative collection development that the availability of electronic material permits; the various cultural, economic, technological, and legal issues to be resolved before any such alternative model is viable; and the need for an adequate

---

[3]The college data were supplied by Anne MacEachern, research coordinator, Williams Project on the Economics of Higher Education.

telecommunications infrastructure capable of moving large quantities of electronic text and data at high speeds.

Consistent with this shift in methodology, the primary sources utilized for Part 2 are quite unlike those used in Part 1. There were few data to be analyzed (apart from those pertaining to recent shifts in the composition of library expenditures, which are discussed in Chapter 4), and we relied instead on such materials as literature published by some of the major bibliographic utilities (the Research Libraries Group, DIALOG Information Services, Inc., and so on); articles in specialized but still "popular" periodicals (including especially *The Chronicle of Higher Education*); and unpublished memoranda and studies of various kinds. While a considerable amount of literature has been consulted, there are many other studies that we would have liked to review and incorporate into this analysis.

The nature of the issues treated dictated the nature of the sources used: the situation is changing very rapidly, and our objective was to ensure that our account of developments be as current as possible. In some ultimate sense that objective proved unattainable, and we cannot claim that our picture of the situation is anything other than a snapshot, taken in the spring of 1992. A snapshot taken subsequently might show a rather different picture. In fact, even as this introduction was being drafted, new articles of importance were appearing on various of the issues treated in Part 2. With this important proviso we feel that Part 2 nonetheless indicates the ways in which new technologies suggest a model for the library of the future that may differ sharply from the traditional one.

OTHER QUESTIONS

Before concluding these introductory remarks, we should say more about what this study does not do, about some of its most obvious limitations in terms of coverage. First of all, the study concerns universities of very different types, some of which have a large complement of graduate and professional schools, some of which do not. The presence or absence of such professional programs clearly affects the character of the library system, expenditures, the sizes of collections, and so on. The available data sets have been compiled in such a way that, in general, they cannot easily be disaggregated; as a consequence, data on medical, law, and business school libraries have not been subtracted from the totals.[4] To some extent, therefore, we are obliged to work with unlike entities.

Moreover, the study does not consider in any depth the different sorts of problems one finds in particular subject areas within the arts and sciences. Scientists and humanists make very different uses of the library, and the collections maintained for each "class" of scholar have different characteristics and pose distinctive problems. We have not specifically addressed these kinds of contrasting needs in any detail, though we do occasionally refer to them.[5]

---

[4]It would have been possible to separate data for law and medical libraries between 1978 and 1990, but this was not done.

[5]For excellent general statements on these kinds of issues, see the materials collected in *Communications in Support of Science and Engineering*, A Report to the National Science Foundation from the Council on Library Resources (Washington, D.C.: Council on Library Resources, August 1990). We are grateful to Warren J. Haas for sending a copy of this publication.

Nor does this study consider the problem of book preservation. Many of the volumes housed at libraries of the type studied here are in danger of disintegration; they were printed on paper manufactured from wood pulp and as a result have a high acid content. The fact that we do not discuss the preservation problem should not be taken as an indication that we do not consider it serious; on the contrary, it must be regarded as one of the most important problems research libraries face. Our sense, however, is that it is one problem that is particularly well understood, at least in relation to the other kinds of problems identified here.

The preservation problem is also more clearly separable from the others, whereas those issues discussed here are in some sense more inextricably linked with one another and therefore must be treated as parts of a whole. Finally, there have been systematic, determined efforts underway for some years now that address preservation issues with visible success. That success is due in no small part to the activities of the Commission on Preservation and Access, ably directed by Patricia Battin, and other similar programs, notably that supported by the National Endowment for the Humanities.[6]

Considered together, as they must be, the panoply of questions, issues, and choices outlined in this study will define in no small measure the nature of the process of scholarly communication in the years ahead. There are implications for both graduate and undergraduate education, for the finances of higher education, for the publication process itself, and perhaps even for the ways in which some ideas are formulated, reviewed, and then revised. While a considerable amount of experimentation and learning as we go is inevitable, we are persuaded that the time is at hand for systematic efforts to define sets of alternatives, test their implications, and devise feasible modes of collaboration across sectors and among different types of entities.

The interconnections among both the questions to be considered and the institutional players are so strong that limited perspectives are likely to lead to unsatisfactory outcomes. The opportunity exists to rethink an entire set of relationships that, if reconstituted appropriately, can give libraries both new dimensions and an even more central role in the educational process than they have enjoyed in the past.

---

[6]For statements of the preservation problem and the efforts to work toward solutions, see the commission's many excellent publications, available from its office at 1400 16th Street, N.W., Washington, D.C. We are most grateful to Patricia Battin for providing a complete set and for useful discussions and correspondence concerning book preservation.

One aspect of the discussion of preservation does impinge directly on the other questions associated with electronic technologies—namely, the debate over the desirability of putting less emphasis on microfilming and more emphasis on the use of digital imaging.

PART 1

Historical Trends: Collections, Expenditures, Publications

CHAPTER TWO

Growth of Library Collections

The most common way of thinking about libraries has been in terms of the sizes of their collections. In recent years more attention has been given to access, as students and scholars have come to realize that a book is of limited value if it cannot be found readily and used, and much of the second part of this study is devoted to the implications of moving away from such a single-minded commitment to the size of collections per se. Still, the size of a collection does matter, and recent developments concerning the use of library materials can be understood only in the context of an appreciation for the historical trends in the numbers of volumes held.

Much has been written on this subject in an attempt to understand underlying patterns and thereby, perhaps, to project future library size and anticipate library needs. Ever since Fremont Rider's well-known assertion, "It seems, as stated, to be a mathematical fact that, ever since college and university libraries started in this country, they have, on the average, doubled in size every sixteen years,"[1] there have been numerous attempts to substantiate or disprove his thesis, particularly with regard to the concept of exponential growth. (Rider's assertion is equivalent to proposing a constant average annual rate of growth of approximately 4.5 percent.)

Our analysis of this aspect of library growth differs in some respects from earlier studies.[2] First, earlier studies were necessarily focused on more limited time spans than is this study, which includes annual data for years from 1912 through 1991. Rider's analysis, for example, was based on the number of volumes held at various libraries in six specific years between 1831 and 1938. A series of studies at Purdue University attempted to predict values of several variables through 1980 on the basis of data collected from 1950–51 through 1971–72. Baumol and Marcus (1973) analyzed Purdue data for the period 1950–51 to 1968–69. Other studies (Drake 1977; Wyllys 1978; Leach 1976) analyzed data from the early 1960s through the mid-

---

[1]Fremont Rider, *The Scholar and the Future of the Research Library* (New York: Hadham Press, 1944), 8.

[2]The best critical overview of this literature is Robert Molyneux's article "Patterns, Processes of Growth, and the Projection of Library Size: A Critical Review of the Literature on Academic Library Growth," *Library and Information Science Research* 8 (January-March 1986): 5-28. In this article the author asserts that "library growth has not been modeled well and that no successful method of projecting growth has been developed." He cites three reasons for the failure to develop reasonable projections: (1) most writers apparently assumed that library growth occurs in one particular pattern; (2) no understanding of the processes of growth underlying the patterns was developed; and (3) the methods used by the writers did not allow for very different patterns of growth during different periods.

1970s.[3] Molyneux analyzed data from 1962–63 through 1983–84 in an attempt to show that library growth had *not* been exponential during the decade of the 1970s.

A second difference has to do with purpose. In contrast to most of the earlier studies, our purpose is not to project future library growth. We do not start with the premise that there is some automatic or inexorable force that drives library growth independent of other variables, both internal to the university library system and external to it. The data themselves show how dangerous it is to make projections based solely on historical patterns. The patterns of growth that have characterized libraries in the past 30 years in no way reflect growth rates up to 1960. Moreover, we expect that changing technology will alter fundamentally the future structure of libraries—with major implications for library growth. (Part 2 of this study is devoted almost entirely to this topic.) Nonetheless, trends in library growth are useful in providing a context for examining some of the factors underlying major developments within the library world—both historical and prospective—and that is the reason for our interest in them.

VOLUMES HELD

The number of volumes held is one widely used measure of the overall size of research libraries.[4] Figure 2.1 shows trends in the numbers of volumes held for two of our composites—Private 1 and Public 1 universities—between 1912 and 1991. (Data for the other two composites do not go back this far.[5]) Over this 79-year period the overall size of these major libraries grew steadily and rapidly. Public 1 libraries grew by a factor of more than 30—from an average of 163,023 volumes held in 1912 to an average of 4,951,155 in 1991; Private 1 libraries (starting from an appreciably larger base) grew by a factor of more than 13—from an average of 455,351 volumes held in 1912 to an average of 6,109,355 in 1991.

The annual percentage increases for both composites can be seen most clearly by examining the bottom panel of figure 2.1, which contains the same data plotted on a semi-log scale (with, therefore, a straight line representing equal percentage increases from year to year). The two composites grew at different rates: Public 1 universities had an average annual rate of increase of 4.5 percent, whereas the

---

[3]Rider, *Scholar and the Future.* W. J. Baumol and M. Marcus, *Economics of Academic Libraries* (Washington, D.C.: American Council on Education, 1973). M.A. Drake, *Academic Research Libraries: A Study of Growth* (West Lafayette, Ind.: Purdue University Libraries and Audio-Visual Center, 1977). R. E. Wyllys, "On the Analysis of Growth Rates of Library Collections and Expenditures," *Collection Management* 2 (1978): 115–128. S. Leach, "The Growth Rates of Major Academic Libraries: Rider and Purdue Reviewed," *College and Research Libraries* 37 (1976): 531–542.

[4]ARL uses the following definition of a volume: "a physical unit of any printed, typewritten, handwritten, mimeographed, or processed work, contained in one binding or portfolio, hardbound or paperbound, which has been cataloged, classified, and made ready for use." Sarah M. Pritchard and Eileen Finer, comps. *ARL Statistics 1990–91* (Washington, D.C.: Association of Research Libraries, 1992), 63.

[5]Nor do data for all twelve of the Research 1 libraries go back to 1912. Data on volumes added gross for the University of North Carolina and the University of Virginia begin in 1922 and 1923, respectively. To maintain consistency in the number of institutions represented in the Public 1 composite over the entire time period, we imputed data for these two institutions for the years in which data were missing. The data were imputed to reflect the pattern of growth of the average of the other four missing years. The levels of the imputed data for each "missing" institution were based on volumes added gross in the first year for which data were available for the respective libraries (1922 for U.N.C., 1923 for the U.Va.).

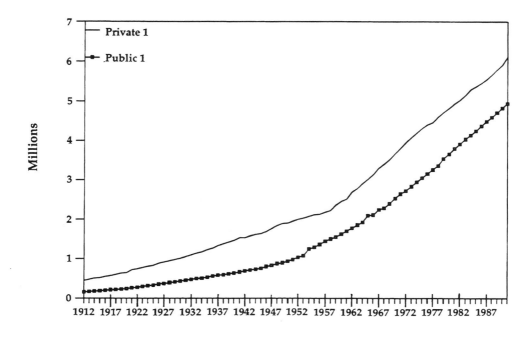

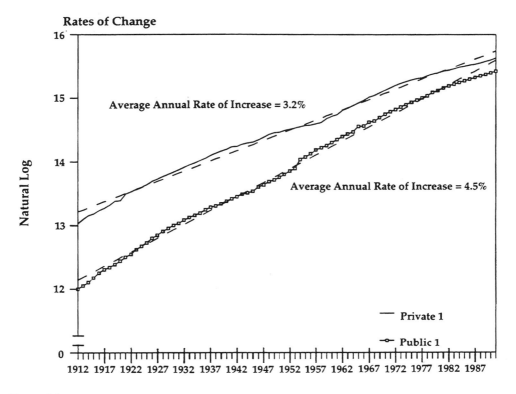

Figure 2.1
Number of volumes held, Private 1 and Public 1 composites, 1912–91

collections at the Private 1 universities grew 3.2 percent per year on average.[6] It is an interesting curiosity (nothing more than that, in our view) that the 4.5 percent average annual growth rate for the Public 1 universities is precisely equivalent to Rider's assertion that libraries double in size every sixteen years. The average annual growth rate of 3.2 percent for the Private 1 universities implies a doubling of collections every 22 years. Of course, the actual annual rates of increase were not constant (the observations do not all lie exactly on the regression line). Annual growth rates for both the Private 1 and the Public 1 composites peaked in the mid- to late 1960s and then fell slowly throughout the 1970s. From about 1940 forward, the absolute size of the difference in scale between the two sets of libraries is fairly consistent, which is one reason why in much of the subsequent analysis we group the Private 1 and Public 1 libraries into a single Research 1 composite.

VOLUMES ADDED GROSS

A more precise picture of library growth can be obtained by using the variable volumes added gross, a measure of annual cataloging activity at each library.[7] While cataloging activity does not represent the number of volumes acquired by the library in any given year, it does measure the overall growth of the collections accessible to users and is therefore a reasonable proxy for acquisitions defined in one highly relevant sense.

Once again, data are available in years before 1963 only for the libraries represented in the Research 1 composite. The growth in this measure was remarkably steady between 1912 and the late 1950s, except for the expected dips that occurred during the two world wars (fig. 2.2). Then, during the 1960s, the number of volumes added annually rose at a record rate of about 10 percent per year—more than doubling, from just under 70,000 volumes in 1960 to a peak of 148,330 in 1970. The retrenchment of the 1970s, which afflicted all of higher education, dramatically reversed this trend.

These sharp fluctuations in the annual numbers of volumes added illustrate clearly that the fortunes of the major libraries have been affected markedly, as one would have expected, by broad trends in higher education. One would expect collections to expand most rapidly when enrollments are rising rapidly, colleges and universities are expanding their offerings, and resources are relatively plentiful. And these were, of course, precisely the defining characteristics of higher education in the United States during the 1960s.[8]

---

[6]The average annual rates of increase were determined by fitting a least-squares regression line to the natural logarithms of the values of each curve and then determining the (constant) annual percentage increase implied by the slope of the regression line.

[7]This measure does not reflect volumes that may be lost, stolen, or deaccessioned for some other reason.

[8]For a summary of broad trends in enrollment and an analysis of changing patterns of degrees conferred, see Sarah E. Turner and William G. Bowen, "The Flight from the Arts and Sciences: Trends in Degrees Conferred," *Science* 250 (October 26, 1990): 517–521. For a more general discussion of trends in higher education in the 1960s and early 1970s, see Earl F. Cheit, *The New Depression in Higher Education: A Study of Financial Conditions at 41 Colleges and Universities* (New York: McGraw Hill, 1971).

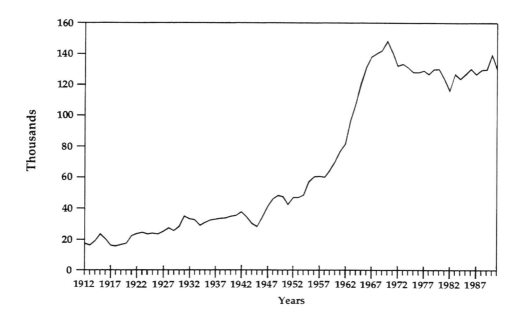

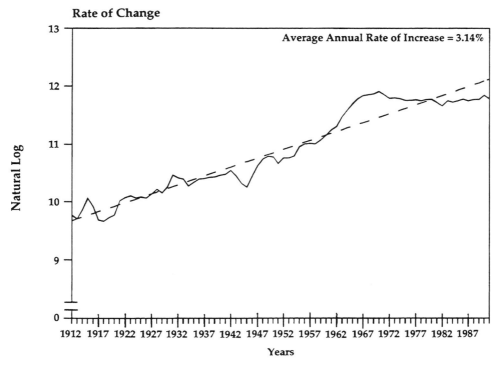

Figure 2.2
Volumes added gross, Research 1 composite, 1912–91

The unprecedented growth in doctoral programs and in doctorates conferred was an additional source of extra pressure on libraries during the 1960s.[9] In essentially all fields of study, doctoral programs can be offered only if library resources are at least reasonably adequate, and any university considering the addition of one or more doctoral programs or even the inclusion of more subfields within an existing program must anticipate pressures for significant growth in library holdings. The number of distinct doctoral programs is a better index of pressures on a research library than is enrollment. It is hardly a coincidence that universities with large numbers of active doctoral programs are the same universities that have large—and growing—collections.

The strong interconnection between graduate education and faculty scholarship and research makes this relationship an even tighter one. Research collections designed to serve expanding graduate programs and faculty who are themselves deeply committed to scholarly and research agendas face unremitting pressures to keep growing; they cannot afford to fail to continue to build their holdings. (The implications of graduate programs for library collections are also reflected in the pronounced differences in library expenditures between universities and colleges, which we note later.)

It is hardly surprising, then, that there is a close correspondence between trends in doctorates conferred and trends in library volumes added (fig. 2.3).[10] Both doctorates conferred annually and annual volumes added gross increased rapidly throughout the decade of the 1960s before a precipitous fall in the early 1970s. The peak year for volumes added gross was a bit earlier (1970) than the peak year for Ph.D.s conferred (1972), and this slight lag is what one might expect given the duration of graduate study; most students who entered graduate programs during the mid- to late 1960s would not have received their degrees until the early to mid-1970s.

Generally speaking, the 1970s and most of the 1980s were years of retrenchment for both graduate programs and libraries. However, reductions in the annual number of volumes added gross were evidently much more modest than the reductions in doctorates conferred. The apparent asymmetry is real. It is generally easier to contemplate reductions in the sizes of entering cohorts of graduate students (in part because external factors, such as declines in the numbers of strong applications and the decreasing availability of financial aid, can be limiting factors) than it is to contemplate reductions in acquisitions. Decisions to invest in building a strong library collection in a certain field usually are—and should be—made for the long run. The figures showing year-to-year movements in volumes added illustrate well that decisions to step up the level of acquisitions are not readily reversed. There is, if you will, a kind of ratchet effect at work here, and any acquisitions policy designed to curtail the growth of a collection is likely to be hotly contested by faculty members and may well prove very difficult to implement.

---

[9]See Bowen and Rudenstine, *In Pursuit of the Ph.D.*, especially chapters 2–5.

[10]Data on trends in the number of doctorates conferred are taken from special tabulations from the National Research Council. The average represented here is a simple average of the Ph.D.s conferred at our Research 1 universities in six fields only (English, history, economics, political science, mathematics, and physics).

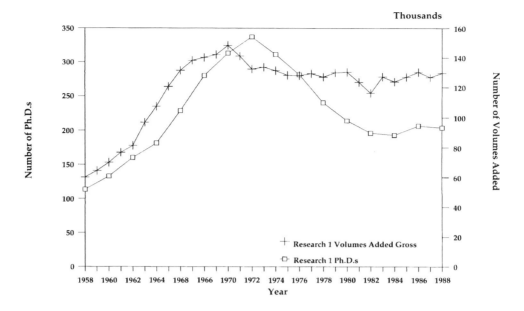

Figure 2.3
Number of volumes added gross vs. number of Ph.D.s awarded, 1958–88

There is one final observation to be made concerning the general comparison between levels of library acquisitions and numbers of doctorates conferred. The modest recovery at the end of the 1980s in number of Ph.D.s conferred was matched, at least in part, by an even more modest recovery in the annual number of volumes added gross. However, as we will attempt to explain later, other factors—including the increasingly severe fiscal problems of universities and the rapidly rising prices of serials—were important in determining the rates at which collections could be augmented.

DIFFERENCES AMONG COMPOSITES

While all our composites followed the same general pattern during the past three decades of expansion and subsequent contraction, there are some variations and some pronounced similarities that merit mention.

Private versus Public

First, among the Research 1 libraries, the public-private distinction does not appear to be significant until the expansion period of the 1960s. At that time the gap between the Private 1 composite's and the Public 1 composite's annual number of volumes added gross widened (fig. 2.4). Subsequently, the rate of acquisitions contracted more within the Private 1 composite than within the Public 1 composite, so that by the early 1980s the difference in annual levels of acquisitions between the two sets of libraries was again roughly what it had been before 1960.

Since the mid-1980s, the Private 1 composite has shown evidence of a recovery, with volumes added increasing each year between 1985 and 1990 (and then declining slightly in 1991). The Public 1 composite, however, has shown little evidence of any persistent recovery in the rate of acquisitions. Considerable year-to-year fluctuations continue to characterize this group of libraries, with a particularly significant drop in 1991. This pattern may result from unusually volatile funding from state governments during much of the 1980s; it illustrates the difficulty that state universities have experienced in planning their acquisitions budgets.

Over longer periods of time the curve showing annual volumes added by the Private 1 libraries has been even more volatile. During the expansion of the 1960s, available resources tended to grow faster at the Private 1 universities than at the Public 1 universities, just as they subsequently tended to fall faster. Whatever the full range of reasons for this pattern, there is no doubt that it is real. The differences just described are not due to the behavior of one or two large libraries in either the Private 1 or the Public 1 composite. The pattern of sharp increases and decreases in annual rates of acquisitions was reported by all six of the Private 1 libraries, and the top half of table 2.1 summarizes the extent to which the average growth rates for this composite differed during expansion and contraction from the average growth rates for the Public 1 libraries.[11]

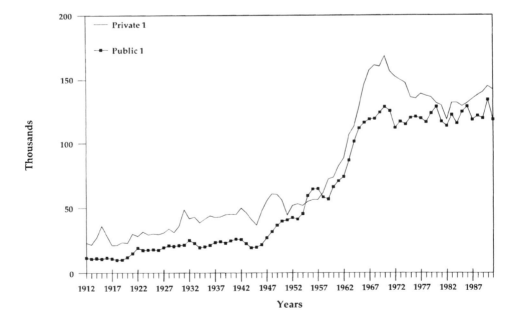

Figure 2.4
Volumes added gross, by type of institution, 1912–91

---

[11]See Appendix Table 2.1 for detail on growth rates for individual libraries in all four composites.

TABLE 2.1
Average Annual Rates of Increase in Volumes Added Gross by Composite (percent)

	Years			
	1952-63	1963–70	1970–82	1982–91
Private 1	6.55	6.94	−2.18	1.70
Public 1	5.87	4.87	−0.19	0.63
Private 2	—	8.8	−0.83	−0.48
Public 2	—	12.2	−2.45	2.68

Notes: Rates are computed as the antilog of the regression line fit to the curve for each composite during each time period. Data are not available for Private 2 and Public 2 composites prior to 1963.

This difference between private and public libraries in the magnitude of swings in rates of acquisitions breaks down, however, when we consider the Research 2 category (bottom half of table 2.1). In fact, between 1963 and 1970 the Public 2 composite increased its annual level of acquisitions faster than any of the other three components (12.2 percent per year). The Private 2 composite recorded the second largest increase in the rate of acquisitions during the 1960s (nearly 9 percent per year), and much of the explanation for such large growth rates at both sets of Research 2 libraries no doubt has to do with the fact that these universities were expanding at more rapid rates (especially at the graduate level) than the longer-established Research 1 institutions. The Public 2 and the Private 2 libraries began in 1963 from a base of volumes added that was about half the size of the base for the Public 1 libraries and about 40 percent of the base for the Private 1 libraries.

Age

We might expect that the age of a library would correlate inversely with the rate of growth, with younger libraries growing faster than older libraries in an attempt to build their collections. After a library reached a certain level of maturity, the rate of growth in number of volumes added might be expected to slow, with emphasis shifting to maintaining rather than building collections.

This proposition is difficult to test with ARL data, since members must achieve a certain scale in order to be considered for ARL membership.[12] Thus, by the time that their data are included within the ARL universe, libraries are at least reasonably well established and may have already passed through an initial period of rapid expansion. It is possible, however, to compare rates of growth for charter (1932)

---

[12] ARL has developed an elaborate quantitative formula based on five variables (total volumes, total staff, serials held, volumes added annually, and total expenditures) by which a library's level of activity and scale are evaluated. To be considered for membership, a library must be above a defined threshold for four years. (The threshold was based on the activity and scale of the ARL charter members. The intent of the four-year requirement is to require a long-term commitment to the development of the library by the parent institution.) The parent institution must have a minimum of 32 Ph.D. programs. Extensive narrative documentation is required, and an ARL committee conducts a site visit to the library that is applying for membership.

members of ARL[13] with rates of growth for those that joined ARL after 1956 (see fig. 2.5). The percentage growth rate has been larger for the younger libraries, as we would have expected, since this set of libraries started from a smaller average base. However, when the curve for the younger libraries is shifted to take account of its smaller base (see the dashed line on fig. 2.5), the two curves are astonishingly similar. This demonstrates that changes in the absolute numbers of volumes added have been nearly identical. The parallel patterns of expansion, modest contraction, and then a leveling off from the 1960s through the 1970s and 1980s for both sets of libraries is strong evidence that common forces (internal and external) have overwhelmed any natural stages of development related to age.

Size

Finally, one might expect that the size of the library would be a significant variable in explaining patterns of growth. In fact, library size does seem to be a significant factor, but the results of this comparison are somewhat counter-intuitive (fig. 2.6).[14] Whereas a plausible hypothesis might have been that smaller libraries

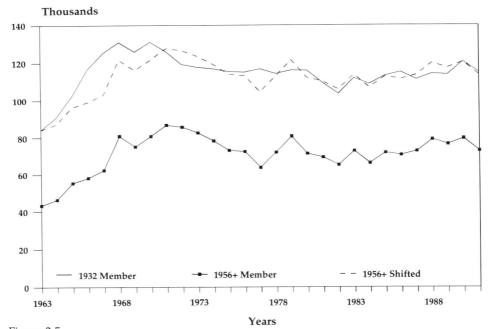

Figure 2.5
Volumes added gross, by year of ARL membership, 1912–91

[13]New York University library is included in the 1932 grouping even though it was not a member of ARL until 1936.

[14]For the purposes of this analysis, the following composites were constructed, based on the number of volumes held in 1963: smaller (<=1,000,000)—Georgetown, Iowa State, Maryland, Boston, Washington State, Washington University, Michigan State; medium (1,000,000 to 2,000,000)—Florida, Southern California, Rutgers, Iowa, Virginia, New York, North Carolina, Wisconsin, Northwestern, Princeton; larger (>=2,000,000)—Chicago, Stanford, Cornell, Berkeley, Columbia, Michigan, Yale.

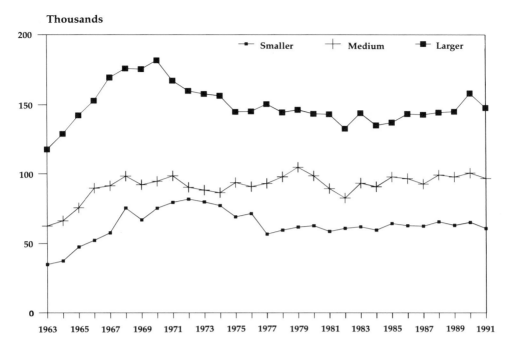

Figure 2.6
Volumes added gross, by size of library, 1963–91

would expand more rapidly than larger libraries during periods of expansion in an attempt to catch up, in fact during the 1960s it was the larger libraries that increased the number of volumes added gross most rapidly. The gap in holdings actually widened between these libraries and those classified for this purpose as medium and smaller. Then, during the 1970s, the larger libraries experienced the most significant degree of contraction, so that the gap in holdings narrowed.

The greater volatility among the larger libraries reflected in these patterns may be due to the factors mentioned earlier in discussing the high volatility of the Private 1 composite during the 1960s and 1970s (since all the Private 1 institutions except Princeton fall into the larger category). In addition, some reduction in the rate of increase in acquisitions may have seemed more realistic for the larger libraries during the 1970s. Their holdings and their continuing rates of acquisition may have seemed large enough to permit them to withstand a period of slower growth without feeling that the integrity of the collections was being threatened. Smaller libraries may have thought that they had less margin for adjustment.

CHAPTER THREE

Growth of Library Expenditures

There are obvious reasons for thinking about library growth in the currency of numbers of acquisitions (volumes added and held), which are measures of real things used by students and scholars. From another perspective, however, it is just as important to know about trends in library expenditures. Libraries consume large quantities of the monetary resources of universities and compete with other valuable activities for limited funds. In this chapter we consider both trends in library expenditures per se (in nominal and real terms) and the relationship between these expenditures and other outlays by universities. We are also interested in the question of whether and to what extent these trends and relationships for research universities differ from corresponding trends and relationships within liberal arts colleges. (We defer until Chapter 4 an analysis of changes in the composition of library expenditures.)

TOTAL EXPENDITURES FOR MATERIALS AND BINDING: 1912–91

Expenditures for materials and binding is the only class of expenditures for which we have consistent data going back to 1912, and we use this category as a rough proxy for total expenditures over this long time period.[1] In nominal terms expenditures for materials and binding by the Research 1 libraries grew at a remarkably steady rate of approximately 7.6 percent per year (fig. 3.1).[2] Only during the war periods, the depression of the 1930s, and the early 1970s did this class of expenditures fail to increase. War periods are of course understood to be atypical, and we return later in this chapter to the factors that caused the decline in expenditures on materials and binding in the early 1970s. We see from this figure also that the typical rate of increase in expenditures has been appreciably greater in the years since World War II than it was before the war. Since 1952, the average annual rate of increase in current dollars has been 9.8 percent per year ($R^2 = 0.99$).

There is always the possibility that a time series expressed in current dollars will be misleading because it will be distorted by changes in the general level of prices. In this instance, however, correcting for changes in the value of the dollar (fig. 3.2) serves mainly to reduce the average rate of increase.[3] In constant dollars, average

---

[1] As we will see in Chapter 4, expenditures for materials have remained a fairly constant share (roughly one-third) of total expenditures between 1963 and 1991. Although binding expenditures declined throughout that same period, they are a very small percentage of all expenditures on materials and binding. Data for total expenditures (including salaries and other operating expenditures) are available on a consistent basis only from 1963 forward.

[2] We limit this analysis to the Research 1 libraries since data for the other libraries included in this study are available only for more recent periods. The R^2 is 0.97.

[3] We use the GNP deflator as our general index of price changes. The Consumer Price Index is not really relevant to library expenditures, and the Higher Education Price Index (HEPI, which should be a somewhat more refined measure) is not available before 1960. A comparison of the GNP deflator and the HEPI after 1960 shows that the movements of the two indices are quite similar in any case.

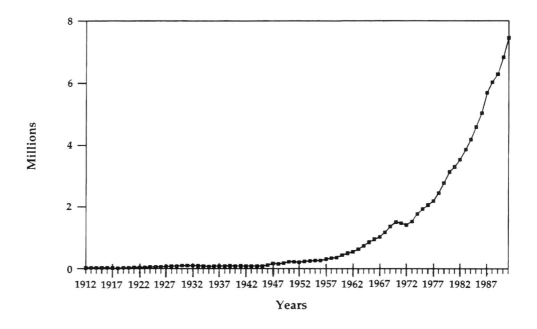

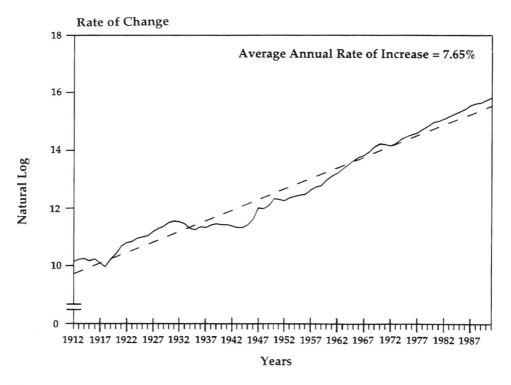

Figure 3.1
Expenditures for materials and binding, Research 1 composite, in nominal dollars, 1912–91

expenditures on materials and binding increased 4.3 percent per year—a far from trivial real rate of growth.

It is revealing that the average annual rate of increase expressed in current dollars is steadier than the average annual rate of increase expressed in constant dollars.[4] This comparison supports the common-sense view that the upward pressures on the library budget have been driven primarily by forces that are not tied closely to the general price index (especially the volume of publications and the prices of those publications). Determined efforts to express every variable in constant dollars can confuse analyses of this kind.

Redoing the analysis of trends in expenditures in constant dollars does serve, however, to account for much of the difference in average rates of increase in current expenditures between the pre- and post-World War II periods noted earlier. The higher inflation rate during much of the post-World War II period undoubtedly escalated library costs, as all other costs. The average annual rate of increase in expenditures measured in constant dollars was 4.7 percent (R^2 = .88) between 1952 and 1991, as compared with 4.3 percent per year for the entire period from 1912 to the present.

This analysis also confirms an important point made earlier: the patterns characteristic of the 1960s are anomalous and not at all consistent with patterns for longer time periods. However one draws the regression lines, the observations for the 1960s are above the long-term trends (see both fig. 3.1 and fig. 3.2). They cannot be taken as any indication of what is "normal." When we confine our analysis to the years after the 1960s, we find that expenditures on materials and binding by the Research 1 libraries have increased, on average, 8.8 percent per year in current dollars and 2.7 percent per year in constant dollars. These are much more modest rates of increase than many observers of the worlds of libraries and university finance would have expected to find, and we shall return to their meaning and interpretation later in this chapter.

If we now place on one figure (fig. 3.3) the data showing the trend in volumes added that we examined in Chapter 2 and the data showing the trend in expenditures on materials and binding expressed in constant dollars, we find that the curves first begin to diverge in the late 1950s and then to move in different directions after about 1970. From about 1970 on, expenditures on materials and binding measured in real terms continued to rise at the same time that the rate of acquisitions actually declined. (We do not present separate data for the various library composites because they all behave similarly in this regard.) In some general sense, libraries began to "pay more for less."[5] This major development is explored in detail in later sections of this study.

---

[4]The R^2 is 0.93 for the regression line in figure 3.2, which measures the trend in expenditures in constant dollars, as contrasted with an R^2 of 0.97 for the regression line in figure 3.1, which measures the trend in expenditures in current dollars.

[5]Moreover, Donald W. Koepp, university librarian at Princeton, has suggested in a conversation with Anthony Cummings that the significance of these trends may be even more dramatic at some institutions than the raw data suggest. Because of efficiencies resulting from the automation of the cataloging function described in the next chapter, arrearage in cataloging has been greatly reduced. Accordingly, rates of increase in volumes added gross may be said to be artificially higher for the period since the automation of the cataloging function, since a larger proportion of volumes acquired has been cataloged expeditiously.

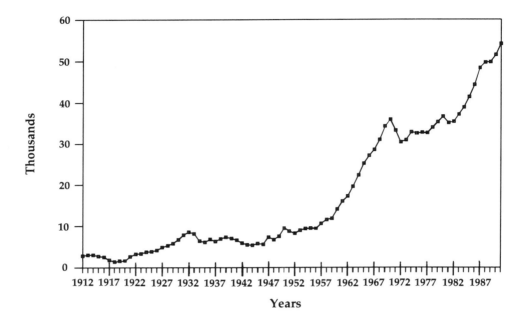

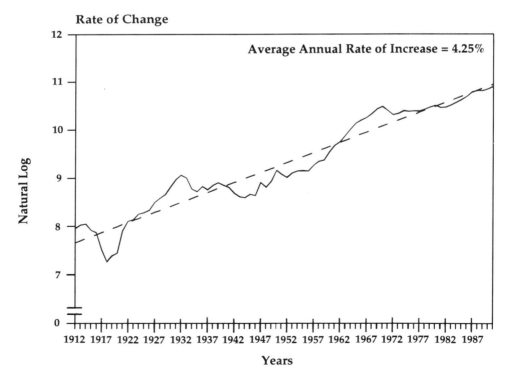

Figure 3.2
Expenditures for materials and binding, Research 1 composite, in real (1982) dollars, 1912–91

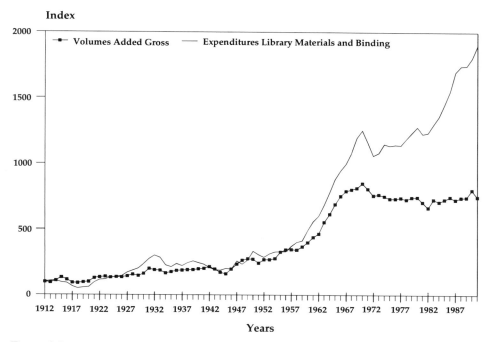

Figure 3.3
Comparison of measures of growth of Research 1 composite, 1912–91 (Index: 1912=100)

TOTAL EXPENDITURES: 1963–91

Starting in 1963, we are able to examine total direct expenditures by university libraries, excluding space costs and the libraries' share of general university overhead. The absolute numbers are far from inconsequential. In 1991 both Berkeley and Stanford reported total library expenditures in excess of $31 million, and the average for the twelve Research 1 libraries included in this study was slightly more than $22 million. Total library expenditures for the twelve Research 2 libraries included in this study averaged almost $15 million in 1991.

Over the entire period 1963–91 the overall rate of growth in total library expenditures was almost precisely the same as the overall rate of growth in expenditures on materials and binding. For the Research 1 composite, the two growth rates were 8.8 percent per year (total expenditures) and 8.79 percent (materials and binding)! For all 24 libraries the corresponding growth rates were 9.2 percent (total expenditures) and 9.12 percent (materials and binding). (This comparison implies an overall consistency in the composition of the budgets of research libraries that is correct for the materials and binding share but not correct for other components, as we shall see in Chapter 4.)

An even more interesting picture emerges when we examine average rates of change in total expenditures within each of our four composites during three subperiods: 1963–70, 1970–82, and 1982–91 (table 3.1). Total library expenditures rose extremely rapidly between 1963 and 1970 within all four composites (at an average annual rate of over 14 percent for all 24 libraries). Not surprisingly, library expenditures rose even more rapidly at the Private 2 and Public 2 libraries, which had lower levels of expenditures at the start of this period of expansion, than at the longer-established Private 1 and Private 2 libraries. (The respective average annual rates of increase were 13.1 percent at the twelve Research 1 libraries versus 16.3 percent at the Research 2 libraries.)

Library expenditures continued to rise faster at the Research 2 libraries than at the Research 1 libraries in both the 1970–82 and 1982–91 intervals, but the differentials were much compressed. The sharpest contraction in the rate of increase in library expenditures in the most recent period occurred within the Public 1 composite, no doubt as a result of the fiscal pressures on state budgets. The Private 1 universities experienced the slowest rate of increase in library expenditures in the 1970-82 period, presumably as a result of the severe financial pressures felt within those universities in the 1970s.

When we examine year-to-year changes in total expenditures within all 24 libraries (fig. 3.4), we see an abrupt change in the slope of the curve in 1970. In effect, two regimes can be distinguished: (1) the expansionary years between 1963 and 1970, when library expenditures rose at what was clearly a nonsustainable rate; and (2) the years since 1970, when library expenditures continued to rise steadily but at an average rate of just over 8 percent per year, as compared with an earlier average rate of about 14 percent. Of course, an 8 percent annual rate of increase—which implies a doubling of library expenditures every eleven years—is hardly trivial. We are reminded again of the strength of upward pressures on library budgets within each of our four composites.

LIBRARY EXPENDITURES IN RELATION TO OTHER UNIVERSITY EXPENDITURES

These data on growth in library expenditures take on much greater meaning when analyzed in the context of broader trends in university finances. A pivotal question is whether libraries have become ever more insistent claimants, consuming ever larger shares of available resources. When we began this study, we assumed that the answer to this question would be an emphatic yes. We were wrong. In fact, we were *very* wrong, as can be seen by examining figure 3.5, which shows library

Table 3.1
Average Annual Rates of Increase in Total Expenditures, Current Dollars, by Composite

	1963–70	1970–82	1982–91	1963–91
Private 1	14.6	7.2	8.3	8.7
Public 1	11.3	9.3	7.4	9.0
Research 1	13.1	8.1	7.9	8.8
Private 2	15.7	9.0	8.3	10.3
Public 2	16.8	8.3	9.2	9.7
Research 2	16.3	8.6	8.7	10.0
All-24 (Current)	14.1	8.3	8.2	9.2
All-24 (Real)	10.0	0.6	4.6	3.0

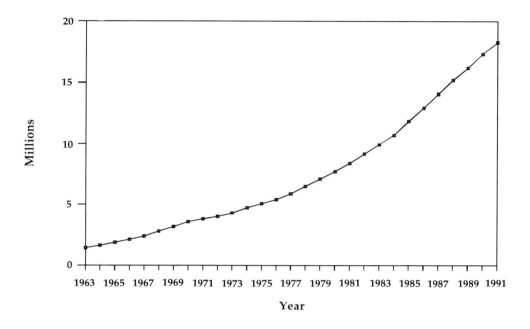

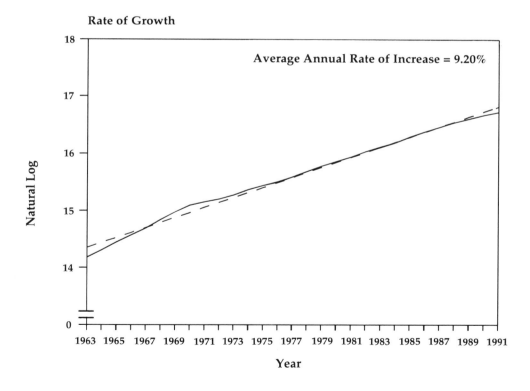

Figure 3.4
Total library expenditures, All-24 composite, in nominal dollars, 1963–91

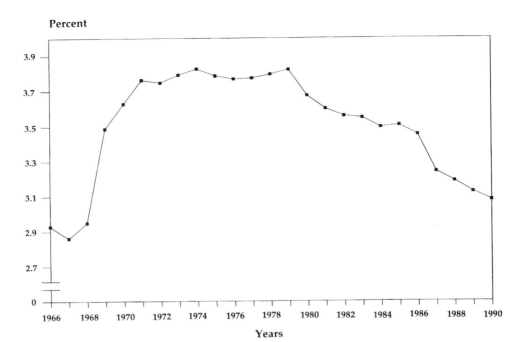

Figure 3.5
Library as a percentage of Educational and General expenditures, 17-university average, 1966–90

expenditures for a subset of 17 of our 24 libraries as a percentage of all Educational and General Expenditures at the same universities.[6]

The sharp rise in the libraries' share of Educational and General Expenditures (hereafter E&G) from the mid-1960s through 1971 indicates that research libraries participated more than fully in the rapid growth in university budgets that occurred

---

[6]We use the U.S. Department of Education survey data for Educational and General Expenditures but continue to rely on the ARL data for library expenditures. For sources and definitions of the Education Department data, see Appendix A. In brief, Educational and General Expenditures include academic and administrative expenditures of all kinds, including sponsored research, maintenance of the plant, and student aid; they exclude such auxiliary activities as dormitories and food services. One advantage of using this broad grouping of expenditures is that it is less influenced than some of its components by changing definitions of the boundaries between subcategories.

The percentages in figure 3.5 are averages of the percentages for the seventeen libraries for which consistent data could be obtained from 1966 through 1990. The 7 libraries (of the total group of 24 included in this study) for which these data could not be calculated back to 1966 are Berkeley, Columbia, Cornell, Maryland, Michigan, Rutgers, and Wisconsin. The missing data are almost always the Educational and General Expenditures. In the cases of a few other libraries, we had to interpolate figures for one or two years to obtain a consistent time series.

These percentages can be computed for all 24 libraries for years from 1972 forward, and the 24-university averages for the 1972–90 period are very similar to the 17-university averages for the same years, except that the 24-university averages are slightly higher in absolute terms (3.20 percent of Educational and General Expenditures in 1990, as compared with 3.08 percent for the 17-university average). With very few exceptions, the year-to-year changes are nearly identical.

during that expansionary period. On average, these libraries increased their share of E&G expenditures from under 3 percent to nearly 4 percent. (This was also the period of the most rapid expansion in doctoral education.)

During the severe retrenchment in higher education that characterized the decade of the 1970s, libraries essentially held their own with respect to share of E&G expenditures. Then, starting in 1980, the libraries' share fell every year but one during the 1980s—until it reached a low point of 3.08 percent in 1990, a level just slightly higher than the level in the mid-1960s.

Is this recent downtrend in the relative emphasis given to library budgets a function of exceptionally rapid increases in expenditures for such purposes as student aid (necessitated by a decline in the relative amount of federal funding available), student services, or central administrative functions? This proposition can be tested, at least roughly, by making use of a more narrowly defined benchmark that focuses solely on more strictly "academic" expenditures—the category called Instruction and Departmental Research on the Department of Education's survey instruments.[7]

Relating library expenditures solely to Instruction and Departmental Research (hereafter I&DR) does not change the basic pattern described above.[8] Library expenditures grew in relation to I&DR during the last half of the 1960s, held constant through 1975, and then declined—at first very sharply and then more gradually (fig. 3.6). In particular, we see again the same kind of steady decline during the decade of the 1980s that is evident when library expenditures are compared with all Educational and General Expenditures. (It should be noted, however, that the relative rate of decline is less rapid for this measure than for library expenditures as a percentage of E&G expenditures.) We also see stronger evidence in this figure of the emergence of a new plateau, since library expenditures have been almost constant as a percentage of I&DR from 1987 through 1990. There are other intriguing aspects of these sets of data, looked at together, but they are more relevant to a broader study of university finance during these decades than to this study of research libraries.[9]

The principal conclusion is inescapable: rather than continuing to claim a larger and larger percentage of the university budget, the typical research library has seen its share of all E&G expenditures fall steadily in recent years. The consistency of

---

[7]This expenditure category consists mainly of the basic budgets of the academic departments and is therefore unaffected by changes in student aid, student services, plant maintenance, and administrative costs. Sponsored Research is another category, also separate from Instruction and Departmental Research, but it is less independent in that gains and losses in Sponsored Research funding can have significant effects on Instruction and Departmental Research by shifting portions of some salaries onto (or off) the regular departmental budget.

[8]For convenience, we express library expenditures as a percentage of expenditures on Instruction and Departmental Research, even though library expenditures are not a component of the I&DR category. This is simply one way of calculating a ratio, thereby scaling the data.

[9]The major difference between figures 3.5 and 3.6 occurs during the period 1974–76, when library expenditures remain essentially constant as a percentage of E&G but decline sharply as a percentage of I&DR. The proximate explanation has nothing directly to do with library expenditures; rather, the I&DR share of total university expenditures rose markedly between 1974 and 1976. This may be nothing more than a statistical artifact, related to some changes in the HEGIS forms and reporting in that interval. The rapid increase in the Consumer Price Index during these years could also be part of the explanation, since universities felt strong pressure to do as much as they could for salaries of faculty and staff, which make up a disproportionately large part of the I&DR category.

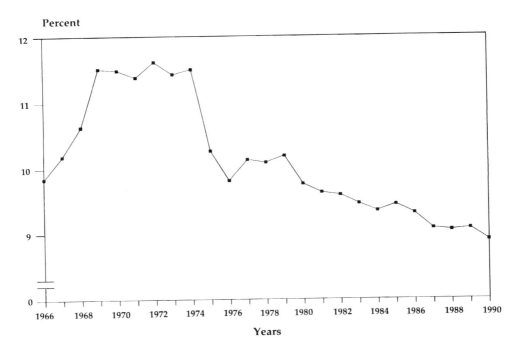

Figure 3.6
Library expenditures as a percentage of Instruction and Departmental Research expenditures,
17-university average, 1966–90

this pattern among the 24 universities included in this study is striking, as can be seen from table 3.2, which compares the library percentages in 1979 with the comparable percentages in 1990. The plethora of minus signs in the last two columns speak for themselves. In all but 2 of the 24 universities, library expenditures declined in relation to all E&G expenditures.[10]

The same pattern is evident when we plot the year-by-year ratios of library expenditures to E&G expenditures values for each of the four library composites, showing the detail for both the 17-university data, going back to 1966, and the 24-university data from 1972 forward (fig. 3.7). The only general comparison to note is that the ratio falls most rapidly for the Private 1 set of libraries, which have had the highest library share in all years. More generally, we find that within each of the four composites the largest decline in the library share occurred at the library that had received the largest absolute share of its university's total expenditures in 1979 (for example, Princeton, Virginia, Northwestern, and Rutgers). Conversely,

---

[10]However, at least one component of library expenditures—serials subscriptions—rose appreciably more rapidly than E&G expenditures, especially in the last decade or so. Kendon Stubbs has found that serials expenditures have even kept pace with national expenditures on research and development, which have grown much faster than E&G expenditures (Letter to Richard Ekman, October 2, 1992). Chapter 4 contains a fuller discussion of shifts in the components of library expenditures.

Table 3.2.
Total Library Expenditures as a Percentage of Total Educational and General Expenditures,
1979 and 1990

	1979	1990	Increment	% Increase
Private 1 Universities				
Chicago	3.95	3.20	−0.75	−18.99
Columbia	3.22	2.93	−0.29	−9.01
Cornell	5.98	5.26	−0.72	−12.04
Princeton	7.76	5.43	−2.33	−30.03
Stanford	4.32	3.34	−0.98	−22.69
Yale	5.42	4.65	−0.77	−14.21
Priv-1 Avg.	5.11	4.14	−0.97	−18.98
Public 1 Universities				
U.C. Berkeley	5.24	4.21	−1.03	−19.66
Iowa	3.40	2.69	−0.71	−20.88
Michigan	2.82	2.60	−0.22	−7.80
North Carolina	3.09	2.57	−0.52	−16.83
Virginia	5.79	4.22	−1.57	−27.12
Wisconsin	2.70	2.57	−0.13	−4.81
Pub-1 Avg.	3.84	3.14	−0.70	−18.23
Private 2 Universities				
Boston	2.36	1.95	−0.41	−17.37
Georgetown	4.37	4.26	−0.11	−2.52
N.Y.U.	2.46	2.45	−0.01	−0.41
Northwestern	4.58	2.89	−1.69	−36.90
Southern California	2.39	2.55	0.16	6.69
Wash U. (St.Louis)	2.71	2.10	−0.61	−22.51
Priv-2 Avg.	3.15	2.70	−0.45	−14.29
Public 2 Universities				
Florida	3.53	2.32	−1.21	−34.28
Iowa State	2.87	2.54	−0.33	−11.50
Maryland	3.89	3.31	−0.58	−14.91
Michigan State	2.07	2.13	0.06	2.90
Rutgers	6.05	3.56	−2.49	−41.16
Washington State	3.89	3.05	−0.84	−21.59
Pub-2 Avg.	3.72	2.82	−0.90	−24.19
24-University Avg.	3.95	3.20	−0.75	−18.99

Notes: Data for Library Expenditures are from ARL. Data Expenditures are from HEGIS/IPEDS
surveys.

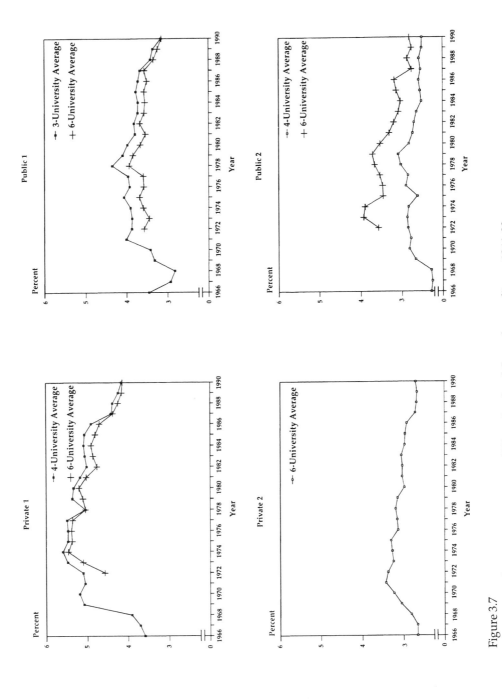

Figure 3.7
Library expenditures as a percentage of Educational and General expenditures, 1966–90

libraries that had rather low ratios of library expenditures to total expenditures in 1979 tended to see the library share decline somewhat less rapidly (though there are exceptions). The tendency for library expenditures to decline in relation to the I&DR category was also pervasive, although somewhat less consistent than in relation to E&G expenditures. In 17 of the 24 universities, library expenditures declined as a percentage of I&DR between 1979 and 1990 (table 3.3). The seven exceptions (Columbia, Michigan, Wisconsin, Georgetown, Southern California, Maryland, and Michigan State) were spread almost evenly among the four composites and can be explained, we believe, primarily with respect to local circumstances. Again, the plot of annual ratios for the four composites (fig. 3.8) provides additional detail of another kind, all of which is consistent with the general pattern that we have been describing.

The 1970s and early 1980s were difficult times for higher education, and the evidence cited here suggests that retrenchment is particularly harsh on libraries. It may be easier to slow the growth of acquisitions than to take other kinds of budgetary actions such as reducing faculty positions, laying off staff members, and reducing financial aid. We do not believe, however, that this is the full explanation for the failure of the library to maintain its share of total expenditures. In our view other developments, including technological changes and steep increases in the prices of serials, led to changed attitudes toward library expenditures and their long-term place in the university budget—differences in fundamental assumptions as to what was both desirable and sustainable. These themes are developed in subsequent chapters. Before turning to these topics, however, we will provide a brief postscript to this chapter's analysis of trends in expenditures in the form of a comparison of research libraries with college libraries.

COLLEGE LIBRARIES

While the subject of this study is research libraries associated with major universities, the characteristics of these libraries can be seen in sharper relief when they are compared with some of the libraries maintained by leading liberal arts colleges. The essential difference, of course, is that the college libraries have no obligation to serve the needs of major doctoral-granting programs. For that reason alone we would expect to find a difference in the level of library expenditures, and so we do. A set of fifteen highly selective, private liberal arts colleges had average annual expenditures of about $2 million in 1990, as contrasted with an average for our 24 research university libraries of just under $18 million.[11]

That ratio of 8:1 or 9:1 can be considered a rough upper bound of what appears to be required at the level of library investments if an institution is to commit itself to doctoral programs in a large way. We say "upper bound" because research

---

[11]The fifteen colleges included in this analysis are Bowdoin, Bryn Mawr, Carleton, Davidson, Grinnell, Haverford, Middlebury, Mount Holyoke, Oberlin, Pomona, Reed, Smith, Swarthmore, Trinity, and Vassar. These fifteen were chosen in part because data were available for them on a reasonably consistent basis from 1977 through 1990. In the case of these institutions, none of which are members of the Association of Research Libraries, data for both library expenditures and other expenditures come from the HEGIS/IPEDS surveys. As a result, we have information on total library expenditures only, and these data are somewhat less reliable than the comparable data collected by ARL for the research universities.

Table 3.3
Total Library Expenditures as a Percentage of Instructional and Departmental Research Expenditures, 1979 and 1990

	1979	1990	Increment	% Increase
Private 1 Universities				
Chicago	9.84	6.29	−3.55	−36.08
Columbia	8.28	9.43	1.15	13.89
Cornell	20.00	16.79	−3.21	−16.05
Princeton	24.09	22.13	−1.96	−8.14
Stanford	16.93	14.31	−2.62	−15.48
Yale	13.66	11.22	−2.44	−17.86
Priv-1 Avg.	15.47	13.36	−2.11	−13.64
Public 1 Universities				
U.C. Berkeley	15.13	13.24	−1.89	−12.49
Iowa	7.63	6.89	−0.74	−9.70
Michigan	7.35	8.10	0.75	10.20
North Carolina	7.16	6.23	−0.93	−12.99
Virginia	14.00	11.63	−2.37	−16.93
Wisconsin	8.33	10.36	2.03	24.37
Pub-1 Avg.	9.93	9.41	−0.52	−5.25
Private 2 Universities				
Boston	7.53	5.08	−2.45	−32.54
Georgetown	9.93	12.68	2.75	27.69
N.Y.U.	5.85	5.45	−0.40	−6.84
Northwestern	9.63	7.70	−1.93	−20.04
Southern California	5.62	6.31	0.69	12.28
Wash U. (St.Louis)	7.02	4.18	−2.84	−40.46
Priv-2 Avg.	7.60	6.90	−0.70	−9.21
Public 2 Universities				
Florida	8.59	7.34	−1.25	−14.55
Iowa State	8.33	8.27	−0.06	−0.72
Maryland	8.93	9.94	1.01	11.31
Michigan State	4.96	5.35	0.39	7.86
Rutgers	14.57	10.16	−4.41	−30.27
Washington State	12.49	10.08	−2.41	−19.30
Pub-2 Avg.	9.64	8.52	−1.12	−11.62
24-University Avg	10.66	9.55	−1.11	−10.41

Notes: Data for Library Expenditures are from ARL. Data for I&DR Expenditures are from HEGIS/IPEDS surveys.

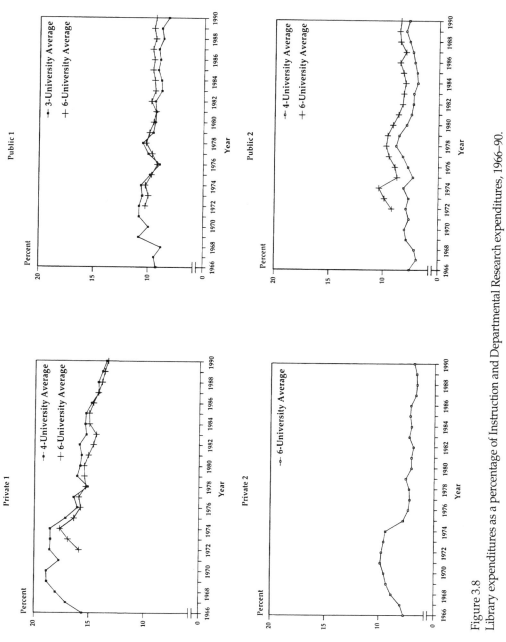

Figure 3.8
Library expenditures as a percentage of Instruction and Departmental Research expenditures, 1966–90.

universities also enroll many more students than do selective liberal arts colleges, and some of the difference in library expenditures noted earlier is simply a matter of scale. Also, research universities usually maintain highly expensive professional libraries in fields such as medicine and law.

It is instructive, therefore, to compare library expenditures at Princeton (which is primarily an arts-and-sciences university, with no professional schools of law, medicine, business, or education, and a total enrollment of about 6,000) with library expenditures at Oberlin and Smith, which have strong libraries and enrollments roughly half as large as enrollment at Princeton. Annual library expenditures at Princeton are four to five times greater than library expenditures at these two colleges, and this ratio is perhaps more indicative of the direct effects of doctoral education and the other features of a research university. If we were to make a generous allowance for differences in enrollment, the ratio of library expenditures at Princeton to library expenditures at Oberlin or Smith might be reduced to something like three or four to one (since no one believes that library outlays need to increase in proportion to the number of undergraduate students). The implications of research-university status for library expenditures are obvious.

While the absolute level of library expenditures is far higher at a research university than at a liberal arts college, the *share* of library expenditures in the overall budget of the institution is significantly higher at the typical liberal arts college. (See Appendix Tables 3.1-3.5.) This finding may come as something of a surprise to those who thought that doctoral education and a heavy emphasis on research would require disproportionate investments in library resources. The apparent explanation is that libraries at liberal arts colleges as well as at universities entail heavy fixed costs (subscriptions to a core set of journals and reference materials, for example), and the far larger enrollments at research universities permit these fixed costs to be spread over larger numbers of students. In short, there may well be substantial economies of scale.

Again, it is instructive to examine the case of Princeton, where differences in enrollment as compared with the liberal arts colleges, while still significant, are less overwhelming than at most other research universities. Even with a larger enrollment (roughly three times the enrollment of the average liberal arts college included in this analysis), Princeton allocated a larger percentage of instruction and departmental research expenditures to the library than did any of the fifteen liberal arts colleges—22 percent in 1990 at Princeton versus a high for the colleges of about 20 percent at Bryn Mawr and Haverford.[12] (Bryn Mawr, of course, has important doctoral programs and is in that sense something of a misfit among the liberal arts colleges.) The average for the fifteen colleges was about 15 percent. Princeton also allocated a slightly higher percentage of all educational and general expenditures to the library (5.4 percent in 1990) than did the typical college (5.1 percent in 1990). In this instance, economies of scale were insufficient to outweigh the additional expenses associated with a heavy emphasis on doctoral education and research.

---

[12]At Oberlin, Total Library Expenditures were also approximately 20 percent of instruction and departmental research expenditures in 1990. However, the value for total library expenditures for this year was imputed, so we do not have as much confidence in its accuracy.

Research universities apparently have to be larger than Princeton before scale effects predominate.[13]

A primary reason for examining library expenditures at colleges is to see if their trends mirror those at the research universities.[14] Overall, library expenditures at the fifteen colleges increased by a factor of about 3.2 between 1977 and 1990, for an average annual growth rate of approximately 9.4 percent per year. This is just slightly higher than the growth rate for library expenditures within the research universities (about 8.7 percent per year).

A more revealing comparison is of trends in the library's share of all educational and general expenditures. As in the case of the universities, library expenditures at the colleges have declined in recent years as a percentage of both E&G and I&DR expenditures (fig. 3.9). Thus, in this sector too we see that, contrary to some popular wisdom, libraries have not absorbed a larger and larger share of the budgets of institutions of higher education.

The rate of decline in the library share of budgets at the colleges has been very modest, however, and does not appear to have become pronounced until about 1985 and thereafter. Between 1979 and 1990 the typical college in our set saw its library expenditures decline from 6.0 percent to 5.1 percent of E&G expenditures and from 16.4 percent to 15.9 percent of I&DR expenditures. The comparable figures for university libraries (tables 3.2 and 3.3) indicate that library shares of university budgets fell somewhat more than library shares of college budgets.

---

[13]It would be interesting and worthwhile to carry out a more detailed analysis of the relationship between enrollment and library expenditures within both the research universities and the liberal arts colleges in an effort to understand better the shapes of the relevant cost curves. However, even cursory inspection of the data collected for this study demonstrates how difficult it would be to control for other important variables such as the number of programs of study, the research emphasis of the institution, the balance between the humanities and the sciences, and the wealth (and perhaps the age) of the institution. In any case, these scale effects may well change markedly as more use is made of some of the new technologies discussed in Part 2 of this study.

[14]For another analysis of college libraries as compared with university libraries, see Richard Hume Werking "Collection Growth and Expenditures in Academic Libraries: A Preliminary Inquiry," *College & Research Libraries* 52 (1991): 5-23. The author uses data primarily from the Bowdoin List for college libraries and ARL for university libraries and finds, as we do, that the college library expenditures grew more rapidly than the university library expenditures between 1977 and 1987. (Our analysis extends to 1990.) He also analyzes both college library collections and components of expenditures *within* total college library expenditures.

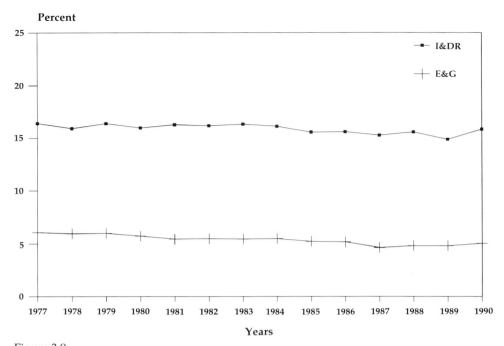

Figure 3.9
Library expenditures as a percentage of I&DR and E&G expenditures, 15-college average, 1977–90

CHAPTER FOUR

Components of Library Expenditures

In this chapter we look behind the library aggregates and consider trends in three major categories of direct library expenditures: staffing and staff salaries; expenditures on materials and binding; and other expenses (in recent years, principally outlays related to automation). In the last part of the chapter we examine the rising fraction of the expenditures for materials that has been devoted to the purchase of serials, a development with broad implications for scholarly communication as well as for the economics of university libraries.

STAFFING

Libraries are labor-intensive entities, and wages and salaries appear to have constituted over half of all current expenditures for as many years as records exist.[1] Salary data, however, are less reliable in early years than figures showing the number of staff employed; therefore, we begin by looking at changes in staff size.

The long-term growth in number of staff in Research 1 libraries was steady between 1912 and the early 1960s, allowing for the inevitable fluctuations associated with two world wars (fig. 4.1). Taking the years since 1912 as a single period, we find that the total number of professional and supporting staff at Research 1 libraries has increased at an average annual rate of approximately 3.7 percent.

While all parts of this record are of historical interest, it is the patterns since World War II (and especially over the last three decades) that are most consequential. Distinct subperiods stand out. Following the war, there was a considerable rebuilding of staff (which lasted from 1944 to about 1949); once this was accomplished, staff size grew only modestly until about 1960. At that time the entire face of higher education began to change rapidly. The general expansion of colleges and univer-

---

[1]Reliable data on shares of total expenditures date back only to 1963. However, cruder data on salary budgets, seen in relation to expenditures on materials and binding, go back to 1912 for at least some libraries. Examination of the relevant ratios suggests strongly that salaries have long been the largest single category of expenditure. (At Berkeley, for example, salaries were approximately 1.5 times expenditures on materials and binding during the decades before World War II; this same ratio was approximately 2.1 in 1963 and 2.2 in 1991.)

In making this statement and in presenting other expenditure ratios in this chapter, we follow—of necessity—the traditional practice of taking total direct expenditures by libraries as the base for all such calculations. This method is seriously misleading in that no weight is given to the costs of space, which are very considerable. (In Part 2, we speculate briefly on the importance of taking the costs of space into account if wise decisions are to be made concerning new publishing forms made possible by electronic technology.) The neglect of space costs is but one example of a more generic problem with university accounting—namely, the tendency either to understate or to ignore altogether capital costs of many kinds. See Gordon Winston, "Why Are Capital Costs Ignored by Colleges and Universities and What Are the Prospects for Change?" Williams Project on the Economics of Higher Education, DP-14, July 1991.

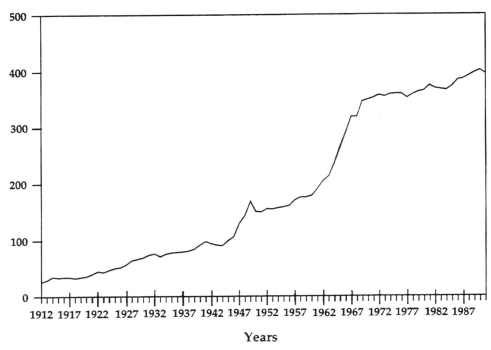

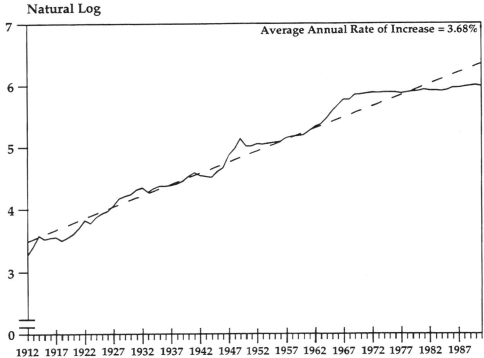

Figure 4.1
Professional and nonprofessional staff, Research 1 composite, 1912–91

sities had a dramatic effect on the size of the library staff as well as on library acquisitions. Between 1960 and 1970 the average size of the staff in the Research 1 libraries almost doubled (increasing by 94.7 percent), or an average of about 7 percent per year. While some of these increases in staffing were no doubt required by higher workloads associated with increased enrollments and the need to cope with an increasing volume of acquisitions (discussed later), another significant part of the explanation for this unprecedented growth in library staffing surely has to do with the equally unprecedented expansion of graduate education that occurred simultaneously. More branch and departmental libraries were established, and bibliographers, catalogers, and reference librarians were needed in larger numbers than ever before.

The growth in staff size then came to an abrupt halt. In the fifteen years between 1970 and 1985 the average size of the library staff at these same Research 1 universities increased by only 6.9 percent (less than 1/2 of 1 percent per year). Most recently, there has been a modest "recovery," in that the average size of the library staff grew by another 5.9 percent over the next six years.

More complete staffing data for all four of our composites (including data on total salaries paid, which are presented later) exist from 1963 on, and they show both the same high rates of increase in staff size during the 1960s and the same virtual halt to net additions during the 1970s (fig. 4.2).[2] While the expansionary period of rapid increases in staff size lasted somewhat longer at the Research 2 universities than at the Research 1 universities, a sharp deceleration in the rate of new hiring followed by a period of essentially no change is evident in the plots for all four composites. In none of these sets of libraries, however, is there evidence of any absolute decline in the size of the staff during the 1970s. (The negative blips in a few individual years appear to be due to shifts in the numbers of temporary employees, associated with the birth and death of special projects.) The essential point is that there was very little net expansion in library staffs between the early 1970s and the mid-1980s.[3]

Another perspective on changes in staffing at Research 1 universities is obtained when we compare the growth in staff with changes in the size of collections. The long-term rates of increase in volumes held and volumes added per year have been roughly comparable to the long-term rate of increase in staff, with the average annual growth rate for volumes held (3.7 percent per year) exactly the same as the growth rate for personnel (3.7 percent per year) and the average annual growth rate

---

[2]The annual data presented in figure 4.2 are calculated as three-year moving averages of the year-to-year change in the size of the total staff.

[3]This virtual halt in the growth of professional and nonprofessional staff was accompanied by an increase in the number of student assistants. In all but the Public 2 composite the ratio of student assistants to total staff increased modestly throughout the 1970s. At the Private 1 composite, for example, this ratio increased from 0.168 to 0.196, an increase of approximately 17 percent. However, not even the larger number of student assistants, when expressed at Full-Time Equivalent (FTE) employees, alters the basic proposition about slow growth of staff during the 1970s. The absolute number of student assistants added during the entire decade ranged from only 10 to 30. The changing mix of staff itself reflects changes in the way that libraries operate.

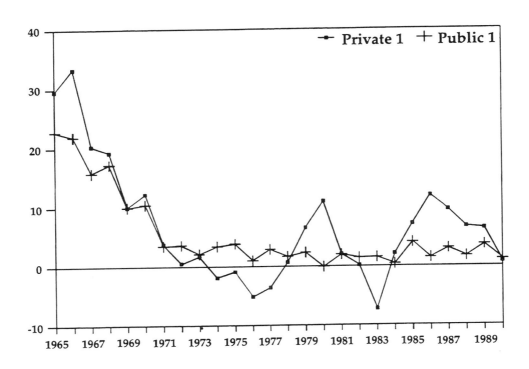

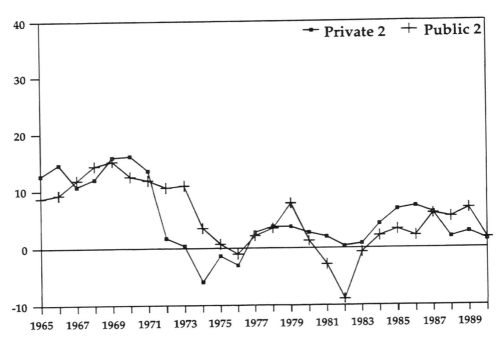

Figure 4.2
Annual change in size of total staff, three-year moving average, 1965–90

for volumes added (3.1 percent per year) only modestly lower.[4] But beneath these long-term similarities are some sharply divergent trends.

The ratio of volumes held per staff member was reasonably steady during the pre-World War II years (fluctuating in the range of 10,000 to 13,000 volumes per staff member); it then fell sharply during World War II (to a low of about 8,000 volumes per staff member in 1948) before climbing back to roughly the 11,000 level in the early 1960s (fig. 4.3a). During the decade of the 1960s the ratio of volumes held per staff member fell sharply and reached a level lower than that observed at any previous time (excepting only the World War II trough year). Since volumes held continued to increase after 1970, when staff size ceased to grow, there has been a steady and steep rise in the number of volumes held per staff member, which has continued to the present day.

An ever-larger collection is being managed by a staff that for the last 20 years has not increased at anything approaching a comparable rate. The result is that volumes held per staff member at the Research 1 universities is now at an all-time high of nearly 15,000 volumes.

The second measure of changes in collections—the annual number of volumes added gross, the measure of annual flow into the system as contrasted with the previous measure of the size of the stock—also declined in relation to staff size during the 1960s (fig. 4.3b). The net additions to library staff were so great that they dominated even the substantial increase in the rate of acquisitions that also occurred during that decade (as well as, *a fortiori*, the increases in volumes held). However, while the ratio of volumes held per staff member then rose sharply, the ratio of volumes added per staff member continued to decline during the 1970s and 1980s (bottom panel of fig. 4.3b). The reason for this decline is very different, however, from the reason for the decline during the 1960s: the retrenchment in higher education that began in the 1970s had an even stronger restraining effect on new acquisitions than it did on new staff.

In sum, then, library staff have faced contradictory trends in the early 1990s. They have had to manage a larger collection per staff member than ever before; at the same time, the number of new acquisitions per staff member has fallen back to the level of the mid-1950s.

BROAD SHARES OF LIBRARY EXPENDITURES

The three principal components of the library budget for which we have reliable data going back to the early 1960s are (1) expenditures for library materials and binding; (2) total salaries and wages, including the compensation of student assistants; and (3) other operating expenditures, which have been affected significantly by outlays for the computerization of libraries.

---

[4]See Chapter 2, figures 2.1 and 2.2. The average rate of increase in volumes held (which is a stock) will normally be greater than the average rate of increase in volumes added (which is a flow). The total number of volumes held would still increase somewhat (albeit at a declining percentage rate) even if the growth rate for volumes added were zero, since a zero growth rate for volumes added would be consistent with a constant annual increase in the absolute number of volumes added. This is, in fact, a reasonably accurate description of what has happened to collections over the last two decades.

Thousands

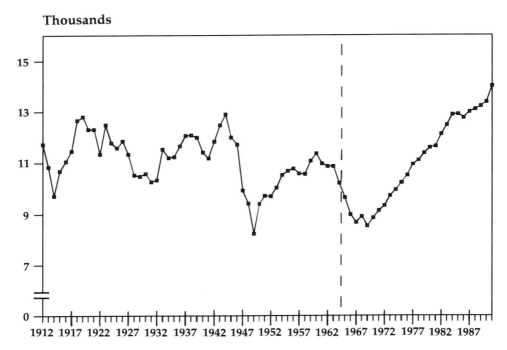

Figure 4.3a
Volumes held per staff member, Research 1 composite only, 1912–91

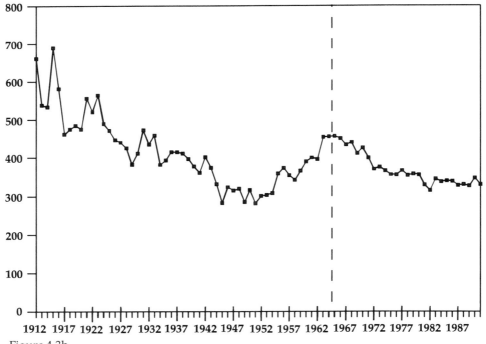

Figure 4.3b
Volumes added gross per staff member, Research 1 composite only, 1912–91

While absolute expenditures in all three categories have of course increased substantially over the last three decades, there have been some noteworthy shifts in relative shares. The basic pattern is most easily presented and described via snapshots taken at four different points in time: 1963, 1970, 1982, and 1991 (fig. 4.4).

Expenditures on materials and binding at these 24 libraries have been a remarkably constant share of total library expenditures, moving from 33 percent to 35 percent, back down to 33 percent, and then back up to 35 percent. The noteworthy trends concern the other two components. Salaries have fallen steadily, from an average of 62 percent of total expenditures in 1963 to 52 percent in 1991. The remaining component, other operating expenditures, has risen just as steadily, climbing from an average of just 6 percent in 1963 to 14 percent in 1991.

These shifts in salary percentage may be more consistent with the trends in number of staff discussed in the preceding section than they first appear to be. What is surprising initially is the sharp decline in the salary share between 1963 and 1970 given the rapid increase in the number of staff between those two years. The explanation, we believe, is that the age distribution of the staff probably changed markedly during the 1960s, since most of the new additions to staff can be assumed to have been relatively young. Rapid increases in staffing are often accompanied by less rapid increases in payroll costs because of the growing fraction of the staff earning entry-level salaries. The post-1970 declines in the salary share of total

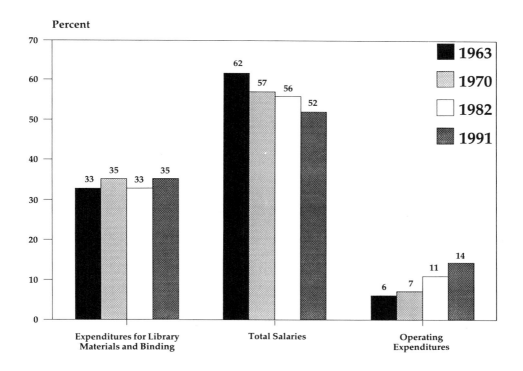

Figure 4.4
Components of library budget (percentage shares), All-24 universities, 1963, 1970, 1982, and 1991

expenditures require no special explanation, since they follow directly from the halt in recruitment described in the previous section.[5]

The increase in the share of total expenditures of the other operating expenditures category has been dramatic by any reckoning. This share has more than doubled, rising from 6 percent to 14 percent. By all accounts, increasing outlays related to computerization have been the driving force, and it is therefore not surprising that the largest jump in share occurred between 1970 and 1982, when the new technology was first introduced on a large scale.

Before commenting further on computerization, it is worth noting that the pattern just described has characterized all four of our library composites (fig. 4.5), with only slight variations among the sets of libraries. Shares of expenditures devoted to other operating expenditures started from a lower base in the Public 1 and Public 2 composites (5 and 4 percent, respectively) than in the private composites and then rose relatively rapidly in these two public composites. But there is little more to be said about differential rates of increase in the shares of any of these components. The point to emphasize is surely the commonality of the trends. (See also fig. 4.6, which provides annual data for each of the four library composites.)

Pronounced similarities in the absolute levels of the shares across composites are also evident. In 1991 the share of total library expenditures devoted to expenditures on materials and binding ranged from a low of 33 percent in the Private 1 composite to a high of 36 percent in the Public 1 composite. The salary share in 1991 ranged from a low of 50 percent in the Private 2 composite to a high of 53 percent in the Public 2 composite (with values of 52 percent in both Private 1 and Private 2). And the share devoted to other operating expenditures in 1991 ranged from lows of 12 percent in Public 1 and Public 2 to a high of 15 percent in Private 1 and Private 2.

OPERATING EXPENDITURES AND COMPUTERIZATION

At this point a brief explanation of three of the functions that have been automated over the past two decades will help provide a better understanding of operating expenditures and the kinds of developments that have encouraged reallocations of funds within the total budget for the library. We will then discuss the issue of budgetary trade-offs more explicitly.

At many institutions the first of the functions to be automated was circulation, which was seen as an obvious candidate for such treatment. At many institutions barcode labels that are optically scanned at the moment the book is charged out have replaced cards, which in the past had to be removed manually from the volume and filed. The advantages of storing the title, call number, and author's name electronically are obvious: any of the elements can be retrieved and a patron need know only one element of the three in order to request information about the volume.

---

[5]These salary figures include the salaries of student assistants.

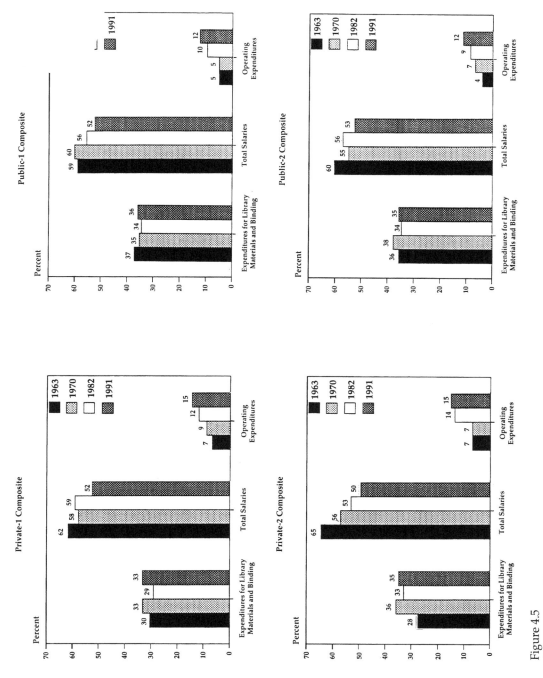

Figure 4.5
Components of library budget (percentage shares), by composite, 1963, 1970, 1982, and 1991

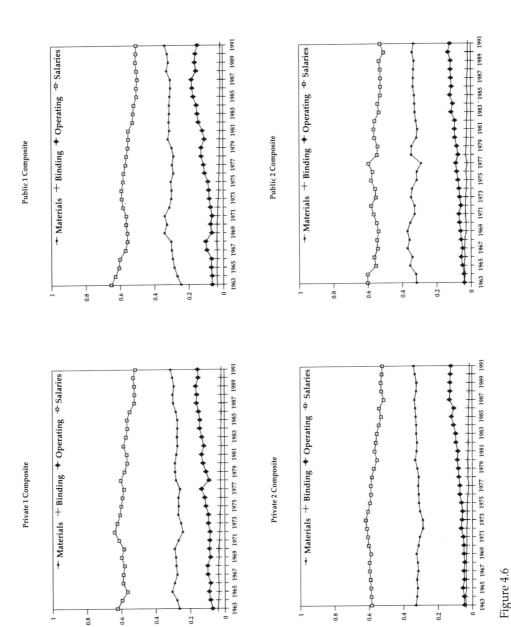

Figure 4.6
Principal components of library budget (share of total expenditures), 1963–91

The automation of the cataloging function has been of even greater importance; indeed, in Warren J. Haas's words, "[c]ataloguing is what turns an accumulation of material into a library collection,"[6] and the technological advances of the past few decades have afforded a degree of standardization within the entire system nationally that previously would have been impossible. In the past a professional cataloger at a particular institution would either write his or her own catalog copy or make use of cards provided by the Library of Congress, which sometimes required revision resulting from a different classification scheme or minor differences between the volume actually in the possession of the cataloger engaged in writing copy and the volume cataloged by the Library of Congress.[7] Subsequently, Library of Congress copy was made available online from one of the national vendors, in particular OCLC (originally the Ohio College Library Center, now the Online Computer Library Center) and RLIN (the Research Library Group's Research Libraries Information Network). Individual member libraries also contribute records written by their professional catalogers to both the RLIN and OCLC databases.

The advantages of this approach are obvious: copy made available online can readily be reformatted to fit specifications peculiar to a particular institution. Moreover, because member institutions contribute copy there are additional sources of records in the absence of Library of Congress copy, which obviates the need for original copy to be written at each individual institution and offers the promise of greater uniformity in the content of the records. In the past the Research Libraries Group charged member institutions that used the RLIN database a per-transaction fee. Members may now purchase transactions in blocks (500,000 searches annually, for example) and are given rebates for each record contributed to the database.

The acquisitions function has also benefitted from automation. The Research Libraries Group, for example, provides a service that enables a member library to search the database for information about items it may wish to purchase, and order forms may then be generated directly from the database. Similarly, invoices in machine-readable form are often included with shipments of books. The information that the invoices contain is integrated into computer files and affords a means of achieving various kinds of control over the acquisitions budget generally and the performance of vendors.

These technological developments mean that while the basic library functions continue to be performed, they are now performed in very different ways. And the costs of performing them are now allocated somewhat differently among categories of expenditure than they were in the past. In effect, trade-offs have been made between staffing and automation—which is not to say that this has been a conscious,

---

[6]See Haas's preface to *The National Coordinated Cataloging Program: An Assessment of the Pilot Project* (Washington, D.C.: Council on Library Resources, 1990), v. It should be noted that under Mr. Haas's leadership the Council on Library Resources played a continuing role in supporting shared cataloging, automated catalogs, and linkage of bibliographic systems.

[7]Since the establishment of the Cataloging in Publication program, moreover, an effort has been made by the Library of Congress to write catalog copy for books *before* their publication, so that it could be printed in the published books. Because various elements of catalog records written prospectively do not always conform precisely to the books in their final published form, the records cannot in all instances be accepted without revision.

carefully articulated process. As Kendon Stubbs has put it, in commenting on an earlier draft of this manuscript:

It is true that other operating expenditures have risen faster than total expenditures and staffing somewhat less. But I doubt that any library director would say that over the past 15 or 20 years there has been a deliberate shifting of money from staff to automation and other "other operating" expenditures. In fact, as you note, the absolute size of ARL staffs has never declined; it has just grown more slowly in recent years. Thus, in the various places in this study where you suggest a conscious trade-off between staffing and automation, I would be more inclined to suggest something less planned. ARL libraries tend to be conservative and to hold onto staff, often for traditional functions even when those functions are no longer cost-efficient (though in the very recent past, under the impact of the recession, there is evidence that the libraries are being more hard-nosed about relinquishing staff in traditional but low-impact functions).

It may be closer to the truth to say that by the mid-seventies new staffing positions were harder to come by than they had been in the sixties, so that increases in staffing (and staffing expenditures) slowed; while the then relatively small amount devoted to other operating expenditures was allowed to grow at its own pace, chiefly driven by automation. I don't know if this formulation comes out sounding really different from yours; but it does propose that the flow of money from staff to other operating was more fortuitous than planned up to very recent years. One piece of evidence for the unplanned nature of the historical trend is that during the late seventies and up to the past few years it was reported as axiomatic in library literature that automation does not save staff. If you were a library director and were requesting funding for an online cataloging system, you had to sell the concept to your administration while at the same time telling them that you could not give up any cataloging staff after you were automated. This was an unrealistic sales job, even if the library community had convinced themselves that it made sense; and university administrations may have reacted by putting reins on new staffing, while hoping that automation would stabilize library costs.[8]

Surely no one would suggest that librarians sat down, plotted the changes in the production possibility curves facing the library that resulted from technological change, superimposed the relative costs of different inputs on the diagram, and then decided to shift "x" amount of resources from staff salaries to automation. The process of reallocating resources was surely far less planned and more evolutionary, as Stubbs suggests. Nonetheless, there has been an inexorable character to these developments, and the results have been much the same as those that one would

---

[8]Letter from Mr. Stubbs, associate librarian for public services, Alderman Library, University of Virginia, to Anthony C. Cummings, January 29, 1991.

have derived from a more formal cost-benefit model.[9] The implications of new technological possibilities could not simply be ignored, and by changing the very nature of key library functions these technologies altered the staffing needs of the library with consequences for both total staff size and the relative mix of staff members in various employment categories.

We conclude this part of the discussion by noting that it is difficult to determine with precision how the effective functioning of the library has been affected by the redistribution of shares of library expenditures from staffing to automation. The reason is that the automation of circulation, cataloging, and acquisitions has changed the nature of these functions. Our strong impression is that the quality of these services has been enhanced, in some instances quite appreciably, but this is hard to prove definitively.

EXPENDITURES WITHIN THE MATERIALS CATEGORY: SERIALS

There is one remaining trend in the composition of library expenditures that must be mentioned because of its potential consequences, even though reliable data are available only since 1976. The overall stability in the share of the total library budget that has been devoted to expenditures on materials and binding conceals a pronounced internal shift in the allocation of the acquisitions budget: a far higher proportion of the acquisitions (or materials) budget is now being spent on serials.[10]

In both the Research 1 and Research 2 composites the percentage of the materials budget devoted to serials increased rapidly during the 1970s and peaked about 1981.[11] After a period of decline in the early 1980s, the serials share began to rise again beginning in 1986 (fig. 4.7). The main difference between the Research 1 and Research 2 composites is the absolute share of the materials budget devoted to serials. Throughout this entire period the Research 2 libraries spent approximately 10 percent more of their materials budget on serials than the Research 1 libraries. This difference apparently results from the fact that the materials budgets of the Research 2 libraries are generally smaller. At the smaller institutions librarians may feel that first priority has to go to purchasing a reasonably comprehensive set of serials.

The somewhat erratic path of this time series is due to varied rates of increase in expenditures for serials. Serials expenditures have increased rapidly for the entire period since 1976, but three subperiods can be distinguished—1976-81, 1981-86, and 1986-91—with the middle period one of somewhat more moderate increase and the

---

[9]We are reminded of a famous controversy in economics in the 1940s in which Fritz Machlup and Richard Lester debated the extent to which business decisions were in fact based on comparisons of marginal costs with marginal revenues. Machlup used the analogy of the driver of an automobile making a decision whether or not to overtake a truck. The driver (we all agree) does not consciously make the complex calculations needed to determine the rate at which he must accelerate under varying conditions; still, he drives *as if* he had made the calculations. See Fritz Machlup, "Marginal Analysis and Empirical Research," *American Economic Review* 36 (1946): 534–535.

[10]For the rest of this discussion we will focus on expenditures for materials only (as opposed to materials and binding). We use the terms "materials" and "acquisitions" interchangeably.

[11]Because data were either not available or unreliable, Cornell University and the University of Florida are not included in their relevant composites for the following discussion of serials and serial expenditures.

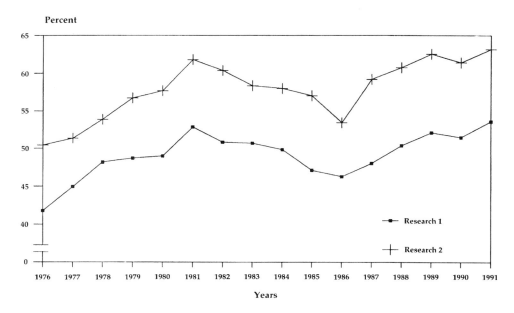

Figure 4.7
Serials expenditures as a percentage of materials expenditures, 1976–91

last the period of most rapid increase (fig. 4.8). Between 1986 and 1990 the All 24 composite increased at an average annual rate of increase more than 11 percent.

Trends in the prices of serials are discussed at some length in Chapter 6. We can anticipate that discussion by noting that the price increases have been the driving force in increases in the serials share of the materials budget. Evidence for this assertion is the fact that larger and larger expenditures for serials have *not* led to a comparable increase in the number of serials acquired (fig. 4.9). In fact, between 1986 and 1990 the number of serials received at Research 1 libraries actually decreased by 6 percent.[12] During this same period, nominal expenditures increased by 73 percent.

As we will discuss in Chapter 6, price increases for journals vary significantly by field, and the experiences of individual universities illustrate the effects of these increases on serials budgets in recent years. For two individual universities for which we were able to collect data (a Public 1 university and a Private 2 university), the percentage of the serials budget expended for science serials has increased steadily since the mid-1980s (table 4.1). At the Private 2 university we calculated the science serials expenditures as a percentage of all serials expenditures for

[12]The data on the number of serials received that are presented in figure 4.8 and discussed here include both serials purchased and serials not purchased. Data for serials received have been collected in these two categories since 1986, and a better comparison with serials expenditures would of course be with serials purchased only. Unfortunately, we included only the total category of serials received when we created the original spreadsheets.

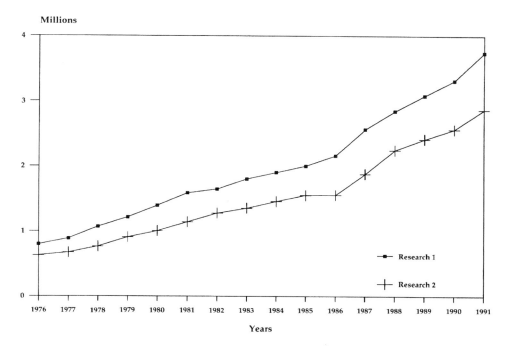

Figure 4.8
Expenditures for serials in nominal dollars, 1976–91

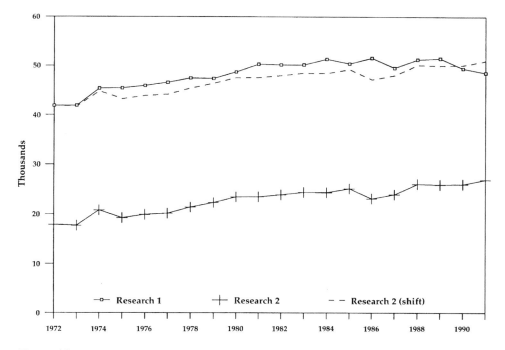

Figure 4.9
Total current serials, 1972–91

Table 4.1
Serials Expenditures by Individual Universities

	1983–84	1984–85	1985–86	1986–87	1987–88	1988–89	1989–90	1990–91
Private 2 University								
Humanities	66,630	64,004			99,128	95,571	111,429	133,616
Social Sciences	141,823	126,851			267,331	298,575	279,736	331,235
Sciences	298,187	317,569			577,991	578,978	621,697	787,435
Total	506,640	508,424			944,450	973,124	1,012,862	1,252,286
Science as % Total	58.9	62.5			61.2	59.5	61.4	62.9
Public 1 University								
Humanities			54,373	82,020	96,402	89,763	92,128	92,290
Social Sciences			190,048	235,284	259,073	269,773	272,921	266,685
Humanities/Social Sciences			3,839	8,310	10,174	10,791	12,475	12,874
Sciences			421,909	596,363	670,454	716,772	728,032	812,975
Other			43,359	67,152	69,730	81,118	81,118	81,428
Total			670,169	921,977	1,036,103	1,087,099	1,105,556	1,184,824
Science as % of Total			63.0	64.7	64.7	65.9	65.9	68.6

Notes: Data were collected from individual universities. Expenditures are in nominal dollars.

humanities, social sciences, and science departments. (General serials expenditures were not included in the total.) This percentage has increased from 58.9 in 1983–84 to 62.9 in 1990–91. Although data on the number of serials were not available, we have been told that the total number of serials stayed relatively constant, with the few serials that were added concentrated in the humanities and social sciences rather than in the sciences.

At the Public 1 university, expenditures for science serials as a percentage of the total were remarkably comparable to those at the Private 2 university. In this instance, expenditures for science serials increased from 59.1 percent of the total (including humanities, social sciences, sciences, nonscience libraries, and area studies) in 1985–86 to 64.2 percent in 1990–91. Again, data on the number of serials are unavailable for those years, but we can get an idea of the magnitude of these figures with data from 1991–92. In this year 1,947 science serials constituted only 28.7 percent of the total number of serials in the same areas included in our total expenditures—that is, expenditures for science serials constituted approximately 65 percent of the serials budget and provided approximately 29 percent of the total number of serials.[13] Conversations with librarians at other universities suggest that percentages such as these are not uncommon.

The rapid increases in serials expenditures documented earlier and the substantial redeployment of materials expenditures toward serials and away from monographs may now be more fully understood as responses to external forces that have had such pronounced effects on the functioning of academic libraries. *Indeed, it would not be an exaggeration to say that of the various factors in the constellation affecting university libraries in recent years, the rapidly rising prices of periodicals have in many respects been the most important.* They explain the de facto encumbering of the materials budget, and they surely go a long way toward explaining the widening gap between the numbers of volumes added gross and of book titles published, since the redeployment of the materials budget toward serials has constrained libraries' ability to purchase monographs.[14] As we have seen, there has been little increase in the number of serials acquired annually, and these developments can

---

[13]Moreover, neither of the two universities mentioned has an engineering department, which would likely have made the science expenditures an even higher percentage of the total.

[14]Universities have attempted to cope with this problem in a variety of ways. At 1 of the 24 institutions studied here, the realization that there was a widening gap between rates of increase in acquisitions and rates of increase in international book title output resulted in a decision to relate levels of funding for acquisitions to increases in the number of titles published in the United Kingdom and the United States, though the decision entailed a substantial increase in the acquisitions budget.

Other universities have attempted resource-sharing initiatives. James Madison University, the University of Virginia, and Virginia Polytechnic Institute and State University, for example, agreed to provide one another with copies of articles from journals not in their own collections; the copies are sent by telefacsimile within 24 hours, and publishers are compensated appropriately. What these initiatives and other, similar ones have in common is that they apply existing services and technologies— interlibrary loan, photocopying, telefacsimile—to the problem of access to materials held elsewhere. It is important to remember that, despite initiatives such as these, the primary way of dealing with the serials crisis has been to redistribute the acquisitions budget towards serials and away from monographs. (Dorothy Milne and Bill Tiffany, "A Survey of the Cost-Effectiveness of Serials: A Cost-Per-Use Method and Its Results," *The Serials Librarian* 19 (1991): 137–149, and "James Madison University, Carrier Library, Documents Express Program." We are grateful to Dennis E. Robison, university librarian at James Madison, for providing a copy of this last item.)

therefore be understood as retarding the growth of the collections. It is not surprising, then, that in writing of the situation, authors have invoked such metaphors as "the library doomsday machine" and "the journal that ate the library."[15]

There are a number of possible ways of looking at the inability of libraries to accommodate fully the changes in the serials and book industries. Both internal and external factors are involved. Emphasis could be placed, on the one hand, on the inadequacy of the materials and binding budget. Since materials and binding expenditures increased at a lower rate than total educational and general expenditures throughout the 1970s and 1980s, one might argue that the level of institutional support for acquisitions was inordinately low and that an appropriate response in light of the increases in both title output (books and serials) and the prices of library materials would have been to increase the percentage of the educational and general budget expended on the acquisition of library materials.

On the other hand, there are always many competing claims on university resources, and each such claim, no matter how important, has to be evaluated in relation to the others. On this basis one could argue that the relevant external forces, no matter how pressing, simply did not justify the extraordinary redeployment of institutional resources that would have been necessary had individual universities attempted more comprehensive coverage. The issues are not unlike those involved in evaluating the continued viability of a need-blind admissions policy, for example. Such a policy remains an exceedingly important objective at many institutions and is considered vitally important to institutional health. Nonetheless, there are other critically important objectives—compensating faculty members adequately, supporting faculty research activity adequately—that also require attention.

In that sense, the forces contributing to the widening gap between rates of increase in volumes added and rates of increase in title output can be said to have been principally external rather than internal, in that the external demands were far too great for individual institutions to undertake the kind of response necessary to meet them more fully. Those demands, in short, were out of phase with institutions' ability to respond.

---

[15]Ann Okerson and Kendon Stubbs, "The Library 'Doomsday Machine,'" *Publishers Weekly* 238 (February 8, 1991): 36–37; Herbert S. White, "The Journal That Ate the Library," *Library Journal* 113 (May 15, 1988): 62–63.

CHAPTER FIVE

Book and Serial Production

For reasons discussed in previous chapters, there was a virtual halt in the rate of increase in the annual number of volumes added at university research libraries during the 1970s and much of the 1980s. The effects of this development on the comprehensiveness of library collections can be understood only by examining the changes in acquisition rates in the context of trends in the numbers of books and periodicals published.

BROAD TRENDS AND THE ISSUE OF QUALITY

The deleterious effects of the slowing in acquisitions during the 1970s and 1980s might have been mitigated to some extent had the shift in the rate of increase in acquisitions been paralleled by a similar slowing in the rate of increase in domestic and international book and serial production. The conventional assumption, however, is that precisely the opposite occurred—that there has been a substantial increase in scholarly output over the past several decades. Indeed, data collected by means of an unpublished 1988 U.S. Department of Education faculty survey suggested that "[e]ach of the nation's estimated 489,000 full-time faculty members produced an average of two refereed journal articles and 0.6 scholarly books, chapters in edited volumes, monographs, or textbooks during the previous two years."[1]

There is certainly no absence of comment, largely negative, on a phenomenon characterized as "academic overdose" in an article in *The New York Times* entitled "Where Information Is All, Pleas Arise for Less of It."[2] The article suggested that "[a]s the population of books and journals continues to explode, librarians complain that shelf space is running out and expenses are spinning out of control" and reported that "[i]n February 1988, Harvard Medical School issued new guidelines for tenure review, recommending that the faculty consider requiring no more than five published works for a candidate for assistant professor, seven for associate professor and 10 for full professor," a decision made against a background of expressions of concern that "the multiplicity of mediocre publications makes it impossible to sift out the ones that contain fresh ideas. The proliferation of books and journals seems to have narrowed access to information instead of widening it."

---

[1] Carolyn J. Mooney, "In 2 Years, a Million Refereed Articles, 300,000 Books, Chapters, Monographs," *The Chronicle of Higher Education* 37 (May 22, 1991):A17. However, in a letter to *The Chronicle* (June 26, 1991), Ann Okerson, director of the Office of Scientific and Academic Publishing at the Association of Research Libraries, observed that Mooney's article failed to take account of the fact that articles typically have more than one author; Okerson suggested that in 1986 the average number of authors per paper was 2.98 and that the number of articles published in a two-year period is therefore closer to 326,000 (two-thirds of 489,000), or fewer than 200,000 per year.

[2] See the July 9, 1989 issue of *The New York Times*.

More recently, Donald Kennedy, then president of Stanford, was quoted as saying that "[t]he overproduction of routine scholarship ... tends to conceal really important work by its sheer volume ... and is a major contributor to the inflation of academic library costs."[3]

Others argue that concerns about a putative decline in quality are unjustified, that they mask other, unstated concerns about how scholarly fields are defined and about changes in methodologies and perspectives with which many of those who express such concerns simply disagree. Two papers, among others, make the very important point that the increase in the number of journal articles and books is in part a function simply of an increase in the size of the professoriate. Any assumption about a decline in quality or an increased emphasis on research based largely on the increase in the number of items published may fail to take adequate account of the statistical fact that these two papers highlight. The per-person output, that is, may not be significantly higher now than before.[4]

On one important issue, however, there seems to be little disagreement: the basic problem, if indeed the phenomenon is a problem, results in large part from the nature of the reward system. Appointment to the professoriate and advancement within it are contingent upon scholarly output, as measured (qualitatively and quantitatively) by one's record of publication.[5] Moreover, the intense competition for places that characterized many academic labor markets in the 1970s and 1980s only intensified the pressure to publish.

We have no new insights to offer on this range of issues concerning the quality of scholarly output, and we can do no more here than acknowledge the importance of the debate. We must limit ourselves to the more mundane task of calibrating output and not attempt judgments as to whether more or less of it is valuable now than was the case in earlier days.

---

[3]Carolyn J. Mooney, "Efforts to Limit 'Trivial' Scholarship Win Backing from Many Academics," *The Chronicle of Higher Education* 37 (May 22, 1991):A13.

[4]See Francis Oakley, "Against Nostalgia: Reflections on Our Present Discontents in Higher Education," *National Humanities Center Newsletter* 12 (spring/summer 1991):1–14, especially p. 5; and Henry W. Riecken, "Scholarly Publication: Are There Viable Options?" Draft for the Research Library Committee [of the Council on Library Resources], October 1989, 5–6.

On the question of quality and its relationship generally to increases in the number of titles published, see also two provocative recent articles on the editing of book manuscripts at commercial publishing houses: Jacob Weisberg, "Rough Trade: The Sad Decline of American Publishing," *The New Republic* 204 (June 17, 1991):16ff.; and Ted Solotaroff, "The Paperbacking of Publishing," *The Nation* 253 (October 7, 1991):399–404.

The decline in editing standards noted by Weisberg in particular, if it in fact exists, is certainly to be related to the phenomenon of overproduction. Any attempt libraries might make to be selective in their acquisition of titles published by commercial houses would involve them inevitably in a debate about quality; Warren J. Haas has argued that "[l]ibrarians cannot make qualitative judgments by themselves, but as senior administrative officers they have the responsibility to see to it that those judgments are made." ("Reflections/Directions," *Council on Library Resources Reports* 3 [February 1989]:2).

[5]On these questions, see Ernest L. Boyer, *Scholarship Reconsidered: Priorities of the Professoriate, A Special Report* (Princeton, New Jersey: The Carnegie Foundation for the Advancement of Teaching, 1990). Boyer (pp. xi, 12–13) describes a "narrowing" of "the standards used to measure academic prestige" in the post-World War II era: "professors were expected to conduct research and publish results. Promotion and tenure depended on such activity....[T]he research mission, which was appropriate for *some* institutions, created a shadow over the entire higher learning enterprise." In "Publish or Perish: The Troubled State of Scholarly Communication," *Scholarly Publishing* 22 (1991):131–142, Dennis Carrigan offers another, briefer history of the developments Boyer describes.

How precisely can we document trends in the production of books and periodicals and relate them to rates of increase in the acquisition of library materials? "Book industry statistics," Chandler Grannis wrote, "may ... be likened to a handful of wet spaghetti. They may be more or less digestible, even a bit nourishing; but they are messy, slippery, elusive, never tidy."[6] Though such statistics have improved in recent years, there nonetheless remain many inconsistencies and anomalies in the reporting. In some instances, for example, it may be that apparent recent increases in the number of titles published is simply a function of improved data collection: a larger percentage of the items produced is now being "captured."

Moreover, all but one of the data sets used here to measure trends in book-title output have an important limitation for purposes of this study: they count items, perhaps even a great many items, that academic libraries would not choose to purchase. The fact that these data include publications written by nonacademics does not necessarily limit their usefulness, since academic libraries purchase many such items. Their usefulness is limited because, in addition to such materials, they also include items of other types—mass market paperbacks in some instances, university theses and government pamphlets in others—that do not figure in the acquisitions practices of many libraries. These limitations notwithstanding, the available data do permit us to make some provisional observations about changing levels of book- title production, seen in relation to acquisitions.[7]

BOOK TITLES PUBLISHED

Book production, not surprisingly, mirrors general economic, historical, and political developments. The numbers of titles published reflect wars, economic depression, and, in the case of university presses, the financial condition of the presses' parent institutions.[8] Thus, a period of rapid increase in the number of titles published in this country in the late 19th and early 20th centuries was followed by periods of contraction in the decade between 1910 and 1920, modest recovery between 1920 and 1929, contraction during the Great Depression, recovery from the mid-1930s to early 1940s, substantial contraction during World War II, and, beginning in 1945, extraordinary expansion (fig. 5.1).[9] This expansion was particularly rapid during the first half of the 1960s.

---

[6]Chandler B. Grannis, "1974: U.S. Book Industry Statistics: Titles, Prices, Sales, Trends," *Publishers Weekly* 207 (February 3, 1975):39.

[7]An additional measurement point we should make is that many sources of data on book production distinguish new titles from new editions of existing titles. Since one cannot assume that a library acquired a particular title when it was first published, our analysis makes use of the combined total of new titles and new editions.

[8]For the relationship of university press activity to the financial circumstances of parent institutions, see Ellen Coughlin, "Face of University Publishing Changed by Years of Adversity, Decades of Growth," *The Chronicle of Higher Education* 36 (June 27, 1990):A1.

[9]The data are taken from *The Book Publishing Annual: Highlights, Analyses and Trends,* 1985 edition (New York and London: R. R. Bowker Company, 1985), 127. See the various qualifications concerning the data in notes a–c of that source. The closer analysis of trends for the years 1970–89 offered below is based on data taken ultimately from the same source (the R. R. Bowker Company).

Thousands

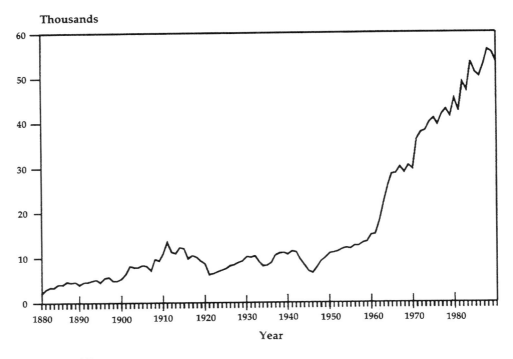

Natural Log

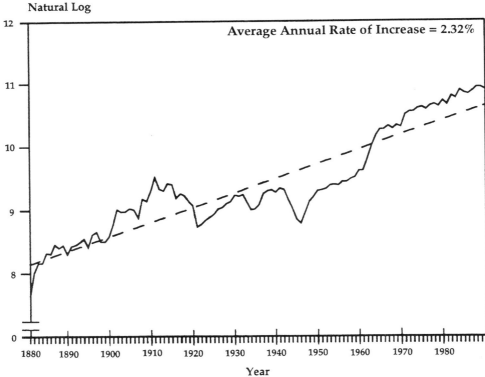

Figure 5.1
Number of titles published annually, domestic presses, 1880–1989

Our principal concern is the relationship between levels of book production and levels of library acquisitions.[10] Since 1912 the overall average annual rate of increase in volumes added gross at our Research 1 composite has been more rapid (3.2 percent) than that of total titles published domestically (2.8 percent). However, most of the growth over the past three-quarters of a century in the number of volumes added gross occurred during the single decade of the 1960s (fig. 5.2). This unprecedented expansion was presumably the result of systematic retrospective purchasing permitted by double-digit increases in the materials and binding budget and, perhaps more important, the founding of many new serials and thus an increase in the number of volumes available for acquisition in any given year. The slopes of the curves diverge dramatically after 1970, with the annual number of volumes added gross staying more or less constant while the number of book titles published continued to rise at a steady rate.[11]

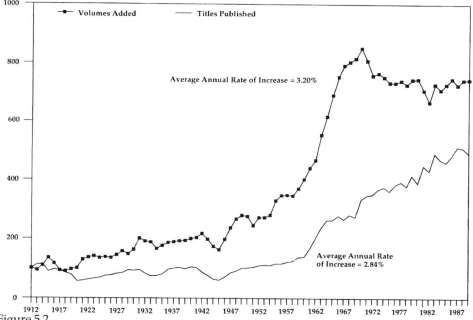

Figure 5.2
Number of volumes added gross (Research 1) vs. total titles published domestically, 1912–89 (Index: 1912=100)

---

[10]For another analysis of this relationship, see Ann L. O'Neill, "Book Production and Library Purchases: Looking Beyond the Thor Ruling," *Publishing Research Quarterly* 7 (Summer 1991):39–51.

The categories that are the subject of comparison in this section have many dissimilarities, one of which is the fact that book production data are reported for the calendar year while volumes added gross are reported for the academic year. The analysis is meant only to provide a sense of the changing levels of book publishing as compared with acquisitions of academic libraries.

[11]An important caveat with regard to this comparison is that the data for volumes added gross include serial titles, while book production data (Bowker here and, later in the discussion, UNESCO and AAUP) include book titles only. However, the important point is that during the 1970s libraries failed to maintain rates of growth in acquisitions equivalent to rates of growth in book titles published annually, and the fact that serials (many of which were founded during the 1970s) are counted in the volumes added gross data simply serves to reinforce the notion that libraries have not been able to acquire a full collection of available materials.

While these data document trends in the entire domestic book industry for the past century, inspection of data for a group of fields more relevant to the acquisitions practices of academic libraries provides a sharper sense of developments during the past two decades (fig. 5.3).[12] The shapes of the two curves are quite similar, with the same peaks and valleys, albeit with publications in the select fields growing at a slightly slower rate during these decades than publications in all fields (2.0 percent versus 2.3 percent). During this same period, the number of volumes added gross at our All 24 library composite actually declined slightly—at an average annual rate of -0.6 percent (fig. 5.4). The steadily growing gap between acquisitions and titles published is evident in the figure.

It is also useful to look even more closely at publications disaggregated by particular fields, since shifts in the relative field-shares are relevant to the acquisitions practices of academic libraries. Just as university curricula are redesigned in response to changes in the nature of scholarship and the emergence of new fields of inquiry, so libraries are expected to be responsive to shifts in the relative shares of title output represented by particular fields, even while continuing at the same time to build collections in fields that previously represented a larger share of the total number of titles produced. Shifts in relative proportions also are important because the price of published materials can differ enormously by subject area (discussed later).

The numbers of titles in many of the traditional arts and sciences fields—such as biography, literature-poetry-drama, and art-music—as well as in education have decreased as a percentage of total publications over the past two decades. (See table 5.1.) The most significant drop is in the share of publications represented by the combined field of literature-poetry-drama, which fell from 17.2 percent in 1970 to 9.1 percent in 1988. Concurrently, there were increases in the shares of many professional-applied fields, including business, law, technology, and particularly medicine. Between 1970 and 1988 there has been an overall shift of approximately 9 percentage points toward the professional-applied fields. Once again, it is important to note that these counts include many titles that academic libraries would not acquire. Insofar as they are indicative of general trends, however, they are illuminating and confirm our impression of "global" shifts in publication patterns.

---

[12]To define a relevant data set, we limited the publications in the select fields to publications in agriculture, art, biography, business, education, history, law, literature, medicine, music, philosophy and psychology, poetry and drama, religion, science, sociology and economics, and technology; we excluded titles in all other fields (fiction, general works, home economics, juveniles, language, sports and recreation, and travel).

While one could certainly challenge this particular choice of fields, there is evidence that supports this classification. Beginning in 1981, a distinction can be drawn between hardbound and trade paperbound only and "all hardbound and paperbound" (which includes mass market paperbound books). We report the latter figure here for all years to maintain consistency with figures before 1981, which were not so disaggregated. When the number of titles in the subject areas we excluded are deducted from the total count, the difference between the total numbers of hardbound and trade paperbound books only and of *all* hardbound and paperbound books almost disappears. In other words, mass market paperbound books—the kinds of items academic libraries would be unlikely to purchase—seem to be concentrated almost entirely in the fields that we excluded from consideration.

These data are taken from the relevant issues of *Publishers Weekly*. Until 1976, the count of titles published in a particular year was as of the beginning of the following year. Beginning in 1976, the count was as of midyear in the following year.

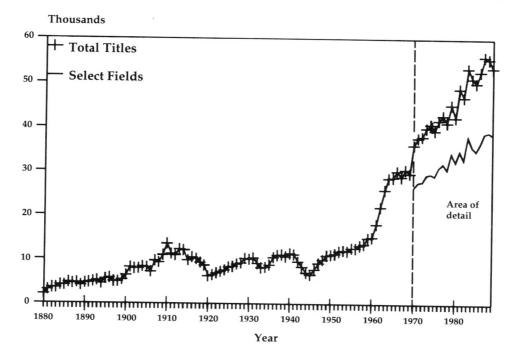

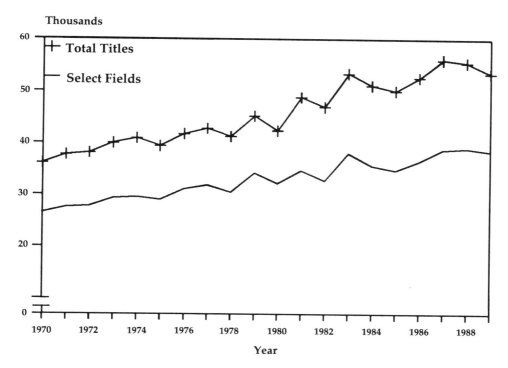

Figure 5.3
Number of titles published annually, domestic presses, total and select fields

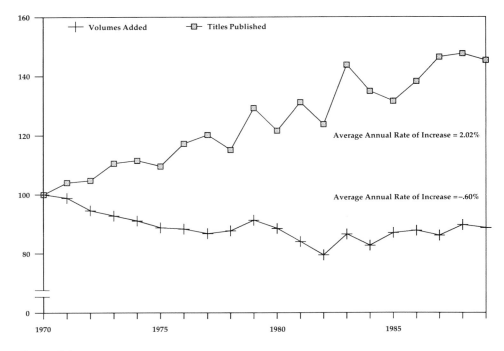

Figure 5.4
Number of volumes added gross (All 24) vs. selected titles published domestically, 1970–89 (Index: 1970=100)

This redistribution of publications by field has had a real impact on library budgets because of differential pricing. Those fields that experienced the most significant gain in percentage share of publications since 1970 are precisely those with the highest average per-volume prices of hardcover copies—business ($37.51), law ($50.85), medicine ($66.59), and technology ($65.26). (Science also had a very high average per-volume price [$66.91], and maintained a fairly constant but significant percentage share of about 9.5 percent.) The fields that experienced the largest losses in percentage share of publications had significantly lower prices—biography ($25.99), education ($33.55), literature ($30.85), and poetry and drama ($28.02).[13]

Some part of the redistribution of publications by field is related, albeit in a complicated way, to shifts in enrollment patterns at both the undergraduate and graduate levels. At the undergraduate level, the arts and sciences share of baccalaureate degrees conferred declined after about 1970, especially at comprehensive institutions, concurrent with increases in degrees conferred in preprofessional subjects.[14] At the graduate level, the number of Ph.D.s peaked in 1973 and then began to decline, particularly rapidly in the arts and sciences. Concurrent with this

[13]Prices are as of 1988. See Chandler B. Grannis, "Titles and Prices, 1988: Final Figures," *Publishers Weekly* 236 (September 29, 1989):26.

[14]See Turner and Bowen, "The Flight from the Arts and Sciences," for a detailed analysis of the factors responsible for this trend.

Table 5.1
Titles Published Annually, by Field (percentage shares)

					Year					
	1970	1972	1974	1976	1978	1980	1982	1984	1986	1988
Arts and Sciences										
Art/Music	5.9	6.8	6.1	6.6	6.3	6.4	6.3	6.2	5.6	4.9
Biography	5.8	7.2	7.5	6.7	6.2	5.9	5.4	5.9	5.9	5.8
History	7.5	5.9	4.4	7.4	6.6	6.9	6.7	6.3	6.8	8.4
Lit./Poet./Drama	17.2	14.5	13.3	10.6	10.2	8.9	8.5	8.9	9.4	9.1
Phil./Psych./Relig.	11.6	10.4	10.9	11.1	11.7	10.8	10.8	11.3	12.2	12.0
Science	8.9	9.3	10.3	9.2	9.5	9.7	9.5	9.1	9.2	9.6
Sociol., Econ.	22.3	23.1	22.5	22.6	21.2	22.2	22.8	21.9	21.6	21.1
Subtotal	79.4	77.1	75.0	74.2	71.7	70.8	70.0	69.6	70.7	70.9
Professional/Applied										
Agriculture	1.0	1.4	1.3	1.9	1.8	1.4	1.3	1.4	1.5	1.7
Business	3.0	2.5	3.1	3.2	4.1	3.7	4.1	4.8	4.4	4.2
Education	4.5	4.7	3.9	3.5	3.5	3.1	3.2	2.9	2.8	2.9
Law	2.3	2.6	3.5	2.8	3.5	3.4	4.4	3.9	3.8	3.4
Medicine	5.6	6.6	7.7	8.3	9.2	10.2	9.9	10.0	9.4	10.0
Technology	4.3	5.1	5.4	6.1	6.2	7.3	7.1	7.4	7.4	6.9
Subtotal	20.6	22.9	25.0	25.8	28.3	29.2	30.0	30.4	29.3	29.1

Source: *Publishers Weekly*, relevant issues.

decline was an increase in the number of degrees awarded in professional fields—especially medicine, law, and business. There was also a shift in the composition of doctoral degrees awarded within broad fields toward more applied subjects; for example, engineering grew faster than the sciences between 1973 and 1988, and, within the social sciences, clinical psychology grew faster than anthropology.[15] This general movement away from the arts and sciences may well have had a dual effect on the book publishing industry—creating both a declining pool of potential authors in the arts and sciences and a declining demand for books in these fields.

Trends in book publishing over the last three decades are reflected also in the experiences of university presses. The activities of this set of publishing institutions are especially relevant for present purposes because academic libraries are likely to purchase a large proportion of the aggregate list of their publications. Data compiled from records maintained by the Association of American University Presses (AAUP) show patterns that are something of an amalgam of the trends shown here for all domestic publishers and the financial histories of the universities that are homes to most of these presses (fig. 5.5).[16]

The AAUP data also show a rapid increase in the number of titles published throughout the 1960s. Beginning in 1969, however, there was a period of very little growth at these presses, a pattern not seen in the Bowker data (which show continued increases until about 1979). This flattening is similar to that documented in the first section of this study with respect to library acquisitions and the number of Ph.D.s awarded nationally. The financial condition of university presses is in some cases linked to that of their parent institutions, and the difficult circumstances of the 1970s inevitably had an impact on the number of titles that they could afford to publish. Moreover, given that academic libraries constitute one of the principal markets for monographs published by university presses, restrictions on their acquisitions budgets are more likely to affect the activity of university presses than of commercial presses, which predominantly serve other markets.

Beginning in 1979, there was a substantial recovery in the number of titles published annually by these university presses, and rapid expansion has continued without abatement through at least 1988 (the last year for which we have these data); the number of titles published annually by the university presses increased by a factor of 1.75 over this eleven-year period (5.2 percent per year). The average annual rate of increase since 1970 for these university presses has also been more rapid (3.6 percent) than the rate over the same period for all domestic presses in our selected fields (2.3 percent), despite the fact that the domestic presses expanded over that

---

[15]See Bowen and Rudenstine, *In Pursuit of the Ph.D.*, particularly chapters 2 and 3.

[16]We use the acronym AAUP throughout this discussion to refer to the Association of American University Presses, not to the American Association of University Professors.

The data on titles published were obtained directly from the AAUP. For purposes of this study a subset of the total membership of the AAUP was selected. In order to define a stable population, the selection was limited to 51 constituent member presses that reported data in 1963 and more or less continuously thereafter: Arizona, Brookings Institution, California, Chicago, Columbia, Cornell, Duke, Florida, Fordham, Georgia, Harvard, Hawaii, Illinois, Indiana, Iowa State, Johns Hopkins, Kansas, Kentucky, Laval, Louisiana State, M.I.T., McGill, Metropolitan Museum, Michigan, Minnesota, Missouri, Nebraska, New Mexico, New York, North Carolina, Notre Dame, Ohio State, Oklahoma, Pennsylvania State, Pittsburgh, Princeton, Rutgers, Smithsonian Institution, South Carolina, Southern Methodist, Stanford, Syracuse, Texas, Toronto, U.S. Naval Institute, Washington, Wayne State, Wisconsin, Yale, Cambridge, and Oxford.

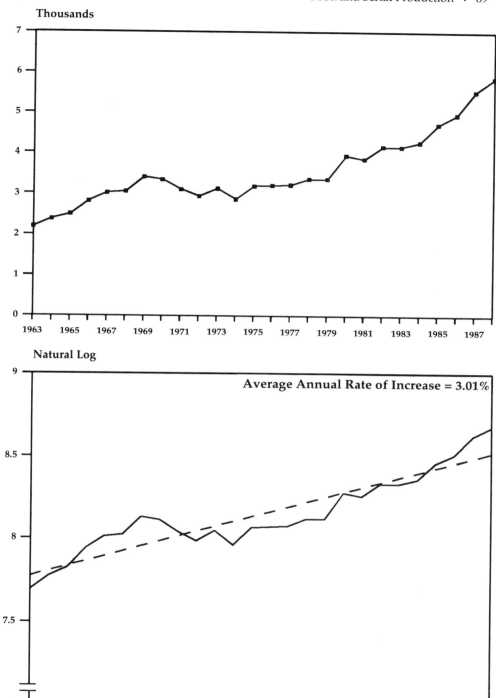

Figure 5.5
Number of titles published annually by the Association of American University Presses
(selected presses), 1963–88

entire time period while the expansion at the university presses did not really begin until 1979. Moreover, growth in the aggregate number of titles published by all AAUP member presses is understated by our data because we have excluded those presses that did not begin to report titles published until after 1963.

This extraordinary increase in titles published by university presses was probably due to a confluence of forces including greater availability of good manuscripts as a result of the shifting boundary between commercial and university presses.[17] The recovery of AAUP presses was probably influenced as well by the desire to respond to the emergence of new scholarly fields. (This latter development is particularly relevant to trends in scholarly periodicals and is discussed in greater detail later.) Significantly, the increase in titles published was *not* a function of a recovery in the purchasing power of acquisitions budgets, since, as we have seen, the average number of volumes added gross has actually declined since 1970. A direct comparison of titles published by university presses and volumes added by all 24 of our research libraries shows clearly that since 1974 new university press publications have far outstripped acquisitions (fig. 5.6).

One other dimension of publishing activity must be considered in assessing the implications of recent trends in acquisitions by research libraries—namely, international publishing trends, since these libraries collect many materials published outside the United States. The United Nations Educational, Scientific and Cultural Organization (UNESCO) has collected data documenting international book production for several decades, and we have sought to construct a subindex that would be particularly useful for our purposes, based this time, however, on countries rather than on subject matter. We have aggregated publishing data for six Western European countries (France, West Germany, Italy, the Netherlands, Swit-

---

[17]Sanford Thatcher, director of the Pennsylvania State University Press, has suggested that some of the traditional distinctions between university and commercial presses and between the profiles of the authors each type serves may no longer be current and indeed may not have been current for some time. ("Scholarly Monographs May Be the Ultimate Victims of the Upheavals in Trade Publishing," *The Chronicle of Higher Education* 37 [October 10, 1990]:B2–B3.) Thatcher suggests that the decision of the management at Random House—to have its subsidiary, Pantheon Books, publish books that would sell more copies than had many of Pantheon's previous titles—would not disadvantage the kinds of authors whom Pantheon had traditionally served. These authors would have another outlet for their work, the university presses, which have been interested for some time in the kinds of "mid-list books" that typified Pantheon's output. Given that they can capitalize on the interest of this new class of authors, the university presses may be increasingly unwilling to publish titles with potential sales of 1,000 copies or fewer. Under such circumstances the authors ultimately likely to be disadvantaged by these changed circumstances are "scholars seeking publication of their monographs in fields where average sales are low."

Solotaroff ("The Paperbacking of Publishing") described the conditions at commercial publishing houses that led to the "shift in boundary" between the commercial and academic sectors of which Thatcher wrote. For other statements of general trends in academic publishing, see Ellen K. Coughlin, "Face of University Publishing Changed," A1, A8–A9; John F. Baker and John Mutter, "University Presses: Weighing the Options," *Publishers Weekly* 238 (August 2, 1991):12–15; and, most important, Herbert S. Bailey, Jr., *The Rate of Publication of Scholarly Monographs in the Humanities and Social Sciences, 1978-1988* (New York: Association of American University Presses, 1990).

zerland, and the United Kingdom) and combined them with comparable data for the United States.[18]

International production of books—predictably—dropped sharply between 1938 and 1944 and then began to rise again in 1945. A period of rapid expansion between 1945 and 1948 was followed by four decades of more moderate but remarkably consistent growth. (See fig. 5.7 and Appendix Table 5.1; data before 1950 are not presented on the figure because they are not complete for all countries.)

The average annual rate of increase in titles published between 1950 and 1988 in Western Europe (3.7 percent) was greater than the annual rate of increase in volumes added at our Research 1 composite during those same years (3.0 percent), but again these overall averages mask major differences in growth rates during specific time periods. Until 1970, the rate of increase in volumes added gross was much greater than the rate of increase in titles published in Western Europe. The rate of increase in volumes added gross peaked in that year and has even declined slightly since

---

[18]This decision was based partly on the practical grounds that it was possible to construct for these countries a fairly continuous data set from the 1930s to the present. Also, titles published in these countries have been of particular interest to the research libraries with which we are concerned in this study. To be sure, as universities in the United States have redesigned their curricula to include course work on the intellectual traditions of other, non-European cultures, their library collections have changed accordingly and will continue to change. Nonetheless, we may assume that until fairly recently, titles published in Western Europe constituted the largest proportion of nondomestic titles purchased by most academic libraries. (For some evidence that Western European countries provide the largest numbers of nondomestic materials to academic libraries, see Sally F. Williams, "Construction and Application of a Periodical Price Index," *Collection Management* 2 (Winter 1978):329–344, especially p. 331, where it was observed that the United States, France, Germany, Great Britain, and Italy were the major sources of periodical titles acquired for the central research collection at Harvard).

These data are taken from the following sources: For 1937–49, *Preliminary Statistical Report on Book Production in Various Countries* (Paris: UNESCO, Statistical Service, 1951), 18, 32, 44, 47, 66, 71, and 74. For 1950–78, *An International Survey of Book Production During the Last Decades,* Statistical Reports and Studies, No. 26 (Paris: UNESCO, Office of Statistics, Division of Statistics on Culture and Communication, 1982), 49–55 and 58–64. For 1979–88 (France, Germany, Italy, Netherlands, Switzerland), appropriate issues of the *UNESCO Statistical Yearbook* (Paris: UNESCO, 1983-). For 1979-84 (United Kingdom), *ibid.* For 1985–87 (United Kingdom), *The Bowker Annual Library and Book Trade Almanac,* 36th Edition 1991, comp. and ed. Filomena Simora (New York: R. R. Bowker, 1991), 445. For 1979–81 (United States), *The Bowker Annual of Library & Book Trade Information,* 30th Edition, 1985, comp. and ed. Julia Moore (New York and London: R. R. Bowker Company, 1985), 492.

The R. R. Bowker Company is the source of UNESCO figures for the United States and the United Kingdom for all years. The Bowker data presented here (hereafter Bowker international data) representing U.S. book production differ from the Bowker data presented earlier in the discussion of book production in the United States in that the latter do not include either university theses or government documents. Beginning in 1965, the R.R. Bowker Company added these additional categories when reporting counts to UNESCO to maintain comparability with reporting standards of other countries.

For 1988 (United Kingdom), the value was projected from the average annual rate of increase in the number of titles for the time period 1937–87. For 1982–88 (United States), data were imputed based on the relationship of Bowker (domestic) data to UNESCO data for the period 1965-81. For 1950, 1956, 1972, and 1973 (West Germany), the values were imputed on the basis of values of neighboring years.

Although the UNESCO data are disaggregated by subject area, the categories are defined in such a way that any of them might contain many titles of interest to academic libraries. One cannot, therefore, easily identify subject categories that are likely to be less pertinent in this context. The 1987 UNESCO questionnaire is included in Gretchen Whitney, "The UNESCO Book Production Statistics," *Book Research Quarterly* 5 (Winter 1989–90):12-29, especially 25–29. See the various issues of *Publishers Weekly* for the items included in the Bowker data.

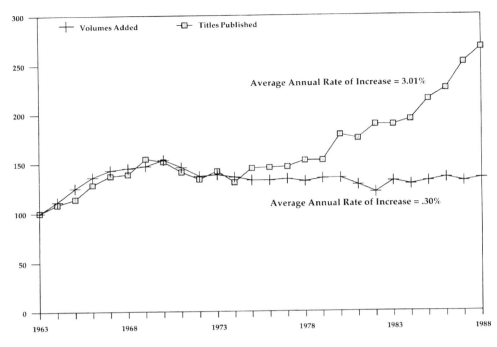

Figure 5.6
Number of volumes added gross (All 24) vs. titles published by the Association of
American University Presses (Index: 1963=100)

then, while the number of titles published has continued to increase steadily over
the past two decades (fig. 5.8).

In this context what is especially important is the relative percentages of the total
represented by output in the United States and in Western Europe, and these
percentages are changing. In 1971 American titles represented almost 40 percent of
the total book production in the United States and these six Western European
nations. By 1988 the U.S. share had dropped by more than 5 percentage points to
about 34 percent.[19] The decrease in the United States's share was due to a flattening
in the number of titles published annually in this country concurrent with a
continued increase in the number of titles published in these Western European
countries. Moreover, with the exception of Germany, the countries that produce the
greatest number of titles annually—the United Kingdom, France, and Italy—are
also those that have had the most rapid rates of increase since 1970 (between 3.5 and
5.0 percent per year compared to 1.1 percent for the Netherlands and 2.7 percent for
Switzerland). Germany, starting from a base larger than any other Western
European country's in this data set, has had a more moderate rate of increase since
1970 (2.6 percent) but a rate still greater than that of the United States (2.1 percent).

---

[19]We discuss relative shares of U.S. and Western European book production only for the post-1970
period because there is reason to believe that 1970 marked the beginning of a period of better reporting.
Accordingly, for purposes of this analysis 1970 perhaps should be considered the beginning of a new
statistical series.

Thousands

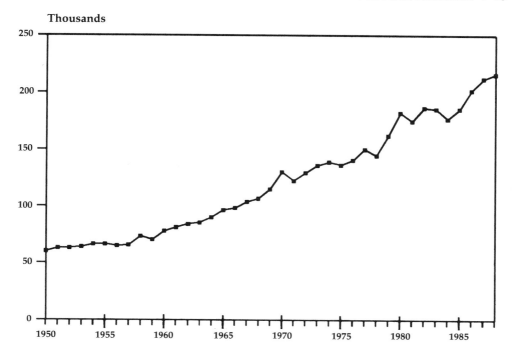

Natural Log

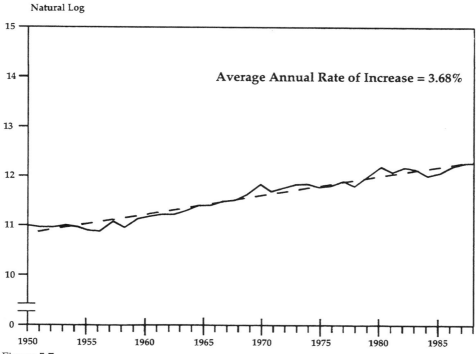

Figure 5.7
Number of titles published, selected Western European countries, 1950–88

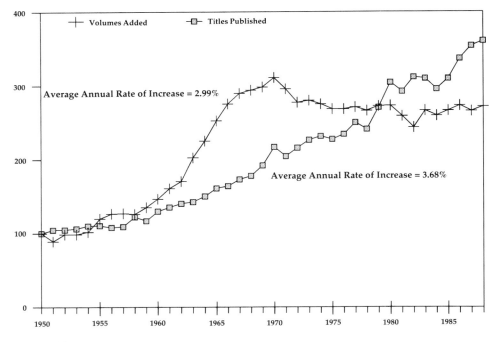

Figure 5.8
Number of volumes added gross (Research 1) vs. titles published in Western Europe, 1950–88 (Index: 1950=100)

In brief, the number of titles published in Western Europe has been greater than the number published in the United States and has increased more rapidly (table 5.2).[20]

Disadvantageous rates of exchange during the late 1970s and the mid- to late 1980s exacerbated the consequences of these trends for the acquisitions practices of American research libraries. Between 1985 (when the Plaza Accord depreciated the U.S. dollar against other major currencies) and 1988, the exchange rates for the dollar fell against these Western European currencies by at least 60 percent. West Germany stands out as the country that published the greatest number of titles annually and for which the rate of exchange was least favorable since the early 1970s.[21] In all countries, however, the confluence of these two factors—rapid increases in book production and unfavorable rates of exchange—has had important consequences

---

[20]Although we have chosen to show trends in book production in Western Europe and the United States only, there is also evidence that book production is increasing more rapidly (in relation to the United States) in other areas of the world as well, particularly Asia. Japan, for example, is among the top five publishing countries, and book production there increased at an average annual rate of 2.8 percent between 1970 and 1986. The rate of increase was particularly rapid during the latter 10 years of that period. (Data are from UNESCO: *An International Survey of Book Production During the Last Decades,* and relevant issues of the *Statistical Yearbook.*)

[21]Moreover, more recent events, including the shift from state-subsidized to private-sector publishing in the former East Germany and the merging of the two German economies, have dramatically increased the prices of German library materials.

Table 5.2.
Average Annual Rates of Increase in Book Title Production, Selected Western European Countries and the United States

	West						W. Europe	
	France	Germany	Italy	Nether.	Switzer.	U.K.	Subtotal	U.S.
1950–88	4.39	4.70	1.86	2.15	3.85	3.29	3.68	—
1970–88	3.49	2.55	4.86	1.14	2.69	3.93	3.17	2.07

Notes: Average annual rate of increase for U.S. is not shown for the period 1950–88 because data collected after 1965 are not comparable with earlier data. See footnote 18 in text for sources of data and qualifications concerning interpretation.

for American academic libraries that wished to maintain collections international in character.[22]

For present purposes what is most important is the disparity between the rates of growth in the number of titles published shown by all these data sets and the number of volumes added by our group of research libraries (table 5.3). During the 1960s the average annual rate of increase in book titles published was comparable to that of volumes added only for the university presses. During this period, university libraries still constituted the principal market of the university presses, and the expansion in higher education during those years surely was the main factor propelling this extraordinary expansion of title production.

Then, however, the number of volumes added yearly within this group of 24 libraries decreased between 1970 and 1982 at an *annual rate of -1.4 percent while the number of titles published, domestically and internationally, was increasing at a rate of greater than 2 percent per year.* Furthermore, the number of titles published (according to all the data reported here) continued to expand into the 1980s. While the contraction in volumes added gross by these libraries appears to have tapered, there is no evidence of any major recovery. It appears, then, that libraries have been able to respond *less* effectively and comprehensively to developments in the publishing industry—in particular, the steady expansion in the number of titles published since the 1960s—than at any previous time in the 20th century.

The potential consequences of these trends are evident. Some members of the library profession are concerned that as acquisitions budgets are less adequate to perceived needs and permit less comprehensive coverage of the world's output of

---

[22]Data on exchange rates are from the *International Financial Statistics Yearbook, 1990* (Washington, D.C.: International Monetary Fund, 1990). Monthly exchange rates of German marks, Dutch guilders, and English pounds per dollar from 1973 to 1988 are graphed in Economic Consulting Services, "A Study of Trends in Average Prices and Costs of Certain Serials Over Time," 13–15; and annual exchange trends between the English pound, the French franc, the German mark, and the Japanese yen from 1975–1988 are graphed in Ann Okerson, "Of Making Many Books There is No End," 26. Both sections are contained in *Report of the ARL Serials Prices Project* (Washington, D.C.: Association of Research Libraries, 1989). For general statements of the difficulties libraries currently encounter in attempting to acquire international materials, see "Research Libraries in a Global Context," prepared by ARL staff, December 1989; "Scholarship, Research Libraries and Foreign Publishing in the 1990s," prepared by ARL staff, March 1991; and Jeffrey J. Gardner, "What They Have and How We Might Get It: Son of Farmington?" Paper read at the Seminar for the Acquisition of Latin American Library Materials, San Diego, California, June 4, 1991.

Table 5.3
Average Annual Rates of Increase in Number of Titles Published (various data sets) and
Number of Volumes Added Gross (All 24 Universities)

	1963–70	1970–82	1982–88
Bowker (All Fields)	3.25%	2.09%	2.27%
Bowker (Selected Fields)		2.03	2.13
AAUP	6.58	2.30	6.48
UNESCO	5.53	3.38	3.04
VOLSADG	7.50	−1.43	1.48

Notes: AAUP data are for selected presses only. UNESCO data are for six Western European countries only. See text for explanation.

books, there is a tendency to concentrate on core materials, with the result that library collections are perhaps beginning to resemble one another more than before and lose some of the variety that previously distinguished them and some of the richness that characterized the entire national collection.[23] To describe the significance of these developments in starkest form: as libraries are increasingly unable to respond effectively to increases in the numbers of book published, the national collection is characterized by less comprehensive coverage of the world's title output, and access to information, the "capital" of scholarship, may be said to be narrowing in this important respect.

SERIAL TITLES PUBLISHED

These statistics on book publishing allow us to document the problems faced by libraries in seeking to acquire some share of the universe of scholarly materials. For many university libraries, however, the more pressing acquisitions problem is that of serial subscriptions. Articles about the rapidly increasing numbers and prices of serials abound, and at many libraries serial subscriptions consume an increasingly

---

[23]That acquisitions practices may be so described was suggested in personal conversation by Dale Flecker of the Office of Systems Planning and Research, Harvard University Library. His view is shared by, among others, members of the staff of the Association of Research Libraries (see the ARL staff paper entitled "Research Libraries in a Global Context").

The tendency for individual libraries to concentrate their acquisitions on a core set of materials may result in collaborative efforts across institutions to preserve the national collection. Such efforts are not without precedent. In 1947, under the leadership of the Association of Research Libraries, more than 60 research libraries participated in a collaborative effort called the Farmington Plan. The intent of the plan was for individual libraries to "take responsibility for collecting and cataloging material from specific countries and/or areas with the intent of building a distributed national collection of foreign materials ensuring coverage of all major areas." However, the effort was abandoned in the early 1970s, with its demise attributed to several factors, "including the lack of a mechanism to monitor the degree of implementation and development of the plan, budgetary constraints of the early seventies that led many libraries to turn inward in their collection development efforts, and real or perceived deficiencies in the services of bookdealers designated for the different parts of the plan" (Jeffrey J. Gardner, "What They Have and How We Might Get It: Son of Farmington?" 5).

larger—and highly significant—proportion of the total acquisitions budget. At our Research 1 and Research 2 composite libraries, for example, we have seen that expenditures for serials were roughly 54 percent and 63 percent, respectively, of the total materials budget in 1991 and that these serials shares were up about 10 percentage points from the comparable percentages in the mid-1970s.

For a variety of reasons, statistics on trends in the production of serials and periodicals are not as easily acquired as those for book production. Unlike monographs, which can be defined clearly albeit arbitrarily by a minimum number of pages,[24] there exists no clear definition as to what constitutes a serial. The Association of Research Libraries, for example, uses a fairly standard definition of a serial as "a publication issued in successive parts, usually at regular intervals, and as a rule intended to be continued indefinitely."[25] Nevertheless, there has been some uncertainty as to whether items such as government documents and monographic serials should be counted in this category. Also illustrative of definitional difficulties is the fact that between 1972 and 1974 ARL used this same definition but called the relevant category "Current Periodicals."[26]

Moreover, what is most relevant to research libraries is not the total universe of serials but the subset of scholarly journals, which are even more difficult to define. In a preliminary report to the Mellon Foundation one economist wrote, "...no existing definitions precisely distinguish between journals and 'other periodicals,' much less, scholarly journals and 'other journals.' Lack of agreement on proper classification criteria has led to an enormous range in estimates of the number of journals published: figures from less than 5,000 to upwards of 100,000 have been cited."[27]

Even if clear definitions of "serials" (or "journals") existed, counting would still be very difficult. "Publication," wrote Allen B. Veaner, "is a living thing, and trying to count its components may be as futile as attempting to number the cells of the human body."[28] This description seems especially characteristic of serial publishing since a single title may be "alive" for several decades or even centuries. Moreover, unlike books, serials may merge, split, or even change title during their lifetimes; publication of particular titles may be assumed by another publisher. In the past few decades commercial publishers, benefiting from economies of scale, have achieved a significant role in the academic serials arena and now publish, for

---

[24]One example is the recommendation adopted by the General Conference of UNESCO in 1964 for the purposes of standardizing international reporting of book production statistics. The Recommendation defined a book as "a non-periodical printed publication of at least 49 pages, exclusive of the cover pages." UNESCO, *An International Survey of Book Production During the Last Decades*, 18.

[25]This definition also appears in Ray Prytherch, comp., *Harrod's Librarians' Glossary*, 7th edition (Brookfield, Vt.: Gower Publishing, 1990):561.

[26]Kendon Stubbs and Robert Molyneux, *Research Library Statistics, 1907-08 through 1987–88; A Guide to the Machine-Readable Version of the Gerould and ARL Statistics* (Washington, D.C.: Association of Research Libraries, 1989), 28.

[27]Lisa Lieberman, Roger Noll, and W. Edward Steinmueller, "Economic Analysis and Empirical Protocol for Examining Scholarly Periodicals Pricing," report submitted to The Andrew W. Mellon Foundation, June 7, 1991, 14.

[28]Allen B. Veaner, "Into the Fourth Century" (College of Information Studies, Drexel University, 1986), 9.

example, the proceedings and other publications of academic societies that were once published by the societies themselves.

Despite these complications, we can document very general trends, particularly with regard to the timing of periods of expansion. This is important because the proliferation in the number of journals has been one of the primary sources of pressure on library budgets both directly and indirectly through effects on serials prices.

The largest serials database that exists is Ulrich's, which includes "all publications that meet the definition of a serial except general daily newspapers, newspapers of local scope or local interest, administrative publications of major government agencies that can be easily found elsewhere, membership directories, comic books, and puzzle and game books." The 30th edition of *Ulrich's International Periodicals Directory* lists more than 118,500 titles.[29]

We can compare the growth in this serials universe to the growth of current serials in our All 24 library composite beginning in 1972 (fig. 5.9).[30] The upward trend in the number of serials contained in the Ulrich's universe was particularly rapid during the 1970s. Beginning in about 1983, however, the growth appears to have tapered. The pattern for current serials was similar; however, the rate of growth was slower during the 1970s, and beginning in the early 1980s the curve was essentially flat. As the proliferation of serials continued, libraries did not—probably could not—respond with more serial subscriptions, and the gap between serials published and serials acquired began to widen. The trends displayed here are not independent of each other; the slowing of the growth in the Ulrich's universe of serials during the mid-1980s may be attributable, at least in part, to the declining demand for serials earlier in the 1980s.

Another way of looking at the question of the timing of expansion in serials publication is to take all periodicals currently available and graph their founding dates. This method does not take into account journals that have ceased publication, but it does give an idea of when the "continuing" journals were first published. We are able to use data from the Science Citation Index with the founding dates of the 1990 Source Publication list graphed in figure 5.10.[31] This figure shows that the real proliferation in science literature began in the 1950s, with the number of journals founded in that decade more than double that of the previous decade. This growth continued into the 1960s and 1970s, with 43 percent of the journals in this

---

[29]*Ulrich's International Periodicals Directory*, 30th Edition (New Providence, NJ: Reed Publishing, 1991), viii. The Ulrich's data used here are taken from Ann Okerson, "Of Making Many Books," 13, 15–16. In this report Okerson uses Bowker-Ulrich's serials database to estimate how the serials universe has grown since 1971–72, from 70,000 titles to 108,590 at present. Okerson then graphs average ARL library serials holdings as a percentage of the serials universe, showing that there has been a substantial drop in the percentage of titles collected in research libraries.

[30]"Current serials" includes items other than periodicals and, more important, items "received but not purchased." A better measure of libraries' ability to acquire serials would be "serials purchased" only, but ARL did not begin to collect data for this category until 1986.

[31]The titles in this universe were taken from the Institute for Scientific Information's printed list of the source publications in the 1990 *Science Citation Index*. Information on founding date and country of publication for each title was taken from *Ulrich's International Periodicals Directory*. When this information was unavailable from *Ulrich's*, we used the OCLC database. In just a few cases information was available from neither source.

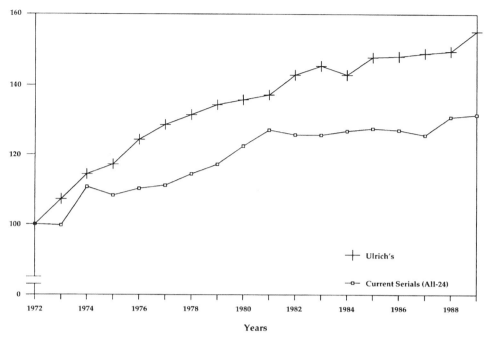

Figure 5.9
Growth in number of serials (Ulrich's and current serials), 1972–89 (Index: 1972=100)

list founded in those two decades alone. The proliferation tapered somewhat during the 1980s, with the number founded almost returning to the 1950s level.[32]

Data on periodicals in the field of modern languages and literature may serve as a rough index of trends in the general availability of scholarly journals outside the sciences.[33] In this field there were substantial increases in the number of journals founded throughout the post-World War II era. The decade of the 1970s, however, stands out, as it alone witnessed the founding of more than 400 new journals (fig. 5.11). Although there was a pronounced slowing in the rate of increase in the 1980s, *more than half of the titles currently available were first published during the last two decades.*

---

[32]These data also allow us to gain some idea of the number of science journals published abroad (which tend to be more expensive than journals published domestically). Of those journals in this list of source publications for which the country of publication is known (3,658 out of 3,680), more than half (55.5 percent) were published outside the United States.

[33]The *MLA Directory of Periodicals* lists titles in modern languages and literatures and the date they were first published, so that one can determine the aggregate number of titles available for acquisition in any given year. See Kathleen L. Kent, comp., *MLA Directory of Periodicals, A Guide to Journals and Series in Languages and Literatures, 1990-91 Edition: Periodicals Published in the United States and Canada* (New York: The Modern Language Association of America, 1990).

In this instance as in others before, the counts will include some number of items that libraries would not choose to acquire; the aim in compiling the *Directory* is to be comprehensive in a way that libraries in their acquisition practices cannot be.

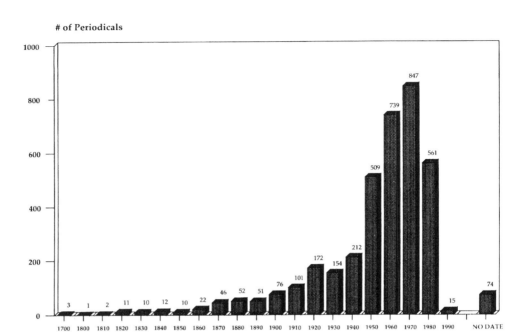

Figure 5.10
Date of founding of journals, 1991 SCI source publications, by decade, 1700–1990

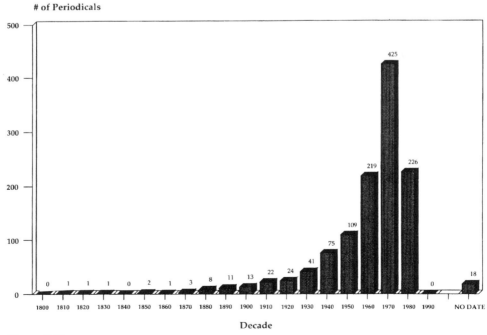

Figure 5.11
Date of founding of periodicals in MLA directory, by decade, 1800–1990

This picture must be modified somewhat by the conclusions reached by Daniel Uchitelle, director of the Center for Information Services at the Modern Language Association, in a very recent unpublished paper in which he tracks the dates when journals in literature ceased publication throughout the 1970s and 1980s. When this information is combined with the more familiar numbers of new journals begun in this period, it appears that the total number of journal titles increased only gradually. Indeed, Uchitelle suggests that the number of journal cessations has been larger than the number of inceptions in recent years.[34]

The founding of so many journals in the decade when the academic labor market was at its weakest point may be attributable in part to a heightened pressure to publish and to the efforts of academics to seek new outlets for their scholarship. Also, it has been argued that the established journals are slow to reflect changes in scholarship and that the resultant founding of new journals is a function of the redefinition of scholarly disciplines. The proliferation of journals in the humanities is surely related in some way to the debates that have occurred in many of these fields (and in some of the related social sciences) about the virtues and limitations of various methodologies and theories.[35] These developments have served to transform the character of scholarly discourse and have led in some instances to the founding of new journals, as have changes in the content of various disciplines (the interest in the experiences of "nonelites," for example, and of women and members of various racial and ethnic minorities). The increase in specialization is yet another force at work here.

Such increases in the number of serials inevitably raise questions about a decline in the quality of scholarship, although the increases do not in themselves substantiate such concerns. One need not enter into arguments about quality, however, or about the virtues of various scholarly approaches to appreciate that the proliferation of journals has had important consequences for academic libraries. Even journals that in some quarters are considered less prestigious or whose methodological approaches are deemed problematic will contain some number of items of interest, and many libraries will want to continue to maintain serials collections that are comprehensive in scope. Nonetheless, despite the substantial redeployment of library acquisitions funds toward the serials budget (see fig. 4.7), the number of current serials acquired has increased only modestly. The obvious inference is that—as all librarians know too well—the prices of serials have also increased significantly, especially during the decade of the 1980s. We now turn to this difficult and complex topic.

---

[34]Daniel Uchitelle, "An Analysis of Data from the *MLA Directory of Periodicals* to Describe Patterns of Journal Publication in the Humanities."

[35]Such debates are reflected, for example, in large-scale changes in scholarly ethos, from the perspectives reflecting the influence of 19th-century German positivism, to the fundamental challenges to that optimistic vision of the potential of scholarship posed above all by deconstructionism, to more recent exhortations to attempt anew to "to negotiate the perceived differences between subject and object, reader and text, interpreter or describer and the external cultural and other structures." On this subject, see Neil Rudenstine's survey in William G. Bowen and Neil L. Rudenstine, *In Pursuit of the Ph.D.*, Appendix F, from which the quotation is taken.

CHAPTER SIX

Book and Serial Pricing

The findings presented in Chapters 3 and 4 demonstrate that in recent years libraries have been spending more of their financial resources to buy fewer materials. Moreover, expenditures for serial subscriptions have been increasing more rapidly than any other component of the materials and binding budget and thus have been consuming an increasingly larger proportion of this budget. This trend has been accompanied by little or no increase in the number of serial subscriptions purchased, and in very recent years this number has declined at many libraries (see figs. 4.7 and 4.8).[1]

It is clear, then, that the rising prices of serial subscriptions and their impact on acquisitions practices are major concerns. Indeed, anyone conversant with recent developments affecting academic libraries will be aware of the so-called serials crisis. The purposes of this chapter are to provide statistical documentation of the magnitude of the problem and then discuss conceptually the interlocking factors that seem responsible for the escalation in prices. While the main emphasis will be on serials, we shall also discuss book prices.

GENERAL TRENDS IN BOOK AND SERIAL PRICING

Some historical perspective is useful in understanding the context of the current concern with the prices of library materials. The recent *Report of the ARL Serials Prices Project* observes that the serials pricing problem has recurred throughout the 20th century but that during the last five years "it has spiraled out of control."[2] We have been able to assemble reasonably reliable national price indexes only for years since 1963 (and, in the case of periodicals, only for U.S. publications). More specific price data are of course of greater interest to individual libraries. Such data are used principally for budgetary planning, and the need is for precise information that is as pertinent to local circumstances as possible. For our purposes—to illustrate broad trends in the prices of library materials and to relate them generally to trends

---

[1]Also, see Ann Okerson, "ARL Libraries React to Projected Serials Price Increases," *ARL: A Bimonthly Newsletter of Research Library Issues and Actions* 153 (November 7, 1990):2; and Ann Okerson, "Monographic and Serial Purchasing in 1992 Projected to Decline Again," *ARL: A Bimonthly Newsletter of Research Library Issues and Actions* 159 (November 12, 1991):8.

[2]*Report of the ARL Serials Prices Project* (Washington, D.C.: Association of Research Libraries, 1989). See therein the report by Ann Okerson, "Of Making Many Books" for a brief overview of the history of concern over serials prices.

in levels of acquisitions—national data on the prices of printed materials are more relevant.[3]

When we compare increases in the average price of hardcover books and the average price of periodicals subscriptions (fig. 6.1), we find that between 1963 and 1970 the respective price indexes increased at comparable rates.[4] Over these seven years the prices of these types of publications also increased roughly in line with the overall price index for all goods and services (the GNP price deflator).

Beginning in 1970, however, the pattern changed profoundly. While the price of books continued to increase at about the same rate as the GNP deflator until about 1978, the price index for periodicals began to increase much more rapidly and to diverge sharply from both the index for books and the overall index. This was precisely the decade when a great many new journals were founded, and there are reasons to believe that the proliferation of specialized journals had a marked effect on the prices of periodicals (see discussion later in this chapter).

Over the entire time period from 1963 through 1990, the average price of periodicals increased at an average annual rate more than one and one-half times that of hardbound books—11.3 percent per year versus 7.2 percent per year. Moreover, the prices of both hardbound books and serials increased more rapidly than the general price level (which increased at an average annual rate of 6.1 percent). In the

---

[3]A number of members of the library profession have noted the limitations of national indexes for their purposes. See Mary E. Clack and Sally F. Williams, "Using Locally and Nationally Produced Periodical Price Indexes In Budget Preparation," *Library Resources & Technical Services* 27 (1983):345–356, especially p. 345; and *Higher Education Price Indexes, 1990 Update* (Washington, D.C.: Research Associates of Washington, n.d.), 19, where it is observed that "a price index reflects a pattern of consumption for a group of consumers, not for the individual. A single national index only approximates the price changes for a single represented consumer." In "German Book Prices," *Book Research Quarterly* 2 (Spring 1986):82–84, Steven E. Thompson published data that revealed that prices listed for books in various subject categories by the vendor Otto Harrassowitz are almost uniformly higher (and often considerably so) than those published in *Buch und Buchhandel in Zahlen*, a standard national index. The prices listed by Harrassowitz are more relevant to the acquisitions practices of American academic libraries because of the nature of the materials surveyed. Similarly, in *Average Prices of British Academic Books, 1974–1984*, Centre for Library and Information Management, Report No. 41 (Loughborough, Leicestershire: Centre for Library and Information Management, Department of Library and Information Studies, Loughborough University, 1985), Lawraine Wood demonstrated that the average price of academic books was higher than that of all books.

[4]Data on prices for hardcover books are from various issues of *Publishers Weekly* (see references cited). For purposes of this analysis the same categories that were excluded from consideration earlier (fiction, general works, home economics, juveniles, language, sports and recreation, and travel) are again excluded here, so as to define a data set that is most relevant to research libraries. Of course, as noted earlier, these data are drawn from national indexes; were one able to define a data set limited to academic materials, the rate of increase almost certainly would be seen to have been even greater.

Price data for periodicals are taken from various issues of the *Library Journal* (again, see references cited). Here too various categories were excluded from consideration. The data set is limited to the following fields: agriculture; business and economics; chemistry and physics; education; engineering; fine and applied arts; history; journalism and communications; labor and industrial relations; law; library science; literature and language; mathematics, botany, geology, and general science; medicine; philosophy and religion; political science; psychology; sociology and anthropology; and zoology. These categories are not identical to those used in *Publishers Weekly*, but they do seem appropriate for our purposes.

The underlying data on which the figures are based are shown in tables 6.1 and 6.2, Appendix B. The overall average prices for books and periodicals (shown in fig. 6.1) are unweighted averages of the values for the separate fields. Book prices do not include philosophy-psychology because data for this category do not begin until 1970.

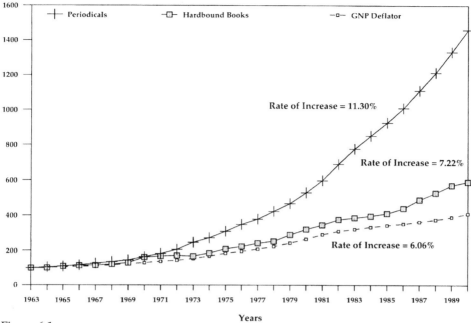

Figure 6.1

Increases in average price per volume, periodicals and books, 1963–90 (Index: 1963=100)

single decade of the 1980s, the GNP deflator increased by a factor of 1.6 while the average prices of books and periodicals increased by factors of 1.9 and 2.8, respectively; the corresponding average annual rates of increase are 3.9 percent, 6.3 percent, and 10.4 percent.

It must be emphasized that the price data included in the periodicals index documents increases in the costs of periodicals published only in the United States, and much of the concern expressed over the rapidly increasing cost of materials has been directed specifically at foreign materials and the pricing practices of foreign publishers.[5] While we cannot provide a reliable estimate of magnitudes, there is no question but that a broader index, which included foreign as well as U.S. publica-

---

[5]See, for example, Deana Astle and Charles Hamaker, "Pricing by Geography: British Journal Pricing 1986, Including Developments in Other Countries" in *Library Acquisitions: Practice & Theory* 10 (1986):165-181; Charles Hamaker, "Library Serials Budgets: Publishers and the Twenty Percent Effect," *Library Acquisitions: Practice & Theory* 12 (1988):211–219; Robert L. Houbeck, Jr., "British Journal Pricing: Enigma Variations, or What *Will* the U.S. Market Bear?" *Library Acquisitions: Practice & Theory* 10 (1986):183–197; Frederick C. Lynden,"Prices of Foreign Library Materials: A Report," *College & Research Libraries* 49 (May 1988):217–231; Kenneth Marks, Steven P. Nielsen, H. Craig Petersen, and Peter E. Wagner, "Longitudinal Study of Scientific Journal Prices in a Research Library," in *College & Research Libraries* 49 (March 1991):125–138; and H. Craig Petersen, "University Libraries and Pricing Practices by Publishers of Scholarly Journals," *Research in Higher Education* 31 (August 1990):307–314. Also see Economic Consulting Services, "A Study of Trends in Average Prices." The ECS report concentrates on four large publishers: Elsevier (Netherlands), Pergamon (U.K.), Plenum (U.S.), and Springer-Verlag (West Germany). The report reviews price data against publishers' estimated costs from 1973 through 1987.

tions, would show an even steeper rate of increase.[6] Furthermore, as we noted in the last chapter, to the extent that foreign periodicals are purchased in the country of origin, the dramatic decline since 1985 in the value of the dollar vis-à-vis foreign currencies has exacerbated the effects of rising prices on the acquisitions budgets of libraries.

Book Prices By Field

Average price increases, of course, vary significantly by field, as well as by type of publication. When we compare trends by broad field over the years since 1970, we find that increases in the prices of science-technology books have far outpaced increases in other fields (fig. 6.2). Prices in these fields veered sharply higher about 1978 and have increased at an average annual rate of 8.9 percent per year since then. In sharp contrast, price increases for books in the arts and humanities, the social sciences, and business have not diverged greatly from the general movements of the GNP deflator over these two decades. Prices of books in medicine also followed similar trajectories until the most recent years, when they increased much faster than the general inflation index.

Trends in book prices take on more meaning when we look at the actual dollar prices of the "average" book in specific fields. (See table 6.1 where fields are ranked by the average price of books in 1990.) Comparisons spanning several decades fail to highlight what has happened most recently, as the data on this table illustrate so well. Between 1980 and 1986 book prices in only four fields increased at a rate greater than inflation, and one of these fields, education, was in the lower half of the range of prices. What is more significant is that between 1986 and 1990 book prices in all fields but one increased at a rate greater than inflation.[7] Books published in only six of the sixteen fields included in table 6.1 had average price increases of less than 30 percent over this four-year interval; five had increases of more than 40 percent, and two more had increases of 39 percent.

It should also be noted that the two fields with the greatest percentage increases in price (technology and medicine) were among the top three fields with respect to the most expensive books. It appears, then, that price increases have been more significant since the mid-1980s and that the most expensive books are also those that have been increasing most rapidly in price. This evidence suggests that book prices are now showing some of the tendencies characteristic of serials—not an encouraging sign for those who must be concerned about library budgets.

---

[6]See Kenneth E. Marks, Steven P. Nielson, H. Craig Petersen, and Peter E. Wagner, "Longitudinal Study of Scientific Journal Prices," for a longitudinal study that attempts to distinguish between foreign and U.S. journals as well as between commercial and noncommercial publishers. The rate of increase in journal prices published by foreign commercial publishers was found to have been greater in the period between 1967 and 1987 than the rate for any other journal type studied (i.e., U.S. commercial, U.S. noncommercial, and foreign noncommercial).

[7]Law is the exception. Book prices in this field increased 15.5 percent, as compared with 16.4 percent for the GNP deflator.

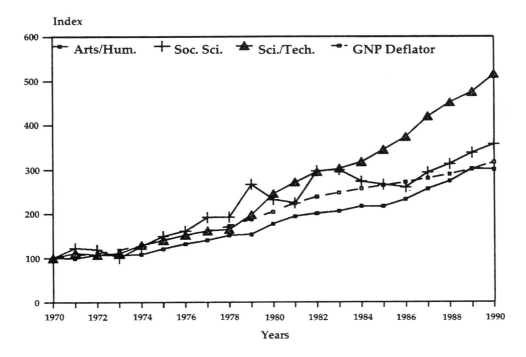

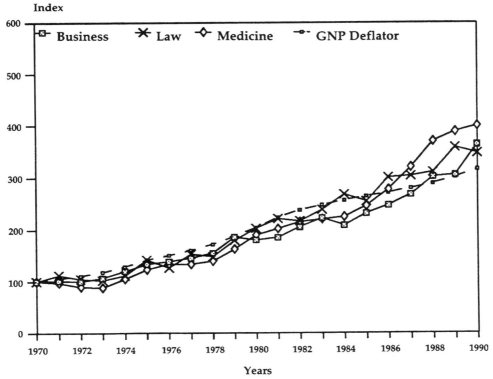

Figure 6.2
Increases in average price per volume by broad field, 1970–90 (Index: 1970=100)

Table 6.1
Average Price per Volume of Hardbound Books, Ranked by Price in 1990

Field	1980	1986	1990	% Change 1980–86	% Change 1986–90
Technology	33.64	55.00	76.61	63.5	39.3
Science	37.45	55.65	75.20	48.6	35.1
Medicine	34.28	49.99	71.87	45.8	43.8
Law	33.25	49.20	56.81	48.0	15.5
Agriculture	27.55	39.26	55.40	42.5	41.1
Business	22.45	30.72	45.17	36.8	47.0
Sociol./Econ.	31.76	30.34	41.97	−4.5	38.3
Art	27.70	35.41	41.74	27.8	17.9
Music	21.79	32.59	41.53	49.6	27.4
Phil./Psych.	21.70	29.65	40.30	36.6	35.9
Education	17.01	26.11	37.80	53.5	44.8
History	22.78	28.44	35.48	24.8	28.3
Literature	18.70	25.73	35.81	37.6	39.2
Poetry/Drama	17.85	25.11	32.27	40.7	28.5
Religion	17.61	21.60	31.24	22.7	44.6
Biography	19.77	22.96	28.95	16.1	26.1
GNP Deflator	85.7	113.8	132.5	32.8	16.4

Notes: See Appendix Table 6.1 for source and more complete data.

Serials Prices by Field

It will come as no surprise to anyone familiar with discussions of the serials crisis that prices of journals also vary considerably by subject matter and that the rapidly rising prices of scientific and technical journals are widely seen as the principal villain of the day. Data from the *Library Journal* suggest a more than eleven-fold increase in the price of scientific and technical journals between 1970 and 1990 (fig. 6.3), which is equivalent to an average price increase of 13.5 percent per year. It is certainly easy to understand why such an extraordinary rate of increase would give a subscriber pause, to say the least. (We discuss later some of the reasons why prices have risen so rapidly.)

While price increases of science and technology journals clearly head the list, prices in *all* fields are seen to have increased since 1970 at a rate significantly greater than inflation.[8] We can illustrate the magnitude of what has transpired more clearly

---

[8]Although the price of periodical subscriptions in the field of business-economics is shown in figure 6.3 as increasing at essentially the same rate as medicine throughout this period (nearly as rapidly as science-technology), it should be noted that business-economics began from a much smaller base—$6.31 per subscription in 1970 compared with $23.44 per subscription for medicine. The business-economics composite in figures 6.3 and 6.5 is an average of the business-economics and labor-industrial relations categories displayed in Appendix Table 6.2.

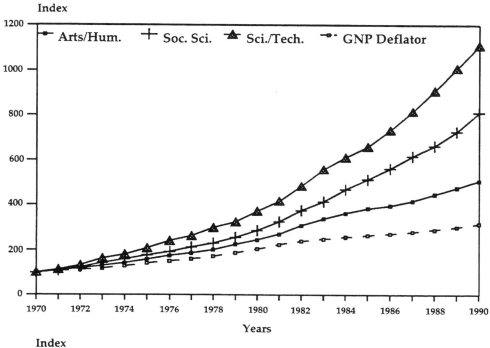

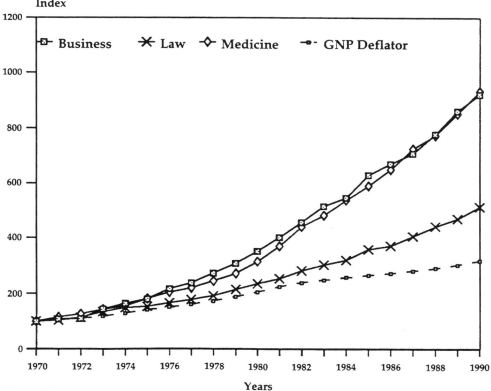

Figure 6.3
Increases in average prices of periodicals by broad field, 1970–90 (Index: 1970=100)

by taking a "snapshot" look at prices in actual dollars for subscriptions in specific fields in specific years (1963, 1970, 1982, and 1990).

In almost every field, by far the largest *relative* price increases occurred during the twelve-year period between 1970 and 1982 (table 6.2 and figs. 6.4 and 6.5).[9] In the fields of chemistry-physics, the "typical" U.S. journal cost $33 in 1970 and $178 in 1982; in engineering, the corresponding dollar figures are $12 and $62; in mathematics and other sciences, $18 and $88. Medicine is the one professional field with a similar experience. In these groups of fields it was normal for serials prices to rise by factors of five-plus over this period (approximately 15 percent per year, on average). In the social sciences, absolute levels of prices are lower and rates of increase, while still rapid, were not quite as great as in the sciences—for example, the typical journal in political science increased in price from $7 in 1970 to $26 in

Table 6.2
Average Price of a Periodical Subscription, by Field, Selected Years, Ranked by Price in 1990

Field	Average Prices (Current $)				% Change		
	1963	1970	1982	1990	1963–70	1970–82	1982–90
Chemistry/Physics	16.07	33.45	177.94	412.66	108.2	432.0	131.9
Medicine	12.22	23.44	102.87	217.87	91.8	338.9	111.8
Math./Bot./Geol./ Genl. Sci.	9.58	18.11	87.99	188.19	89.0	385.9	113.9
Zoology	9.51	16.86	61.07	153.78	77.3	262.2	151.8
Engineering	6.69	12.07	61.54	138.84	80.4	409.9	125.6
Psychology	11.45	17.12	54.21	125.31	49.5	216.6	131.2
Sociol./Anthrop.	4.91	7.31	36.38	77.61	48.9	397.7	113.3
Business/Econ.	6.06	9.03	32.67	63.25	49.0	261.8	93.6
Jrnlsm./Communic.	4.67	6.36	33.91	60.85	36.2	433.2	79.4
Library Science	4.43	7.88	33.52	57.34	77.9	325.4	71.1
Education	4.90	7.09	28.18	56.33	44.7	297.5	99.9
Labor/Indust Rel.	2.51	3.59	24.72	52.74	43.0	588.6	113.3
Law	6.93	9.84	27.53	50.32	42.0	179.8	82.8
Political Science	5.23	6.72	25.89	49.67	28.5	285.3	91.9
Agriculture	3.49	5.17	19.76	42.43	48.1	282.2	114.7
Fine/Applied Arts	5.89	7.50	23.35	36.89	27.3	211.3	58.0
History	5.29	6.90	20.37	35.51	30.4	195.2	74.3
Phil./Religion	4.39	5.84	17.92	30.76	33.0	206.8	71.7
Liter./Language	4.56	6.15	19.39	30.63	34.9	215.3	58.0
GNP Deflator	32.4	42	100	132.5	29.6	138.1	32.5

Notes: See Appendix Table 6.2 for source and more complete data.

[9]To facilitate comparisons, the GNP deflator in figures 6.4 and 6.5 has been indexed to the average price of a periodical subscription in each broad field. In the arts and humanities, for example, the GNP deflator was set equal to $5 in 1963, which is a simple average of the average price of periodicals in 1963 of fine and applied arts, history, literature-language, and philosophy-religion.

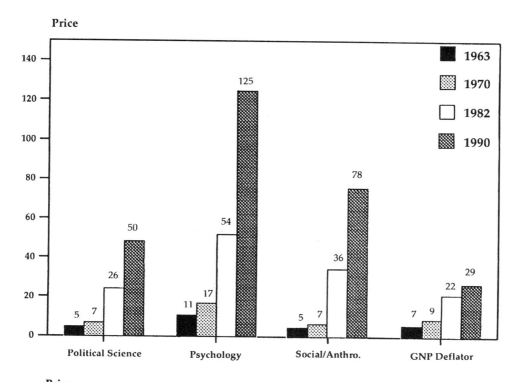

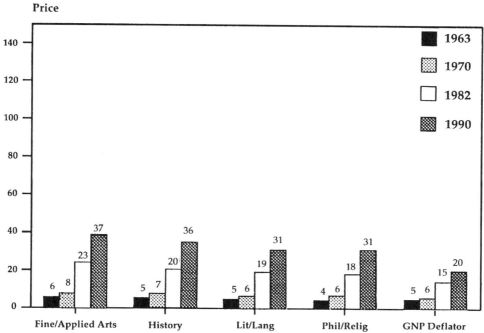

Figure 6.4
Increase in average price of periodicals in nominal dollars, 1963, 1970, 1982, and 1990 (arts, humanities, social sciences)

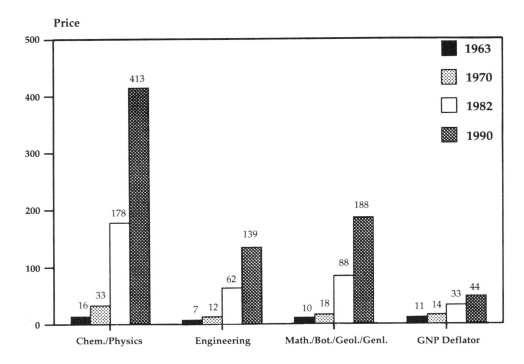

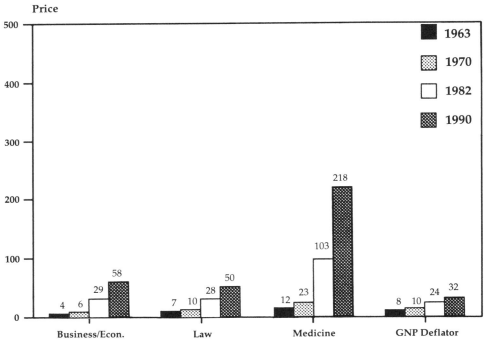

Figure 6.5
Increase in average price of periodicals in nominal dollars, 1963, 1970, 1982, and 1990
(science, technology, professional fields)

1982.[10] The experience in the arts and humanities was roughly comparable to that in the social sciences. In history, for example, the average journal cost $7 in 1970 and $20 in 1982; and in literature and languages, the corresponding costs were $8 and $19. In the humanities and social sciences, serials prices rose rather consistently at average annual rates of about 10 percent per year over this period, a rate of increase that looks modest only in comparison with the 15 percent-per-year rate of increase that occurred in the sciences, engineering, and medicine.[11]

During the eight years between 1982 and 1990, serials prices continued to rise very rapidly but not quite as rapidly as previously. Prices in chemistry-physics, mathematics and the other sciences grouped with it, and in engineering rose at average annual rates of roughly 10 to 11 percent (as compared with increases averaging about 15 percent per year during the 1970-82 period). In the humanities and social sciences, average rates of increase fell to 6 to 7 percent (as compared with increases of 10 percent per year in the period 1970-82). Of course, the absolute dollar increases were much greater in the more recent period as a result of higher base values. The most extreme case is, again, chemistry-physics, where the average price of a journal in 1990 was $413, as compared with $178 in 1982. When confronting such prices, it is small consolation to be told that the relative rate of increase has slowed.[12]

Three more general points can be made:

- First, in all three subperiods we have been examining serials prices rose faster than the GNP deflator. Only between 1963 and 1970 was the relationship at all similar, and even then prices of science and technology journals frequently rose twice as rapidly as the general price index; it was the journals in the humanities and social sciences that had price increases roughly comparable to the GNP deflator.

- Second, there is a striking consistency of rates of increase within similar groups of fields (in the humanities, history, literature-languages, and philosophy-religion; in the sciences, chemistry-physics, mathematics and other sciences, and engineering); clearly subject matter and associated variables count for a great deal in explaining both price levels and differential rates of increase in price.

- Third, the data reveal a persistent tendency for the most expensive serials to experience the largest relative price increases. One consequence is that the relative price differential between serials in, say, chemistry-physics and in literature-languages has steadily expanded: this ratio was 3.5 in 1963 (that is, the average serial in chemistry-physics was 3.5 times more expensive than

---

[10]Psychology is something of a middle case, standing between the natural sciences and the social sciences in price behavior, as it tends to stand between them substantively as well.

[11]Since the GNP deflator rose at an unusually rapid rate during this period, the real rates of increase obtained by dividing by the deflator appear more modest. However, many of the factors driving up the GNP price deflator (for example, the extraordinary increases in the price of energy related to the Arab oil embargo) had little to do with increases in serials prices. This is a good example of a situation in which nominal price increases for a particular commodity or service are more revealing than real price increases. Working only with deflated values would obscure the power of some of the forces pushing up serials prices, such as the proliferation in the number of journals.

[12]A variation of the pattern is well documented in Warren T. Seibert and Marjorie A. Kuenz, *Growth and Change in 67 Medical School Libraries, 1975–1989* (Bethesda, Md.: National Library of Medicine, 1992).

the average serial in literature-languages), 5.4 in 1970, 9.2 in 1982, and 13.5 in 1990.

ORIGINS OF THE SERIALS CRISIS

These developments—not surprisingly, given their obvious importance—have spawned a substantial literature that has attempted to determine the reasons for the rapid price increases, explored the potential consequences of the trends if left unchecked, and proposed possible responses on the part of libraries and the institutions they serve.[13]

Several studies have identified the principal distinguishing attributes of the serials that command the higher prices and have witnessed more rapid price increases.[14] Subject matter, as we have seen, is of particular importance: scientific and technical periodicals are generally more expensive. Titles published by commercial publishers tend to be more expensive than those published by learned societies or associations or other scholarly publishers (universities, university departments, university presses, museums, and research institutions). Other specific attributes that affect costs—a larger number of issues per year, a larger number of pages per issue, the presence of art work—naturally correlate positively with price. Journals that contain advertising were found to have lower prices.

Other studies have specifically considered the pricing practices of foreign commercial publishers, whose titles often command the highest prices.[15] Some price differential is, of course, to be expected, since increased distribution costs have to be recovered in some way. The question has been raised, however, whether the differential between what is charged local subscribers to European periodicals and what is charged North American subscribers is justified by the cost differentials. Prices of foreign periodicals often appear to correlate with various indicators of use and value, which suggests that in those instances pricing practices are largely value-based rather than cost-based.

It has also been argued that some publishers are engaging in discriminatory pricing. The producer can charge different prices in different markets when (1) the various markets for a particular product are clearly distinguishable, (2) the demand for the product within each differs, and (3) there is little or no possibility for resale of the product from one market to another. Discriminatory pricing of journals apparently originated in the early 1980s, when foreign publishers were seeking to offset losses resulting from disadvantageous exchange rates; however, there were no compensatory decreases when the U.S. dollar subsequently weakened. The pricing practices of a small number of foreign commercial publishers—Elsevier Science Publishers, Gordon and Breach, Pergamon Press, Springer-Verlag, Taylor and Francis, and others—have been subject to particular scrutiny, and one institutional study revealed that subscriptions to titles published by Elsevier, Pergamon,

---

[13]For an excellent general treatment of the question of serials prices, see Ann Okerson, "Periodical Prices: A History and Discussion," *Advances in Serials Management* 1 (1986):101–134.

[14]See, for example, Henry H. Barschall, "The Cost-Effectiveness of Physics Journals," *Physics Today* 41 (July 1988):56–59; Sandra R. Moline, "The Influence of Subject, Publisher Type, and Quantity Published on Journal Prices," *The Journal of Academic Librarianship* 15 (1989):12–18; and H. Craig Petersen, "University Libraries."

[15]See references given in n. 5.

and Springer alone accounted for 43 percent of the increase in serials expenditures at the university in question between 1986 and 1987.[16] Elsevier's acquisition of Pergamon in the spring of 1991 intensified concerns about possible oligopolistic control of the market.[17]

This synopsis of views represents some of the concerns expressed by members of the library profession. Publishers, for their part, have argued that any valid analysis has to take account of cost increases resulting from such factors as increases in the number of pages per issue, and some of the more elaborate studies (such as the one described here) are concerned with trends in subscription price per page.

The most fully articulated model of journal pricing has been developed by Roger Noll and W. Edward Steinmueller and their colleagues at the Center for Economic Policy Research at Stanford University.[18] The Stanford group proposes a model that explains the interaction of various attributes of domestic journals, especially their cost structure and the nature of the demand for them.

The principal elements of the underlying cost structure of scholarly publishing, which is shared with other media products, are relatively high first-copy costs (the costs incurred in producing the first copy of the title—editorial work, typesetting, and so on) and relatively low marginal or incremental costs (the costs of printing and distributing each subsequent copy of the title). The publisher has to recover first-copy costs by charging a sufficiently high unit price—that is, in the case of scholarly journals, the price of a subscription. The average cost of each copy produced decreases as the number of subscriptions increases, and a small subscription base compels the publisher to charge a relatively high price in order to recover first-copy costs.

Critical to the degree of market control is limited substitutability of products (the *Musical Quarterly* cannot be substituted for the *Journal of the American Musicological Society*; research libraries must subscribe to both) and relatively inelastic demand (a market in which sales are relatively unresponsive to price increases because of the inability of the purchaser to find a good substitute and the perceived need of the

---

[16]This finding was reported by Hamaker of Louisiana State University and quoted in Richard Dougherty, "Periodical Price Escalation: A Library Response," *Library Journal* 113 (May 15, 1988):27–29.

[17]For a sampling of general reactions, see "Librarians Fear Elsevier Purchase of Pergamon," *The Chronicle of Higher Education* 37 (April 10, 1991):A5; and "Journal Prices Increase 52%," *The Chronicle of Higher Education* 37 (June 26, 1991):A5.

[18]Some of the preliminary results of this study, still in progress, are summarized in papers submitted to The Andrew W. Mellon Foundation, which is funding the research: Lisa Lieberman, Roger Noll, and W. Edward Steinmueller, "Proposal to the Mellon Foundation: Economic Analysis of Scholarly Periodical Costs," "An Economic Analysis of Scientific Journal Prices: Preliminary Results," and "Economic Analysis and Empirical Protocol for Examining Scholarly Periodicals Pricing." Their preliminary analysis appears in published form in Roger Noll and W. Edward Steinmueller, "An Economic Analysis of Scientific Journal Prices: Preliminary Results," *Serials Review* 18 (1992):32–37. This research concentrates on domestic journals only because patterns of circulation are critical to the analysis; accurate time-series data on this statistic are available only for domestic journals, since U.S. publishers must publish circulation information in order to receive second-class mail privileges.

Some of the propositions reflected in the Stanford model are anticipated in two excellent studies: David W. Lewis, "Economics of the Scholarly Journal," *College and Research Libraries* 50 (November 1989):674–688, and Paul M. Gherman and Paul Metz, "Serials Pricing and the Role of the Electronic Journal," *College and Research Libraries* 52 (July 1991):315–327.

For another conceptualization of journal pricing and how it may be affected by electronic technologies, see: Malcolm Getz, "Electronic Publishing: An Economic View," *Serials Review* 18 (1992):25–31.

purchaser for the product). Demand for periodicals tends to be less elastic than demand for monographs, either because of an implicit assumption about the greater importance of the scholarly journal as a vehicle for scholarly communication or because, in Richard De Gennaro's words, "[l]ibrarians have a weakness for journals and numbered series of all kinds. Once they get volume 1, number 1 of a series, they are hooked until the end. They love neat and orderly serials records and complete runs of periodicals on their shelves. Journals, in short, are the sacred cows of libraries."[19]

The basic cost structure, moreover, has further important effects in a market where new entrants compete for limited resources. Subscriptions gained by new entrants almost inevitably serve to reduce the subscription base of existing journals, in turn resulting in upward pressure on unit prices as publishers are compelled to spread first-copy costs over a smaller number of subscriptions.[20] Preliminary results from the Stanford study suggest that subscription price indeed correlates strongly with circulation; other things being equal, titles with smaller subscription bases ordinarily command higher prices and vice versa.

The demand side of the equation (that is, the demand for a particular journal) is affected by both library budgets and the pressures exerted by readers, especially faculty members, to purchase journals. Noll and Steinmueller make the important if obvious point that "to understand the market for journals requires an understanding of faculty utilization of them."[21] After describing the role of publication (especially in the "best" journals) in determining promotions and salary increases, they observe that:

> ... [A]s more faculty seek publication outlets, the demand to be published in a fixed number of "best" journals grows, and a smaller proportion of scholars succeed in publishing at the top of hierarchy. Recognizing this, both publishers and scholars seek to create new publishing outlets that create a new hierarchy, rather than enter at the bottom of an established one. Thus, scholars and publishers seek to narrow the scope of journals, attempting to create an outlet that will be read by people in a subspecialty and that will attain the status of being the second best place to publish for that subspecialty, rather than the twentieth or thirtieth best place to publish in the entire discipline. The result is a special kind of journal proliferation. As more academics seek to publish, and as more universities try to promote faculty research and reward scholarly publication, faculty and publishers jointly seek to create not only more journals, but ever more specialized

---

[19] "Escalating Journal Prices: Time to Fight Back," in De Gennaro, *Libraries, Technology, and the Information Marketplace, Selected Papers* (Boston, Mass.: G. K. Hall & Co., 1987), 103–113, especially p. 104. One study suggested that faculty expectations are also involved. Richard M. Dougherty reported that in conversations with faculty members at the University of Michigan who served as editors of scholarly journals, he discovered that "the economic stress libraries were feeling was not generally understood or appreciated" and that "serials cancellations can ... be a very volatile issue to some faculty and that they will rise to defend the library's materials budget."

[20] A number of members of the library profession have suggested in private conversations that when a new journal title is added to their collection, an existing subscription has to be cancelled, which suggests that successful new entrants do indeed affect the subscription bases of existing titles.

[21] Noll and Steinmueller, "Economic Analysis," 33.

journals that become important to all scholars in a subspecialty, although irrelevant to most scholars and students in a discipline.[22]

From the standpoint of market structure, we find here a kind of monopolistic competition, in which producers differentiate their products and focus on serving particular subsets of an overall market. This permits each producer to set a price above marginal cost. New entrants seek to chip away at the markets of established journals, and the results are an erosion of the subscriptions to the "first" journal and upward pressure on subscription prices. Circulation, then, is a key variable in explaining prices. Noll and Steinmueller note:

> Journal proliferation and specialization drive down the average circulation of journals, which drives up the average subscription price. Moreover, because faculty prefer to avoid a lengthy hierarchy of journals in a discipline, in some sense all new journals are "essential" in that they constitute a natural home for articles of value. In a sense, all journals become at least second best in the hierarchy for a small number of scholars. Hence, libraries face not only increasing average prices owing to declining average circulation, but also intense demand to subscribe to all journals because every one is in some sense important.... The resulting performance of the journals market is socially undesirable and economically inefficient....[23]

This conceptual model helps explain the rapid increase in journal prices during the 1970s as in no small part a direct result of the proliferation of journals during the 1970s (as documented in Chapter 5). This model also offers a particularly persuasive explanation of the nature of the interaction between library acquisitions practices and the publishing entities with which they interact. Any study that neglects the essential link between circulation and subscription price will fail to explain the relevant phenomena.

It is also easy to see why prices of titles published by commercial publishers are almost inevitably higher than prices charged by nonprofit publishers. Nonprofit publishers—scholarly societies, for example—have a variety of ways of reducing first-copy costs so that unit prices can be kept relatively low. There are a variety of hidden subsidies that are unlikely to appear in the calculus of commercial publishers: in some instances societies levy page charges, which provide revenues denied the commercial publisher;[24] and in many instances, perhaps most, the editor of a scholarly journal published by a nonprofit press is either not compensated at all or receives only modest compensation. Ironically, the potential for revenue from advertising would appear to be greater for commercial publishers. Such revenue could, in theory at least, be applied primarily against first-copy costs.

This set of relationships, which underlies production of the scholarly journal, is likely to produce exactly the pattern we have seen: the size of the periodicals universe increases; relatively fixed materials budgets at libraries result in a decrease in the number of subscriptions per title, as available resources are redistributed

---

[22]Ibid., 33-34.

[23]Ibid., 35.

[24]In "Combating High Journal Costs," *Science* 244 (June 9, 1989):1125, Philip H. Abelson sketched a brief history of the emergence of commercial publishers as important participants in the process of scientific communication. Abelson suggests that the levying of page charges by the societies is among the factors that may have created the opportunity for commercial publishers to enter the market.

among a greater aggregate number of available titles in the periodicals universe; prices per title increase as publishers seek to recover first-copy costs from smaller subscription bases; libraries redeploy materials expenditures in response to periodical price increases, protecting serials subscriptions at the expense of other library materials but still cutting back on some subscriptions; and library budgets are encumbered by rapidly rising outlays for serials.

Although the existing literature principally concerns the economics of the scholarly journal, there is some evidence of a similar kind of market dynamic in the production and acquisition of scholarly monographs. At one academic press whose experience is thought to be representative, the average number of hardcover copies sold per title in the humanities and social sciences declined between 1976 and 1986, from between 1,250 and 1,500 to fewer than 1,000. The smaller press runs caused by this decline in copies sold per title unquestionably put upward pressure on unit prices, since here too first-copy costs must be spread over the relevant number of units sold. Concomitantly, there was an increase in the number of titles published.

One explanation offered by several university press directors was that there have been fewer sales of each title to academic libraries, one of the principal markets for university press books.[25] Here again, we see the interaction between acquisitions practices and an underlying cost structure.

More generally, this set of interrelationships—among cost structures, patterns of demand, market characteristics, and the forces leading to more scholarly output—are entirely consistent with the empirical realities. They explain why in recent years increases in dollars spent on library materials have yielded little or no increase in the overall rate of acquisitions, while at the same time the number of items available for purchase has continued to increase. They are the explanation for the widening gap between the number of volumes added gross and book titles published.

Over the short term, libraries have responded to these circumstances primarily by redistributing their resources.[26] This mode of response cannot be sustained indefinitely, however, and it is already under challenge as both temporizing and inadequate. Increasingly, there is the realization that *no* institution, no matter how amply endowed with resources, can hope to maintain a self-sufficient collection into the indefinite future. The decisions of some of the wealthier institutions to increase acquisitions expenditures may be seen as only an interim expedient, although a critically important one, since maintaining reasonable continuity of coverage of the world's scholarly output must be considered an important objective, in order that the even more fundamental objective of maintaining access to the capital of scholarship can be met.

A more viable long-term solution will almost certainly entail fundamental reconfiguration of the dynamics of scholarly communication: perhaps some modifications to a reward system that in part explains the proliferation of scholarly journals and monographs; certainly some application of developing technologies to the problem of first-copy costs; surely much fuller use of new technologies to facilitate greater sharing of resources; and, conceivably, even alterations in the law that

[25]Bailey, *The Rate of Publication of Scholarly Monographs*, 14–17. Explanations by the university press directors were offered in personal conversations.

[26]Some institutions have also attempted various collaborative efforts as discussed in Chapter 4, n. 14. However, even with these efforts institutions have found it necessary to redistribute resources toward serial subscriptions and away from monographs.

governs the rights to "published" material. Part 2 of this study discusses a range of options, most of which depend on greater use of new technologies, that could lead to quite different patterns of scholarly communication.

PART 2

Information Needs and New Technologies

CHAPTER SEVEN

Information as a Commodity

We have suggested elsewhere in this study that libraries and the books they contain are products of a culture of print. Until very recently, scholarly information needs have been served almost exclusively by the technology of printing developed in Europe in the late Middle Ages.[1] In all of its essential characteristics, that technology was simply a different means of doing what had been done in Europe for more than a millennium: the recording of text (and visual images, musical notation, and so on) on sheets of material, whether parchment or paper. The great virtue of printing, of course, was that unlike manual copying it permitted multiple copies of a text to be produced with almost trivial ease.[2] It permitted the creation of the first media products with the characteristics described in Chapter 6: relatively high cost associated with producing the first copy of the product, relatively low cost associated with producing each subsequent copy. It also ensured that all copies of the text could be virtually identical, which gave it considerable advantages over manual copying in that the variant readings resulting from scribal error or the effects of deliberate emendation or interpolation could be eliminated.[3]

The technology of printing, of course, has other characteristics that are either virtues or limitations depending on one's perspective or on the specific information needs at issue. Its principal characteristic, which it shares with manual copying, is that it produces a physical object—a book, a journal, a magazine, a newspaper—containing a fixed, immutable text permitting the reader to interact with it only in limited ways, as contrasted with conversation, for example;[4] the information flow, that is, is one-way. The information, moreover, is universal—it is not tailored to the

---

[1]Many of the questions in this section are addressed in a series of excellent articles in a special issue of *Scientific American* 265 (September 1991) entitled "Communications, Computers and Networks: How to Work, Play and Thrive in Cyberspace."

[2]That characteristic was not regarded as a virtue, however, by all who witnessed the invention of printing. Angelo Poliziano, the famous fifteenth-century Florentine humanist, dismissed the invention with a remark to the effect that "[t]he most stupid ideas can now in a moment be transferred into a thousand volumes and spread abroad"; see Alan Moorehead, "The Angel in May," *New Yorker* 27 (February 24, 1951):34–65, especially p. 60.

[3]We say "could" rather than "would" because students of early printed books have demonstrated that surviving copies of a given title do not necessarily contain identical texts. In some instances there are corrected copies of a particular issue of the title; in other instances there are new issues of the title not identified as such and known to be new only because of the variant readings they contain.

[4]One of the arguments made about the advantages of electronic texts is that, unlike printed texts, they permit the reader to interact with them. It is possible, however, to exaggerate the extent to which printed texts preclude interaction. One has only to think of the medieval tradition of glossing or commenting upon authoritative texts; in that instance the principal text was not altered, to be sure, but there was nonetheless a considerable degree of readers' engagement and even interaction with it, and the commentary in many instances was entered in the margin alongside the principal text. The reader's relationship to and attitude toward the text, however, were indeed different from what the information technologies of the late 20th century permit.

specific information needs of particular readers—and in almost all instances is arranged in some kind of linear sequence. Absent the kinds of devices developed in a print culture to facilitate access to information in printed form (for example, tables of contents and indexes), readers with particular needs are compelled to ferret out the pertinent information by systematic reading. The means of facilitating access to printed information are therefore to be contrasted with those permitted by electronic information technologies, which afford almost instantaneous, random access to any portion of the text.[5]

FROM A PRINT TECHNOLOGY TO AN ELECTRONIC TECHNOLOGY

Inevitably, the medium of print in which text-based information has traditionally been disseminated has shaped one's most fundamental understanding of the nature of text-based discourse and communication. To some extent, that is, terms rooted in the nature of the medium—print products—rather than in the nature of the resource—the intellectual content—shape the discourse. The nonmateriality of text-based information as exemplified by the technologies of the late 20th century, in contrast, entails different terms. Texts are no longer necessarily immutable; rather, they are dynamic. Given that characteristic, interactivity is eminently possible; readers can alter the received texts and reformat the information they contain to suit individual information needs by means of various scanning and sorting mechanisms. Late 20th century technologies, in short, uncouple the material object—the book, the journal, the newspaper—from the intellectual content—the information the material objects contain.

Such fundamental changes in our perceptions of the nature of information were described a decade ago by Harlan Cleveland in his essay in *The Futurist:*

[w]e have carried over into our thinking about *information* ... concepts developed for the management of *things*—concepts such as property, depletion, depreciation, monopoly, market economics.... The inherent characteristics of information now coming into focus give us clues to the vigorous rethinking that must now begin:

1. Information is expandable.... [T]he facts are never all in....

2. Information is compressible. Paradoxically, this infinitely expandable resource can be concentrated, integrated, summarized—miniaturized, if you will—for easier handling....

3. Information is substitutable. It can replace capital, labor, or physical materials....

4. Information is transportable—at the speed of light....

5. Information is diffusive. It tends to leak....

6. Information is shareable.... [I]nformation by nature cannot give rise to exchange transactions, only to *sharing* transactions. *Things* are exchanged:

---

[5]On the ways in which the capabilities of electronic information technologies serve to profile the limitations of print, see two stimulating articles in May Katzen, ed., *Scholarship and Technology in the Humanities: Proceedings of a Conference held at Elvetham Hall, Hampshire, UK, 9th-12th May 1990* (London, Melbourne, Munich, New York: Bowker-Saur, 1991): J. Hillis Miller, "Literary Theory, Telecommunications, and the Making of History," 11–20, especially p. 17; and George P. Landow, "Connected Images: Hypermedia and the Future of Art Historical Studies," 77–94, especially pp. 82–83.

if I ... sell you my automobile, you have it and I don't. But if I sell you an idea, we both have it....

So it has to be a mistake to carry over uncritically to the management of information those concepts that have proved so useful during the centuries when things were the dominant resources and the prime objects of commerce, politics, and prestige. These concepts include scarcity, bulk, limited substitutability, trouble in transporting them, and the notion of hiding and hoarding a resource....

Furthermore, Cleveland observes, these changes in our understanding of the nature of information will have widespread consequences, reaching beyond print and libraries, into political economy and the law.

- In political economy, won't the concept of market "exchange" have to take account of the fact that more and more of our economic activity now consists of what are by nature "sharing" transactions?...
- In law, how should we adapt the concept of property in facts and ideas when the widespread violation of copyrights and the shortened life of patent rights have become the unenforceable Prohibition of our time? Aren't we going to have to invent different ways to reward intellectual labor that are compatible with a resource that is both diffusive and shareable?[6]

One observer has suggested that the technology of print, as contrasted with the information technologies of the late 20th century, has had even more fundamental effects on the social and intellectual experience of modern society:

Television is not symbiotic with literature in the way that print was. Literary values—authors, great works, deep meanings—fitted hand-in-glove with print, but television both weakens literacy (the skill on which literature depends) and undercuts literature's basic function. The replacement of the printed word by the image and the voice substitutes immediate, powerful one-dimensional pictures and simple continuities for the ironies, ambiguities, and complex structures fostered by print and idealized in literature. Where the fixity of the printed book encouraged the conception of masterworks and permanent truths so central to literature, databases in which items easily intermix and television programs that flicker fleetingly past make literary ideas like originality, form, and permanence seem quaint ideas of another age.[7]

Literature, that is, is perhaps "so much a product of print culture and industrial capitalism, as bardic poetry and heroic epic were of tribal oral society, that, like chivalry in the age of gunpowder, it will simply disappear in the electronic age."[8] As a kind of discourse, it is an expression of the technology of print, and new technologies may ultimately spawn a new kind of discourse with fundamentally different features.

---

[6]Harlan Cleveland, "Information as a Resource," *The Futurist* 16 (December 1982):34–39, especially pp. 35–38.

[7]Alvin B. Kernan, "The Death of Literature," *Princeton Alumni Weekly* 92 (January 22, 1992):11–15, especially p. 15. Kernan's essay is based on his book *The Death of Literature* (New Haven, Conn.: Yale University Press, 1990).

[8]Kernan, "Radical Literary Criticism May Represent the Last Phases of an Old Order Collapsing," *The Chronicle of Higher Education* 37 (September 19, 1990):B1, B3, especially B1.

The characteristics of print therefore have had profoundly important implications for the storage and dissemination of information, including scholarly information, and thus for the most fundamental aspects of the processes of scholarly activity and communication. The essential distinguishing characteristics of research libraries are themselves expressions of the technology of print, as are those of the various publishing industries that have grown up over the past half millennium. Because printing produces physical objects, libraries, in fulfilling their role as participants in the process of scholarly communication, have accordingly acquired certain fundamental characteristics determined by the nature of the technology and appropriate to the nature of their role in the process of scholarly communication, as currently defined. Libraries have been and continue to be physical spaces where printed materials are collected, classified, and stored in a way that facilitates access to them. They contain spaces where readers can consult materials in the collection rather than take them elsewhere,[9] and the proximity of members of the library staff—specialists in information management—similarly facilitates access. (Members of the library profession have observed that theirs is one of the few professions identified with a particular facility; librarians ordinarily work only in libraries, whereas attorneys are not exclusively identified with any one kind of facility.) There are constraints of space and time (and of other kinds) resulting from the nature of the prevailing information technology that limit readers' access to scholarly information: the only such information they have immediate access to is local information that the local research library has been able to acquire, and they have access to it only when the library is open.

The technology of printing, further, has defined the role publishers play in the process of scholarly communication. Indeed, publishers became players in the first instance in part because of their professional expertise in the technical aspects of publishing and because of the economies of scale resulting from centralization and specialization in that function. It is important to observe, however, that publishers make other critical contributions as well, including coordinating the peer review process, termed the "gate-keeping" function by some observers. They solicit opinion regarding the quality of manuscripts proposed for dissemination and make judgments about the importance of their contribution to scholarship. The information technologies of the late 20th century, some argue, may transform publishing in that the publishers' role in the actual process of dissemination may change; there will presumably continue to be a need for the gate-keeping function, however, and the new technologies will not obviate that need.

For the moment, the technology of print requires that both publishers and libraries anticipate demand. It is cost-ineffective for publishers to print either too few or too many copies of a particular title. Given the logistical complexities of disseminating information in printed form (printing and binding, transportation of the resulting material objects to clients, whether individuals or institutions, libraries

---

[9]It must be said that for many scholars, libraries are inviting, welcoming places, powerful material expressions of human intellectual accomplishment. For this reason many scholars regard wistfully the "de-institutionalization" of information permitted by late 20th century technologies; as we argue later, however, print has some advantages over electronic media, especially in some scholarly disciplines and for some scholarly purposes, and since there will presumably continue to be a collection of printed materials, it is difficult to imagine a situation where libraries as they are now known will cease to exist altogether.

or vendors), publishers project demand in an attempt to ensure that titles will be available to clients at the moment when they are in need of them.

A similar set of assumptions underlies the acquisitions practices of research libraries. Scholarly publications often go out of print quickly; research libraries therefore wish to acquire them as soon as possible after their publication so as to ensure access to the information they contain. Moreover, the same concern about the ready availability of material governing publishers' behavior is also operative here. Although interlibrary loan services afford access to material owned elsewhere, for many readers such services seem inefficient. The most desirable option is ownership, and for that reason acquisitions have attempted to be as comprehensive as institutional resources have permitted, so as to build a self-sufficient collection with all the advantages of ready access it entails.

This model has been described as the "just-in-case" model;[10] libraries acquire materials in anticipation of readers' needs, in accordance with an assumption that a particular reader may at some future time wish to consult a particular volume. Given the prevailing information technology, this model in many respects has indeed been the most appropriate. It may be added that for many scholars a rich, self-sufficient collection of millions of volumes has another, critically important advantage: it permits serendipitous, potentially interesting discoveries that result when scholars chance upon titles while browsing in the stacks.

The information technologies of the late 20th century compel us to rethink the most basic assumptions underlying the processes of research and scholarly communication. They affect not only the nature of scholarly activity in the first instance but also the nature of the contributions of other agents—publishers of scholarly materials, academic booksellers, research libraries—participating in the process of scholarly communication.

Some of these technologies have already been effectively employed to streamline and improve various library functions, especially acquisitions, cataloging, and circulation. The cataloging function in particular has been transformed as a result of the new technologies. As we saw in a previous section of this study, individual institutions contribute catalog copy to databases maintained collaboratively and can retrieve and easily reformat records contributed by other institutions, so that there is a degree of uniformity previously unachievable. The automation of cataloging has had the added beneficial effect of permitting collaborative collection development; the catalog copy in the database serves as a record of other institutions' holdings, so that individual institutions, building on local strengths, can make informed decisions about acquisitions that do not replicate decisions made elsewhere within the consortium.[11] While the implementation of collaborative collection development schemes is not perfect, the new technologies make these efforts feasible on a scale that would have been impractical in an earlier era.

---

[10]See, for example, "An Interview with Richard R. Rowe, President and CEO, The Faxon Company," *Library Acquisitions: Practice and Theory* 16 (1992):93–102, especially pp. 93–94.

[11]See, for example, Nancy E. Gwinn and Paul H. Mosher, "Coordinating Collection Development: The RLG Conspectus," *College & Research Libraries* 44 (March 1983):128–140. The importance of the new technologies to collaborative collection development will be discussed more fully below.

THE RECONFIGURATION OF SCHOLARLY COMMUNICATION

Until very recently, however, the new technologies have been employed simply to automate *existing* functions. They hold enormous potential for a much more fundamental reconfiguration of the entire process of scholarly communication and for libraries' role in that process. Nina W. Matheson, professor of medical information and director of the Welch Medical Library at Johns Hopkins, has written of the "de-materialization" and "de-institutionalization" of information:[12] it need no longer be made available to us in printed, immutable forms collected by libraries, where access to the universe of scholarly information is governed by local constraints affecting the size of the acquisitions budget and the physical plant where the print products are stored. Rather, just as automatic teller machines have revolutionized banking (an individual's banking needs are now met by machines that are located everywhere, function 24 hours a day, and afford access to global information),[13] so the information technologies of the late 20th century facilitate access to an ever-larger universe of scholarly information beyond that contained in one's own local research library.

To anticipate the content of much of the remainder of this section, we might summarize some of the characteristics of the new technologies. There is, first, the possibility of ever-greater bibliographic control over the professional literature. The automation of cataloging and the availability of catalog records on the Research Libraries Group's Research Libraries Information Network (RLIN) afford scholars remote access to an extraordinarily rich store of information about the existence and location of scholarly materials held elsewhere and bibliographic information on those materials. As various observers have suggested, however, library catalogs ordinarily contain complete bibliographic information solely on the monographic literature. Since the most current information is often contained in the serial literature and intellectual advances often occur on the basis of interpretations argued in that literature, especially in particular disciplines, it is a limitation that the bibliographic record ordinarily does not extend to the level of the individual article.[14] Increasingly, however, there are bibliographic services available in electronic form that index and abstract the serial literature. By no means are there adequate services of this kind in all disciplines, and the existing ones are expensive to use. Nonetheless, scholars in some fields are certainly closer than before to being able to achieve relatively complete bibliographic control over the literature of their disciplines.

Increasingly, the technologies are being applied not solely to problems of access to information about information but to problems of assembling and ordering the primary information itself and of providing access to it. In all disciplines, including the humanities, the advantages to particular kinds of scholarly activity of the availability of electronic versions of texts and data are clear. As many observers have suggested, such databases are dynamic phenomena; because "the facts are never all in," in Harlan Cleveland's words, it is useful to be able to assemble them

---

[12]Nina W. Matheson, "The Academic Library Nexus," *College and Research Libraries* 45 (May 1984):207–213, especially p. 208.

[13]The analogy with automatic teller machines was suggested by Brewster Kahle of Thinking Machines Corporation in an unpublished paper of 1991 entitled "Electronic Publishing and Public Libraries."

[14]See Matheson, "The Academic Library Nexus."

in a form that allows one to make additions and refinements easily and manipulate the texts or data in various ways. For many scholars the new means of storing text not only facilitates traditional kinds of research but also permits one to ask new kinds of questions that would have been literally impossible to pursue with text and data in printed form. And although the availability of the full texts of secondary literature—works of synthesis and interpretation—in electronic form is still a very recent phenomenon, there can be no question that such material will increasingly be available.

The potential utility for libraries of these means of capturing text-based information is obvious. "Information is transportable—at the speed of light," Cleveland has written. The dematerialization of information may ultimately permit specialization in collection development and collaborative collection development in that the full texts of materials not owned locally would be readily available from other institutions within the consortia to which individual libraries belong. It would permit the ideal of resource sharing, which depends upon more-or-less immediate access to materials owned elsewhere, to become a reality. That these technological developments are occurring at a time when resources do not permit the traditional model of the self-sufficient library to be sustained is perhaps fortuitous, perhaps not.

One must not underestimate the difficulties involved in realizing such a reconfiguration, however. Some of them will be explored in greater detail in the chapters that follow. There are, first, enormous cost implications. The sharing of information in electronic form assumes greatly upgraded computing and telecommunications networks, and many institutions will simply not be in a position to absorb their share of the capital expense. Moreover, electronic versions of material challenge some of the most fundamental assumptions underlying copyright legislation. There are, further, issues of standardization. Over the course of the past half millennium, we have become accustomed to using text-based information in printed form and are conversant with its conventions, while text-based communication in an electronic environment will require different conventions and protocols that have not yet been settled upon.

It is important to add that print products have some considerable advantages over electronic products, especially for certain purposes. Alvin Kernan has observed that print yields particular kinds of text-based discourse, and although his observation pertained principally to literature, it might be extended to include certain kinds of scholarly discourse as well. The utility of electronic versions of primary texts and data is, for many scholars, unarguable. Using search engines one can readily locate references and patterns in the texts or data, conduct particular kinds of analyses, and retrieve virtually all the pertinent material. Works of synthesis and interpretation based on the underlying data or texts, however, especially in the humanities, might share with literature some of the ambiguities, deep meanings, and complex structures for which print is a more appropriate medium. Print's suitability to some kinds of scholarly purposes should not be underestimated, and one needs to be attentive to differences among disciplines. Humanists work differently from scientists and may therefore have some different kinds of information needs. A great advantage of the present situation is that a choice between print products and electronic products need not be made, at least on technological grounds. Cost factors will, however, force almost all institutions to make certain choices irrespective of technological constraints or possibilities. Such choices can be made on the basis of the suitability of various options to specific scholarly objectives.[15]

These late 20th century technological developments have still another implication for libraries. Once the preeminent information service for research and scholarly communication, the library is now complemented by an entirely new set of information services provided by computing, each being the expression of a particular technology.

Librarians have experience in thinking about the nature of information as a commodity, about how one establishes its authenticity and orders and classifies it so as to facilitate access. Some institutions have undertaken an administrative re-organization that may reflect their belief in the importance of integration of computing and library services.[16] Information is regarded as one of the institution's most important resources, like its financial and human resources. At some universities, accordingly, a single vice president for information services, comparable in stature and in the scope of his or her responsibilities to the vice presidents for finance and human resources, has responsibility for both the library and the computing and telecommunications services. Such an administrative structure permits decisions about the allocation of resources for information services to be made in a centralized, coherent way.

We turn now to a more complete consideration of some of these developments and their importance both for scholarly communication and for libraries' role in the process. To many observers it is clear that we are in a period of transition. What many envision, ultimately, is a situation in which the full range of information services and products would be available to the individual end-user at his or her own workstation:[17] fully machine-searchable bibliographic services that abstract and index the existing printed literature;[18] databases of primary material; the full,

---

[15]For example, at some point in the process of scholarly communication it would be useful to be able to convert to print texts stored and transmitted electronically, presumably at the point when the end-user is ready to read them.

[16]"New Job Proliferates on Campuses," *The Chronicle of Higher Education* 38 (October 23, 1991):A18. On the general subject of the need for integration of various information services and therefore for a centralized long-range planning capacity and recast budgeting process, see Patricia Battin's excellent article "The Library: Center of the Restructured University," *College and Research Libraries* 45 (May 1984):170–176 (especially p. 174), which in the library profession has achieved something of the status of a classic.

[17]See, for example, Richard M. Dougherty and Carol Hughes, *Preferred Futures for Libraries: A Summary of Six Workshops with University Provosts and Library Directors* (Mountain View, Calif.: The Research Libraries Group, Inc., 1991); Richard N. Katz and Richard P. West, "Implementing the Vision: A Framework and Agenda for Investing in Academic Computing," *EDUCOM Review* 25 (1990):32–37; and William Y. Arms, "Scholarly Publishing on the National Networks," *Scholarly Publishing* 23 (April 1992):158–169. On the economic implications in particular of such a reconfiguration, see the articles in *Serials Review*, A Special Issue on Economic Models for Networked Information, ed. Czeslaw Jan Grycz, Volume 18, Numbers 1–2 (1992).

[18]Of course, abstracting and indexing services are in some respects products of a transitional phase; when the full texts of the professional literature are themselves available electronically, one will be able to search them directly for references of interest and will perhaps not need to resort to bibliographic services to gain access to the literature. In this way, and in many others, electronic information technologies challenge some basic distinctions traditionally made. On this point, see Ann Okerson, "Scholarly Publishing in the NREN," *ARL: A Bimonthly Newsletter of Research Library Issues and Actions* 151 (July 4, 1990):1–4.

machine-searchable texts of works of analysis with primary material integrated with it through sophisticated windowing and hypertext functions (these would lead the reader to the entire literature and substantiating primary material on any point he or she wishes to pursue); downloading and print options that would permit the end-user to excerpt and reorder portions of the full range of material available and print it locally; flexible protocols for communicating among heterogeneous systems, what one member of the library profession has called "systems with rich and varied access vocabularies [that address the] individual needs, sophistication level, and viewpoint of the user."[19] One cannot know precisely where in the transition we presently are, though we are surely much closer to the beginning than the end. The objective in Part 2 is to describe some elements of the transition and assess their potential utility.[20]

---

[19]Pat Moholt, "Research Issues in Information Access," *Rethinking the Library in the Information Age: A Summary of Issues in Library Research*, Vol. 1 (n.p. [Washington, D.C.]: U.S. Department of Education, Office of Educational Research and Improvement, Office of Library Programs, October 1988), 9.

[20]For a lively account of the kinds of access to information facilitated by its availability in electronic form, see Timothy C. Weiskel, "Environmental Information Resources and Electronic Research Systems (ERSs): Eco-Link as an Example of Future Tools," *Library Hi Tech* 9 (1991):7-19. In Weiskel's words (p. 9), Eco-Link "integrates a wide variety of data from electronic sources relating to the environment. The heart of the system consists of download-filter-manage software routines that automate access to electronic databases and process the acquired information so as to merge data from a broad range of different sources in a common set of locally constructed databases. These ... can be updated regularly and made cumulative—providing an increasingly valuable archive of information for any field in question."

CHAPTER EIGHT

Bibliographic Information in Electronic Form

Whatever promise the new technologies hold, one may be certain that printed scholarly literature will continue to exist for a long time and that adequate bibliographic control is essential to scholarship. We might begin, therefore, with a fuller description of the ways in which the new technologies have been applied to the problem of access to global bibliographic information about the existing printed literature—in the first instance, information on the monographic or booklength literature and, in the second, information on the serial literature.[1]

ELECTRONIC ACCESS TO THE MONOGRAPHIC LITERATURE

Since the early 1970s, university libraries have contributed catalog records to databases maintained collaboratively. A critically important role in the collaboration has been played by two organizations, the OCLC (originally the Ohio College Library Center, now the Online Computer Library Center) and RLG (the Research Libraries Group).

Online Computer Library Center (OCLC)

OCLC[2] was founded in 1971, and its database, the Online Union Catalog, currently contains information on more than 24 million books and other materials held by more than 4,800 member libraries. The database is accessed by nearly 14,000 libraries in 46 countries for cataloging and reference purposes and in order to arrange interlibrary loans. It is growing by more than 2 million records annually; every seven days the Library of Congress adds an average of 4,200 machine-readable records. The database is extraordinarily useful not only because it permits uniformity in the content of catalog copy but also because it affords access to information about the existence of materials and serves as a record of the location of particular titles within the national system.

OCLC's database has traditionally been used principally by library professionals. In October 1991, however, the organization made available a service called First-

---

[1]By global information we mean information on scholarly literature beyond that contained in one's own local research library. For purposes of this discussion the term "monographic literature" applies not only to monographs but also to textbooks, editions of primary texts, and other such materials where the bibliographic record would ordinarily consist solely of information on the entire volume. That literature is to be contrasted with the serial literature and related kinds of writings (a collection of essays by several different authors, a conference report, a *festschrift*), where the most useful bibliographic information would extend to the level of the individual article within the collection.

[2]The information in the following two paragraphs was taken from two articles: "Bibliographic Data Base Marks 20th Anniversary," *The Chronicle of Higher Education* 38 (September 4, 1991):A26; and David L. Wilson, "Researchers Get Direct Access to Huge Data Base" *The Chronicle of Higher Education* 38 (October 9, 1991):A24–A25, A28.

Search, which permits individual patrons to access the database directly to search for materials. FirstSearch employs a menu that guides readers through a series of options; whereas the database was previously searchable only by author or title or a few other categories, the individual reader can now access the records by subject as well. Patrons pay a fixed fee for each search rather than by the minute. The system can be accessed either over the Internet, described in greater detail later, or in some instances over OCLC's new, high-speed, $70 million private telecommunications network, soon to be completed. OCLC has contracted with vendors such as H. W. Wilson Company to provide databases containing information on materials other than monographs.[3]

Research Libraries Group (RLG)

Of at least equal importance to research libraries of the type considered here are the achievements of the Research Libraries Group.[4] Founded in 1975, the RLG by 1991 had 112 members, among them universities, independent research libraries, archives, museums, and learned societies. In September 1991 its bibliographic database, the Research Libraries Information Network (RLIN), an online information system reflecting the combined holdings of the member institutions, contained 50 million catalog records for books, serials and their contents, musical scores, sound recordings, archival collections, maps, computer files, visual materials (films and photographs), and art sales catalogs. In 1992 RLG is adding a number of specialized indexes to RLIN that are now available only in print. Among the important databases already available are the *Avery Index to Architectural Periodicals* online, which analyzes articles from more than 700 publications; the *Eighteenth Century Short Title Catalogue*; and SCIPIO, the art sales catalog database, which provides citations for catalogs of sales dating from 1599 to the present, often valuable sources of information on the provenance of art objects, collection patterns, and so on.

RLIN is available to individual scholars, and readers need a personal computer and modem, a telephone line, and a searching account and password to access the records over the GTE Telenet communications network. Through one's local campus mainframe computer, the database is accessible also over the Internet. (There is currently no communications charge for this means of access.) The database is searchable by personal names, title words in any order, subject headings, and more than 40 additional categories, including the International Standard Book Number. Search results can be limited by language, date and place of publication, and holding library.

The organization is currently engaged in efforts to make RLIN records available on local campus online library catalogs. Library patrons at a particular institution

---

[3]On the responses at one institution to FirstSearch, see Henry S. Whitlow, "Verdict Is In on FirstSearch at Bluefield College," *SOLINEWS* 18 (Spring 1992):9–10.

[4]Information on RLG is taken from David L. Wilson, "Research Libraries Group Seeks New Focus and New Members," *The Chronicle of Higher Education* 38 (January 22, 1992):A21–A22 and two promotional pieces: *RLG* and *Personal Access to RLIN: How Individuals Can Search an On-Line Catalog of Research Libraries' and Archives' Collections* (The Research Libraries Group, Inc. 1989).

will be able to search for records in RLIN as they would in their own institution's online catalog.[5] To cite an early example, at New York University, where the first phase of a three-phase project has already been completed, since March 1990 a daily average of 350 bibliographic records has been transferred electronically from the RLIN system to the Geac system at New York University's Bobst Library. The next phase entails the transfer of records created or updated on NYU's Geac system to RLIN for incorporation into the database, and the final phase will permit online searching of the RLIN database locally by NYU's faculty and students. Other libraries are proceeding with similar plans. What is envisioned, ultimately, is a situation in which all RLG libraries are linked electronically.

Of particular importance is RLG's interest in improving the quality of bibliographic information on what might be called nontraditional materials. Increasingly, scholars, specifically in the humanities and related social sciences, are making use of images, the texts of musical compositions, unpublished archival sources, ephemerae, and other such materials. Access to these sorts of materials is difficult because bibliographic information about them is either not available or is not organized in the same way as information on the published scholarly literature. As boundaries between existing humanistic disciplines are re-negotiated and scholarly information needs change in response to this development and others, the information services designed to address those needs may change accordingly. In this respect RLG's interest in developing appropriate services is potentially of great importance.[6]

Other Initiatives

In addition to the catalog records maintained by OCLC and RLG, many research libraries have also made their own online catalogs available on the Internet. Information about the existence and location of materials not contained in the OCLC and RLG databases is thus provided. Moreover, catalog copy written locally may contain idiosyncratic bibliographic information, potentially of great interest to library professionals and scholars elsewhere. One of the difficulties in making information of this type available on the Internet, however, is that there is a great

---

[5]See *RLG*; also, Jennifer Hartzell, "RLG and NYU Complete Phase One of Project for Electronic Record Exchanges Between RLIN and Geac Local Systems," Press Release, The Research Libraries Group, Inc. (September 21, 1990).

[6]On changing scholarly information needs and their implications for libraries, see in particular *Scholars and Research Libraries in the 21st Century*, ACLS Occasional Paper, no. 14 (New York: American Council of Learned Societies, 1990); and Lawrence Dowler, "Among Harvard's Libraries: Conference on Research Trends and Library Resources," *Harvard Library Bulletin*, n.s. 1 (Summer 1990):5–14. On RLG's initiatives in this area, see Wilson, "Research Libraries Group."

deal of such information. Two publications in particular, *NYSERNet: New User's Guide to Useful and Unique Resources on the Internet* and *Internet Resource Guide*, serve as invaluable guides to some of the more important resources.[7]

The much more significant problem is that the bibliographic record was not automated at most research libraries before the late 1970s. As a result there are hundreds of thousands (in some instances millions) of catalog records not contained in individual institutions' online catalogs. Libraries will have to undertake the retrospective conversion of their card catalogs to have a single integrated record of their monographic collections. This conversion can be done manually for small collections with efficiencies being achieved by searching the OCLC or RLG databases for records matching local holdings. But for major research libraries manual conversion will be so costly as to seem unfeasible. Ultimately, all research libraries will need to put their entire catalogs into machine-readable form. The cost of doing so will be high but may be appropriate in relation to the ongoing costs of library operations and catalog maintenance. More than half of ARL member libraries report that they have already converted 90 percent or more of their card catalogs to machine-readable form. One challenge, of course, is to prevent invaluable local cataloging information from being lost in the process.

Princeton's university librarian, Donald Koepp, and its vice president for computing and information technology, Ira Fuchs, have proposed to convert the university's printed catalog records in a different way. In the first of two phases, high-speed scanning technology would be used to produce digital, bit-mapped replicates of the cards;[8] the resulting images would be stored on optical platters. Although the images would be electronically searchable only in ways approximating the kind of manual searching one does in a card catalog, they would be available online; readers would thus be able to access the entire catalog electronically, although in a two-step process, and from any properly equipped remote station anywhere in the world, since the catalog would be available on the Internet. The second phase, which would entail converting the optical, bit-mapped records into MARC (machine-readable cataloging) format, in which author, title, and other such

---

[7]*NYSERNet: New User's Guide to Useful and Unique Resources on the Internet, A Project of the NYSERNet K-12 Networking Interest Group and the NYSERNet/NYS Library Networking Interest Group for Libraries*, Version 2.0 (Syracuse, New York: NYSERNet, 1991) and *Internet Resource Guide* (Cambridge, Mass.: NSF Network Service Center, BBN Systems and Technologies Corporation, 1989). The second of these publications provides periodic updates as new resources become available on the Internet. Both publications list online library catalogs that are available; among them are the SUNY Buffalo Online Catalog, Colorado Association of Research Libraries, City University of New York Online Catalog, SUNY Binghamton Online Catalog, and the New York Public Library Online Catalog (listed in *NYSERNet: New User's Guide*), and Boston University, University of California and California State University, The University of Michigan's Online Catalog, Emory University Libraries Online, The Library Catalog for the University of Colorado at Colorado Springs, The Catalog of the University of Pennsylvania Libraries, The University of Wisconsin Madison and Milwaukee Campuses Network Library System, University of Utah Card Catalog System, Northwestern University LUIS Online Catalog, University of Maine System Library Catalog, University of Illinois at Chicago, Cleveland Public Library Catalog, Penn State University Library Information and Access System, Harvard Online Library Information System, Cataloging from the Library of Congress, The Online Catalog, Princeton University Libraries, The Cal Poly, San Luis Obispo, Kennedy Library's Online Catalog, and University of Iowa Libraries (listed in *Internet Resource Guide*).

[8]The technology is similar to that used for billing purposes by American Express to produce an image of the triplicate form a client signs at the time of a transaction.

information were adequately distinguished, would employ optical character recognition technology and automatic error-handling algorithms, rather than having the MARC tags assigned manually to each field in each record. The records could then be integrated with those in the online catalog.[9] Princeton's approach may prove to be stopgap, as the costs of other technologies decline, but would be a step forward in any event.

ELECTRONIC ACCESS TO THE SERIAL LITERATURE

The automation of the bibliographic record of the monographic literature has been paralleled by similar services providing information about the serial literature. There is an important difference between the two kinds of service, however. Libraries themselves assumed responsibility for providing bibliographic information in electronic form about their monographic collections, as a continuation of the traditional cataloging activity. Information in electronic form about the serial literature, on the other hand, is in many instances provided by commercial services. The cost implication for libraries is significant: if they wish to offer a comprehensive array of bibliographic services, they must absorb the substantial cost of acquiring the commercial services, and in many instances members of the university community demand such services in addition to traditional acquisitions.

RILA, RILM, INFO-SOUTH

The array of information such bibliographic services can provide is illustrated by RILA, *Répertoire International de la Littérature de l'Art* and RILM, *Répertoire International de la Littérature Musicale*, RILA's prototype. RILA provides bibliographic information (and in many instances abstracts) for current publications in the history of Western art: monographs, book reviews, conference reports, exhibition catalogs, periodical articles, *festschriften*, and other publications. It is produced by the Getty Art History Information Program (AHIP) and has recently merged with the *Répertoire d'Art et d'Archaeologie*, a parallel French bibliography produced by the Centre Nationale de la Recherche Scientifique. More than half the records contain abstracts written by staff members of the AHIP whose responsibility it is to review the current literature, locate and identify publications worthy of being indexed and abstracted, and write brief synopses. As of January 1991 the database contained more than 130,000 records on items published from 1973 on. The bibliographic records and abstracts are available in printed and electronic form. The comparable publication in the history of music, RILM, is produced by the International Musicological Society and the International Association of Music Libraries. It shares many of its essential characteristics with RILA, with two exceptions: there is a five-year interval between publication of the literature and publication of the index, and many RILM abstracts are written by the authors themselves.

Both databases are available online through the DIALOG Information Retrieval Service, from Dialog Information Services, Inc., a Knight Ridder Company. Similar

---

[9]There would remain the considerable problem of converting catalog records in nonroman type. For a general discussion of the issue of retrospective catalog conversion, see the special issue on retrospective conversion of the *IFLA Journal* 16 no. 1 (1990).

databases are available through WILSONLINE, from H. W. Wilson, and ORBIT Search Service, a division of Maxwell Online, Inc., which provides electronic versions of such scientific indexes as *Chemical Abstracts*.[10]

Another example is INFO-SOUTH, the Latin American Information System, which is a comprehensive database of abstracts of the contents of 1,600 publications on all aspects of society and change in South America, Central America, and the Caribbean. Included are newspapers, news magazines, and journals. The University of Miami manages INFO-SOUTH and permits subscription by either hourly rate or annual fee for unlimited use.[11]

It would be difficult to exaggerate the advantages to scholars of having such bibliographic information available in electronic form, in part because of the nature of the information itself, which extends to the level of the individual item (the individual article or book review), and in part because of the ability to search the literature completely for virtually all items of interest and, in contrast with manual searching, with considerable ease. As Michael L. Dertouzos has noted, such services "relieve many of the repetitive, boring and unpleasant tasks related to processing and communicating information."[12] However, one should not underestimate the cost of utilizing such services. DIALOG's promotional literature suggests that "[a] typical 10-minute search can cost from $6 to $16.50. (These examples include telecommunications costs but do not include offline print charges.)"[13] Accordingly, while some university library systems have chosen to make such online services available directly to the individual reader, others, understandably, have restricted their use to members of the library staff so as to keep searching costs to a minimum.

SERVICES OFFERING INDIVIDUAL ACCESS TO DATABASES

Many scholars have argued for individual access to the databases for the reason that "scholars need to be guided by their instincts when they search databases just

---

[10]See, for example, the *Directory of Online Databases* Volume 12, Nos. 1 and 2, January 1991 (New York: Cuadra/Elsevier, 1991).

[11]Mick O'Leary, "INFO-SOUTH Fills Foreign Data Gap," *Information Today* 9 (June 1992):13–14.

[12]"Communications, Computers and Networks," *Scientific American* (September 1991):30–37, especially p. 37.

It is important to remember, however, that the automated record in most disciplines extends back only a few years. Here again, the scholarly community faces the enormous problem of retrospective conversion of the bibliographic record of the serial literature so that comprehensive searching is possible. Clearly, information needs differ between the sciences and the humanities in this respect; in most scientific disciplines it is nowhere nearly as important to be able to search last decade's literature as it is in the humanities (although historians of science will want to be able to do so). On this point, see Douglas Greenberg, vice president of the American Council of Learned Societies, "Technology, Scholarship, and Democracy, or, You Can't Always Get What You Want," a talk delivered at the fall 1991 meeting of the Coalition for Networked Information, Washington, D.C. A revised and condensed version of the talk was published under the same title in *EDUCOM Review* 27 (May-June 1992):46–51. Here we think it is important to add, once again, that abstracting and indexing services are tools appropriate to print literature. Electronic versions of full texts that are fully machine searchable may to some extent obviate the need for such services.

[13]See *DIALOG Database Catalog 1991* (Palo Alto, Calif.: Dialog Information Services, Inc., 1991).

as when they search card catalogues or browse the stacks," as one proponent of individual access has phrased it.[14] In response to the interest of individual scholars in having direct access to indexes of the type described here, some institutions have purchased computer tapes containing the bibliographic records and the requisite software from the vendors and have made the databases available on local-area networks, which saves the cost of the long-distance telecommunications connection. In such instances individual users may have a menu of options available to them listing various kinds of campus information services: the online library catalog, various bibliographic services, and so on. Individual patrons may then search whichever database is pertinent to their purposes. In other instances vendors have made portions of their complete databases available on CD-ROM, and libraries have made the discs available as they would traditional printed indexes. Although the discs share with other electronic media the advantage that one can easily search the database, vendors have tended to stipulate in the rental or sales agreement that they not be mounted on a local network.[15] In such cases they share with printed indexes the disadvantage of being available to only a single patron at a time, as contrasted with the online databases, accessible by more than one patron simultaneously.[16]

Both OCLC and RLG offer yet a third option; they have acquired some of the existing indexes directly from the vendors and have mounted them on their information systems. OCLC, for example, has contracted with vendors such as the H. W. Wilson Company to add to the existing databases already available on OCLC's system.[17] RLG, too, has added various indexes to those available on RLIN. For a fixed annual fee institutions are permitted unlimited searching of some of the files and thus enjoy the advantages of having such indexes accessible locally without

---

[14]Greenberg, "Technology, Scholarship, and Democracy," 11.

[15]In some instances individual institutions have sought permission from the publishers for networked access, but the publishers for the most part have prohibited such access and have instead limited it to a single person at a time. Such limitations by publishers are likely to change—indeed, are already changing—as concerns about revenue are shaped by different factors.

[16]Clearly, the situation with respect to the available kinds of services and options of this type is changing rapidly. For information about some of the choices institutions are currently making in response, we are grateful to Patricia Battin, president of the Commission on Preservation and Access, Marvin Bielawski, assistant university librarian for technical services at Princeton University, Paula Kaufman, dean of libraries at the University of Tennessee, Knoxville, Daniel Oberst, director of advanced technology and applications, Office of Computing and Information Technology at Princeton University, and David Penniman, president of the Council on Library Resources.

On the general situation as it is at present, see also Fran Spigai, "Information Pricing," *Annual Review of Information Science and Technology* 26 (1991):39–73. For this reference, we are indebted to David Penniman.

[17]Wilson, "Researchers Get Direct Access." The indexing and abstracting services already available through FirstSearch are listed on pp. A24–A25.

having had to assume responsibility for the technical demands involved in mounting them.[18]

A further important issue is that many disciplines, in the humanities and related social sciences in particular, either do not have bibliographic services of the type described here or are dissatisfied with the ones they do have.[19] Here again, the Research Libraries Group has played an important role in working with learned societies to identify information needs and assess the adequacies (or inadequacies) of existing bibliographic services.[20]

An experiment conducted by Dialog Information Services at Earlham College in Indiana was designed to gauge faculty and student response to the availability of

---

[18]On RLG's service, called CitaDel, see the promotional piece *CitaDel: The Complete Citation and Document-Delivery Service from the Research Libraries Group* (Mountain View, California: The Research Libraries Group, 1992). Among the abstracting services available are *Dissertation Abstracts, Newspaper Abstracts,* and *Periodical Abstracts.* In addition, RLG has mounted a number of indexes previously available only in print, including the *Hispanic-American Periodicals Index,* the *Index to Foreign Legal Periodicals,* and *Technology and Culture's* bibliography for the history of technology. RLG also offers a companion service, to be discussed in more detail later, that delivers the full texts of most articles cited in the CitaDel files.

One of the general problems institutions face in making information resources of this type available to patrons is the wide variety of user interfaces; there can be as many different kinds of protocols for access to such resources as there are vendors, media, and so on. This point will be discussed in greater detail in Chapter 11.

[19]In "Information Access: Our Elitist System Must Be Reformed," *The Chronicle of Higher Education* 38 (October 23, 1991):A48, Douglas Greenberg suggests that adequate bibliographies in electronic form are generally unavailable and argues for the development of such services. For a differing opinion on the question of the general availability of bibliographic services, see David Lewis, "Letters to the Editor: Is Access Equitable?" *The Chronicle of Higher Education* 38 (November 20, 1991):B4.

Richard P. Kollin and James E. Shea, in "New Trends in Information Delivery," *Information Services and Use,* 4 (1984):225–227 (especially p. 227), and Miriam A. Drake and Kathy G. Tomajko, in "The Journal, Scholarly Communication, and the Future," *Serials Librarian* 10 (1986):289–298 (especially p. 292), discussed the further problems of overlap (two or more services indexing an article) and "underlap" (no coverage of some journals by such services); one possible solution they suggest is "gatewaying," which permits complementary databases to be integrated with one another in a way that prevents duplication.

[20]In the general promotional piece *RLG* (p. 15), the charge of the Task Force on Scholarly Bibliographies is described as follows: "Despite the annual bibliographies produced by many of America's learned societies, access to periodical literature and informal publications is still inadequate for many fields and interdisciplinary areas. During 1992 RLG is working with the American Council of Learned Societies and some of its constituent societies, especially in history and area studies, to assess the inadequacies of bibliographic access, to define useful enhancements, and to establish a pilot project for cooperative production of an online, multipurpose bibliography."

See also RLG's two excellent publications *Information Needs in the Humanities: An Assessment,* prepared for the Program for Research Information Management of the Research Libraries Group, Inc., Principal Author: Constance C. Gould (Stanford, Calif.: The Research Libraries Group, Inc., 1988) and *Information Needs in the Social Sciences: An Assessment,* prepared for the Program for Research Information Management of the Research Libraries Group, Inc., Principal Authors: Constance C. Gould (Economics, Political Science, Psychology), Mark Handler (Sociology, Anthropology) (Stanford, Calif.: The Research Libraries Group, Inc., 1989). Both publications contain expert analyses of changing scholarly practices and information needs in various disciplines and what the RLG might do to help address them.

We are also grateful to RLG for sharing various informative memoranda and unpublished materials on their initiatives.

its services and gather information about their use of the databases.[21] Dialog provided Earlham with a year's free access to its bibliographic and full-text databases and absorbed the telecommunications charges during the academic year 1990–91 and during the following academic year permitted unlimited searching at a discounted rate. The college has received a $200,000 gift from an alumnus to endow online searching. During the first year of the experiment, more than 90 percent of the faculty and 80 percent of the students accessed the databases at some time, although the percentages of those making extensive use of the services were probably lower. Many faculty members testified to the promise these services hold for scholarship and, notably, for teaching. As one faculty member observed:

> In *Notes on Virginia*, Jefferson described the process[:] "A patient pursuit of facts, and cautious combination and comparison of them, is the drudgery to which man is subjected... if he wishes to attain sure knowledge." Jefferson is still right about the patient pursuit of facts.... We have, however, taken much of the drudgery out of the process and made it easier to find sources, but we still have to read carefully— probably more carefully than ever— and we still have to think. The difference is that searching no longer takes much time and energy from the scholarship of thought.[22]

The experience at Earlham gives some sense of the utility of these services and of the importance to scholarship of facilitating access to information about information. To be sure, there is a superabundance of information available, and in attempting to establish bibliographic control over the literature on a particular topic, scholars face formidable challenges resulting from that very superabundance. Moreover, as some faculty members at Earlham suggested, there is the risk that easy access to information will lead some students to substitute the exhaustive assembling of facts and others' opinions for their own critical evaluation and interpretation of issues.

Relatively complete access to global bibliographic information is a critically important objective. Scholarly arguments based on thorough knowledge of the professional literature are at minimum better informed and obviously to be preferred over those that are less firmly grounded. At the same time the cost to institutions of the services that provide access to such information should not be minimized. In an era of limited resources, difficult decisions will have to made about possible tradeoffs in acquisitions between traditional printed materials, which will continue to be fundamental, and services like those described here. Indeed, one of our purposes is to highlight some of the tensions that now exist and will continue as the new information technologies are found to have ever more useful applications to scholarship. The argument is that providing scholars with readily accessible information about the existence and location of scholarly materials held elsewhere is in many respects a more important objective than building a free-standing, self-sufficient local collection.[23]

---

[21]On the experiment, see Amy Beth, "When Cost is No Factor: The Impact on Faculty of Unlimited Access to DIALOG," *Information Searcher* 4 (1991):3ff., and Jerry Woolpy, "The World in a Keystroke," *Earlhamite* 111 (Fall 1991):5–6.

[22]Woolpy, "World in a Keystroke," 5–6.

[23]See, for example, Paul Gherman, "Setting Budgets for Libraries in Electronic Era," *The Chronicle of Higher Education* 37 (August 14, 1991):A36.

CHAPTER NINE

Electronic Publishing

Scholarly activity ordinarily culminates in publication (literally, the act of making public), the communication to colleagues and students of results, observations, and interpretations emerging from one's research. It is at this point that libraries have traditionally entered the process; they have collected and classified printed products published by academic and commercial publishers that serve as vehicles of scholarly communication. But libraries are, of course, indispensable to scholarship from its very inception. They give scholars access to past work and thus make future contributions possible. Those contributions represent not only a culmination, in that they communicate results of work brought to the point where publication is deemed warranted, but also a beginning, in that they furnish material that supports new scholarly ventures and stimulates new analyses.

PRIMARY AND SECONDARY TEXTS: THE GENBANK EXAMPLE

One characteristic of electronic information technologies is that they establish a different relationship between interpretive works and the underlying data or primary texts on which they are based. Consider the difference between the more traditional approach to assembling and publishing data and the electronic procedures of GenBank, the national repository for nucleic acid sequence data.[1] In the past scholars and scientists gathered data in an attempt to test a particular hypothesis. When sufficiently important results were obtained, a paper describing them would be published and the authors would typically include some of the data substantiating their conclusions. After electronic databases such as GenBank were established, the data contained in such articles would then be extracted and stored electronically. There were limitations inherent in such a model, however: the period between the submission of the manuscript of an article and its publication was inordinately long; and as the volume of data increased, publishers were understandably reluctant to include anything more than excerpts, especially given that sequence data in printed form was of limited usefulness.

These features of the current model argued for different procedures altogether. It was proposed that the full range of substantiating data be made available electronically at the same time that a paper presenting conclusions based on them appeared in print. The scientists responsible for maintaining GenBank have secured the cooperation of journal editors so that submission of the data to GenBank would be a necessary condition to publication of a paper based on them. Authors are required, further, to submit data in "machine-parsable" form. The direction of flow of the data between published articles and the databank has therefore reversed. Authors are now able simply to excerpt or cite data from the database. Readers are

---

[1]What follows is based entirely on Christian Burks, Michael J. Cinkosky, James W. Fickett, and Paul Gilna, "Electronic Data Publishing and GenBank," *Science* 252 (1991):1273–1277.

able to retrieve the underlying base data at the same time that they receive the articles themselves.

Such a model might apply to humanistic scholarship and scholarly communication as well. Many humanists would be as interested as scientists in having ready access to the full range of primary material underlying scholarly arguments (in this instance, of course, the material is ordinarily different in kind, usually text rather than data). In historical disciplines, for example, one can distinguish between the sources—contemporary chronicles and narrative accounts, letters, diaries, works of art, literature, and music, debit-credit registers, data on demographic trends, government statutes, and so on—and analyses that make use of such material and attempt to package and interpret it in particular ways. It is in the comprehensive assembling of the primary material that electronic information technologies are especially flexible and powerful tools, in part because "the facts are never all in," as Harlan Cleveland has said, and one therefore wants to be able to assemble material in a way that is appropriate to the dynamic quality of scholarship, and in part because the new technologies permit one to search the assembled primary material with ease and reorder and reassemble it in ways appropriate to one's purposes.

In the humanities, as in the sciences, many publishers are increasingly unwilling to print lengthy original source material because it is so costly to do so. "[P]rinting costs," wrote the late Eric Cochrane of the University of Chicago, "have all but extinguished the four-century-old tradition of European text editing."[2]

These developments highlight the virtues and limitations of each medium and the appropriateness of particular media to particular material. Electronic media are better suited to storing underlying raw material, whether data or texts. Print, in contrast, is better suited to presenting works of synthesis and interpretation that make use of the raw material. As Henry Riecken has suggested, "It may be no more sensible to publish a commentary on the *Miller's Tale* in electronic format than to embalm in a printed work the data from the *Current Population Survey....* The text of the *Federalist Papers* was put into machine-readable form in order to carry out an analysis that resolved questions of disputed authorship of some of the papers; but the new format did not replace the bound volume for readers who want to absorb the thoughts and reflect on the aspirations of this stately document."[3]

The example of GenBank suggests that, at least in some scientific disciplines, printed journal articles need not contain the documentation for the argument they advance. A more appropriate means to handle documentation might be through reference to the contents of the dynamic electronic database, thus consigning the type of material to the medium that handles it best. One advantage of this approach is that it may lead to shorter, less expensive print products that contain little or no

---

[2]Eric Cochrane, *Historians and Historiography in the Italian Renaissance* (Chicago and London: The University of Chicago Press, 1981), xv.

[3]Henry W. Riecken, "Scholarly Publication: Are There Viable Options?" Draft for the Research Library Committee [of the Council on Library Resources], October 1989, 16, 18 (We are grateful to Dr. Riecken for permitting us to quote from his paper). In quoting this portion of his article, we do not want to give the impression that he was necessarily arguing for publication of the *Federalist Papers* or a commentary on the *Miller's Tale* in printed form. On the contrary, he observed earlier (p. 14) that "the accumulated evidence suggests that scholars . . . much prefer to read printed material than screens, and much prefer the portability, browsability, and other familiar characteristics of a book or journal to the electronic formats now available. For this reason, it seems probably that a print option will have to be part of the *output* (not necessarily the input, processing, or storage) of electronic publishing."

documentation. Storing the raw material in electronic form, conversely, would in principle permit individual readers to manipulate it in ways that print clearly does not. The GenBank model of publication also avoids what might be characterized as the compromises and half measures typical of the traditional vehicles of scholarly communication—printed articles that contain the scholarly argument in the main text with brief excerpts from the underlying documentation in footnotes, tables, and appendixes.

But the GenBank example assumes that secondary works will appear in print. The new technologies will also permit a fully integrated process in which works of synthesis and interpretation are also published electronically and linked to underlying base data or texts through flexible, sophisticated hypertext and windowing functions,[4] which offer considerable advantages over print in their ability to connect primary and secondary material.[5]

To be sure, various kinds of intellectual material (we purposely avoid the word "information") have distinctive characteristics and purposes. But that need not imply that literary or philosophical writing or scholarly works of analysis and interpretation should be exempt from electronic publication in the first instance. It is rather that the arguments for electronic publication of such works are not the same as for substantiating data or documentation. Print continues to be the preferred medium for certain purposes: the printed page is still more readable than a computer screen; a book is more transportable than a portable computer; a subtle argument that unfolds over many "pages" is often more accessible in print than on a computer screen.[6] These are arguments for a print option *at some point* in the

---

[4]Windowing is the ability to view sets of data, text, or graphics simultaneously on a computer screen. Hypertext is a class of software that provides the ability to explore a body of text-based information in a non-linear way. Users are able to link concepts by jumping directly to facts needed and by following links and pathways to other related information within the document.

[5]Implicit in the GenBank model, further, are two different retrieval modes. The main text is retrieved as it traditionally has been; one picks up the printed volume and reads the text. The underlying base data, however, are retrieved electronically. Clearly, full integration of retrieval modes would offer considerable advantages. On this point, see also Malcolm Getz, "Electronic Publishing," 27–28; Getz observes that *"The Mathematica Journal* has both a print and software component. The software component is readily available via the network at my workstation. To see the print component, I must go to the science library."

[6]Here we feel it is important to refer once again to the suggestions several observers have made concerning the relationship between the technology of print and the kinds of discourse it produces. Print permits discourse with the characteristics of literary or philosophical writing, among other genres; electronic information technologies may ultimately produce fundamentally different kinds of discourse with characteristics and values different from those familiar from print genres. Whatever the characteristics and values of these new genres will be, we envision an interim period where the new technologies will be applied to existing genres and used to streamline, enhance, and extend existing information practices. Indeed, the earliest European printed books were in many cases designed so as to resemble manuscripts as much as possible; the typefaces replicated familiar lettering styles and space was left for illuminated initials. It is likely, therefore, that the electronic information technologies of the late 20th century will be utilized in this way for some time; eventually, their distinctive characteristics will almost certainly produce fundamentally different kinds of genres.

Perhaps the most important characteristic of electronic information technologies that will serve to produce a new kind of writing is precisely that the technologies permit almost instantaneous communication. The fact that the technology of print often entails an extended process from the time a manuscript is submitted to its publication may perhaps be related, though not in an uncomplicated way, to the deep meanings, ambiguities, and complex structures characteristic of print genres; electronic technologies, conversely, encourage the communication of fresh, immediate observations.

process of scholarly communication because of the advantages that print affords; they are not necessarily arguments for the production of texts, whatever the genre or intellectual purpose, in printed form in the first instance. Even in the case of a commentary on the *Miller's Tale*, there are advantages to having the text stored electronically, in that a reader can instantly locate a passage in the commentary of particular interest using a search-engine. Electronic media may also be more appropriate media of distribution, with respect to economic cost-effectiveness, in very specialized fields where monographs can, at best, be expected to sell just a few hundred copies.

The availability of text in electronic form has important potential advantages, moreover, for purposes of resource sharing among institutions, in that texts stored electronically are almost instantaneously transmittable. One of the main impediments to resource sharing—the cost and perceived inefficiency of traditional interlibrary loan services—is therefore resolvable, at least in principle. Current interlibrary services, which have been described as "a bulky process in which a dozen people [labor to bring] forth a mouse,"[7] could be completely transformed. A reader at a university library in California might be able to review, on a read-only basis, the first few panels of a text maintained electronically at a library in Massachusetts and decide whether to request that the text be downloaded and printed. A transaction that may take weeks under present circumstances could take seconds, and the reader could choose not to request the text at all after having reviewed a small portion of it.

Electronic storage of text also permits the reader or end-user to tailor universal information to individual needs. McGraw-Hill, Inc., has developed a program that permits faculty members at the University of California at San Diego to design their own textbooks;[8] they can search an online catalog from a computer in the university's bookstore for materials in McGraw-Hill's Primis database, which contains the full texts of books, journal articles, and so on. The on-site publishing center compiles the materials, creates a title page, and adds an index, table of contents, and page numbers; the entire process can be completed in 48 hours. McGraw-Hill has been granted permission from copyright holders to reprint all materials in the database. Because the texts are created and "published" on demand, faculty members need not anticipate class enrollments weeks or months in advance to order books. More important, faculty members can design texts more precisely suited to

---

[7]Riecken, "Scholarly Publication," 9–10. As Riecken also observes, "[t]he requested item may be out on loan, not due back for weeks or months." This, too, is an argument for electronic versions of texts: they do not circulate and are thus always available, at least in principle (it is in this sense that information in electronic form, as contrasted with print form, leads to sharing transactions rather than exchange transactions, to borrow Harlan Cleveland's words). By extension, while printed volumes can be mutilated or stolen and must be handled, bound, and shelved, electronic texts have advantages in these respects (that is not to say, however, that they are not susceptible to the electronic equivalent of theft or mutilation, nor that there are no costs associated with their handling). On some of these characteristics of electronic texts and their advantages, see Gherman and Metz, "Serials Pricing," 315–327, especially p. 324; and, on the issue of theft particularly, "Library Thieves Take All but the Covers," *The New York Times* (April 7, 1992). For this last reference, we are grateful to Thomas Nygren.

[8]Information on McGraw-Hill's service is taken from Beverly T. Watkins, "San Diego Campus and McGraw-Hill Create Custom Texts," *The Chronicle of Higher Education* 38 (November 6, 1991):A25.

their pedagogical purposes.[9] The economic implication of such a capability, as one economist observed, is that "[l]argely because of the changes in costs due to electronics, the size of the minimum press run for a title has become smaller. Indeed, McGraw-Hill publishes textbooks on demand from a database of articles or chapters.... The minimum press run is approaching one. The number of titles produced grows in part as titles for narrower audiences become economic."[10]

Electronic publication, finally, has the virtue that it is the only existing medium appropriate for publishing material of certain types, as Jerome Yavarkovsky, director of the New York State Library, has observed:

> In some instances, research results are not published by conventional, printed means because the results can't be printed and still be meaningful. This is true, for example, when the results are three dimensional, graphic, moving simulations, or animations, or when the outputs are dynamic visual representations of variable processes or theoretical constructs. Traditional, printed publication is completely inadequate for disseminating research of this kind. Yet, this research should be included in what we refer to as "the literature."[11]

Because few electronic journals presently exist, no one can confidently predict what new paradigms of scholarly communication in the electronic age will eventually emerge. Our objective in this section is simply to offer a few suggestions as to how scholarly publication might work.[12] We would do well to heed the challenge issued by Ann Okerson, director of the Office of Scientific and Academic Publishing at the Association of Research Libraries:

> It is critical that in starting virtually "from scratch" with a brand new "making public" vehicle, we are unfettered by old modes of viewing and doing publishing: by existing notions of publishing offices; marginal cost structure of publishing; the idea of "circulation;" indexing and abstracting; "monographs" and "serials;" advertising; ownership; possibly even profits. We have the opportunity to begin with a blank page—even that notion needs a new metaphor.[13]

---

[9]An individual reader's ability to reformat existing texts so as to create new texts that suit particular information needs can perhaps be related to the discussions in current literary-theoretical writings of "writerly" versus "readerly" texts. Electronic information technologies permit an entirely different attitude on the part of the reader toward the authority of the received text and elevate the role of the reader. Whether the new technologies are responsible for such discussions would be difficult to say; the fact that both are late 20th century developments, however, can hardly be entirely coincidental. At minimum, the McGraw-Hill service may serve as an example of a new kind of intellectual creativity permitted by the new technologies.

[10]Getz, "Electronic Publishing," 2.

[11]Jerome Yavarkovsky, "A University-based Electronic Publishing Network," *EDUCOM Review* 25 (1990):14–20, especially p. 15. Yavarkovsky's remarks, of course, suggest an extension of options beyond hypertext to "hypermedia," a term used to describe the coexistence of different forms of electronic information within the same document: text, images (whether still or moving), or sound, or, to use J. Hillis Miller's terms, "alphabetic," "iconic," and "auditory signs" (see "Literary Theory, Telecommunications, and the Making of History," in Katzen, ed., *Scholarship and Technology in the Humanities*, p. 15).

[12]Several papers in particular have proven to be particularly thoughtful and incisive attempts to envision how scholarly communication might work in the electronic age: see Riecken, "Scholarly Publication," Getz, "Electronic Publishing," Gherman and Metz, "Serials Pricing," and Yavarkovsky, "University-based Electronic Publishing Network."

[13]Ann Okerson, "Scholarly Publishing," 1–4, especially p. 1.

ELECTRONIC PRODUCTION AND DISTRIBUTION

Assuming that the principal current document formats—monographs and periodicals—will continue to exist in an electronic environment, at least for a time, the new technologies will no doubt first be applied to the tasks of producing and distributing traditional kinds of documents.[14] Let us begin with production.

When a scholar finishes the manuscript of a journal article and sends it to a publisher, it is ordinarily subjected to editorial and peer review. Some observers have suggested that the traditional editorial and peer review processes might be circumvented altogether because electronic information technologies so facilitate communication among scholars. In Henry Riecken's words, "[a] jaundiced view might hold that desktop publishing suffers from the same blight as computer network 'bulletin boards'—anyone with the equipment can 'publish' whatever he wants, of whatever merit or interest, and the potential audience is left with the task of sifting through the midden." In our view, however, as in Riecken's, the peer review process is so fundamental to scholarly practice that it will continue to be critically important, whatever the medium of distribution.[15] However, the new technologies may well expand the review process and change its character, with preliminary versions of manuscripts being made available on a network for comment by interested readers. The author would then prepare a final version, incorporating any suggestions that seem to have particular merit.[16] Even if this expanded process does not develop, the traditional one is greatly expedited in an electronic environment. Editors can send manuscripts to reviewers and receive responses much more quickly, thus reducing the period between the time of the manuscript's submission and editorial decisions.[17]

The manuscript then goes into production, and here electronic technologies have already been effectively employed. If the author has submitted his or her text in electronic form, the cost of original typesetting is considerably lower, since the compositor's task is simply to edit the electronic version of the text, and original

---

[14]Indeed, it is telling that the TULIP project of Elsevier Science Publishers makes use of a technology that produces images of the pages of the printed journal, which therefore cannot be searched, reformatted, or excerpted in the way that texts in alphanumeric form can. Imaging technology nevertheless offers advantages over print largely for reasons of ease of transmission. Many observers are urging that the distinctive characteristics of electronic technologies be fully exploited, that texts be made available in such a way as to permit full interactivity.

[15]See also Douglas Greenberg's paper "Technology, Scholarship and Democracy, or, You Can't Always Get What You Want," 13, on peer review as "the distinguishing sign of all scholarship"; Yavarkovsky, "University-based Electronic Publishing Network," 19; and Stephen Cole, "The Role of Journals in the Social Construction of Scientific Knowledge," (Paper read at The Role of Journals in Scholarly Communication, A Centennial Conference in Memory of George J. Stigler, The University of Chicago, April 10–11, 1992).

[16]Charlene S. Hurt and Sharon J. Rogers, "How Scholarly Communication Should Work in the 21st Century," *The Chronicle of Higher Education* 36 (October 18, 1989):A56; Yavarkovsky, "University-based Electronic Publishing Network," 19. On the possibilities inherent in any kind of pre-publication scheme, see also n. 40.

[17]Yavarkovsky, "University-based Electronic Publishing Network," 19; Riecken, "Scholarly Publication," 13.

keying of characters is kept to a minimum.[18] Both author and editor can have changes made readily, using global search and change functions.

Whether the new technologies will result in other significant production cost savings is difficult to determine at this point. Many of the principal costs have less to do with the medium than with the nature of the activity. For example, many of the costs associated with the highly labor-intensive editorial and peer review processes will remain, while some costs associated with the actual production of the text—typesetting, in particular—can almost certainly be reduced.[19]

Once author and editor have settled upon a final version of the text, it is distributed. Traditionally, distribution has consisted of shipping or mailing printed and bound copies of the first copy to individuals, vendors, and libraries. In an electronic environment there might be a variety of distribution media.[20] Publishers might continue to make hard copy available on demand from their own printers to clients who do not yet have the means to make use of electronic versions of texts (or prefer paper). Alternatively, they might issue titles on CD-ROM or floppy disc; these have an advantage over printed volumes in that they miniaturize the text, so that the considerable space problems libraries face might be addressed by this kind of distribution.[21] Such products might either be sold to the user, whether individual or institutional, or leased. In either case the option to download and print the text or any portion thereof might be controlled by the sales or rental agreement. If the CD-ROM or floppy disc is sold or leased to an institution, the publisher might also specify in the agreement that the text is not to be mounted on a local-area network, so that more than one reader can have access to it simultaneously.[22] In any of these cases the cost of printing, if it is permitted, could be the responsibility of the individual user, just as now the individual ordinarily incurs the cost of photocopying printed material in a library's collection.[23]

The option that appears to be of unusual interest is that texts will be mounted on a local-area or wide-area network and clients provided with direct access to them online. Under such circumstances one can envision a variety of retrieval architectures. Individual institutions—colleges and universities—might choose to main-

---

[18]Prospero Hernandez, business manager and assistant director at Rutgers University Press, suggested in conversation that there is a savings of "several hundred dollars" in production costs when an author submits a manuscript on disc.

[19]On some of these costs and how they might be reduced in a fully electronic environment, see Riecken, "Scholarly Publication," 13; Gherman and Metz, "Serials Pricing," 322 and 324; and Brett Butler, "Scholarly Journals, Electronic Publishing, and Library Networks: From 1986 to 2000," *Serials Review* 12 (Summer and Fall 1986):47–52, especially p. 49.

[20]The remainder of this paragraph is indebted in good part to Riecken, "Scholarly Publication."

[21]On some of the storage costs associated with the current model of scholarly communication, see Getz, "Electronic Publishing," 5.

[22]Currently, if a library wishes to make a printed text available to more than one reader simultaneously, it must either purchase multiple copies of the text or make photocopies; copyright legislation controls photocopying that can occur and the circumstances under which it is permissible. Publishers are understandably concerned about the ease with which electronic versions of texts can be made available to several readers at one time.

[23]One hypothetical but plausible model of how such a system might work in practice is the one developed by Marvin Sirbu and Paul Zahray of the Information Networking Institute at Carnegie Mellon University. See Marvin Sirbu and Paul Zahray, "The Provision of Scholarly Journals by Libraries via Electronic Technologies: An Economic Analysis," *Information and Economics Policy* 4 (1991):127–154.

tain local electronic repositories of frequently used titles they had purchased out-right from the publishers; in that case the cost of the telecommunications connection with the publishers would be eliminated.[24] Alternatively, some publishers might choose not to sell titles but rather maintain them at central sites themselves and charge users on a fee-per-use basis. Yet a third kind of architecture may eventually evolve in which libraries at different institutions collaborate in collecting electronic materials; under those circumstances the consortium will own a full complement of resources but will distribute them among the different members of the consortium. Malcolm Getz has described an architecture of this type as "decentralized ... with multiple, autonomous nodes subject to a standard protocol that allows participants to search multiple sites easily."[25]

To what extent any of these methods of distribution will result in cost savings is difficult to determine now with any precision. Any of them could have significant positive implications for libraries' space problems, as we have suggested, although there will continue to be substantial costs associated with storage, especially if texts are maintained in online databases. William Y. Arms suggests that "[t]oday, storing a document on a computer is more expensive than on paper, but prices are falling rapidly. By the end of the decade, online computing will be much cheaper than storing books on library shelves."[26]

There are other costs entailed in distribution. Let us consider, for example, a journal published by a university press that is currently mailed to subscribers; if the texts of the articles are instead mounted at the university's BITNET node and subscribers elsewhere retrieve them from the network, the cost of mailing, currently recovered in the subscription price, is eliminated, as are the costs of printing and binding on the publisher's part. On the other hand, both the university where the journal is produced and the university where it is received incur costs associated with the operation of the computing and telecommunications facilities supporting the electronic distribution; such costs are ordinarily hidden, at least from the individual subscriber, yet they nonetheless exist.[27] How the costs for various phases of the process of scholarly communication in a fully electronic environment will compare to those incurred now is clearly a subject for considerable further investigation, as is the associated question of who will absorb which costs.

---

[24]Getz, "Electronic Publishing," 3; Yavarkovsky, "University-based Electronic Publishing Network," 16.

[25]Getz, "Electronic Publishing," 3.

[26]William Y. Arms, "Scholarly Publishing on the National Networks," *Scholarly Publishing* 23 (April 1992):158–169, especially p. 160.

[27]As Ann Okerson suggested ("Scholarly Publishing," 3), "[p]resently, network development is a heavily subsidized activity: subsidized by government, its agencies, the universities, and private industry to some extent. Although capital costs appear to be being met via special funds, there is a question of whether that will continue." Although Okerson's remarks pertain to capital costs, there is also subsidization of operating costs. For example, a faculty member who has an individual subscription to a journal pays a subscription price, set so as to recover a portion of the costs associated with its distribution. If the journal is instead mounted on a network and the faculty member downloads and prints articles at a workstation provided by his university, at least some of the cost of production and distribution he would otherwise indirectly incur is passed off to his university instead. Disaggregating and comparing some of the elements of these contrasting cost structures would be extremely difficult. On the structure underlying the present system, see Chapter 6 and the literature cited there, especially Roger Noll and W. Edward Steinmueller, "An Economic Analysis of Scientific Journal Prices: Preliminary Results," *Serials Review* 18 (1992):32–37.

Now let us consider some of the possibilities inherent in these various options. First, individual readers could tailor the information to particular needs. The reader might be able to excerpt and print a single chapter (or page) of a monograph or a single article of a journal issue.[28] Indeed, as several observers have suggested, the very concept of an issue of a journal is challenged by electronic information technologies.[29] Articles are currently collected together and an issue published when there is a sufficient number of articles available to make up an issue. In an electronic environment one can envision a situation where a single article will be mounted on a network as soon as it clears editorial review; there will be no need to wait for other articles to reach the same point in the process. It is in this sense that some of the distinctions entailed by the technology of print invite reconsideration, as Ann Okerson has suggested.[30]

Precisely because electronic technologies permit individual information needs to be met, different subscription and pricing schemes and practices will almost surely develop, whether for individuals or institutions. For example, publishers or vendors would presumably be able to charge on the basis of the amount of material retrieved: the entire text of a monograph or any part thereof, an individual journal article, a page or even a few paragraphs of material downloaded selectively. Case Western Reserve University and IBM are attempting to monitor this process within the university through a software that functions as a kind of royalties manager. On a larger scale CitaDel, the new citation and document-delivery service of the Research Libraries Group, allows for online ordering, delivering, and billing.[31]

Publishers, moreover, may choose to offer various services of other kinds. Although many subscribers will wish to continue to receive routinely all the articles published in a particular journal, it will be possible for publishers to facilitate selective acquisition as well.[32] A comprehensive, fully integrated service could provide tables of contents, lists of article titles, or abstracts of periodical articles or monographs, as INFO-SOUTH now begins to do for Latin American studies. Prospective buyers could skim portions of a full text on a read-only, not-keep basis.[33] Readers could order individual items of interest by means of a simple command; the document could then be delivered by any number of methods.[34]

Some redefinition of the traditional roles of publisher, vendor, and library and of the relationships among them is almost inevitable. Because individual end-users will be able to purchase information tailored specifically to their needs, they will

---

[28]Moreover, readers will presumably be able to enhance, alter, or reformat the document physically, as well as define a textual subset; that is, they may be able to select their own typography, paging, and so on.

[29]Riecken, "Scholarly Publication," 14; Gherman and Metz, "Serials Pricing," 323; Getz, "Electronic Publishing," 5.

[30]Okerson, "Scholarly Publishing."

[31]"Rutgers and BYU to Showcase RLG's CitaDel Service," *Information Today* 9 (June 1992):11–12.

[32]Getz, "Electronic Publishing," 5.

[33]Riecken, "Scholarly Publication," 14.

[34]On precisely this kind of service, see the discussion of document delivery options in Chapter 10.

perhaps be more inclined to interact directly with publishers or vendors—that is, readers may not need to rely as much on the library. (One makes certain assumptions about the pricing by publishers and vendors of such services).[35]

Libraries, for their part, may develop a different approach to acquiring materials, more appropriate to the characteristics of electronic technologies. Such an approach has been termed the "just-in-time" model, as contrasted with the "just-in-case" model currently governing libraries' acquisition practices.[36] Because libraries will ultimately have ready access to electronic versions of texts stored elsewhere, they will be able to base acquisition practices on immediate reader needs rather than on *a priori* assumptions about what those needs might be. Instead of subscribing to a certain number of journals, for example, libraries may instead negotiate contracts for a certain number of discrete articles from a national database of articles, acquired in response to readers' requests.[37]

It also seems clear that there may be some blurring in the distinctions among the historical roles of publishers as producers, vendors as intermediaries, and librarians as archivists. Scholarly publishers have traditionally allowed titles to go out of print because of libraries' willingness to serve as "a sort of secondary distribution system and warehouse," to quote Henry Riecken.[38] The costs associated with archiving materials have been the responsibility of the library. In an electronic environment, where texts can be miniaturized and storage costs greatly reduced, publishers and vendors may be more inclined to maintain archives of texts for many years.

It may also be that traditional models of resource sharing among libraries will be affected. Libraries have historically turned to other libraries for materials not owned locally; if such materials continue to be available from publishers or vendors, libraries might be inclined to acquire them directly, if resources permit and the demand justifies acquisition. Under any of these circumstances, the rapidly changing state of the technology is likely to be an important dynamic. As Jerome Yavarkovsky suggested, "A necessary feature of online accessibility and network publishing is a commitment to archival storage. Once an article is accepted and published online, the publisher, or some other agency, must keep that publication available in perpetuity, in the same way that traditional publications are held permanently by research libraries. This archival responsibility might even be one of the roles possible for research libraries in the future."[39]

---

[35]One characteristic of the cost structure underlying some electronic media is that advertising is often not included in the parallel electronic version of many print products, for the reason that publishers know that readers will not read it, given that their access to the text is random—by means of searches of key words, for example—rather than based on systematic reading. In order to recover revenues lost when the version is made available electronically, therefore, publishers may charge a higher price for the electronic version of the text. For useful discussion on this point, we are grateful to Ira Fuchs.

[36]See the general promotional piece entitled *Faxon Research Services, Inc.* (Cambridge, Mass.: Faxon Research Services, Inc., n.d.).

[37]Gherman, "Setting Budgets," A36. Gherman's models presumably include the British Document Center in London Spa, which delivers the texts of journal articles upon request within a certain time period (24 hours, say). A proposal in this country for a National Periodicals Center, similar to the British one, was not adopted, in part because of publishers' concerns about fair compensation.

[38]Riecken, "Scholarly Publication," 2.

[39]Yavarkovsky, "University-based Electronic Publishing Network," 15.

CHANGES IN SCHOLARLY ETHOS AND COMMUNICATION

Electronic information technologies may, some observers think, bring about far more significant changes. Indeed, some envision fundamental changes in scholarly ethos and practices of scholarly communication as a result of their introduction. Apart from the expanded processes of peer review described earlier, the new technologies could permit immediate and public response from readers to electronic publications and allow them access to the reactions of prior readers.[40] Further, since their invention centuries ago, footnotes and bibliographic references have connected texts to prior pertinent writings and documented the arguments authors wish to advance. As such, they serve as print equivalents of hypertext, as we have suggested.[41] But the analogy is far from perfect. Footnotes and bibliographic references are always selected samples of the full range of material that might be related to the text at issue. Electronic technologies such as hypertext permit access to a much wider range of relevant materials—both primary and secondary, substantiating and contradictory—than those authors have elected to call to readers' attention. In this new environment readers need not rely on authors' selective presentations of related materials and can, if they choose, seek additional references for themselves using electronic media.

Some have suggested that the technologies may permit the emergence of new institutions or infrastructures supporting scholarly communication. As Patricia Battin has observed, "The advent of electronic capabilities provides the university with the potential for becoming the primary publisher in the scholarly communication process. At the present time, we are in the untenable position of generating knowledge, giving it away to the commercial publisher, and then buying it back for our scholars at increasingly prohibitive prices. The electronic revolution provides

---

[40]Gherman and Metz, "Serials Pricing," 323; Getz, "Electronic Publishing," 2. Earlier (p. 322), Gherman and Metz observed that "[t]here is nothing to stop commercial publishers from 'prepublishing' solely in electronic form, and then selling the archival and canonical version of the same journal in print a year or so later. The paper version could quite likely contain modifications based on electronic dialogues between readers and authors of the original version." Gherman and Metz's observation expresses a concern about the possibility that commercial publishers might exploit one characteristic of electronic texts, their mutability, for economic gain. Implicit in their observation, however, is the further possibility that such texts might undergo many iterations, precisely because one can make changes with ease: the author's original text might be revised in light of the reviewers' comments; once the revised text is mounted on the network ("published"), subsequent readers' responses might be incorporated in yet another iteration. Here again, electronic technologies serve to challenge traditional distinctions; the peer review process could ultimately be only the first in a series of ongoing reviews of the text that result in new versions as new information comes to light and new perspectives serve to refine the arguments originally made. In this way scholarly exchanges would exploit the dynamic quality of electronic texts, which contrast with the fixity of printed texts.

[41]See articles by Miller and Landow in Katzen, ed., *Scholarship and Technology in the Humanities*.

the potential for developing university controlled publishing enterprises through scholarly networks supported either by individual institutions or consortia."[42]

How might such a system function? One proponent envisions two broad types of campus network nodes, editorial and distributing. The first of these would offer editorial software for creating and reviewing papers. As demand dictated, it might also store publications held by an editorial node at another campus, a redundancy that would reduce telecommunications costs and network traffic. The second type of node would exist solely to distribute publications by making them accessible online and would resemble traditional libraries by serving as repositories of publications created and issued elsewhere. The distinction expressed in this scenario is familiar and approximates the distinction between the collecting or archiving function currently performed by libraries and the production function performed by university presses. In the new environment librarians might continue to be responsible for decisions about which materials are made directly available to local readers. Access to materials stored elsewhere, however, might well be more directly controlled by the individual reader than is the case under the terms of current interlibrary loan services.[43]

A variety of pricing and compensation schemes, similar to those anticipated earlier, might emerge: a licensing fee paid to a particular publisher might permit a local node to provide access to all the publisher's works; subscription fees might be based on anticipated use of subsets of a node's publications, with users—institutions or individuals—paying for access to parts of the node's holdings; alternatively, access might be on a fee-per-use basis. For individual institutions there will continue to be important and difficult questions to resolve concerning the extent to which the costs of these services are assumed by the institution or passed off to the individual user.[44]

One can envision how the system might operate. Individual scholars interested in accessing particular titles at their own workstations might first determine whether the titles were among those purchased by their institutions and loaded at the local campus network node. If the texts were available locally, the individual readers might be able to access them on a read-only basis, just as now they access printed materials in the university library on a read-only basis. If they chose to download and print portions of the text retrieved, they might be expected to assume some of the cost of doing so, just as now they assume the cost of photocopying printed material. If the text were not available locally, they might be able to scan the first few panels of text on a read-only, not-keep basis by means of a telecommunications connection, either with the publisher's (editorial) node or with the

---

[42]Battin, "The Library: Center of the Restructured University," 175. Battin's observations concerning the untenability of the present situation are echoed by James C. Thompson in an important editorial entitled "Journal Costs: Perception and Reality in the Dialogue," *College and Research Libraries* 49 (November 1988):481–482, especially p. 482. See also Riecken, "Scholarly Publication," 11, where it is argued that "[t]he idea that a university might be the most appropriate publisher of its own faculty's work is appealing. It recognizes that publication is the final phase of the sustained support and collaboration that existed between scholar and institution through the earlier phases of the research." Here we would add only that faculty members who are active as scholars but employed at institutions not having a research mission ought to be assured of adequate means of disseminating their work.

[43]Yavarkovsky, "University-based Electronic Publishing Network," 16–17.

[44]Ibid., 18.

distributing node at another campus within the consortium (in this instance, the local library or its descendant institution might continue to act as mediator in the process). If they decided, once again, to retrieve and print all or part of the text, they might be charged according to whether the title was acquired directly from the publisher or from a fellow member of the consortium.

What any of these scenarios might permit is an assertion (or reassertion) of the university's direct role in scholarly communication, as Battin suggested.[45] The commercial publishers entered the market because they offered economies of scale and technical expertise to professional societies interested in publishing conference proceedings and professional papers. To a considerable extent these new technologies may eventually obviate the need to rely so much on the commercial publishers for their expertise, especially since many of those involved in editorial work for learned journals, even those published by commercial publishers, are academics with university appointments; copyright, if it remains in force in anything like its present form, can be held either by the author or the sponsoring university.[46]

ISSUES TO BE RESOLVED: ADULTERATION OF TEXT, FUNCTIONING OF THE NETWORK

Clearly, a number of issues must be successfully addressed and resolved by all the relevant parties before electronic technologies, whatever their virtues, will be seen as preferable to print as a medium of distribution. There is, first, the question of ensuring the authenticity and integrity of the text. "Electronic text," Riecken notes, "is far more susceptible to distortion, adulteration, and mischievous or criminal alteration than printed pages are."[47] Text on CD-ROMs (read-only memory discs) cannot be changed and thereby prevent alterations of the sort that concern Riecken.

The very characteristic of electronic text that permits easy adulteration is in another way a source of concern to publishers, and in what follows here we are anticipating some of the substance of the later discussion on copyright. A technology (photocopying) already exists that provides prospective buyers of a printed media product with an alternative to buying it (although a less satisfactory one). Anyone who would otherwise subscribe to a journal who instead photocopies selected articles of interest takes advantage of an existing technology to avoid subscribing, and the publisher is denied revenue. Publishers are understandably concerned that making texts of scholarly material available electronically will

---

[45]Battin, "Library: Center of the Restructured University," 175. See also Ann Okerson, "Back to Academia? The Case for American Universities to Publish Their Own Research," *LOGOS* 2 (1991):106–112.

[46]This scenario, however, assumes agreement in the interpretation of current copyright law, which in practice may be much harder to come by. See, for example, Scott Bennett and Nina Matheson, "Scholarly Articles: Valuable Commodities for Universities," *The Chronicle of Higher Education* 38 (May 27, 1992):B1–B3; and the sharp responses of Frank G. Genovese and Allen Lichtenstein, "Treating Scholarly Articles as Valuable Commodities," *The Chronicle of Higher Education* 38 (July 1, 1992):B3. We shall discuss copyright problems in Chapter 11.

[47]Riecken, "Scholarly Publication," 15. There is always the possibility, of course, that these are the concerns of a print culture and that fundamentally different assumptions about such questions will eventually emerge.

greatly facilitate this kind of circumvention.[48] Publishers of computer software programs, for example, are aware that there are a great many pirate copies of their products.[49] Their response is to charge substantially for every copy legitimately sold to offset the economic effects of illegal copying, just as University Microfilms, Inc. does for photocopies of journal articles.

It will be important, moreover, to refine and extend electronic access functions approximating the kind of intellectual activity occurring when a scholar browses in a library or skims the pages of a learned journal. When the latest issue of a core journal in a particular discipline is published, many scholars at least skim the opening pages of articles outside their own subspecialty to have some sense of what colleagues are writing about generally in the discipline. If one had to retrieve the text of the latest issue from a network, would one be more inclined to retrieve and print only the articles in one's own subspecialty? Would one's own interests become ever narrower as a result? As suggested, a related issue concerns the ability to browse in a library. Some interesting discoveries are made serendipitously; will scholars be able to make such discoveries as easily in an electronic environment?[50]

Illustrative material—black-and-white or color reproductions of works of art or other images, graphs, and charts—presents particular problems, which may explain why until very recently there was not a single peer-reviewed electronic journal in the sciences, where scholars make extensive use of such material.[51] It is certainly technologically possible to offer such material and with fully satisfactory results; the issue is rather that to do so assumes the availability of specific equipment and software.[52] There are not yet universally accepted conventions for representing images digitally, and the inconsistent methods of representing and resolving such information are an added complexity.[53]

Finally, there are many questions to be resolved concerning the functioning of the network and the principles governing scholarly publication therein, some of

---

[48]Gherman and Metz, "Serials Pricing," 321.

[49]There is the possibility of technological controls on copying, but many of these are readily circumvented.

[50]The issue of browsing is discussed by Brewster Kahle of Thinking Machines Corporation in an unpublished paper entitled "Electronic Publishing and Public Libraries," where Kahle suggests that "[w]e still have a ways to go to improve browsing, but great strides are being made." See also Jennifer Eberhardt, Dennis E. Egan, Louis M. Gomez, Thomas K. Landauer, Carol C. Lochbaum, and Joel R. Remde, "Formative Design-Evaluation of SuperBook," *ACM Transactions on Information Systems* 7 (January 1989):30–57.

[51]David L. Wilson, "Testing Time for Electronic Journals," *The Chronicle of Higher Education* 38 (September 11, 1991): A22–A24, especially p. A23.

[52]David L. Wilson, "New Electronic Journal to Focus on Research on Medical Treatments," *The Chronicle of Higher Education* 38 (October 2, 1991):A27; Ellen Dorschner, Marilyn Geller, Marlene Manoff, Keith Morgan, Carter Snowden, "Report of the Electronic Journals Task Force, MIT Libraries," Submitted to Carol Fleischauer, Associate Director for Collection Services, MIT Libraries, November 6, 1991, pp. 15, 17. This informative report, available to us when not yet published, has now appeared in *Serials Review* 18 (1992):113–129.

[53]For useful discussion on this point, we are grateful to Ira Fuchs.

which have been discussed by Ann Okerson.[54] Among them are issues of availability, affordability, and friendly access; the consequences of a shift from the current subsidization of the network to its eventual commercialization;[55] intellectual standards (the integrity of texts and privacy); underlying cost structure (cost recovery, methods of collecting and distributing revenues, and so on); ownership and copyright practices; and academic culture (incentives or disincentives associated with publishing one's work on the network instead of by traditional means). In the culture of print, the fundamental issues of this type were addressed and resolved many years ago, and paradigms governing scholarly practices and the functioning of the entire system, with all its complexities, have been widely accepted. The new technologies provoke fundamental reconsideration.

The various scenarios sketched here suggest both the potential and flexibility of electronic technologies and also some of their current limitations. The discussion to this point has been relatively abstract; one means of achieving greater specificity is by surveying some of the characteristics of the relatively few electronic journals currently existing[56] and some of the issues libraries encounter in collecting them.[57]

One electronic journal attracting particular attention is *The Online Journal of Current Clinical Trials*, edited by Edward J. Huth, M.D., former editor of the *Annals of Internal Medicine*.[58] For our purposes *The Online Journal* is an especially serviceable example since it typifies some of the issues presented by materials of this sort. It is believed to be the first peer-reviewed electronic journal containing illustrative material.[59] It will, moreover, be available only to subscribers who meet particular hardware and system requirements, at least initially, though eventually subscribers will be able to retrieve it using other systems as well. The contents will be machine-searchable by key words, subject, author, and title; in this instance the distinctive advantages of electronic text are thus exploited. They are further exploited in that texts will be corrected after their initial publication and marked to indicate that they have been so revised. Moreover, readers will be able to customize their subscrip-

---

[54]Okerson, "Scholarly Publishing," 4–7.

[55]On this question, see the discussion in Chapter 12 of the National Research and Education Network (NREN), which may be conceptualized as an upgraded, rationalized, and harmonized extension of the Internet.

[56]See Diane Kovacs and Michael Strangelove, comps., *Directory of Electronic Journals, Newsletters,* and *Academic Discussion Lists,* 2d ed. (Washington, D.C.: Association of Research Libraries, 1992). The directory lists 36 journals, 697 scholarly lists, and 80 newsletters.

[57]See generally Wilson, "Testing Time for Electronic Journals." We do not specifically discuss electronic publications of other kinds, such as reference works, though they are obvious candidates for publication in electronic form, specifically because the readers who use them have very particular, immediate information needs that are best met by electronic access. See Peggy Langstaff's article "Just the Facts: With a Growing Mass of Easily Manipulated Data, and Some Exciting New Technologies, Reference Publishers Are Riding High and Aiming a Slew of New Products at the Retail Market," *Publishers Weekly* (March 2, 1992):37–45.

[58]On *The Online Journal*, see Wilson, "New Electronic Journal," from which much of the material summarized here was taken. See also Edward J. Huth, "Medical Journals Yesterday and Today: Implications for Tomorrow" (Paper delivered at The Role of Journals in Scholarly Communication, A Centennial Conference in Memory of George J. Stigler, University of Chicago, April 10-11, 1992).

[59]For an instance of another journal making use of such material, see "Experimental Graphic Included in Electronic Journal," *The Chronicle of Higher Education* 38 (April 15, 1992):A21.

tion, specifying topics of particular interest on which they especially wish to receive articles and to some extent controlling format specifications.

The TULIP project of Elsevier Science Publishers mentioned earlier makes bitmapped images of articles in some of its printed materials-science journals available on the Internet.[60] Elsevier will be responsible for mounting the journals on the network; each of the clients—colleges and universities—will be responsible for determining how it will retrieve them. Materials science journals were selected precisely because they contain graphs, illustrations, and other such matter. Unlike completely electronic texts, which are transmitted in alphanumeric form, the bitmapped images made available through TULIP cannot be altered or customized by users nor are they searchable. In these respects TULIP's capabilities differ markedly from those provided by *The Online Journal of Current Clinical Trials*. Elsevier does plan, however, to supplement the bitmapped image of a text with searchable bibliographic information: author, title, and so on.

These initiatives present challenges to library staff members and others involved in providing information services to the members of an academic community. Many of the challenges have been discussed in a valuable study by members of the library staff at M.I.T.[61] Among them are issues of selection (including the matter of simply being aware of the existence of particular electronic journals), acquisition (knowing the correct subscription information and successfully placing orders and retrieving and downloading the texts), cataloging (providing readers with adequate access information, including information about the medium, how one subscribes, how one specifies the "location" of electronic materials within the "collection"), access and retrieval (including "adding value," such as the possibility of doing keyword or simple string searches of the ASCII text), indexing of contents, archiving, and so on.

Various initiatives at a number of institutions are likely to yield lessons of value to many others. At Carnegie Mellon University, the Mercury Electronic Library now stores information resources of various types, including the page images of the journals included in Elsevier's TULIP program. These can be read online over the campus network. The key feature of CMU's practical success is the early adoption of a distributed approach to computing—that is, acceptance of diverse types of workstations and formats for the storage of information, as well as of the concept of dispersed storage of information.[62] At Stevens Institute of Technology, students and faculty will be able to retrieve the texts of journals published by Engineering Information, Inc., from the campus network.[63] At Cornell University, readers located at their own workstations will be able to retrieve bibliographic information and abstracts of articles published in twenty of the American Chemical Society's principal journals since 1980, as well as the full, machine-searchable ASCII texts and

---

[60]See the text of n. 14, this chapter.

[61]See Ellen Dorschner, et al., "Report of the Electronic Journals Task Force." Some of these same issues have also been identified by Gherman and Metz, "Serials Pricing," 326.

[62]Arms, "Scholarly Publishing on the National Networks," 163–164, 167.

[63]"Engineering Articles Available on Campus Computer," *The Chronicle of Higher Education* (May 13, 1992):A21.

images of illustrative material: line drawings of apparatus, plots of spectograms, chemical structures, photographs.[64]

More important than the differences among these projects is their common assumption that the roles of the component institutions in the process of scholarly communication are changing and in ways that can be understood only by practical attempts to discover what is effective.

---

[64]For an interesting and informative description of the Cornell project, see Michael Lesk, "The Core Electronic Chemistry Library," (unpublished paper).

CHAPTER TEN

Resource Sharing:
Collection Development and Document Delivery

Thus far we have considered various bibliographic services and publishing ventures that make information about information and scholarly information itself available in electronic form. The availability of text and data in that form—whether so produced in the first instance or converted retrospectively from print products[1]— in principle permits a degree of resource sharing among institutions that was unimaginable in the past. The extent to which institutions will practice it, however, will depend upon a host of other considerations.

Two broad types of information service, bibliographic and full text, constitute the minimal necessary preconditions for successful resource sharing. Sharing depends on adequate information about the existence of materials and their location, which the various bibliographic services described earlier furnish, and on the availability of full texts in electronic form, which are more easily transmittable than printed texts. What many envision, ultimately, is a situation in which the individual reader at a particular institution is led easily through a series of options culminating in direct access to the aggregate content of the nation's principal research collections, in which local and remote library catalog entries and bibliographic records merge with readily retrievable electronic versions of full texts that can be downloaded and printed locally at one's own workstation.[2] Just as the texts of secondary works in electronic form can be integrated with the underlying base data in a more fully electronic environment, so there might eventually be an unbroken continuum of types of information, from entries in the bibliographic record of monographic

---

[1]Our study does not consider the problem of book preservation, for the reasons given in the introduction. However, the issue of preservation of a book's intellectual content (as opposed to the conservation of the actual physical object) is clearly related to the issues discussed here. The technological means chosen to preserve the texts of books in danger of disintegration might also be appropriate to the task of converting the texts of books not at risk to electronic form to expedite transmission for purposes of resource sharing. In the fall of 1990 Xerox Corporation announced an important new technology that may play a significant role in efforts to convert printed material; their DocuTech Production Publisher can scan, digitize, and reproduce printed texts and, conversely, turn texts stored electronically into bound volumes in minutes. Although the texts converted as the result of scanning are stored as digitized images rather than in alphanumeric form and are therefore not machine-searchable, they can be transmitted electronically over telecommunications networks and converted to alphanumeric form at a later time. See Laurence Hooper, "High-Tech Gamble: Xerox Tries to Shed Its Has-Been Image with Big New Machine," *Wall Street Journal* September 20, 1990, and "Cornell, Xerox, Commission on Preservation and Access Join in Book Preservation Project," Cornell University News (Ithaca, New York: Cornell University News Service, June 26, 1990). See also Michael Lesk, *Image Formats for Preservation and Access, A Report of the Technology Assessment Advisory Committee to the Commission on Preservation and Access* (Washington, D.C.: The Commission on Preservation and Access, July 1990).

[2]In such a context there will, of course, have to be a distinction between works that are no longer protected by copyright provisions and those that are. For protected works fees will have to be collected in some way and distributed to the copyright holder.

collections, to records in various bibliographic, indexing, and abstracting services, to full texts of databases of primary material and studies based on them. The sharp distinctions we now make among these different kinds of information are implicitly challenged by electronic technologies.

Although university libraries have practiced resource sharing for years, for many the preferable option nonetheless remains local ownership of as much of the universe of published scholarly material as resources permit. Interlibrary loan services are thought to be inefficient; the lending library, understandably, attends to its own readers' needs before addressing those of readers elsewhere. The difficult economic circumstances in which research libraries currently find themselves argue for new models, and electronic information technologies seem to hold particular promise.

The degree to which such sharing will necessarily result in cost savings to individual institutions is difficult to determine at this juncture. New paradigms governing local collecting and sharing within consortia will entail new economic relationships among publishers, vendors, and libraries. New pricing schemes will be related to the resolution of copyright issues.[3]

Another important argument for the new technologies is that they will streamline and extend the entire process of scholarly communication in some of the ways considered in the previous section. If such a vision is to be realized, however, it will require reallocation of resources away from expenditures associated with building a self-sufficient collection and toward those associated with cooperative collection development and sharing. The aggregate cost to individual institutions may not be lower, but access to larger universes of material may be facilitated.

EXAMPLES OF DOCUMENT DELIVERY MECHANISMS

In this section we will consider the characteristics of some of the resource sharing and document delivery arrangements various consortia have already attempted. In Chapter 4, we briefly described one such initiative at James Madison University, the University of Virginia, and Virginia Polytechnic Institute and State University.[4] What this initiative and other, similar ones have in common is that they apply existing services and technologies—interlibrary loan, photocopying, telefacsimile—to the problem of access to materials held elsewhere, a problem resulting from the prices of scholarly materials and the consequent inability of any individual institution to provide comprehensive access. Although they assume the medium of print and therefore do not adequately suggest how such sharing might function in a more fully electronic environment, they nonetheless might serve as prototypes of the kinds of infrastructures and organizational principles that might eventually emerge, instances of responses to the current situation anticipating what more might be possible in a fully electronic environment.

---

[3]As Ann Okerson suggested: "ILL delivery delays, copyright restrictions, diverse and unpredictable costs, and evolving pay-for-use strategies undo the benefits of non-purchase and of cancellation." ("Scholarly Publishing," 3).

[4]See Milne and Tiffany, "Cost-Effectiveness of Serials," 137–149, and "James Madison University/ Carrier Library/Documents Express Program."

Conspectus

The Research Libraries Group has played a critical role in collaborative collection development initiatives from its founding; indeed, cooperative action has been fundamental to RLG's mission from the very beginning. In January 1980 RLG's Collection Management and Development Committee endorsed the recommendation of a subcommittee that

> the committee develop an RLG collection policy statement ... to serve as a vehicle for cooperation with the Library of Congress and other major research libraries in developing an eventual national research resource collection of materials held ... by RLG and other major research libraries, *with primary collecting responsibilities distributed among those libraries and LC,* and with LC acting as a kind of "system equalizer" to minimize the impact of local program change on national research library resources.[5] [emphasis added]

The result was the RLG Conspectus, which permitted participating institutions to build collections complementing those of other institutions, thus ensuring the availability of rare titles.

How does such a scheme work? The designers of the Conspectus recognized, first, that it had to respect the autonomy of individual institutions, to facilitate planning but not have the prescriptive force of a policy. Each institution was free to base collecting practices on the profile of its academic program, for example, or on the availability of resources locally. The Conspectus was seen simply as a means to facilitate coordination of individual institutional efforts.

The Collection Management and Development Committee envisioned an interactive, online format that would allow one to search the Conspectus database by subject, institution, Library of Congress classification, and so on. If bibliographers at a particular university had to decide whether to purchase a certain title, they could first search the RLIN database to determine if any other RLG library had purchased or ordered it. If no record were found, they could then search the Conspectus database for information about collection strength in the field in question at other institutions. If they discovered, for example, that another RLG library had both a comprehensive collection in that field and a commitment to continue to collect at the current level, they would have the option of choosing to rely on the other institution's collection.

If there were at least three collections in a particular subject at levels termed "research" or "comprehensive," coverage was thought to be adequate; if two or fewer RLG libraries had research-level collections, it was thought that a member should be identified who could accept primary collecting responsibility. The Library of Congress agreed to consider assuming a primary responsibility in fields where there was neither an RLG member with a strong academic program in that field nor one interested in increasing its collecting to a level considered desirable by the membership. In return, the Library of Congress hoped to be able to depend on the collecting responsibilities of other research libraries in the country.[6]

---

[5]Gwinn and Mosher, "Coordinating Collection Development," 128–140, especially p. 130. The following paragraphs on the RLG Conspectus are based entirely on Gwinn and Mosher's article.

[6]On the RLG Conspectus, see also Anthony W. Ferguson, Joan Grant, and Joel S. Rutstein, "The RLG Conspectus: Its Uses and Benefits," *College and Research Libraries* 49 (May 1988):197–206.

Although the Conspectus was first designed for purposes of collaborative collection development, it has a number of other uses, as the authors suggest: it is being used to assign responsibilities in preservation; it can help identify materials for storage, in that diminishing local emphases in collection development might suggest lower use, a usual qualification for storage; and it can be used for purposes of allocation of staff and materials expenditures, in that it aids in collection assessment and therefore in appropriate allocation of resources.[7]

Collection interdependence remains central to RLG's mission.[8] There is currently an initiative designed to ensure that critical resources in particular journals remain accessible. Titles in chemistry, business, and mathematics considered essential to scholarship have been identified by subject specialists, and one or more institutions have agreed to continue their subscriptions to particular titles, regardless of other claims on the materials budget. Lists of the titles in question, annotated with information about collecting responsibility, are available on RLIN. The initiative will be expanded to include periodical titles in foreign law, geology, physics, and German literature, as well as art exhibition catalogs, German monographic series, and foreign newspapers.

As we have suggested, efficient document delivery services go hand-in-hand with collaborative collecting initiatives. The effort RLG is currently engaged in, for example, also involves the development of access and delivery procedures; the Task Force on Interdependent Collections is responsible for designing a service that would expedite delivery of copies of articles from the core titles to members requesting them.[9]

Before the development of electronic delivery technologies, document delivery relied entirely on methods familiar from traditional interlibrary loan services. Under the terms of the understanding that led to the RLG Conspectus, for example, members agreed to give priority to loan requests from other members, to respond within three days to any request, and to ship materials by United Parcel Service.[10] Electronic technologies, telefacsimile in particular, have greatly expedited transmission of shorter items; for book-length materials, telefacsimile is clearly not an appropriate distribution medium.

UnCover and Ariel

Two organizations in particular—the Colorado Alliance of Research Libraries (CARL)[11] and RLG once again—have prominently featured document delivery by electronic means among their services. CARL's UnCover service, for example, furnishes bibliographic information on articles from some 10,000 periodicals in a variety of disciplines; the information is entered into the CARL database when the

---

[7]The material in this paragraph is drawn exclusively from the study cited in the previous note.

[8]*RLG*, 14–15.

[9]*RLG*, 15.

[10]Gwinn and Mosher, "Coordinating Collection Development," 134 (footnote).

[11]Information on CARL may be found in various issues of *On CARL: The Quarterly Newsletter for CARL System Users*. Information on the services described in this paragraph are taken from the Winter 1992 issue.

latest journal issues are received by the CARL libraries.[12] UnCover2, the companion delivery service, delivers the full texts of articles from the journals indexed in the UnCover service. More than 97 percent of requests are met, all within 24 hours; 40 percent of the articles requested are sent by telefacsimile within the same working day, and optically stored articles are delivered in less than an hour. A copyright royalty fee is collected for each article ordered; publishers are compensated either directly or by arrangement with the Copyright Clearance Center. CARL offers a variety of payment schemes: clients may either pay by credit card or maintain deposit accounts; the average size of an account is $500 to $700, and reports on account use are provided monthly.

Of special interest and importance is RLG's new document transmission system called Ariel.[13] Any printed material can be scanned, stored, transmitted, and printed, including material containing photographic plates, charts, formulae, and tables; the system affords its users rapid, error-free transmission and print images of high quality and is designed for transmission of images over the Internet from one user's workstation to another and local printing on laser printers (the telecommunications charge incurred when telefacsimile is used instead is thus avoided).

What many of these initiatives and services involve is the prior conversion of printed material to electronic form; if scholarly materials are increasingly produced and distributed in electronic form in the first instance, sharing of materials will be easier still. In the case of distribution by telefacsimile, an existing technology was exploited almost immediately for purposes of resource sharing among libraries. The Ariel system offers advantages over that technology. Documents of any size up to $8\frac{1}{2} \times 14$ inches can be scanned directly; there is no need to photocopy them first. The transmitted images can be printed on bond paper of various sizes. Scanning, transmission, and printing are more rapid, and multiple transmissions of the original document are permitted. The user has access to the stored documents, so that any of them can be selected for transmission to other destinations; for copyright purposes a count of the number of times the document is transmitted to different destinations is displayed on the screen when the file is accessed.[14]

It should also be noted that many of the commercial bibliographic services described earlier also deliver full texts in electronic form. Dialog Information Services, for example, in addition to the abstracting and indexing services described earlier, also offers the full texts of such publications as the *Atlantic*, the *Boston Globe*, *Consumer Reports*, *Harvard Business Review*, *Scientific American*, *Time*, and the

---

[12]CARL also offers other kinds of bibliographic services. For example, ERIC, a database of bibliographic information on materials on education maintained by the Educational Resources Information Center, has been licensed by CARL and will be available to institutions within the consortium via the CARL Systems network. It covers materials that have appeared since 1966 and as of 1991 consisted of more than 700,000 records; it is updated monthly. CARL's decision to license the database is another instance of the practice of some organizations of acquiring databases directly and mounting them on the organizations' own local networks; see Chapter 8, nn. 17–18 and the accompanying text. On CARL's decision to license the database, see the Winter 1992 issue of *On CARL*.

[13]On Ariel, see *Ariel: The Document Transmission System from The Research Libraries Group, Inc.*, and *Ariel: The Document Transmission System, User's Guide* (Mountain View, Calif.: The Research Libraries Group, Inc., October 1991). We are also grateful to Marilyn M. Roche, Senior Program Officer at RLG, for providing further information about Ariel.

[14]These characteristics of the Ariel system as contrasted with telefacsimile are outlined in the material provided by Marilyn M. Roche of RLG.

Washington Post, among a great many others; most of the full-text databases are machine-searchable.[15] Although such services are examples of document delivery services, they are obviously different in kind from the sorts of services considered thus far in that they are provided by commercial vendors; they are not the sorts of services, therefore, that would complement collaborative collection development efforts within library consortia. Moreover, the kinds of texts they deliver represent only a small portion of the kinds of materials academic libraries collect. They do, nonetheless, give some sense of how the full texts of materials of various kinds are increasingly available to individual scholars at their own workstations.

Faxon Finder

Of potentially far greater significance for academics (because of the nature of the material) is a service OCLC and Faxon Research Services, Inc., have recently initiated. Called Faxon Finder, it provides bibliographic information through OCLC's FirstSearch and EPIC services; alternatively, institutions may purchase a site license and load the database locally.[16] The companion delivery service, Faxon Xpress, delivers copies of journal articles located in the Faxon Finder database. The scanned document, which may contain images, illustrations, and other nontext material, is delivered to the user's telefacsimile machine or to a computer facsimile board; orders received by 6:00 P.M. are shipped by 6:00 A.M. the following day. Faxon offers a variety of accounting and billing plans: institutions may arrange for a deposit account; individuals may have their credit card accounts charged. The user is charged a fixed price and applicable copyright fees, and to ensure compliance with copyright provisions Faxon retains the bit-mapped image of the article only so long as to complete the transaction.[17]

At present, users of the Faxon service are able to receive copies of articles from a limited number of journals; eventually, the service will extend to all journal titles. Further, "[i]n five years," according to K. Wayne Smith, OCLC's president and chief executive officer, "you will look up a journal through OCLC databases, punch a button on the computer, and get the document in your hand."[18]

---

[15]For a list of the full-text databases available, see *DIALOG Database Catalog 1991*, 87–92.

[16]Faxon Finder is a table of contents index to journals and serial literatures. More than 11,000 titles in the humanities and fine arts, social sciences, sciences and engineering, business, and health sciences are indexed, organized by subject so that a patron can retrieve materials on that basis. The index includes citations for all the relevant contents of each issue of the titles covered, including articles, reviews, editorials, commentaries, letters, and errata. Other material on the title page, such as an abstract or translation, is also included in the record; eventually, all records will be expanded to include abstracts. See the promotional pieces *Faxon Research Services, Inc., Faxon Finder*, and *Faxon Xpress*, all available from Faxon Research Services, Inc., Cambridge, Mass.

[17]See the promotional pieces *Faxon Research Services, Inc., Faxon Finder*, and *Faxon Xpress*.

[18]See David L. Wilson, "Researchers Get Direct Access," A24–A25, A28.

As suggested earlier, RLG also offers a document-delivery service that is the companion to its citation service. One can automatically order the full texts of many items cited in the citation files by means of a command, and in most cases orders are filled within one to two days; see *CitaDel: The Complete Citation and Document-Delivery Service from the Research Libraries Group* (Mountain View, California: The Research Libraries Group, 1992). The documents are delivered either to the patron's interlibrary loan office or directly to the patron.

These various current initiatives permit one at least to envision what kinds of creative, productive resource sharing arrangements and document delivery services might eventually emerge in the electronic age, even if the current services will ultimately be seen as only first approximations of what is possible. The services of the Colorado Alliance in particular illustrate the kinds of advantages consortial arrangements offer; no one institution in the consortium could envision offering the full range of information services the members acting together can offer one another. The alliance could serve usefully as a prototype of similar arrangements other institutions might attempt. Only when there is fuller experience with such arrangements, moreover, might institutions undertake careful analyses of the contrasting cost implications of either attempting to build self-sufficient collections or instead distributing resources and delivering copies of materials not owned locally to fellow consortium members.[19] Among the costs of the latter model are those of electronically sharing bibliographic information on one another's holdings to permit collaborative collection development; disseminating copies of materials, either by telefacsimile or some other means; and compensating publishers in accordance with copyright provisions. Fuller data on these different elements of the cost structure should permit at least some preliminary analyses of the relative cost to individual institutions of each of the two principal models of scholarly communication considered in this study.

---

[19]Virtually the only comprehensive study of such questions we are aware of is the unpublished "Report on the Conoco Project in German Literature and Geology," written in 1987 by Scott Bennett, now Sheridan director of the Milton S. Eisenhower Library at Johns Hopkins, and James Coleman, senior program officer at the Research Libraries Group. We are grateful to Mr. Bennett for bringing this excellent and important study to our attention and to Mr. Coleman for providing us with a copy of it; some of its findings will be considered in the section on copyright.

CHAPTER ELEVEN

Economic and Legal Issues

We have postponed until now full discussion of some of the more important and difficult issues to be resolved if the model of scholarly communication described here is to be viable. Some issues, principally of a technical nature, were identified earlier, in the discussion of the electronic publication of full texts. The issues discussed here might be described instead as more social or cultural in character, and their resolution will involve the participation of others besides specialists in computing, telecommunications, and other technical aspects of the electronic dissemination of information.

TENURE AND NONTRADITIONAL PUBLICATIONS

Among these factors is the nature of the reward system.[1] Scholarly achievement, a crucial basis for appointment and promotion at institutions of the type studied here, is measured by established methods and assumes publication by means of traditional vehicles: the scholarly monograph and journal article. What incentives are there for disseminating one's work over the Internet when the rewards are for publication by the traditional means? How might committees on appointment and promotion assess contributions made, perhaps collaboratively, to a database? One scholar has described the problem this way: "[T]enure is the incentive, and building up resources, such as a database, as opposed to, say, summarizing, is less valued in tenure considerations."[2] Moreover, electronic journals are few in number, and fewer still make use of the peer-review process. Some argue that scholars' inevitable tendency is to publish their manuscripts in the traditional way, because the status of the established vehicles is understood.[3]

COSTS OF UPGRADING LOCAL TELECOMMUNICATIONS

An issue of exceptional importance is the cost of upgrading local campus computing and telecommunications infrastructures.[4] The amount authorized by

---

[1] On this general issue, see Okerson, "Scholarly Publishing," 4, and Yavarkovsky, "A University-based Electronic Publishing Network," 19.

[2] See the remarks of Gregory Crane of the Classics Department at Harvard University in Lawrence Dowler, "Among Harvard's Libraries: Conference on Research Trends and Library Resources," *Harvard Library Bulletin* n.s. 1 (Summer 1990):7. Roberta Miller of the National Science Foundation reminded participants at the same symposium at which Crane made his remarks that "[s]ome works lend themselves to being recorded on electronic rather than print media."

[3] See Beverly T. Watkins, "Acceptance of Electronic Journals Will Be Gradual," *The Chronicle of Higher Education* 37 (April 24, 1991):A18.

[4] On the general issue of the cost of computing, see David L. Wilson, "Many Public Colleges Curb Spending on Computing," *The Chronicle of Higher Education* 38 (December 18, 1991):A20–A22.

the U.S. Congress for the National Research and Education Network (NREN), the data superhighway that will succeed the Internet, will be only a fraction of the total needed to link university libraries and research laboratories electronically. An aide to Sen. Albert Gore, Jr., of Tennessee, one of the chief proponents of the NREN, has acknowledged that for every dollar appropriated by the federal government, state and local governments and private institutions may have to appropriate five to ten dollars. The federal government's role in making its appropriation was principally to encourage development of the entire infrastructure and bring the NREN only so far as "the gates of academe."[5] One observer suggested that it may require between 10 and 100 billion dollars to develop or improve campus networks.[6] A more fully integrated resource allocation process may be called for, and under such circumstances some renegotiation of the boundary between the library and computing-telecommunications budgets is almost inevitable.

STANDARDIZING ACCESS AND RETRIEVAL PROTOCOLS

There is, further, the substantial problem of the heterogeneity of access and retrieval protocols and means of representing information digitally.[7] In the culture of print, retrieval of material from an open-stack library usually consists of little more than determining the call number, which is as much a key to a physical location within the building as an element in a classification scheme, and locating the material. In an electronic environment, access and retrieval are clearly altogether different in kind. To facilitate access the National Information Standards Organization (NISO), the organization that created the International Standard Book Number (ISBN), has sought, first, to recast and expand bibliographic records so that their various elements are appropriate to the distinctive features of electronic products.[8] In addition to information about the author, title, publisher, and place and date of publication familiar from records for monographs, for example, the record for a computer program might include information about the medium,[9] the date of update or revision (this element reflects the dynamic

---

[5]The phrase is David L. Wilson's; see his "High Cost Could Deny Big Computer Advance to Some Colleges," *The Chronicle of Higher Education* 38 (December 4, 1991):A1, A32, especially p. A32. See also the remarks of Ira Fuchs, vice president for computing and information technology at Princeton University, ibid; Fuchs argues, similarly, that "[t]he largest fraction of the overall investment will be at the campus level, not the national level."

[6]Fuchs, ibid.

[7]On this general question, see Vinton G. Cerf, "Networks," *Scientific American* 265 (September 1991):42–51, especially p. 43, where Cerf writes that "[i]n computer networking, it is essential that the communicating programs share conventions for representing the information in digital form and procedures for coordinating communication paths." See also the concluding paragraphs of Chapter 9, where some retrieval issues and hardware and software requirements involved in collecting electronic materials and journals are discussed.

[8]"Documentation—Bibliographic references—Electronic documents or parts thereof," Information Standards Organization-Committee Draft 10956, January 21, 1991. For sending us a copy of this important document, we are grateful to Ann Okerson of the Association of Research Libraries.

[9]The draft specifies that "[t]he words 'computer program' or their equivalent shall be placed in square brackets after the title. If an additional type of medium is necessary for the running of the computer program, the media are listed together, e.g. '[computer program + videodisc].'"

quality of many electronic products),[10] and the system requirements (such information might include the specific model of computer on which the program is designed to run, the amount of memory required, the name of the operating system and its version, the software requirements, and so on).[11] Bibliographic records for databases, similarly, might specify "database" and the medium,[12] an indication as to the beginning date of the database with a reference to the effect that it is still being updated, and system requirements. The record for such a product might therefore have the following form:

> *World cultures* [database on disk] (La Jolla, California: World Cultures, 1987–). Quarterly. Computer disks: 5¼ in., double sided, double density, 320+ KB; program and data diskettes MAPTAB and programs and data utility diskettes MAP and SORT. Accompanied by: codebook; companion publication *World Cultures Quorum*. ISSN 1045–0564. System requirements: DOS 3.3; 256K RAM; disk drive.[13]

Clearly, such information is of extraordinary utility to readers, since retrieval depends upon the adequacy of the information concerning the medium and system requirements.

Of even greater importance are NISO's efforts to standardize access protocols themselves, to permit readers to negotiate their way among systems with various kinds of conventions and characteristics. Many of the online library catalogs available on the Internet, for example, employ distinctive search conventions. The NISO's Linked Systems Protocol (Z39.50) is a standard for system-to-system communication for purposes of retrieval of bibliographic information;[14] it permits a reader to use the conventions of his or her own institution's online catalog to access and retrieve information from other catalogs without having to master the

---

[10]The draft specifies that "[s]ince computer programs are frequently updated or revised between editions or versions, this date shall be given following the date of the original, as 'updated Jan. 1990' or 'rev. March 1, 1989.'"

[11]Committee Draft 10956, as in n. 8, p. 10.

[12]"The word 'database' or its equivalent, followed by the medium, shall be placed in square brackets after the title, as '[database online]', '[database on magnetic tape]', '[database on disk]', or '[database on CD-ROM]'."

[13]Adapted from Committee Draft 10956, as in n. 8, p. 18.

[14]See Carol A. Parkhurst, ed., *Library Perspectives on NREN: The National Research and Education Network* (Chicago: Library and Information Technology Association, A Division of the American Library Association, 1990), 73. On the new, updated standard, identified as ANSI/NISO Z39.50-199X to distinguish it from the existing standard (ANSI/NISO Z39.50-1988), see two memoranda of December 2, 1991, from Patricia Harris and Ray Denenberg to NISO voting members and alternates and other interested parties, available from the National Information Standards Organization, P.O. Box 1056, Bethesda, Maryland, and *ANSI/NISO Z39.50-199X (Revision ANSI/NISO Z39.50-1988): Proposed American National Standard Information Retrieval Application Service and Definition and Protocol Specification for Open Systems Interconnection*, Developed by the National Information Standards Organization (Bethesda, Md.: National Information Standards Organization, 1991). Clifford A. Lynch's *Z39.50 in Plain English: A Non-technical Guide to the New NISO Standard for Library Automation Networking* third edition (St. Louis, Mo., and Marlboro, Mass.: distributed by Data Research and Digital, 1990) is a useful brief explanation and description of the standard.

idiosyncrasies of the search conventions of each.[15] At the Pennsylvania State University the Protocol also enables readers to search various subject databases like AGRICOLA, ERIC, and MEDLINE using familiar commands.[16]

Eventually, efforts to standardize (or to facilitate access) will be extended to the primary information itself, currently formatted in a bewildering variety of ways, specifically as contrasted with print, which requires minimal standardization.[17] Under the worst circumstances a reader may have to master as many different user interfaces, software packages, and system conventions as there are electronic products to be accessed. Such efforts would fulfill the objective of organizing "[a]ccess to diverse technical environments and information resources ... to appear to be coming from a single system."[18] Natural language is increasingly being incorporated into interfaces to facilitate retrieval; expert systems will operate within heterogeneous environments and make the requisite translations among computer languages so that material retrieved from various databases has a uniform appearance to the end-user.[19]

---

[15]See the remarks of Nancy M. Cline, dean of university libraries at the Pennsylvania State University, in "Statement ... on behalf of the Association of Research Libraries before the Subcommittee on Government Information, Justice, and Agriculture, Committee on Government Operations," February 19, 1992, pp. 3–4. For sending us a copy of this piece and other useful information on the Linked Systems Protocol and for helpful discussion, we are grateful to G. Jaia Barrett of the Association of Research Libraries.

[16]AGRICOLA is the database of the National Agricultural Library. ERIC is the database on educational materials from the Educational Resources Information Center; it corresponds to two print indexes—*Current Index to Journals in Education* and *Resources in Education*. MEDLINE, produced by the National Library of Medicine, is one major source for biomedical literature; it corresponds to three print indexes—*Index Medicus, Index to Dental Literature*, and *International Nursing Index*. On the three databases, see *DIALOG Database Catalog 1991*, pp. 20, 43, and 58–59. On the service available at Pennsylvania State, see Cline, "Statement ... on behalf of the Association of Research Libraries," 4.

To simplify, the Linked Systems Protocol functions as follows: the system software where the reader initiates the search (the client software) prompts the reader to enter a request; the software then translates the search words into the terms of the Linked Systems Protocol and presents the search request to the server where the requested information resides; the server software matches the search words to the pertinent records; the client software receives the search results and presents the reader with a list of the pertinent records found. See the unpublished paper by Eliot J. Christian and Timothy L. Gauslin, "Wide Area Information Servers (WAIS)"; for sending us a copy of this paper, we are grateful to Jaia Barrett.

[17]See, for example, Judith Axler Turner, "Group Begins Work on Electronic-Information Standards," *The Chronicle of Higher Education* 37 (September 19, 1990):A23, which reports on the efforts of the NISO to develop standards for the storage, transmission, and use of electronic information.

[18]Richard N. Katz and Richard P. West, "Implementing the Vision: A Framework and Agenda for Investing in Academic Computing," *EDUCOM Review* 25 (1990):32–37, especially p. 33.

[19]Miriam A. Drake and Kathy G. Tomajko, "The Journal, Scholarly Communication, and the Future," 293.

On such expert systems, see also Michael L. Dertouzos, "Communications, Computers and Networks," *Scientific American* 265 (September 1991):30–37. Dertouzos writes specifically (p. 35) of the Knowbot, or Knowledge Robot, first developed by Vinton G. Cerf and Robert E. Kahn of the Corporation for National Research Initiatives (CNRI): "Knowbots are programs designed by their users to travel through a network, inspecting and understanding similar kinds of information, regardless of the language or form in which they are expressed.... Your Knowbot would understand enough about the different ways the same kind of information may be represented to glean the relevant details from each entry. It would then process and present the information to you in a useful and familiar way."

CHALLENGES TO COPYRIGHT LEGISLATION

There are, finally, the critical issues resulting from the challenges to copyright legislation the new technologies implicitly pose. These issues are of such importance that we will consider them here in detail.[20]

American copyright practices have their origin ultimately in the U.S. Constitution, where in Section 8 of Article 1 it is stated that "Congress shall have the power ... To promote the Progress of Science and useful Arts, by securing for limited Times to Authors and Inventors the exclusive Right to their respective Writings and Discoveries."[21] The original intent, therefore, was to encourage intellectual productivity, specifically by granting "to Authors ... the ... Right to their ... Writings." By the late 20th century, of course, it had become the practice for many scholars to assign copyright to their publishers; the incentives for scholars, therefore, are now "diffusely economic," as Henry Riecken points out, "through the bearing that scholarly publication has upon professional recognition and occupational success":

> [T]he producers of scholarly work rarely receive more than a token pecuniary reward.... Instead, they are usually supported by an institutional salary paid in part for the performance of duties other than producing publishable scholarly work, but a salary whose continuance and ... magnitude is dependent in part upon the quantity and quality of published scholarly work—i.e., tenure and promotion are granted partly if not mainly on the basis of scholarly achievement evidenced by published work. Such achievement can also be necessary and sufficient to persuade private foundations, government agencies, or the scholar's employing institution to provide money for research, study, travel, and publication.... Instead of rewarding the producer, the economic arrangements nourish the distributor of scholarly work. Publishers ordinarily retain copyright to the work, sell permission for its use in other publication (e.g., anthologies), and attempt to collect fees for photoduplication.[22]

Publishers, one might say, are assigned copyright in return for the substantial contribution they make to scholarly communication.[23]

---

[20]On these issues generally, see Richard De Gennaro, "Copyright, Resource Sharing, and Hard Times: A View from the Field," *Libraries, Technology, and the Information Marketplace: Selected Papers* (Boston: G. K. Hall & Co., 1987), 90–103, and Ann Okerson, "With Feathers: Effects of Copyright and Ownership on Scholarly Publishing," *College and Research Libraries* 52 (September 1991):425–438.

[21]See Robert L. Oakley, *Copyright and Preservation: A Serious Problem in Need of a Thoughtful Solution* (Washington, D.C.: The Commission on Preservation and Access, 1990), p. 6, n. 24. Oakley's report is an extremely clear and cogent presentation of the implications for libraries of copyright legislation; although it specifically addresses the relevance of the legislation to preservation, it is a very useful general summary of the principal elements of the copyright laws of 1909 and 1976, and we have made extensive use of it throughout this entire section. For a shorter general summary of the provisions of the 1976 law, see Dennis Drabelle, "Copyright and Its Constituencies: Reconciling the Interests of Scholars, Publishers, and Librarians," *Scholarly Communication: Notes on Publishing, Library Trends, and Research in the Humanities* 3 (Winter 1986):4–7.

[22]Riecken, "Scholarly Publication," 3, 5. On the noneconomic incentives for scholarly publication, see also Ann Okerson, "With Feathers," 425–438.

[23]On this issue, see, for example, Gherman and Metz, "Serials Pricing," 321; and John R. Garrett, "Copyright Compliance in the Electronic Age: Conceptual Issues," *Publishing Research Quarterly* 7 (Winter 1991–92):13–20, especially p. 20.

What rights does the 1976 copyright law specifically grant, and what are their implications for academic libraries and the process of scholarly communication? The exclusive rights of the copyright holder include the right to (1) make copies for sale or distribution; (2) prepare derivative works (scripts based on novels, for example, or translations into foreign languages); (3) distribute copies by sale, transfer of ownership, lease, or lending; and (4), in the case of a literary, musical, dramatic, choreographic, or audiovisual work, perform or display it publicly.[24]

The holder's rights are then limited by a series of provisions balancing those rights with the rights of information users. Section 109 of the law, for example, limits somewhat the holder's right to control the distribution of a work: the lawful owner of a particular *copy* of the work is permitted to sell or otherwise dispose of it or display it publicly. This doctrine, known as the first sale doctrine, provides the legal foundation for interlibrary lending. Similarly, Section 107 was intended, in the language of the House and Senate Committee Reports, "to restate the present judicial doctrine of fair use," which permits the use of excerpts from a protected work for scholarly, critical, or journalistic purposes. The statue states that

> the fair use of a copyrighted work ... for purposes such as criticism, comment, news reporting, teaching (including multiple copies for classroom use), scholarship, or research, is not an infringement.... In determining whether the use made...is a fair use the factors to be considered shall include—
>
> (1) the purpose and character of the use, including whether such use is of a commercial nature or is for nonprofit educational purposes;
>
> (2) the nature of the copyrighted work;
>
> (3) the amount and substantiality of the portion used in relation to the copyrighted work as a whole; and
>
> (4) the effect of the use upon the potential market for or value of the copyrighted work.[25]

For our purposes the most important provisions are stated in Section 108, which specifies the conditions under which copying of library materials is permitted. All such copying, first, is limited to single copies, which must be undertaken without any purpose of "commercial advantage." Moreover, before a library can "copy ... a published work ... for the purpose of replacement of a copy ... that is damaged, deteriorating, lost, or stolen," it must first determine "that an unused replacement cannot be obtained at a fair price."[26] Finally—and this provision is of crucial importance—Section 108 states:

> The rights of reproduction and distribution under this section extend to the isolated and unrelated reproduction or distribution of a single copy ... of the same material on separate occasions, but do not extend to cases where the library...
>
> (1) is aware or has substantial reason to believe that it is engaging in the related or concerted reproduction or distribution of multiple copies of the same material, whether made on one occasion or over a period of time, and

---

[24]Oakley, *Copyright and Preservation*, 15–19.

[25]Ibid., 16–20.

[26]Ibid., 23–24.

whether intended for aggregate use by one or more individuals or for separate use by the individual members of a group; or

(2) engages in the systematic reproduction or distribution of single or multiple copies ... of material described in subsection (d):[27] *Provided*, That nothing in this clause prevents a library ... from participating in interlibrary arrangements that do not have, as their purpose or effect, that the library ... receiving such copies ... for distribution does so in such aggregate quantities as to substitute for a subscription to or purchase of such work.[28]

We have quoted these provisions at such length because they have important consequences for libraries' efforts to form consortia and share resources with other institutions. The phrase "systematic reproduction" is left undefined in the statute but is explained by example in the report of the Senate Judiciary Committee, to which the bill was referred for consideration:

> While it is not possible to formulate specific definitions of "systematic copying," the following examples serve to illustrate some of the copying prohibited....
>
> (1) A library with a collection of journals in biology informs other libraries with similar collections that it will maintain and build its own collection and will make copies of articles from these journals available to them and their patrons on request. Accordingly, the other libraries discontinue or refrain from purchasing subscriptions to these journals and fulfill their patrons' requests for articles by obtaining photocopies from the source library.[29]

As Robert Oakley noted, the language of the Senate Committee Report "is similar to the analysis of fair use that suggests that the most important of the four factors is the one dealing with the effect of the use on the potential market for the work."[30]

Clearly, the legislation was intended to address precisely the kind of arrangement typified by the Colorado Alliance of Research Libraries, for example, and for that

---

[27]Subsection (d) permits copying of "one article or other contribution to a copyrighted collection or periodical issue, or ... a small part of any other copyrighted work, if— (1) the copy ... becomes the property of the user, and the library ... has had no notice that the copy ... would be used for any purpose other than private study, scholarship, or research; and, (2) the library ... displays prominently, at the place where orders are accepted, and includes on its order form, a warning of copyright in accordance with requirements that the Register of Copyrights shall prescribe by regulation"; see *Library Photocopying and the U.S. Copyright Law of 1976: An Overview for Librarians and Their Counsel* (New York: Special Libraries Association, 1978), Appendix A, Public Law 94–553, 6.

[28]Oakley, *Copyright and Preservation*, 27. In an attempt to specify what might be intended by the phrase "such aggregate quantities as to substitute for a subscription to or purchase of such work," the guidelines of the National Commission on New Technological Uses of Copyrighted Works, which can be found in Appendix Three to the *General Guide to The Copyright Act of 1976* (Washington, D.C.: Library of Congress, U.S. Copyright Office, 1977), define the phrase to mean, in the case of a periodical, "filled requests ... within any calendar year for a total of six or more copies of an article or articles published in such periodical within five years prior to the date of the request." As Dennis Drabelle suggests "[t]he ... guidelines ... do not have the force of law—though almost.... [They] are part of the Act's legislative history." (Drabelle, *Copyright and Its Constituencies*, 5). The guidelines may not have "the force of law," but RLG's "Report on the Conoco Project in German Literature and Geology," to be discussed more fully later, nonetheless accepts that "cooperative uses of a title ... above six will involve a fee" (p. 25).

[29] *Library Photocopying and the U.S. Copyright Law*, Appendix B, Excerpts from Senate Report 94–473, 70.

[30]Oakley, *Copyright and Preservation*, 28.

reason CARL is properly careful to compensate publishers so as not to violate copyright. It is difficult to contrast the relative costs to individual institutions of either maintaining journal subscriptions locally or distributing and sharing such resources, absent full studies comparing the underlying cost structures of the two models. It is difficult, therefore, to gauge the precise economic effects of compliance with copyright as one of the costs underlying the distributive model.[31] (We should also note that a local decision to cancel a subscription and share resources with other institutions might lead to an increase in unit price, given the marginal cost structure underlying the printed scholarly journal; the price is therefore a moving target, which makes it more difficult still to predict and contrast costs. Producing journals electronically may have a different economic effect in this respect.)

Electronic information technologies, for the first time in history, permit acceptable alternatives to the purchase of entire printed books or journals and greatly complicate the enforcement of copyright legislation. As Paul M. Gherman and Paul Metz suggested, "[T]he critical point about the print medium is that it converts intellectual property into a physical commodity whose use can be limited and monitored and whose replication and redistribution is inconvenient and unsatisfactory. These limitations in reproducibility and transportability, while serious drawbacks to libraries and their users, are highly valuable strategic advantages to publishers."[32] Electronic technologies afford possibilities one simply could not have envisioned in the culture of print. Indeed, one might say that the most fundamental assumptions underlying copyright legislation are as much an expression of that culture as are literary writing and the other genres sharing its values and characteristics. In *Williams and Wilkins* v. *U.S.*, for example, the Court of Claims held that "it is almost unanimously accepted that a scholar can make a handwritten copy of an entire copyrighted article for his own use;"[33] the "effect ... upon the potential market for ... the copyrighted work" specified as a factor to be considered in attempting to determine fair use would clearly be minimal. The making of

---

[31]We have had occasion before to refer briefly to the study by Scott Bennett and James Coleman, "Report on the Conoco Project in German Literature and Geology" (April 7, 1987), available from The Research Libraries Group, Inc., Mountain View, Calif. Bennett and Coleman's study is one of the most comprehensive attempts to contrast elements of the cost structures of the self-sufficient and distributive models. The study identifies the various kinds of expense associated with each and proposes a methodology for calibrating the budgetary effects of greater reliance on resource sharing and interlibrary loan services. Institutions can insert their pertinent local data into the proposed formulae and model the results. Among the elements of the formulae to be calibrated are (1) probable increases in the number of interlibrary loan transactions; (2) probable cost increases resulting from cooperative selection (for interlibrary loan service, interlibrary loan communication, duplication, copyright payments, document delivery, and supplies and other administrative overhead); and (3) probable cost decreases resulting from cooperative selection (for library materials, binding, cataloging, acquisition, circulation, and storage) (Bennett and Coleman, pp. 22–29). We recommend Bennett and Coleman's carefully qualified argument and suggest that there is a great need for more such studies; in their absence, discussion of genuine collaborative collection development and resource sharing will not advance beyond abstractions. Their study represents an important effort to clarify the central issues to be resolved before any large-scale reconfiguration of current practices can be envisioned. See also Richard Hacken, "The RLG Conoco Study and Its Aftermath: Is Resource Sharing in Limbo?" *Journal of Academic Librarianship* 18 (March 1992):17–23.

[32]Gherman and Metz, "Serials Pricing," 321.

[33]Oakley, *Copyright and Preservation*, 21.

multiple copies by means of a high-speed photocopier, on the other hand, would have considerable economic effects.[34]

The instances of copyright violation or careful compliance suggested by the practices of Kinko's Graphics Corporation on the one hand and McGraw-Hill, Inc. on the other give some sense of what is possible. In the first instance, a U.S. District Court judge rejected Kinko's claim that photocopying excerpts from books and selling them in anthologies constituted fair use.[35] In the second instance, as we have seen, texts stored electronically in McGraw-Hill's database can be assembled in an almost endless number of ways; McGraw-Hill, however, has been granted permission by copyright holders to reproduce the texts.[36] In both instances a new technology was used to create personalized information products that were not possible in an earlier era.

The 1976 law recast and extended (or, to use the more highly charged language of one observer, "stretched"[37]) the provisions of the existing legislation in an attempt to cover such new situations. The legislation also implicitly recognizes, however, that under some circumstances enforcement is difficult if not impossible: Subsection (f), Clause (1), of Section 108 states that "[n]othing in this section ... shall be construed to impose liability for ... infringement upon a library ... or its employees for the unsupervised use of reproducing equipment located on its premises: *Provided*, That such equipment displays a notice that the making of a copy may be subject to the copyright law."[38] Photocopying services offices dutifully post such notices,[39] but publishers suspect—correctly, to be sure—that infringements regularly occur. In this way "the widespread violation of copyrights and the shortened life of patent rights have become the unenforceable Prohibition of our time," observes Harland Cleveland.

---

[34]Ibid.

[35]"Kinko's Pays $1.9 Million to Settle Copyright Suit," *Publishers Weekly* 238 (November 1, 1991):14; and "New Push Planned Against Copyright Infringement," *The Chronicle of Higher Education* 38 (January 8, 1992):A15. For a similar instance of alleged violation, see Denise K. Magner, "Publishers Sue to Enforce Copyrights," *The Chronicle of Higher Education* 38 (April 22, 1992):A23.

In response to one of the difficulties cited by copy-shop owners—that of obtaining permission in a timely fashion—the Copyright Clearance Center, the National Association of College Stores, and the Association of American Publishers are providing services designed to aid in securing permission; see "CCC and NACS to Help with Copyrights," *The Chronicle of Higher Education* 37 (June 5, 1991):A11.

Finally, on this issue (and the related one of the amount charged for permissions), see also Debra E. Blum, "Use of Photocopied Anthologies for Courses Snarled by Delays and Costs of Copyright Permission Process," *The Chronicle of Higher Education* 38 (September 11, 1991):A19-A20; and Parker Ladd's letter in response, "Copyright Infringement Criticized by Publishers," *The Chronicle of Higher Education* 38 (October 16, 1991):B6.

[36]See Chapter 9.

[37]Francis Dummer Fisher, "The Electronic Lumberyard and Builders' Rights: Technology, Copyrights, Patents, and Academe," *Change* 21 (May-June, 1989):13–21, especially p. 21. One principal point made in Fisher's article is that we have essentially lost sight of the initial impetus behind American copyright practices, which was to stimulate intellectual productivity. A return to that fundamental tenet, he argues in effect, may well result in very different principles from those currently governing the adjudication of copyright disputes.

[38]*Library Copying and the U.S. Copyright Law*, Appendix A, Public Law 94–553, 6.

[39]See, for example, "Rules Issued on Warning of Copyright for Use by Libraries on Photocopier Machines," *Business Officer: Newsmagazine of the National Association of College and University Business Officers (NACUBO)* 11 (January 1978):3.

Sony v. *Universal Studios* suggests some of the other possible complicating effects of new technologies. In that case it was ruled that "the practice of recording a program to view it once at a later time, and thereafter erasing it" constituted fair use: "Time-shifting enables viewers to see programs they would otherwise miss because they are not at home, are occupied with other tasks, or are viewing a program on another station at the time of a broadcast they desire to watch."[40] Oakley suggested the argument made in the *Sony* case might easily be applied to other situations, specifically when the electronic transmission of a protected work is at issue; in that instance the justification might be "location shifting" rather than "time shifting":

> [S]uppose the only copy of a 1963 medical journal needed by a physician in Oregon for research purposes was held by the National Library of Medicine in Bethesda.... [I]f that material were transmitted electronically and read with no permanent copies being made, there is little difference in circumstances from the *Sony* case, and a court might find fair use. If, however, researchers used such arrangements to create their own paper or disk-based libraries then the copying would clearly be beyond what is permitted under *Sony*.

Oakley's final sentence, of course, states the central point; depending upon what kinds of controls are in place under the circumstances he describes, individuals might well find it easy to engage in what are infringing practices, knowingly or not, just as now photocopying machines enable them to do so. In the culture of print, the only kinds of transactions possible are exchange transactions. Electronic technologies, in contrast, permit sharing transactions in the following sense: if a particular volume owned by one library is lent to another, the first still owns it; if, however, the text is available electronically, it is more easily shared; absent adequate technical controls limiting use to a read-only option, both can own it in some sense, yet only the first has compensated the publisher.

The new technologies have even more far-reaching effects. To return to the examples of the Colorado Alliance and the consortium formed by the three Virginia universities: one might say that it is electronic information technologies that make such consortia viable in the first instance, that in the absence of the technologies such arrangements would be very difficult to undertake and sustain. They depend on electronic bibliographic tools that permit institutions to share information about collecting practices with one another, build complementary collections, and facilitate rapid document delivery. Such arrangements are clearly systematic, and copying of materials for other institutions within the consortium would therefore be in violation of the 1976 law, as explained by the language of the Senate Judiciary Committee Report, if publishers were not duly compensated. But what if a single institution decided unilaterally to reduce expenditures for the acquisition of printed materials in order to improve its interlibrary loan services and acquire electronic bibliographic tools to locate materials held elsewhere? Would such an internal reallocation be considered systematic and in violation of copyright? It would certainly constitute an alternative to purchase of materials and would therefore affect publishers' revenue streams.

---

[40]Oakley, *Copyright and Preservation*, 20.

Copyright practices have been crafted in response to the traditional model of scholarly communication and implicitly assume many of its elements, including the technology of print. The legislation has been extended piecemeal in an effort to apply it to an emerging model fundamentally different in kind. The 1976 law, one might say, attempts through a series of controls to preserve the *effects* of the conditions created by print (little alternative to purchase other than hand copying, exchange rather than sharing transactions, and so on), but the characteristics of the new technologies are such that altogether different conditions are created.

The new technologies serve to raise more basic questions, still John Garrett notes that "the idea of a work changes fundamentally in an electronic world. Questions that have never been answered in the print world—such as whether there is a core unit of a work (word? sentence? paragraph? image?) in which copyright ownership remains imbedded forever, like Chomsky's grammar—will need to be debated and resolved."[41] Francis Fisher suggested, similarly, that under the terms of the current law,

> works that were derivative of protected works were... protected, but deriva-
> tive works were generally adaptations of the entirety or a large portion of
> it.... But now the new technology makes it much easier to use pieces of a
> work. It is easy to search an enormous database and locate the exact piece
> of information that could be usefully combined into a new product. The
> combining is made easier because the pieces of expressed ideas to be
> combined are already in the same electronic form as the new product.
> Indeed... the pieces may be used simply by being pointed at by the re-
> creator.[42]

Under such circumstances what responses are possible? What new models might be considered that would be appropriate to the distinctive characteristics of electronic products, as contrasted with those of print products? A number of observers have suggested a transactional approach in which information users would be charged on a per-use basis.[43] Computers, they rightly argue, are "good at counting things," and in principle a fee structure of this kind would therefore be easy to manage. There are disadvantages, however. Consensus on precisely what constitutes use would be extraordinarily difficult to achieve.[44] There would, moreover, be significant costs involved in tracking use.[45] Finally, there is the difficulty of controlling access to information in electronic form;[46] if photocopy

---

[41]Garrett, "Copyright Compliance," 16, 17. See also Robert L. Oakley, "Pathways to Electronic Information: Copyright Issues for the Creators and Users of Information in the Electronic Environment," (Paper prepared for the Faxon Institute, Reston, Va., 29–30 April 1991), 24. Summarizing the argument advanced by some that "copyright is fundamentally flawed," Oakley goes on to suggest that "[i]t worked, they say, when an intellectual work was represented in something tangible.... But the concept of a stable 'work' that can be protected is meaningless in an environment where ideas are nothing more than a string of bits and bytes in cyberspace that can be transmitted instantaneously for use anywhere else in the world with or without making a physical 'copy.'"

[42]Fisher, "Electronic Lumberyard," 18.

[43]See, for example, Fisher, "Electronic Lumberyard," 18-20; and Garrett, "Copyright Compliance," 15–16.

[44]For some examples, see Fisher, "Electronic Lumberyard," 19–20; and Garrett, "Copyright Compliance," 15–16.

[45].Ibid.

[46]Ibid.

machines already provide one with an alternative to purchase, what will be the effects of the ready availability of large amounts of information in electronic form? "Digits," declares Fisher, "ooze from their containers."[47]

Others have suggested accordingly that a more effective alternative would be licensing.[48] In situations where use is difficult to control, a license, by statutory means, grants blanket permission to use works in return for the payment of a fee to a central agency.[49] Many of the difficulties of the transactional approach are thereby avoided; on the other hand, one would lose the data one could otherwise use to determine prices.[50]

There are, finally, the proposals that universities (1) claim joint ownership of scholarly writings with members of their faculties, remunerating them and prohibiting them from assigning copyright to a third party; (2) request that faculty members first submit manuscripts to publishers whose pricing practices are, in effect, more consonant with larger educational objectives; and (3) grant unlimited copying to libraries and individual scholars and specify that such permission has been granted in the copyright statement.[51] These proposals, of course, are extensions of the broader proposal that universities reclaim responsibility for disseminating the results of faculty scholarship.[52]

"Law is born old," Nino Tamassia, the Italian legal historian, used to say,[53] and we envision a situation where the new technologies will continue to challenge the assumptions underlying current legislation and permit possibilities that existing copyright practices were not specifically designed to address and to which they are not well suited. Under such circumstances, new legislation will be crafted in response to situations predating it, as Tamassia's apt metaphor suggests.

---

[47]Fisher, "Electronic Lumberyard," 19.

[48]Garrett, "Copyright Compliance," 16; Oakley, *Copyright and Preservation*, 31–32. Oakley in particular discusses the services of the Copyright Clearance Center (CCC) (p. 32), "established to provide a clearinghouse for the copying of journals beyond what is permitted under the statute. Originally, payment to the CCC was made on a per-copy basis, and royalties were distributed accordingly. In recent years the CCC has developed an annual license program for its major corporate users. In that program, payments are based on industry surveys and sophisticated econometric modeling."

[49]Oakley, *Copyright and Preservation*, 31. See also John R. Garrett and Joseph S. Alen, *Toward a Copyright Management System for Digital Libraries* (Washington, D.C.: ARL/CAUSE/EDUCOM Coalition for Networked Information, 1992). Garrett and Alen note that the Bern Convention makes it unlikely that unilateral action by the publishers of one country will change fundamental copyright law anytime soon.

[50]Garrett, "Copyright Compliance," 16.

[51]Okerson, "Scholarly Publishing," 4. There would, of course, be the problem of determining who is a "scholar"; perhaps membership in a professional society or affiliation with a university could be criteria.

[52]See, however, Garrett, "Copyright Compliance," 20, who properly asks whether universities can in fact "assume ownership of copyrights ... and develop their own efficient, time-sensitive journal publishing programs.... It would be difficult and costly to replicate the peer review, solicitation, editing, production, and distribution systems evolved by existing publishers. Despite the clamor, it may be long while before the bauble of university-controlled publication and dissemination—whether print or electronic—becomes a major factor in the rights and royalties world."

[53]Tamassia, as quoted in *Medieval Trade in the Mediterranean World, Illustrative Documents*, translated with introductions and notes by Robert S. Lopez and Irving W. Raymond (New York: W. W. Norton & Company, Inc., n.d.), 6.

CHAPTER TWELVE

Networks and the National Telecommunications Infrastructure

The full realization of the model of scholarly communication described here depends, finally, upon the development of an adequate national telecommunications infrastructure, capable of moving vast quantities of text and data at very high speeds. Such an infrastructure could provide a scholar or student at a particular institution almost instantaneous access to bibliographic information stored elsewhere and facilitate the rapid delivery of full texts. Although the library community was not represented during the beginning stages of planning for the National Research and Education Network (NREN),[1] its interests are now certainly reflected in thinking about the aims and purposes of the network; indeed, the vision of a virtual library[2]—a national collection of digitized texts, distributed among institutions and accessible from anywhere at any time—is fundamental to many individuals' conception of the NREN.

NATIONAL RESEARCH AND EDUCATION NETWORK (NREN)

Although computing and telecommunications networks have existed for several decades, their proliferation has been ad hoc. One principal objective of the NREN is a kind of harmonization of the existing variety of architectures, systems, and protocols. Dr. Robert Kahn, president of the Corporation for National Research Initiatives, a coalition of major telecommunications and computer corporations, government agencies, and educational institutions that have agreed to undertake the research necessary to create an integrated network,[3] likens the developing infrastructure to the nation's highway system, as his colleague John Garrett reports:

> Kahn ... likes to draw an analogy between the emerging electronic systems for managing and conveying information ... and the nation's highways.... [R]elative ease of travel [is] dependent on a long, complex process of generation and integration of highways from community to community.... Robert Frost did not know or care whether his road less traveled was under town, state, or interstate jurisdiction, and I suspect most of the rest of us don't care either. Why should we? The system functions seamlessly (except for an occasional toll or overzealous state trooper) and transparently to the user: because it is there, and it works, it can safely be ignored. If we

---

[1]Charles R. McClure, Ann P. Bishop, Philip Doty, and Howard Rosenbaum, *The National Research and Education Network (NREN): Research and Policy Perspectives* (Norwood, N.J.: Ablex Publishing Company, n.d. [1991], 30–32.

[2]Graceanne A. DeCandido and Michael Rogers, "'Virtual Library' Promulgated by Library/Education Coalition," *Library Journal* 115 (April 15, 1990):14.

[3]John Markoff, "Robert Kahn's Vision of a National Network of Information Begins to Take Hold," *The New York Times* September 2, 1990.

are very fortunate, the comprehensive infrastructure that will link sources of information and users will be as invisible as the national network of highways.[4]

The first of the prototypes of the NREN was ARPANET, funded in 1969 by the Defense Advanced Research Projects Agency (DARPA) of the Department of Defense.[5] One important characteristic of ARPANET and other networks funded by DARPA was the commitment to a standard communications protocol (TCP/IP), which permits transmission of text and data among systems of different kinds.[6] Since the mid-1980s the National Science Foundation has established a number of supercomputer centers; a high-speed communications network known as the NSFNET links the centers electronically and provides users with electronic access to the data stored on the computers. The NSFNET has now effectively superseded the ARPANET and is the domestic "spinal column" of the Internet, a network of local, regional, national, and international networks. Also founded in the 1980s was BITNET, described as the first major network to be based solely on interest and willingness to connect rather than disciplinary specialty, mainframe type, or funding source.[7] Among the standard options available on these networks are electronic mail and file transfer services;[8] in addition, many universities, as we have seen, have mounted their online library catalogs on the Internet.[9]

In part because of the rapid, ad hoc growth of the networks[10] and the resultant patchwork quality of the current situation (the Internet "consists of autonomous entities that are interconnected" in the words of one observer[11]), in part because of broad agreement on the extraordinary economic and social importance of an adequate information infrastructure, the federal government recently enacted legislation designed to rationalize and upgrade the Internet. It is this upgraded, harmonized network that is the NREN.

---

[4]Garrett, "Copyright Compliance," 14. See also Daniel J. Oberst and Sheldon B. Smith, "BITNET: Past, Present, Future," *EDUCOM Bulletin* 21 (Summer 1986):10–17, especially p. 17, where the authors refer to "a seamless vision of interconnectivity," and Dertouzos, "Communications, Computers and Networks," 33, where Dertouzos draws analogies with existing infrastructures like "the telephone network and the electric power grid."

[5]Of the many publications on the NREN and the background to its development, two in particular have proved to be especially valuable: McClure et al., *NREN: Research and Policy Perspectives*, and Parkhurst, *Library Perspectives on NREN*. On the ARPANET, see Bishop et al., *NREN: Research and Policy Perspectives*, 9.

[6]See Eric Aupperle, "USA NSF Backbone," *Internet Society News* 1 (Winter 1992):6, on the insistence on using the TCP/IP in building the NSFNET as well.

[7]Oberst and Smith, "BITNET," 10.

[8]McClure et al., *NREN: Research and Policy Perspectives*, 2, 9; and Oberst and Smith, "BITNET," 13–15.

[9]See Chapter 8.

[10]As Brian Kahin suggested, the rapid growth is the product of leveraging. There is "top-to-bottom" leveraging, in the sense that investment at each of the three tiers of the NSFNET (the national spinal column, the regional networks, and the local area networks operating within individual universities) serves to leverage investment at other levels. In addition, leveraging operates across functions; users conversant with one type of function—electronic mail, for example—demand services, which generates political support at the institutional level. See Brian Kahin, "Libraries and Information Infrastructure," Draft Discussion Paper, Prepared for the Council on Library Resources (January 3, 1992), 2–3 See also Aupperle, "USA NSF Backbone," on the effects of leveraged funding.

[11]McClure et al., *NREN: Research and Policy Perspectives*, 9.

Fundamental to the conception of the NREN is a three-tiered hierarchy of networks, which replicates the structure of the present Internet.[12] The NSFNET currently includes 13 nodes, each the hub in turn of a regional network, which in its turn comprises local campus networks linked to one another. The first tier—the spinal column—is to be managed by an independent, nonprofit organization created by Merit, Inc., IBM, and MCI Communications Corporation.[13] The second tier—the regional networks—have as their prototypes such existing regional networks as the New York State Education and Research Network (NYSERNet), the John von Neumann Computer Network (JvNCnet),[14] and the Bay Area Regional Research Network. The third tier will consist of networks operating within individual educational institutions or research laboratories.

In technical terms, the upgrading consists in part of replacing twisted copper cable with fiber-optic cable, pure-glass filaments that carry the data in the form of light pulses;[15] the resultant transmission speeds are considerably faster than the fastest permitted by the Internet. At the highest speeds currently attainable, for example, some 50 pages of text can be transmitted per second. The NREN is intended to be a gigabit network, capable of moving some one billion bits (or binary digits) of data per second, or the equivalent of about 30,000 pages of text.[16] Such increased capacity is important not solely for purposes of speed of transmission, however; it is also demanded by information existing in particular forms (sound, for example, or high resolution graphics, moving graphic images, video, and multimedia formats).[17] The increased capacity should also serve to relieve the highway congestion occurring on the Internet.[18] Of course, not all users will need

---

[12]McClure et al., *NREN: Research and Policy Perspectives*, 11, and EDUCOM Networking and Telecommunications Task Force, *The National Research and Education Network, A Policy Paper*, revised ed. (Princeton, N.J.: EDUCOM, March 1990), 1, 7.

[13]McClure et al., *NREN: Research and Policy Perspectives*, 11. See also David Wilson, "High-Speed Network for Research Stirs Controversy," *The Chronicle of Higher Education* 38 (March 4, 1992):A22, A24, on some fears about the provisions for management of the NREN.

[14]On the JvNCnet, see, for example, the following descriptive literature available from the Office of Computing and Information Technology at Princeton University: JvNCnet, John von Neumann Computer Network, *The Robust Gateway to the Internet: An Overview of JvNCnet Services* (Princeton, N.J.: JvNCnet, The John von Neumann Computer Network, January 1992).

[15]John Schwartz, "The Highway to the Future: Thanks to Fiber Optics, the United States Has Broken Ground for a Computer Expressway," *Newsweek* (January 13, 1992):56–57, and McClure et al., *NREN: Research and Policy Perspectives*, 2.

[16]On the contrasting speeds of the Internet and NREN, see, for example, Mike Roberts, "National Network Legislation Enacted in U.S.A.," *Internet Society News* 1 (Winter 1992):40, and David L. Wilson, "High Cost Could Deny Big Computer Advance," A1, A32.

[17]On the need for an infrastructure capable of transmitting information in various media, see, for example, Markoff, "Robert Kahn's Vision," 1; Dertouzos, "Communications, Computers and Networks," 34; *The National Research and Education Network, A Policy Paper*, 5; Wilson, "High Cost Could Deny Big Computer Advance," A32; and Larry Masinter, "Multimedia," *Internet Society News* 1 (Winter 1992):29.

[18]On the issue of congestion, see, for example, Kahin, "Libraries and Information Infrastructure," 12, and Wilson, "High Cost Could Deny Big Computer Advance," A32.

to exploit the NREN's full capacity at all times. "If users ... can set ... 'levers,'" explains Michael Dertouzos,

> choose the combination of transmission speed, security and reliability appropriate for their task, then they need only pay for the service they want. The alternative—a highly secure and lightning-fast transport service that would satisfy all potential needs—would be so expensive that it would never become widely used.[19]

The NREN should to an unprecedented degree facilitate the collaboration of colleagues widely separated geographically in that remote, immediate access to the contents of databases assembled and maintained cooperatively will be greatly enhanced.[20] It is also envisioned that the network will contain a number of information resources and services: directories of users and files, the texts of monographs and periodicals, the contents of databases of bibliographic and primary information, user support systems, and so on.[21] As indicated earlier, Robert Kahn's vision extends to a type of information service called a Knowbot, or Knowledge Robot. Because information resources are widely distributed—because they do not exist in a single, centralized computer but instead in local systems subject to specialized protocols—there will be a need for a service that assembles information from a wide variety of sources and packages it in a way that is familiar and accessible to end-users. Here, too, there is a need for increased network and local storage capacity commensurate with the quantity of data to be accumulated by Knowbots, which could be programmed to scan every monograph and periodical in a particular discipline and assemble all the references on a particular topic.[22]

Before concluding this section on the NREN, it is only proper to note that there are some reasonably serious concerns about it—its management[23] and its purposes. Some, in fact, might argue that its purposes risk becoming confused. There are those who hope that the kinds of services the network will support might eventually be extended to almost every household in the country, in the way that almost every household is connected to local telephone and electric power infrastructures. In that way all Americans would potentially have access to some subset of the information resources available in databases to be linked to the network. Others argue for a much more limited set of objectives like those described here, a network designed to connect large institutional repositories of information resources—research laboratories, libraries, and so on. Given the projected costs and the involvement of the federal government, resolution of such disagreements is not likely to be easily or rapidly achieved.

---

[19]Dertouzos, "Communications, Computers and Networks," 33; see also Wilson, "High Cost Could Deny Big Computer Advance," A32.

[20]See, for example, *The National Research and Education Network, A Policy Paper*, 5, and the promotional piece *NREN: The National Research and Education Network* (Washington, D.C.: Coalition for the National Research and Education Network, 1989), 8–9.

[21]The print publication *NYSERNet: New User's Guide*, discussed in Chapter 8, may serve as an example of the kinds of directories and aids to users envisioned; see also *The National Research and Education Network, A Policy Paper*, 5.

[22]See Markoff, "Robert Kahn's vision," and the earlier reference to Knowbots in Chapter 11, n. 19.

[23]Wilson, "High-Speed Network," A22, A24.

TRANSFORMATION OF SCHOLARLY COMMUNICATION

Our objective in Part 2 was to identify some of the principal pieces of an alternative model of scholarly communication proposed by many observers. That model is the expression of electronic information technologies that permit one to envision entirely different ways of structuring scholarly activity and communicating the results. As suggested earlier, it is difficult to determine precisely where we are in the transition to a new paradigm, although it is clear that the thinking is more advanced about some elements of the alternative model than others. At all major research universities, for example, electronic technologies have been effectively employed in automating the bibliographic record, although at only a few (New York University and the University of Michigan among them) is the retrospective conversion of the existing card catalog complete or nearly so. In addition, in many disciplines though not all there are exceedingly useful abstracting and indexing services providing bibliographic information on the serial literature. The electronic publication of full texts, on the other hand, is a more recent development, and we have yet to settle upon equally well-developed conventions and practices.

Similarly, the central organizational and logistical components of the distributive as contrasted with the self-sufficient model—collaborative collection development and document delivery services—have yet to be adequately considered, although in the Colorado Alliance of Research Libraries there is an excellent prototype for the kinds of arrangements that might eventually emerge. In some respects the national telecommunications infrastructure, as an element of the alternative model, is like the automation of the bibliographic record in that we are farther along in its development, in part because of the direct involvement of the federal government.

It is extremely unlikely—we would say almost inconceivable—that any alternative model will completely supplant the existing one at any point in the foreseeable future. Rather, we envision a situation where incremental modifications to the current model will be made. We would also argue, however, that it is equally inconceivable that there will *not* eventually be a more-or-less complete transformation of scholarly communication. The new technologies are too powerful and their advantages too clear for current practices to continue indefinitely. However one might regard present technological developments, no amount of nostalgic longing for traditional practices, in our view, will serve to forestall the application of the new technologies to scholarly communication, just as Angelo Poliziano's dismissal of printing[24] did not forestall its ascendancy. Manuscripts and printed books coexisted for many decades after the invention of printing, to be sure; eventually, however, print all but supplanted manual copying as the favored means of disseminating information of the type we are concerned with in this study.

Just as print, as contrasted with manual copying, yielded text products and information industries with certain fundamental characteristics of the type described at the beginning of this section—multiple, identical copies of a text, media products whose first copy is relatively costly to produce and whose subsequent copies are produced relatively inexpensively—so electronic technologies, as contrasted with print, yield products with features correspondingly different in kind from those produced by the existing technology. Among others, they are the dynamic quality of texts stored electronically, the capacity for interactivity and

---

[24]See Chapter 7, n. 2.

creating personalized information products, instantaneous, random access to the text, the dematerialization of the text, which permits almost instantaneous transmission and remote access, the possibility of miniaturization and its implications for storage, and so on.

As we have also tried to suggest, a given technology fits hand-in-glove with economic and legal practices appropriate to it and particular kinds of relationships among the relevant players (print leads to prospective acquisition of library materials in anticipation of readers' needs, for example). New technologies bring new economic and legal practices accordingly, which will have to be completely and carefully rethought. Such issues have been fully addressed and resolved in the culture of print; the new technologies complicate existing practices. That is not to say that such issues are necessarily inherently difficult to resolve; it is rather that many of the elements of the existing model are implicit, and in envisioning alternatives one has to attempt to recognize first principles and anticipate explicitly as many of the ways as possible in which current arrangements must be rethought under different circumstances.

But in saying such issues are not necessarily difficult to resolve, neither do we wish to suggest that anything about the transition to a new model will be easy or that new technologies promise easy solutions to difficult problems. It is rather that some of these developments, in our view, are almost inevitable. The challenge for those participating in the process of scholarly communication is to employ the technologies in a way consistent with fundamental scholarly objectives and practices.

References Cited

Arms, William Y. "Scholarly Publishing on the National Networks." *Scholarly Publishing* 23 (April 1992):158–169.

Bailey, Herbert S. Jr. *The Rate of Publication of Scholarly Monographs in the Humanities and Social Sciences, 1978–1988*. New York: Association of American University Presses, 1990.

Barschall, Henry H. "The Cost–Effectiveness of Physics Journals." *Physics Today* 41 (July 1988):56–59.

Battin, Patricia. "The Library: Center of the Restructured University." *College and Research Libraries* 45 (May 1984):170–176.

Baumol, W.J. and M. Marcus. *Economics of Academic Libraries*. Washington, DC: American Council on Education, 1973.

Bennett, Scott and James Coleman. *Report on the Conoco Project in German Literature and Geology*. Mountain View, CA: Research Libraries Group, Inc., 1987.

Bennett, Scott and Nina Matheson. "Scholarly Articles: Valuable Commodities for Universities." *The Chronicle of Higher Education* 38 (July 1, 1992):B1–B3.

Beth, Amy. "When Cost is No Factor: The Impact on Faculty of Unlimited Access to DIALOG." *Information Searcher* 4 (1991):3 ff.

Bowen, William G. and Neil L. Rudenstine. *In Pursuit of the Ph.D.* Princeton, NJ: Princeton University Press, 1992.

Bowen, William G. and Julie Ann Sosa. *Prospects for Faculty in the Arts and Sciences*. Princeton, NJ: Princeton University Press, 1989.

Burks, Christian, Michael J. Cinkosky, James W. Fickett and Paul Gilna. "Electronic Data Publishing and GenBank." *Science* 252 (1991):1273–1277.

Boyer, Ernest. *Scholarship Reconsidered: Priorities of the Professoriate, a Special Report*. Princeton, NJ: Carnegie Foundation for the Advancement of Teaching, 1990.

Butler, Brett. "Scholarly Journals, Electronic Publishing, and Library Networks: From 1986 to 2000." *Serials Review* 12 (Summer-Fall 1986):47–52.

Carrigan, Dennis. "Publish or Perish: The Troubled State of Scholarly Communication." *Scholarly Publishing* 22 (April 1991):131–142.

Cerf, Vinton G. "Networks." *Scientific American* 265 (September 1991):42–51.

Cheit, Earl F. *The New Depression in Higher Education: A Study of Financial Conditions at 41 Colleges and Universities.* New York: McGraw Hill, 1971.

Clack, Mary E. and Sally F. Williams. "Using Locally and Nationally Produced Periodical Price Indexes in Budget Preparation." *Library Resources and Technical Services* 27 (October 1983):345–356.

Cleveland, Harland. "Information As a Resource." *Futurist* 16 (December 1982):34–39.

Cole, Stephen. "The Role of Journals in the Social Construction of Scientific Knowledge." Paper Presented at The Role of Journals in Scholarly Communication, A Centennial Conference in Memory of George J. Stigler, University of Chicago, 10–11 April 1992.

Communications in Support of Science and Engineering: A Report to the National Science Foundation from the Council on Library Resources. Washington, DC: Council on Library Resources, August 1990.

DeGennaro, Richard. *Libraries, Technology and the Information Marketplace: Selected Papers.* Boston, MA: G.K. Hall and Co., 1987.

Dertouzos, Michael. "Communications, Computers and Networks." *Scientific American* 265 (September 1991):30–37.

Dougherty, Richard M. "Periodical Price Escalation: A Library Response." *Library Journal* 113 (15 May 1988):27–29.

Dougherty, Richard M. and Carol Hughes. *Preferred Futures for Libraries: A Summary of Six Workshops With University Provosts and Library Directors.* Mountain View, CA: Research Libraries Group, Inc., 1991.

Dowler, Lawrence. "Among Harvard's Libraries: Conference on Research Trends and Library Resources." *Harvard Library Bulletin* N.S. 1 (Summer 1990):5–14.

Drabelle, Dennis. "Copyright and Its Constituencies: Reconciling the Interests of Scholars, Publishers and Librarians." *Scholarly Communication: Notes on Publishing, Library Trends, and Research in the Humanities* 3 (Winter 1986):4–7.

Drake, Miriam A. *Academic Research Libraries: A Study of Growth.* West Lafayette, IN: Purdue University Libraries and Audio-Visual Center, 1977.

Drake, Miriam A. and Kathy G. Tomajko. "The Journal, Scholarly Communication, and the Future." *Serials Librarian* 10 (Fall 1985-Winter 1986):289–298.

Economic Consulting Services. "A Study of Trends in Average Prices and Costs of Certain Serials Over Time." In *Report of the ARL Serials Prices Project.* Washington, DC: Association of Research Libraries, 1989.

Fisher, Francis Drummer. "The Electronic Lumberyard and Builders' Rights: Technology, Copyright, Patents and Academe." *Change* 21 (May/June 1989):13–21.

Gardner, Jeffrey J. "What They Have and How We Might Get It: Son of Farmington?" Paper Read at the Seminar for the Acquisition of Latin American Library Materials (SALALM), San Diego, CA, 4 June 1991.

Garrett, John R. "Copyright Compliance in the Electronic Age: Conceptual Issues." *Publishing Research Quarterly* 7 (Winter 1991/92):13–20.

Getz, Malcolm. "Electronic Publishing: An Economic View." *Serials Review* 18 (1992):25–31.

Gherman, Paul M. and Paul Metz. "Serials Pricing and the Role of the Electronic Journal." *College and Research Libraries* 52 (July 1991):315–327.

Gould, Constance. *Information Needs in the Humanities: An Assessment.* Stanford, CA: Research Libraries Group, Inc., 1988.

Gould, Constance and Mark Handler. *Information Needs in the Social Sciences: An Assessment.* Stanford, CA: Research Libraries Group, Inc., 1989.

Greenberg, Douglas. "Technology, Scholarship, and Democracy, or You Can't Always Get What You Want." Paper Delivered at the Fall 1991 Meeting of the Coalition for Networked Information, Washington, DC. [Revised and Condensed in *Educom Review* 27 (May-June 1992):46–51].

Gwinn, Nancy E. and Paul H. Mosher. "Coordinating Collection Development: The RLG Conspectus." *College and Research Libraries* 44 (March 1983):128–140.

Hacken, Richard. "The RLG Conoco Study and Its Aftermath: Is Resource Sharing in Limbo?" *Journal of Academic Librarianship* 18 (March 1992):17–23.

Hamaker, Charles. "Library Serials Budgets: Publishers and the Twenty Percent Effect." *Library Acquisitions: Practice and Theory* 12 (1988):211–219.

Hurt, Charlene S. and Sharon J. Rogers. "How Scholarly Communication Should Work in the 21st Century." *The Chronicle of Higher Education* 36 (18 October 1989):A56.

Huth, Edward J. "Medical Journals Yesterday and Today: Implications for Tomorrow." Paper Delivered at The Role of Journals in Scholarly Communication, A Centennial Conference in Memory of George J. Stigler, University of Chicago, 10–11 April 1992.

Kahle, Brewster. "Electronic Publishing and Public Libraries." Unpublished paper, 1992.

Katz, Richard N. and Richard P. West. "Implementing the Vision: A Framework and Agenda for Investing in Academic Computing." *Educom Review* 25 (1990):32–37.

Katzen, May, ed. *Scholarship and Technology in the Humanities: Proceedings of a Conference Held at Elvetham Hall, Hampshire, UK, 9–12 May 1990*. New York: Bowker-Saur, 1991.

Kernan, Alvin B. "The Death of Literature." *Princeton Alumni Weekly* 92 (22 January 1992):11–15.

Kollin, Richard P. and James E. Shea. "New Trends in Information Delivery." *Information Services and Use* 4 (1984):225–227.

Kovacs, Diane and Michael Strangelove, comps. *Directory of Electronic Journals, Newsletters, and Academic Discussion Lists*. 2d ed. Washington, DC: Association of Research Libraries, 1992.

Leach, S. "The Growth Rates of Major Academic Libraries: Rider and Purdue Reviewed." *College and Research Libraries* 37 (1976):531–542.

Lesk, Michael. "The Core Electronic Chemistry Library." Unpublished Paper.

— — —. *Image Formats for Preservation and Access, A Report of the Technology Assessment Advisory Committee to the Commission on Preservation and Access*. Washington, DC: Commission on Preservation and Access, July 1990.

Lewis, David W. "Economics of the Scholarly Journal." *College and Research Libraries* 50 (November 1989):674–688.

Library Perspectives on NREN: The National Research and Education Network, ed. Carol A. Parkhurst. Chicago: American Library Association, 1990.

Library Photocopying and the U.S. Copyright Law of 1976: An Overview for Librarians and Their Counsel. New York: Special Libraries Association, 1978.

Lieberman, Lisa, Roger Noll and W. Edward Steinmueller. "Economic Analysis and Empirical Protocol for Examining Scholarly Periodicals Pricing." Paper Submitted to The Andrew W. Mellon Foundation, 1991.

— — —. "Economic Analysis of Scientific Journal Prices: Preliminary Results." Paper Submitted to The Andrew W. Mellon Foundation, 1991.

— — —. "Proposal to the Mellon Foundation: Economic Analysis of Scholarly Periodical Costs." Paper Submitted to The Andrew W. Mellon Foundation, 1991.

Lynch, Clifford. *Z 39.50 In Plain English*. 3d ed. St. Louis, MO: Data Research, 1990.

Lynden, Frederick C. "Prices of Foreign Library Materials: A Report." *College and Research Libraries* 49 (1988):217–231.

Machlup, Fritz. "Marginal Analysis and Empirical Research." *American Economic Review* 36 (1946):534–535.

Marks, Kenneth E., Steven P. Neilson, H. Craig Petersen and Peter E. Wagner. "Longitudinal Study of Scientific Journal Prices in a Research Library." *College and Research Libraries* 52 (March 1991):125–138.

Matheson, Nina W. "The Academic Library Nexus." *College and Research Libraries* 45 (May 1984):207–213.

McClure, Charles, Ann P. Bishop, Philip Doty, and Howard Rosenbaum. *The National Research and Education Network (NREN): Research and Policy Perspectives.* Norwood, NJ: Ablex Publishing Co., 1991.

Milne, Dorothy and Bill Tiffany. "A Survey of the Cost-Effectiveness of Serials: A Cost-Per-Use Method and Its Results." *Serials Librarian* 19 (1991):137–149.

Moline, Sandra R. "The Influence of Subject, Publisher Type, and Quantity Published on Journal Prices." *Journal of Academic Librarianship* 15 (1989):12–18.

Molyneux, Robert. "Patterns, Processes of Growth, and the Projection of Library Size: A Critical Review of the Literature on Academic Library Growth." *Library and Information Service Research* 8 (January-March 1986):5–28.

National Coordinated Cataloging Program: An Assessment of the Pilot Project. Washington, DC: Council on Library Resources, 1990.

Noll, Roger and W. Edward Steinmueller. "An Economic Analysis of Scientific Journal Prices: Preliminary Results." *Serials Review* 18 (1992):32–37.

Oakley, Francis. "Against Nostalgia: Reflections on Our Present Discontents in Higher Education." *National Humanities Center Newsletter* 12 (Spring/Summer 1991):1–14.

Oakley, Robert L. *Copyright and Preservation: A Serious Problem in Need of a Thoughtful Solution.* Washington, DC: Commission on Preservation and Access, 1990.

— — —. "Pathways to Electronic Information: Copyright Issues for the Creators and Users of Information in the Electronic Age." Paper Presented at the Faxon Institute, Reston, VA, 29–30 April 1991.

Okerson, Ann L. "Back to Academia? The Case for American Universities to Publish Their Own Research." *Logos* 2 (1991):106–112.

— — —. "Of Making Many Books There Is No End." In *Report of the ARL Serials Prices Project.* Washington, DC: Association of Research Libraries, 1989.

— — —. "Periodical Prices: A History and Discussion." *Advances in Serials Management* 1 (1986):101–134.

— — —. "Scholarly Publishing in the NREN." *ARL: A Bimonthly Newsletter of Research Library Issues and Actions* 151 (July 4, 1990):1–4.

— — —. "With Feathers: Effects of Copyright and Ownership on Scholarly Publishing." *College and Research Libraries* 52 (September 1991):425–438.

O'Neill, Ann L. "Book Production and Library Purchases: Looking Beyond the Thor Ruling." *Publishing Research Quarterly* 7 (Summer 1991):39–51.

Petersen, H. Craig. "University Libraries and Pricing Practices by Publishers of Scholarly Journals." *Research in Higher Education* 31 (August 1990):307–314.

"Research Libraries in a Global Context." Paper Prepared by ARL [Association of Research Libraries] Staff, December 1989.

Rider, Fremont. *The Scholar and the Future of the Research Library*. New York: Hadham Press, 1944.

Rieken, Henry W. "Scholarly Publication: Are There Viable Options?" Draft for the Research Library Committee [of the Council on Library Resources], October 1989.

Scholars and Research Libraries in the 21st Century. ACLS Occasional Paper 14. New York: American Council of Learned Societies, 1990.

"Scholarship, Research Libraries, and Foreign Publishing in the 1990s." Paper Prepared by ARL [Association of Research Libraries] Staff, March 1991.

Seibert, Warren T. and Marjorie A. Kuenz. *Growth and Change in 67 Medical School Libraries, 1975–1989*. Bethesda, MD: National Library of Medicine, 1992.

Sirbu, Marvin and Paul Zahray. "The Provision of Scholarly Journals by Libraries via Electronic Technologies: An Economic Analysis." *Information and Economics Policy* 4 (1991):127–154.

Solotaroff, Ted. "The Paperbacking of Publishing." *Nation* 253 (7 October 1991):399–404.

Spigai, Fran. "Information Pricing." *Annual Review of Information Science and Technology* 26 (1991):39–73.

Thompson, James C. "Journal Costs: Perception and Reality in the Dialogue." *College and Research Libraries* 49 (November 1988):481–482.

Turner, Sarah E. and William G. Bowen. "The Flight From the Arts and Sciences: Trends in Degrees Conferred." *Science* 250 (26 October 1990):517–521.

Uchitelle, Daniel. "An Analysis of Data from the MLA Directory of Periodicals to Describe Patterns of Journal Publication in the Humanities." Unpublished Paper.

United Nations Education and Social Commission. *International Survey of Book Production During the Last Decades.* Paris: UNESCO, 1985.

United States. Copyright Office. *General Guide to the Copyright Act of 1976.* Washington, DC: Library of Congress, Copyright Office, 1977.

Veaner, Allen B. *Into the Fourth Century.* Philadelphia, PA: Drexel University, College of Information Studies, 1986.

Weisberg, Jacob. "Rough Trade: The Sad Decline of American Publishing." *The New Republic* 204 (17 June 1991):16 ff.

Werking, Richard Hume. "Collection Growth and Expenditures in Academic Libraries: A Preliminary Inquiry." *College and Research Libraries* 52 (January 1991):5–23.

Whitney, Gretchen. "The UNESCO Book Production Statistics." *Book Research Quarterly* 5 (Winter 1989–90):12–29.

Winston, Gordon. "Why Are Capital Costs Ignored by Colleges and Universities and What Are the Prospects for Change?" Paper DP-14, Williams Project on the Economics of Higher Education, July 1991.

Woolpy, Jerry. "The World in a Keystroke." *Earlhamite* 111 (Fall 1991):5–6.

Wyllys, R.E. "On the Analysis of Growth Rates of Library Collections and Expenditures." *Collection Management* 2 (1978):115–128.

Yavarkovsky, Jerome. "A University-based Electronic Publishing Network." *Educom Review* 25 (1990):14–20.

Appendix A
ARL Data Categories

The following ARL data categories were used in our analysis:

Pertaining to <u>collections</u>:

1. Number of Volumes Held

2. Number of Volumes Added Gross

3. Number of Volumes Added Net

4. Total Number of Current Serials Received

Pertaining to <u>personnel</u>:

1. Number of Professional Staff

2. Number of Non-Professional Staff

3. Total Number of Professional and Non-Professional Staff

4. Number of Student Assistants

Pertaining to <u>expenditures</u>:

1. Expenditures for Monographs

2. Expenditures for Current Serials

3. Expenditures for Other Library Materials

4. Miscellaneous Expenditures

5. Total Expenditures for Library Materials

6. Expenditures for Contract Binding

7. Salaries and Wages for Professional Staff

8. Salaries and Wages for Non-Professional Staff

9. Salaries and Wages for Student Assistants

10. Total Salaries and Wages

11. Other Operating Expenditures

12. Total Library Expenditures

HEGIS/IPEDS Data Categories and Definitions

The following HEGIS/IPEDS data categories were included in our analysis:

<u>Instruction</u>: The category Instruction and Research (entitled simply Instruction beginning in 1974/75) refers to the budgets of academic departments. According to the HEGIS questionnaire, it includes expenditures "of the colleges, schools, departments, and other instructional divisions of the institution and expenditures for departmental research and public service which are not separately budgeted."

<u>Libraries</u>: The HEGIS questionnaire simply states "expenditures for libraries."

<u>Total Educational and General Expenditures and Mandatory Transfers</u>: This category is the sum of "Instruction," "Research," "Public Service," "Academic Support" (which includes "Libraries"), "Student Services," "Institutional Support," "Operation and Maintenance of Plant," "Scholarships and Fellowships," and "Educational and General Mandatory Transfers."

ARL STATISTICS QUESTIONNAIRE, 1990–91

Please do not leave any lines blank. If an exact figure is unavailable, use "U/A." If a question is not applicable in your library, use "N/A." If the appropriate answer is zero or none, use "0".

Reporting Institution _____ Date Returned to ARL _____
Questionnaire Completed by (Name) _____
Position _____ Phone _____
Contact Person (if different) _____
Position _____ Phone _____

COLLECTIONS (*See instructions 7-11*)

1. **Volumes held June 30, 1990** (*See instruction 7*)
   (Exclude microforms, uncataloged govt. docs., maps, a/v material. Record figure reported last year or footnote adjusted figure on p. 4.)   _____

2. **Volumes added during year — Gross** (*See instruction 8*)
   (Exclude microforms, uncataloged govt. docs., maps, a/v material.)   _____

3. **Volumes withdrawn during year**
   (Exclude microforms, uncataloged govt. docs., maps, a/v material.)   _____

4. **Volumes added during year — Net** (Subtract line 3 from line 2)   _____

5. **Volumes held June 30, 1991** (Add line 1 to line 4)   _____

6. **Number of monographic volumes purchased** (*See instruction 9*)
   Volumes for which expenditures are reported on line 16. Footnote if titles.)   _____

7. **Number of current serials, including periodicals, purchased** (*See instruction 10*)   _____

8. **Number of current serials, including periodicals, received but not purchased** (Exchanges, gifts, deposits, etc.) (*See instructions 10-11*)   _____

9. **Total number of current serials received** (Add line 7 to line 8) (*See instruction 11*)   _____

10. **Total microform units held June 30, 1990** (*See instruction 12*) _____

11. **Total government documents <u>not counted above</u>** (pieces) (*See instruction 13*) _____

PERSONNEL (*See instructions 14-16. Round figures to nearest whole number.*)

12. **Number of professional staff, FTE** (*See instruction 15*) _____

13. **Number of nonprofessional staff, FTE** _____

14. **Number of student assistants, FTE** (*See instruction 16*) _____

15. **Total FTE staff (Add lines 12, 13, 14)** _____

	Dollars Canadian libraries only)	Dollars U.S. (Divide Canadian dollars by 1.1547)

EXPENDITURES (*See instructions 17-25*)

16. **Monographs** (Expenditures for volumes reported on line 6) (*See instruction 18*) _____ _____

17. **Current serials including periodicals** (*See instruction 19*) _____ _____

18. **Other library materials** (e.g., microforms, a/v, etc.) (*See instruction 20*) _____ _____

19. **Miscellaneous** (All materials fund expenditures not included above) (*See instruction 21*) _____ _____

20. **Total library materials** (Add lines 16, 17, 18, 19) _____ _____

21. **Contract binding** (*See instruction 22*) _____ _____

22. **Salaries and wages — professional staff** (*See instruction 23*) _____ _____

23. **Salaries and wages — nonprofessional staff** (*See instruction 23*) _____ _____

24. **Salaries and wages — student assistants** (*See instruction 24*) _____ _____

25. Total salaries and wages (Add lines 22,23,24)
(*See instruction* 23) \underline{\hspace{3cm}} \underline{\hspace{2cm}}

26. Other operating expenditures (*See instruction* 25) \underline{\hspace{3cm}} \underline{\hspace{2cm}}

27. Total library expenditures (Add lines 20, 21, 25, 26) \underline{\hspace{3cm}} \underline{\hspace{2cm}}

INTERLIBRARY LOANS (*See instruction* 26)

28. Total number of filled requests for materials <u>provided</u> to other libraries

29. Total number of filled requests for materials <u>received</u> from other libraries

PH.D. DEGREES (*See instructions 27-28*)

30. Number of Ph.D.s awarded in FY1990-91

31. Number of fields in which Ph.D.s can be awarded (*See instruction 28*)

ENROLLMENT — FALL 1990 (*See instruction 29; line numbers refer to IPEDS survey form*)

32. Total full-time students (Add line 8, columns 15 & 16, and line 14, cols. 15 & 16)

33. Total part-time students (Add line 22, columns 15 & 16, and line 28, cols. 15 & 16)

34. Total full-time graduate students (Line 14, columns 15 & 16)

35. Total part-time graduate students (Line 28, columns 15 & 16)

FACULTY (*See instruction 30*)

36. Number of full-time instructional faculty in FY1990–91

FOOTNOTES FOR ARL STATISTICS, 1990–91

(See instruction 31. Compare footnotes from previous year as they appear in the published ARL Statistics and revise as appropriate. For your convenience, a copy of your library's footnotes from last year is given on p. 4 of this questionnaire.)

1. **Law Library statistics are included.**

   _____ Yes _____ No _____ We do not have a Law Library

2. **Medical Library statistics are included.**

   _____ Yes _____ No _____ We do not have a Medical Library

3. **Other main campus libraries not included:**

   _____
   _____
   _____

4. **Figures include reports from branch campus libraries.** *(See instruction 5)*

   _____ Yes _____ No _____ We have only one campus.

5. **If branch campus libraries are included, please specify which campuses.**

   _____
   _____

6. **If branch campus libraries are <u>not</u> included, please specify which campuses:**

   _____
   _____

7. **Basis of volume count is:** _____ Physical _____ Bibliographic

8. **Count of current serials** (Questions 7-9) **includes government document serials.**

   _____ Yes _____ No

9. **Fringe benefits are included in expenditures for salaries and wages** (Questions 22-25).

   _____ Yes _____ No

10. **Other comments:**

    _____
    _____
    _____
    _____

FOOTNOTES FOR ARL STATISTICS, 1990–91

11. **Footnotes as published in the 1989–90** *ARL Statistics.* (Please indicate revisions, additions, and deletions as appropriate. If any footnotes published last year are unchanged, please mark to indicate that they are still valid. Note: number in ( ) refers to the column in Library Data Tables in 1989–90 *ARL Statistics*.)

PLEASE RETURN COMPLETED QUESTIONNAIRE TO THE ARL OFFICE BY **OCTOBER 11, 1991.**

Reporting Institution: _____

Library Director's Signature: _____

Association of Research Libraries, 1527 New Hampshire Avenue, N.W., Washington, D.C. 20036. (202) 232-2466; Fax (202) 462-7849. Please call Sarah Pritchard or Eileen Finer for assistance with the questionnaire; E-mail PRITCHAR@UMDC.BITNET or PRITCHAR@UMDC.UMD.EDU.

ARL STATISTICS, 1990–91

Instructions for Completing the Questionnaire

1. Definitions of the statistical categories used in this questionnaire can be found in *American National Standard for Library and Information Sciences and Related Publishing Practices - Library Statistics. Z39.7-1983.* (New York, American National Standards Institute, 1983.)

2. The questionnaire assumes a fiscal year ending June 30, 1991. If your fiscal year is different, please provide a footnote on p. 4 of the questionnaire.

3. **Please do not use decimals.** All figures should be rounded to the nearest whole number.

4. **Please do not leave any lines blank.** If an exact figure is unavailable, use **U/A**. If a question is not applicable to your library, use **N/A**. If the appropriate answer is zero or none, use **0**.

5. In a university that includes both main and branch campuses, <u>an effort should be made to report figures for the main campus only.</u> (The U.S. National Center for Education Statistics in its Integrated Postsecondary Education Data System (IPEDS) survey describes a **branch campus** as one "located in a community different from that of its parent institution ... beyond a reasonable commuting distance from the main campus ... The educational activities at the location must be organized on a relatively permanent basis ... and include course offerings for one or more complete college-level programs of at least one full year.") If figures for libraries located on branch campuses are reported, please provide an explanatory footnote on p. 4 of the questionnaire.

6. A **branch library** is defined as an auxiliary library service outlet with quarters separate from the central library of a system, which has a basic collection of books and other materials, a regular staffing level, and an established schedule. A branch library is administered <u>either</u> by the central library or (as in the case of some law and medical libraries) through the administrative structure of other units within the university. Departmental study/reading rooms are not included.

7. **Questions 1-6. Collections.** Use the ANSI Z39.7-1983 definition for **volume** as follows:

   a physical unit of any printed, typewritten, handwritten, mimeographed, or processed work, contained in one binding or portfolio, hardbound or paperbound, that has been cataloged, classified, and made ready for use.

   Include duplicates and bound volumes of periodicals. For purposes of this questionnaire, unclassified bound serials arranged in alphabetical order are considered classified. Exclude microforms, maps, nonprint materials, and uncataloged items. If any of these items cannot be excluded, please provide an explanatory footnote on p. 4 of the questionnaire.

Include government document volumes that are accessible through the library's catalogs regardless of whether they are separately shelved. "Classified" includes documents arranged by Superintendent of Documents, CODOC, or similar numbers. "Cataloged" includes documents for which records are provided by the library or downloaded from other sources into the library's card or online catalogs. Documents should, to the extent possible, be counted as they would if they were in bound volumes (e.g., 12 issues of an annual serial would be one or two volumes). Title and piece counts should not be considered the same as volume counts. If a volume count has not been kept, it may be estimated through sampling a representative group of title records and determining the corresponding number of volumes, then extrapolating to the rest of the collection. As an alternative, an estimate may be made using the following formulae:

> 52 *documents pieces per foot*
> 10 *"traditional" volumes per foot*
> 5.2 *documents pieces per volume*

If either formulas or sampling are used for deriving your count, please indicate in a footnote.

8. **Question 2.** Include only volumes cataloged, classified, and made ready for use. Include government documents if they have been included in the count of volumes on line 1.

9. **Question 6.** Report number of volumes purchased. Include all volumes for which an expenditure was made during 1990-91, including volumes paid for in advance but not received during the fiscal year. Include monographs in series and continuations. If only number of titles purchased can be reported, please report the data and provide an explanatory footnote on p. 4 of the questionnaire. **Note:** This question is concerned with volumes purchased rather than volumes received or cataloged. Question 16 requests the expenditure for the volumes counted here.

10. **Questions 7-9. Serials.** Report the total number of subscriptions, not titles. Include duplicate subscriptions and, to the extent possible, all government document serials even if housed in a separate documents collection. Verify the inclusion or exclusion of document serials in the notes section on p. 3. Exclude monographic and publishers' series. A **serial** is

    a publication issued in successive parts, usually at regular intervals, and as a rule, intended to be continued indefinitely. Serials include periodicals, newspapers, annuals (reports, yearbooks, etc.), memoirs, proceedings, and transactions of societies.

11. **Question 8.** If separate counts of nonpurchased and purchased serials are not available, report only the total number of current serials received on line 9, and report U/A for lines 7 and 8.

12. **Question 10. Microforms.** Report the total number of physical units: reels of microfilm, microcards, and microprint and microfiche sheets. Include all government documents in microform; footnote on p.4 if documents are excluded.

13. **Question 11. Government documents.** Report the total number of physical units (pieces) of government documents in paper format that have not already been counted in any of the above categories. Include local, state, national and international documents; include documents purchased from a commercial source if shelved with separate documents collections and not counted above. Include serials and monographs. To estimate pieces from a measurement of linear feet, use the formula *1 foot = 52 pieces* and indicate in a footnote that the count is based on this estimate. Exclude microforms and nonprint formats such as maps or CD-ROMs.

14. **Questions 12-15. Personnel.** Report the number of staff in filled positions, or positions that are only temporarily vacant. Include cost recovery positions and staff hired for special projects and grants, but provide an explanatory footnote indicating the number of such staff. If such staff cannot be included, provide a footnote on p. 4 of the questionnaire. To compute full-time equivalents of part-time employees and student assistants, take the total number of hours worked by part-time employees in each category and divide it by the number of hours considered by the reporting library to be a full-time work week. **Round figures to the nearest whole numbers.**

15. **Question 12.** Since the criteria for determining professional status vary among libraries, there is no attempt to define the term "professional." Each library should report those staff members it considers professional, including, when appropriate, staff who are not librarians in the strict sense of the term, for example computer experts, systems analysts, or budget officers.

16. **Question 14.** Report the total FTE (see instruction 14) of student assistants employed on an hourly basis whose wages are paid from funds under library control or from a budget other than the library's, including federal work-study programs. Exclude maintenance and custodial staff.

17. **Questions 16-27. Expenditures.** Report all expenditures of funds that come to the library from the regular institutional budget, and from sources such as research grants, special projects, gifts and endowments, and fees for service. (For question 24 include non-library funds; see instruction #24.) Do not report encumbrances of funds that have not yet been expended. Canadian libraries should report expenditures in both Canadian and U.S. dollars. To determine figures in U.S. dollars, divide Canadian dollar amounts by 1.1547, the average monthly noon exchange rate published in the Bank of Canada *Review* for the period July 1990-June 1991. **Please round figures to the nearest dollar.**

18. **Question 16.** Report expenditures for volumes counted on line 6.

19. **Question 17.** Exclude monographic and publishers' series, and encumbrances.

20. **Question 18.** Include all materials except monographs and current serials, e.g. microforms, backfiles of serials, charts and maps, audiovisual materials, manuscripts, electronic media, etc. If expenditures for these materials are included in lines 16 and/or 17 and cannot be disaggregated, please report U/A and provide a footnote on page 4. Do not include encumbrances.

21. **Question 19.** Include any other **materials funds expenditures** not included in questions 16-18, e.g., expenditures for bibliographic utilities, literature searching, security devices, memberships for the purposes of publications, etc. Please list categories, with amounts, in a footnote on p. 4 of the questionnaire. **Note:** If your library does <u>not</u> use materials funds for non-materials expenditures — i.e., such expenditures are included in "Other Operating Expenditures" — **report 0, not U/A**, on line 19.

22. **Question 21.** Include only <u>contract</u> expenditures for binding done outside the library. If all binding is done in-house, state this fact and give in-house expenditures in a footnote on p. 4 of the questionnaire; do not include personnel expenditures.

23. **Questions 22-25.** Exclude fringe benefits. If professional and nonprofessional salaries cannot be separated, enter U/A on lines 22 and 23 and enter total staff on line 25.

24. **Questions 24-25.** Report 100% of student wages regardless of budgetary source of funds. Include federal and local funds for work study students.

25. **Question 26.** Exclude expenditures for buildings, maintenance, and fringe benefits.

26. **Questions 28-29. Interlibrary Loan.** Report the number of filled requests for material provided to other libraries on line 28. Report the number of filled requests for material received from other libraries <u>or document delivery services</u> on line 29. On both lines, include originals, photocopies, and materials sent by telefacsimile or other forms of electronic transmission. Do not include transactions between libraries covered by this questionnaire.

27. **Questions 30-31. Ph.D. Degrees.** Report the number awarded during the 1990-91 fiscal year. Please note that only the number of <u>Ph.D.</u> degrees are to be counted. Statistics on all other advanced degrees (e.g., D.Ed., D.P.A., M.D., J.D.) are not included in this survey. If you are unable to provide a figure for Ph.D.s only, please add a footnote on p. 4 of the questionnaire.

28. **Question 31.** For the purposes of this report, Ph.D. fields are defined as the specific discipline specialties enumerated in the U.S. Department of Education's Integrated Postsecondary Education Data System (IPEDS) "Completions" Survey. Although the IPEDS form requests figures for all doctoral degrees, only fields in which <u>Ph.D.s</u> are awarded should be reported on the ARL questionnaire. Any exceptions should be footnoted on p. 4 of the questionnaire.

186 · Appendix A

29. **Questions 32-35.** Enrollment. U.S. libraries should use the Fall 1990 enrollment figures reported to the Department of Education on the form entitled "Integrated Postsecondary Education Data System, Fall Enrollment 1990." The line and column numbers on the IPEDS form for each category are noted on the questionnaire. Please check these figures against the enrollment figures reported to ARL last year to ensure consistency and accuracy. **Note:** In the past, the number of part-time students reported was FTE; the number now reported to IPEDS is a head count of part-time students. Canadian libraries should note that the category "graduate students" as reported here includes all post-baccalaureate students.

30. **Question 36. Instructional Faculty.** Instructional faculty are defined by the U.S. Dept. of Education as

    "those members of the instruction/research staff who are employed full-time as defined by the institution, including faculty with released time for research and faculty on sabbatical leave. Full-time counts <u>exclude</u> faculty who are employed to teach fewer than two semesters, three quarters, two trimesters, or two four-month sessions; replacements for faculty on sabbatical leave or leave without pay; faculty for preclinical and clinical medicine; faculty who are donating their services; faculty who are members of military organizations and paid on a different pay scale from civilian employees; academic officers, whose   primary duties are administrative; and graduate students who assist in the instruction of courses."

    Please be sure the number reported, and the basis for counting, are consistent with those for 1989–90 (unless in previous years faculty were counted who should have been excluded according to the above definition). Please footnote any discrepancies.

31. **Footnotes.** Reporting libraries are urged to record in the footnote section any information that would clarify the figures submitted, e.g.,   the inclusion of branch campus libraries (see instruction #5 for definition of branch campus libraries). Explanatory footnotes will be included with the published statistics. Please make an effort to word your footnotes in a manner consistent with notes appearing in the published report, so that the ARL Office can interpret your footnotes correctly. For your convenience, a copy of your footnotes from the 1989–90 ARL Statistics is included in the questionnaire. **Please update these notes, delete them, or indicate that they remain valid.** Note that the number in parentheses refers to the appropriate column on the Library Data Tables in the published Statistics, not to a line number on the questionnaire.)

30. After the questionnaire has been completed, compare the figures with those submitted last year. On occasion, an error will be detected because of an unusual difference between numbers submitted this year and those for the preceding year. If an unusual change has occurred, provide an explanatory footnote on p. 4 of the questionnaire.

31. Before returning the questionnaire, **please check all arithmetic**. Many follow-up telephone calls can be avoided if calculation errors are corrected before the questionnaire is submitted.

32. Return one copy of the questionnaire to the ARL Office by **October 11, 1991**. If there are any questions about the procedure to be followed in completing these questionnaires, contact the ARL Office. Please be sure the library director has signed the questionnaire before it is returned.

Appendix B
Appendix Tables

Chapter 2

Appendix Table 2.1: Volumes Added Gross, by University, 1963–91

Chapter 3

Appendix Table 3.1: Total Library Expenditures as a Percent of Educational and General Expenditures, by University, 1966–90

Appendix Table 2.3: Total Library Expenditures as a Percent of Instruction and Departmental Research Expenditures, by University, 1966–90

Appendix Table 3.3: Total Library Expenditures, by College, 1977–90

Appendix Table 3.4: Total Library Expenditures as a Percent of Educational and General Expenditures, by College, 1977–90

Appendix Table 3.5: Total Library Expenditures as a Percent of Instruction and Departmental Research Expenditures, by College, 1977–90

Chapter 5

Appendix Table 5.1: UNESCO Counts of Numbers of Titles Published in Selected Countries, 1937-88

Chapter 5

Appendix Table 6.1: Average Price for Hardbound Books in Various Fields, 1963–90

Appendix Table 6.2: Average Price for Periodicals in Various Fields, 1960–90

Appendix Table 2.1
Volumes Added Gross, by University

	1963	1964	1965	1966	1967	1968	1969	1970	1971	1972	1973	1974	1975	1976	1977
Priv-1 Universities															
Chicago	85,913	94,763	109,390	122,560	126,513	161,807	152,778	150,517	128,822	151,165	141,232	166,813	147,594	151,584	136,621
Columbia	97,430	103,143	123,311	121,894	137,395	132,281	126,675	131,381	138,874	153,308	135,671	117,795	121,963	118,569	133,838
Cornell	141,932	167,969	152,822	171,012	177,979	194,903	195,756	177,418	175,232	130,976	158,024	127,274	125,716	112,609	113,315
Princeton	85,800	67,711	78,733	106,390	108,480	81,340	97,029	95,911	121,356	99,824	108,687	103,510	106,983	101,527	101,083
Stanford	108,119	101,381	181,745	177,684	204,053	195,450	214,397	254,355	173,721	159,229	160,337	177,926	134,377	145,367	142,515
Yale	119,946	146,978	128,281	178,937	189,484	200,031	173,642	198,324	200,788	219,719	195,366	190,750	179,298	180,882	204,903
Private-1 Avg	106,523	113,658	129,047	146,413	157,317	160,969	160,046	167,984	156,466	152,370	149,886	147,345	135,989	135,090	138,713
Pub-1 Universities															
UC Berkeley	143,864	152,288	165,594	155,175	172,814	162,167	159,950	176,688	176,308	156,379	159,855	174,820	167,155	167,877	166,718
Iowa	47,715	46,259	51,864	63,762	72,385	69,300	71,705	75,183	96,540	91,218	80,487	71,015	72,615	94,977	101,933
Michigan	125,756	135,894	134,811	142,859	178,406	185,421	205,100	183,748	176,963	148,826	154,156	139,669	137,857	138,999	155,000
N Carolina	71,120	62,855	96,336	70,962	74,149	91,200	76,899	102,328	101,748	83,562	76,667	88,974	88,613	77,030	89,186
Virginia	59,839	60,696	87,719	156,460	79,569	78,606	84,521	91,002	83,258	83,277	93,304	99,355	100,873	83,325	94,437
Wisconsin	72,536	149,397	135,792	108,647	136,225	129,783	147,618	143,114	118,194	109,430	138,350	116,047	153,448	162,683	110,666
Public-1 Avg	86,805	101,232	112,019	116,311	118,925	119,413	124,299	128,677	125,502	112,115	117,137	114,980	120,094	120,815	119,657
Priv-2 Universities															
Boston	28,529	36,280	34,709	32,324	56,722	61,994	63,851	77,874	80,049	89,029	83,354	70,985	64,295	62,830	48,754
Georgetown	28,825	29,094	42,443	28,496	28,995	25,482	28,810	38,663	47,683	54,859	47,667	49,430	55,552	49,214	47,356
New York Univ.	74,702	56,439	62,264	114,505	166,746	216,780	102,323	97,093	101,200	107,815	68,662	85,470	107,354	89,316	110,062
Northwestern	58,481	59,150	68,796	65,605	77,416	90,617	84,828	79,883	89,046	65,925	78,032	78,690	80,366	89,984	92,907
Southern California	45,049	53,532	47,177	57,331	49,046	58,101	59,403	50,946	72,113	82,927	61,329	49,133	58,788	60,941	73,718
Wash U. (St. Louis)	38,467	34,038	42,600	86,675	75,762	73,730	74,229	79,376	78,415	83,918	73,850	62,978	60,430	63,204	55,877
Private-2 Avg	45,676	44,756	49,665	64,156	75,781	87,784	68,907	70,639	78,084	80,746	68,816	66,114	71,131	69,248	71,446
Pub-2 Universities															
Florida	46,976	44,336	52,268	65,592	68,014	62,304	73,645	63,958	67,127	63,398	70,822	75,421	54,376	49,085	47,266
Iowa State	14,468	15,658	20,091	22,215	26,310	31,620	46,493	61,509	55,740	63,092	60,219	68,699	62,758	63,742	60,015
Maryland	52,317	60,072	70,768	85,495	76,647	170,705	93,323	100,528	109,530	123,400	128,688	132,067	93,284	104,055	60,448
Michigan State	66,770	65,194	97,660	80,840	102,269	123,698	118,508	129,633	136,823	113,768	118,077	110,595	104,146	101,403	91,760
Rutgers	61,151	60,073	72,781	85,993	80,859	104,869	122,148	145,855	133,530	114,932	105,737	95,425	113,178	97,175	108,352
Washington State	16,518	22,500	24,672	29,094	35,786	39,136	41,975	38,045	46,643	43,232	45,023	43,661	41,416	54,227	31,991
Public-2 Avg	43,033	44,639	56,373	61,538	64,981	88,722	82,682	89,921	91,566	86,970	88,094	87,645	78,193	78,281	66,639

Notes: Some figures have been modified to adjust for missing data and anomolies.

Appendix B · 191

Appendix Table 2.1 (continued)
Volumes Added Gross, by University

	1978	1979	1980	1981	1982	1983	1984	1985	1986	1987	1988	1989	1990	1991
Priv-1 Universities														
Chicago	144,349	175,566	144,844	147,928	132,269	130,629	113,234	107,187	101,139	113,277	111,663	96,350	133,000	140,573
Columbia	126,679	116,343	119,830	113,313	99,053	103,145	113,319	113,182	121,669	121,276	140,135	166,476	148,872	122,219
Cornell	122,417	118,031	119,880	117,666	109,564	126,398	119,467	121,347	129,755	136,220	141,067	126,812	189,070	145,157
Princeton	101,492	82,632	90,722	78,284	72,843	95,131	123,993	121,724	107,393	109,948	114,716	110,908	105,659	135,239
Stanford	145,360	134,807	141,208	131,303	137,403	163,099	145,725	159,118	154,742	167,055	161,451	150,725	144,450	142,689
Yale	182,703	189,195	173,003	190,521	161,097	172,165	175,623	153,258	174,739	160,953	156,767	188,616	147,841	166,244
Private-1 Avg	137,167	136,096	131,581	129,836	118,705	131,761	131,894	129,303	131,573	134,788	137,633	139,981	144,815	142,020
Pub-1 Universities														
UC Berkeley	163,666	170,683	175,785	164,148	160,755	169,389	162,708	171,751	175,963	165,623	168,629	166,727	202,202	188,270
Iowa	89,905	89,522	87,154	74,813	64,437	87,282	88,818	88,085	99,184	89,049	96,134	93,259	91,083	77,204
Michigan	125,901	119,465	129,046	136,571	128,911	142,708	115,645	133,971	145,349	135,011	130,358	119,296	141,606	128,783
N Carolina	104,093	120,668	129,652	127,764	123,940	121,501	118,048	128,456	120,512	118,308	121,680	127,838	123,899	112,134
Virginia	93,244	112,121	92,357	94,088	90,164	91,553	86,975	106,668	110,519	102,177	112,535	102,040	106,577	93,717
Wisconsin	122,815	129,271	158,344	105,136	113,953	121,531	121,685	119,204	121,882	101,202	100,070	108,834	139,194	111,900
Public-1 Avg	116,604	123,622	128,723	117,087	113,693	122,327	115,647	124,689	128,902	118,562	121,568	119,666	134,094	118,668
Priv-2 Universities														
Boston	47,043	42,098	45,177	47,504	59,367	64,566	54,739	62,603	56,764	54,674	57,964	53,264	58,075	54,835
Georgetown	47,392	68,377	56,036	46,328	57,336	65,155	63,351	72,228	65,104	66,530	60,872	71,282	64,921	60,718
New York Univ	112,067	104,658	93,966	91,911	89,290	60,479	66,984	76,763	74,656	72,755	73,914	74,628	73,877	74,899
Northwestern	70,062	81,433	84,113	75,208	75,707	103,280	81,186	101,153	97,577	80,511	88,466	89,619	80,284	85,912
Southern California	79,862	96,881	87,981	81,278	76,293	82,782	87,318	82,878	68,058	57,372	61,762	55,566	54,528	67,119
Wash U. (St Louis)	53,474	53,133	51,166	43,638	47,950	45,795	46,645	47,519	43,333	49,487	53,136	53,549	59,093	70,316
Private-2 Avg	68,317	74,430	69,740	64,311	67,657	70,343	66,704	73,857	67,582	63,555	66,019	66,318	65,130	68,967
Pub-2 Universities														
Florida	93,653	139,413	84,840	75,578	57,737	69,272	69,487	70,284	78,902	79,610	105,778	100,629	127,167	110,496
Iowa State	69,588	59,446	64,326	56,984	50,271	55,590	59,158	60,563	63,139	55,895	55,534	43,218	43,204	44,848
Maryland	62,539	57,712	74,427	75,903	62,969	53,113	49,211	78,889	87,563	83,642	76,396	68,531	67,348	71,330
Michigan State	94,469	101,898	103,284	101,118	105,928	103,774	103,386	89,768	81,521	86,578	116,564	114,521	114,116	81,083
Rutgers	110,176	90,402	75,109	88,432	59,730	99,269	61,146	80,856	86,082	114,490	116,017	113,110	102,635	97,601
Washington State	40,725	48,477	43,015	37,392	40,821	43,998	39,353	36,555	39,594	38,511	36,280	34,616	47,300	39,714
Public-2 Avg	78,525	82,891	74,167	72,568	62,909	70,836	63,624	69,486	72,800	76,454	84,428	79,104	83,628	74,179

Notes: Some figures have been modified to adjust for missing data and anomolies.

Appendix Table 3.1
Total Library Expenditures as a Percent of Educational and General Expenditures (Universities)

	1966	1967	1968	1969	1970	1971	1972	1973	1974	1975	1976	1977	1978	1979	1980	1981	1982	1983	1984	1985	1986	1987	1988	1989	1990
Private 1 Universities																									
Chicago	1.45	1.47	1.71	2.98	2.77	2.72	2.73	3.66	3.74	3.99	4.04	4.20	3.45	3.95	4.00	4.01	3.68	3.90	3.94	4.14	4.19	3.86	3.68	3.60	3.20
Columbia	2.99	2.67	—	—	—	3.35	3.52	3.46	3.42	3.49	3.60	3.41	3.23	3.22	3.35	3.19	3.10	3.22	3.25	3.15	3.23	3.41	3.26	2.99	2.93
Cornell	3.86	—	—	—	6.00	6.44	3.49	5.24	6.97	6.85	6.81	6.78	6.85	5.98	6.55	6.30	5.43	5.69	5.87	5.44	5.36	5.19	4.71	4.96	5.26
Princeton	3.51	3.93	4.44	5.46	5.26	5.23	6.49	6.86	6.66	6.82	7.29	7.09	7.22	7.76	7.97	7.63	7.45	7.51	7.51	7.57	6.58	5.73	5.54	5.37	5.43
Stanford	3.45	3.39	3.72	5.22	5.26	5.83	5.57	5.33	5.59	4.72	4.62	4.65	4.19	4.32	4.25	4.11	4.09	3.91	4.12	4.07	4.18	3.34	3.34	3.26	3.34
Yale	5.93	6.02	5.76	6.68	6.71	5.06	5.61	6.05	6.36	6.33	5.92	5.99	5.33	5.42	5.10	4.94	4.83	4.94	4.77	4.50	4.69	4.70	4.94	4.72	4.65
Four University Avg	3.59	3.70	3.91	5.09	5.00	4.71	5.10	5.48	5.59	5.46	5.47	5.48	5.05	5.36	5.33	5.17	5.01	5.06	5.09	5.07	4.91	4.41	4.38	4.24	4.16
Six University Avg	3.53	3.50	3.91	5.09	5.20	4.77	4.57	5.10	5.46	5.37	5.38	5.35	5.05	5.11	5.20	5.03	4.76	4.86	4.91	4.81	4.70	4.37	4.25	4.15	4.14
Public 1 Universities																									
UC Berkeley	—	—	—	—	—	—	4.16	3.97	4.22	4.27	4.27	4.34	5.07	5.24	4.38	4.08	4.62	4.41	4.49	4.41	4.26	4.56	4.39	4.32	4.21
Iowa	2.53	2.58	2.44	2.66	2.45	2.50	2.30	2.21	2.23	3.16	3.29	3.16	3.63	3.40	3.17	3.22	3.12	2.99	2.82	2.85	2.92	3.17	2.85	2.63	2.69
Michigan-Ann Arbor	—	—	—	—	—	3.37	3.06	3.00	3.05	3.00	3.04	3.15	2.86	2.82	2.93	3.03	3.09	3.07	2.78	2.82	3.00	3.16	2.82	2.65	2.60
N Carolina-Chap Hill	3.34	3.14	3.17	3.58	3.58	3.73	3.26	3.19	2.93	2.46	2.96	3.10	3.24	3.09	3.11	3.14	3.25	3.12	3.26	3.10	3.12	3.16	3.05	2.93	2.57
Virginia	4.49	3.07	2.87	3.72	4.23	5.78	6.04	6.18	6.54	6.56	5.51	5.63	6.18	5.79	5.64	5.00	5.06	5.05	5.06	5.36	5.10	4.67	4.35	4.52	4.22
Wisconsin-Madison	—	—	—	—	—	2.48	2.61	2.10	2.56	2.64	2.37	2.62	2.62	2.70	2.74	2.73	2.88	2.77	2.88	2.89	2.61	2.66	2.58	2.42	2.57
Three University Avg	3.45	2.93	2.83	3.32	3.42	4.00	3.86	3.86	3.90	4.06	3.92	3.96	4.35	4.09	3.97	3.79	3.81	3.72	3.72	3.77	3.71	3.67	3.42	3.36	3.16
Six University Avg	—	—	—	—	—	—	3.57	3.44	3.59	3.68	3.57	3.59	3.93	3.84	3.66	3.53	3.67	3.57	3.55	3.57	3.50	3.56	3.34	3.24	3.14
Private 2 Universities																									
Boston	2.63	2.52	2.68	3.17	3.86	3.96	3.92	3.38	3.12	2.91	2.80	2.71	2.52	2.36	2.58	2.64	2.73	2.55	2.34	2.30	2.40	2.25	2.00	2.01	1.95
Georgetown	1.73	1.53	1.66	2.99	3.16	3.63	3.60	3.61	3.87	4.18	3.62	3.81	4.14	4.37	4.31	4.57	4.18	4.54	4.76	5.13	4.78	3.87	3.98	4.04	4.26
New York Univ	1.70	1.55	1.79	1.64	1.71	1.80	1.90	2.01	2.24	2.49	2.36	2.52	2.55	2.46	2.27	2.39	2.49	2.49	2.53	2.47	2.50	2.45	2.32	2.43	2.45
Northwestern	3.32	3.69	4.22	3.82	3.96	4.51	4.62	4.47	4.47	4.51	4.53	4.50	4.75	4.58	3.66	3.50	3.60	3.59	3.10	3.09	3.20	2.83	2.91	2.97	2.89
Southern California	2.99	3.10	2.70	2.72	2.68	2.86	2.65	2.54	2.62	2.52	2.38	2.32	2.40	2.39	2.39	2.45	2.52	2.48	2.39	2.33	2.28	2.55	2.58	2.38	2.55
Wash U-St. Louis	3.59	3.57	3.83	3.96	4.00	3.82	3.57	3.45	3.31	3.21	3.11	3.22	2.77	2.71	2.67	2.65	2.66	2.64	2.70	2.44	2.37	2.34	2.26	2.18	2.10
Six University Avg	2.66	2.66	2.81	3.05	3.23	3.43	3.38	3.24	3.27	3.30	3.13	3.15	3.19	3.15	2.98	3.03	3.03	3.05	2.97	2.96	2.92	2.71	2.68	2.67	2.70
Six University Avg	2.66	2.66	2.81	3.05	3.23	3.43	3.38	3.24	3.27	3.30	3.13	3.15	3.19	3.15	2.98	3.03	3.03	3.05	2.97	2.96	2.92	2.71	2.68	2.67	2.70
Public 2 Universities																									
Florida	2.68	2.52	2.25	2.24	2.21	2.10	2.13	2.36	2.39	2.21	2.02	2.06	3.31	3.53	2.70	2.63	2.30	2.20	1.85	2.06	2.10	2.15	2.32	2.28	2.32
Iowa State	1.29	1.53	1.66	2.74	3.34	3.41	3.64	3.51	3.03	2.70	3.43	3.39	2.89	2.87	2.73	2.77	2.86	2.69	2.78	2.66	2.53	2.48	2.25	2.26	2.54
Maryland	2.30	2.61	—	—	—	4.64	4.67	5.33	5.91	4.34	4.40	3.92	3.97	3.89	4.22	4.10	3.35	2.95	3.03	3.15	3.29	3.11	2.92	2.68	3.31
Michigan State	1.98	2.00	2.29	2.26	2.38	2.14	2.15	2.04	2.17	2.06	2.04	2.14	2.05	2.07	2.12	2.14	2.31	2.30	2.28	2.31	2.30	2.20	2.24	2.24	2.13
Rutgers	3.16	—	—	—	—	4.41	5.31	6.76	6.13	5.89	4.78	5.87	5.90	6.05	5.63	4.81	5.02	4.96	5.07	5.42	5.43	3.31	3.98	3.81	3.56
Washington State	3.20	3.00	2.96	3.43	3.34	3.47	3.50	3.58	3.76	3.52	4.13	3.83	3.86	3.89	3.77	3.43	3.36	3.39	3.21	3.21	3.45	3.35	3.54	3.30	3.05
Four University Avg	2.28	2.26	2.29	2.67	2.82	2.78	2.86	2.87	2.84	2.62	2.91	2.85	3.03	3.09	2.83	2.74	2.71	2.65	2.53	2.56	2.59	2.55	2.59	2.52	2.51
Six University Avg	—	—	—	—	—	3.36	3.57	3.93	3.90	3.45	3.47	3.53	3.66	3.72	3.53	3.31	3.20	3.08	3.03	3.14	3.18	2.77	2.87	2.76	2.82
Seventeen Univ Avg	2.93	2.86	2.95	3.49	3.63	3.76	3.75	3.79	3.83	3.79	3.77	3.77	3.79	3.82	3.67	3.60	3.56	3.55	3.49	3.51	3.45	3.24	3.19	3.13	3.08
Twenty-four Univ Avg	—	—	—	—	—	—	3.77	3.93	4.05	3.95	3.89	3.91	3.96	3.95	3.84	3.73	3.67	3.64	3.62	3.62	3.58	3.35	3.28	3.21	3.20

Appendix Table 3.2
Total Library Expenditures as a Percent of Instruction and Departmental Research (Universities)

	1966	1967	1968	1969	1970	1971	1972	1973	1974	1975	1976	1977	1978	1979	1980	1981	1982	1983	1984	1985	1986	1987	1988	1989	1990
Private 1 Universities																									
Chicago	12.35	11.47	11.69	11.00	11.17	11.11	11.99	12.37	13.79	10.45	10.04	10.44	8.61	9.84	8.74	8.68	7.73	7.70	7.84	8.40	8.47	7.92	7.25	6.97	6.29
Columbia	8.91	7.35	—	—	—	8.01	8.57	10.19	9.79	9.33	9.69	8.64	8.49	8.28	9.00	8.05	7.34	7.38	10.08	10.45	10.34	10.55	10.01	9.51	9.43
Cornell	15.87	—	—	—	—	—	12.59	17.32	22.11	20.37	20.71	21.42	22.96	20.00	20.46	19.55	16.80	17.67	18.23	18.26	18.44	18.17	16.34	16.97	16.79
Princeton	20.84	22.36	24.92	25.15	26.32	24.98	25.14	26.09	24.08	23.33	21.41	21.08	21.88	24.09	25.30	24.34	25.96	25.06	24.60	25.05	21.74	22.46	22.51	22.53	22.13
Stanford	12.27	16.67	16.07	16.65	16.36	15.76	16.68	15.20	15.97	18.16	17.65	18.26	16.68	16.93	16.29	17.24	17.19	15.43	16.72	16.50	16.95	14.58	14.61	14.25	14.31
Yale	17.05	18.01	19.60	22.71	21.77	19.21	20.61	20.51	20.40	16.79	15.29	15.92	13.42	13.66	13.08	12.71	12.84	13.09	12.61	11.53	12.08	11.81	12.61	11.73	11.22
Four University Avg	15.63	17.13	18.07	18.88	18.91	17.76	18.61	18.54	18.56	17.18	16.10	16.42	15.15	16.13	15.85	15.74	15.93	15.32	15.44	15.37	14.81	14.19	14.24	13.87	13.49
Six University Avg							15.93	16.95	17.69	16.41	15.80	15.96	15.34	15.47	15.48	15.09	14.64	14.39	15.02	15.03	14.67	14.25	13.89	13.66	13.36
Public 1 Universities																									
UC Berkeley	8.29	8.27	7.26	9.05	7.36		11.29	11.44	11.95	12.12	12.15	12.45	14.57	15.13	12.75	11.57	13.20	13.01	13.53	13.08	12.78	13.07	12.96	13.22	13.24
Iowa						7.58	8.44	8.42	8.46	7.02	7.17	7.76	7.88	7.63	7.39	7.31	6.94	6.66	6.29	6.48	6.87	7.47	6.92	6.94	6.89
Michigan-Ann Arbor						10.26	9.24	9.09	8.83	8.26	7.91	8.00	7.26	7.35	7.75	7.99	8.17	8.21	7.56	7.81	8.51	8.44	8.55	8.01	8.10
N Carolina-Chap Hill	7.52	7.10	7.25	10.39	9.75	9.49	8.49	8.07	7.26	7.41	7.60	7.85	8.02	7.16	6.62	7.90	8.02	7.57	7.88	7.44	7.32	7.45	7.58	7.29	6.23
Virginia	12.02	13.01	11.94	13.12	12.89	15.40	15.55	15.21	16.29	15.09	12.15	14.52	15.72	14.00	14.20	12.75	13.31	12.26	12.43	13.63	12.80	12.52	11.61	12.40	11.63
Wisconsin-Madison						7.87	8.65	7.88	8.85	8.33	8.16	7.40	7.91	8.33	8.72	8.55	9.07	8.84	9.28	9.59	9.00	9.15	8.91	9.55	10.36
Three University Avg	9.28	9.46	8.81	10.85	10.00		11.78	11.57	11.83	11.54	10.63	11.61	12.77	12.10	11.19	10.74	11.51	10.95	11.28	11.38	10.97	11.01	10.72	10.97	10.37
Six University Avg							10.28	10.02	10.27	9.70	9.19	9.66	10.23	9.93	9.57	9.35	9.79	9.42	9.49	9.67	9.55	9.68	9.42	9.57	9.41
Private 2 Universities																									
Boston	6.53	7.07	7.92	9.92	10.88	10.42	10.57	9.33	9.10	9.04	8.38	8.25	7.77	7.53	8.06	7.77	7.43	7.13	6.55	6.44	6.85	5.77	4.92	5.05	5.08
Georgetown	7.36	6.49	7.68	9.74	10.25	11.25	10.88	10.47	10.45	7.56	6.73	6.74	7.48	9.93	9.49	10.15	9.95	10.87	11.70	12.84	11.67	10.08	10.37	11.15	12.68
New York Univ	6.72	6.80	7.72	7.19	7.60	8.23	8.80	9.30	10.30	7.55	6.75	6.16	6.08	5.85	5.17	5.32	5.47	5.31	5.19	5.38	5.41	5.42	5.17	5.35	5.45
Northwestern	8.64	9.51	10.74	10.20	10.35	11.88	12.74	11.65	11.04	9.24	9.27	9.21	9.91	9.63	7.72	7.40	8.17	8.50	7.60	7.49	7.97	7.52	7.90	7.74	7.70
Southern California	6.31	6.62	5.92	5.53	5.59	5.73	4.92	6.38	6.31	5.61	5.42	5.28	5.67	5.62	5.32	5.34	5.33	5.21	4.92	5.05	5.05	5.88	5.77	5.31	6.31
Wash U-St. Louis	10.91	11.90	13.39	13.50	12.71	11.75	10.83	10.37	9.35	8.00	7.73	7.79	6.96	7.02	6.82	6.66	5.26	6.72	6.65	6.16	6.09	5.88	5.72	5.43	4.18
Six University Avg	7.75	8.06	8.90	9.35	9.56	9.88	9.79	9.58	9.43	7.83	7.38	7.24	7.31	7.60	7.10	7.11	6.94	7.29	7.10	7.22	7.17	6.73	6.64	6.67	6.90
Six University Avg							9.79	9.58	9.43	7.83	7.38	7.24	7.31	7.60	7.10	7.11	6.94	7.29	7.10	7.22	7.17	6.73	6.64	6.67	6.90
Public 2 Universities																									
Florida	9.66	8.67	7.20	7.56	6.66	5.87	6.14	6.73	6.71	4.33	4.07	6.46	10.19	8.59	6.35	6.40	5.18	5.39	4.70	5.24	5.52	6.34	6.87	8.57	7.34
Iowa State	5.01	5.13	5.93	6.87	8.22	8.21	8.78	8.43	9.62	8.80	8.95	9.46	8.32	8.33	7.99	7.77	7.85	7.51	7.80	7.43	7.26	7.42	7.63	7.69	8.27
Maryland	5.97	6.85	—	—	—	10.21	10.55	11.94	13.44	9.82	9.93	8.00	9.03	8.93	9.99	10.61	8.67	8.23	8.19	8.50	9.09	9.25	9.21	8.90	9.94
Michigan State	5.24	5.29	6.08	5.99	6.30	5.41	5.30	5.11	5.49	5.19	4.95	5.23	4.81	4.96	4.90	4.94	5.39	5.51	5.44	5.62	5.65	5.55	5.62	5.61	5.35
Rutgers	8.25	—	—	—	—	11.64	13.15	16.73	16.30	13.47	12.70	16.14	14.14	14.57	12.41	11.43	11.82	11.84	12.26	12.97	13.40	9.32	11.28	10.78	10.16
Washington State	10.52	8.81	9.48	11.13	11.10	11.24	11.58	10.66	10.91	10.98	13.17	11.81	12.13	12.49	12.41	10.92	10.92	10.77	9.88	9.77	10.47	10.31	10.68	10.20	10.08
Four University Avg	7.61	6.97	7.17	7.89	8.07	7.68	7.95	7.73	8.18	7.33	7.78	8.24	8.86	8.59	7.91	7.51	7.33	7.29	6.95	7.01	7.23	7.41	7.70	8.02	7.76
Six University Avg							9.25	9.93	10.41	8.77	8.96	9.52	9.77	9.64	9.17	8.68	8.30	8.21	8.04	8.25	8.57	8.03	8.55	8.62	8.52
Seventeen Univ Avg	9.84	10.19	10.63	11.51	11.49	11.38	11.61	11.43	11.50	10.27	9.81	10.13	10.09	10.19	9.76	9.62	9.59	9.45	9.34	9.44	9.30	9.07	9.04	9.07	8.89
Twenty-four Univ Avg							11.31	11.62	11.95	10.68	10.33	10.60	10.66	10.66	10.33	10.06	9.92	9.83	9.91	10.05	9.99	9.67	9.62	9.63	9.55

Appendix Table 3.3
Total Library Expenditures of Colleges

	1989 FTE Enroll	1977	1978	1979	1980	1981	1982	1983	1984	1985	1986	1987	1988	1989	1990	Average (1977–90)	Average (1977–84)	Average (1985–90)
Bowdoin	1,418	525,290	562,050	633,650	672,240	714,550	822,060	905,400	995,550	1,144,860	1,349,122	1,357,000	1,574,000	1,671,659	1,926,718	990,277	728,849	1,289,051
Bryn Mawr	1,629	1,021,310	1,086,190	1,251,100	1,374,960	1,298,210	1,489,740	1,549,300	1,806,090	1,862,380	1,874,792	1,980,942	2,362,404	1,804,953	2,333,349	1,539,715	1,359,613	1,745,546
Carleton	1,889	575,500	591,310	608,020	486,600	821,330	891,620	1,007,310	1,091,070	965,280	1,226,273	1,398,163	1,470,058	1,575,642	1,719,029	961,814	759,095	1,193,492
Davidson	1,391	402,640	432,690	476,690	520,950	585,700	656,500	723,670	805,610	857,230	917,621	962,799	1,139,317	1,230,273	1,262,543	731,616	575,556	909,969
Grinnell	1,293	323,210	357,560	393,300	444,070	566,750	667,040	697,420	789,730	867,840	991,147	1,112,557	1,269,631	1,336,964	1,540,956	757,212	529,885	1,017,014
Haverford	1,103	539,440	519,850	521,560	572,110	631,110	714,910	828,070	881,030	950,850	696,488	838,399	827,697	954,625	1,570,135	736,418	651,010	834,028
Middlebury	2,050	557,000	596,000	684,000	743,000	829,000	938,000	1,083,180	1,173,000	1,272,000	1,417,000	1,629,000	1,819,000	2,036,000	2,122,000	1,126,545	825,398	1,470,714
Mount Holyoke	1,976	603,750	632,040	676,220	771,640	899,050	1,021,210	1,136,970	1,233,920	1,284,600	1,377,121	1,534,000	1,618,000	1,719,000	1,981,282	1,099,254	871,850	1,359,143
Oberlin	2,797	1,021,950	1,158,070	1,293,620	1,436,700	1,613,410	1,833,150	2,115,240	2,417,210	2,561,990	2,643,273	2,685,778	3,388,789	3,611,556	4,162,602	2,129,556	1,611,169	2,721,998
Pomona	1,421	452,440	513,620	542,970	550,200	638,000	673,000	868,000	926,000	1,021,000	1,026,000	1,160,000	1,276,169	1,337,604	1,452,391	829,160	645,529	1,039,023
Reed	1,234	313,575	334,720	350,390	370,320	441,600	444,260	515,430	503,160	536,910	564,451	613,224	676,091	837,156	942,327	496,241	409,182	595,737
Smith	2,928	1,349,710	1,420,940	1,534,350	1,613,690	1,756,760	1,978,910	2,237,820	2,407,880	2,660,390	3,580,040	3,023,660	3,116,493	3,321,361	3,671,509	2,244,901	1,787,508	2,767,636
Swarthmore	1,355	786,550	830,230	936,930	930,330	1,022,100	1,133,000	1,209,000	1,406,000	1,435,000	1,509,000	1,579,000	1,730,700	1,882,400	2,353,397	1,249,576	1,031,768	1,498,500
Trinity	1,844	586,970	609,480	678,760	765,800	852,140	962,900	1,110,820	1,236,520	1,303,160	1,491,134	1,619,518	1,747,901	2,027,348	2,183,205	1,145,044	850,424	1,481,752
Vassar	2,312	933,150	1,021,560	1,124,610	1,240,810	711,820	1,598,120	1,759,620	1,909,980	1,969,750	2,202,914	2,023,920	2,138,000	2,527,000	2,905,000	1,604,417	1,287,459	1,966,655
Average	1,776	666,166	711,087	780,411	832,895	892,102	1,054,961	1,183,150	1,305,517	1,379,549	1,524,425	1,567,864	1,743,617	1,858,236	2,141,763	1,176,116	928,286	1,459,351

Notes: Swarthmore (1988) and Trinity (1987) were calculated as the average of the neighboring years. (True values were missing.) Reed (1977), Oberlin (1989, 1990), Smith (1989), Mount Holyoke (1990), Grinnell (1990), and Bowdoin (1990) were imputed so as to reflect rate of change of other component institutions between missing and subsequent (in the case of Reed) or previous (in the case of Oberlin, Smith, Mount Holyoke, Grinnell, and Bowdoin) years.

Appendix Table 3.4
Total Library Expenditures as a Percent of Educational and General Expenditures (Colleges)

	1989 FTE Enroll	1977	1978	1979	1980	1981	1982	1983	1984	1985	1986	1987	1988	1989	1990	Average (1977–90)	Average (1977–84)	Average (1985–90)
Bowdoin	1,418	5.09	4.94	5.25	5.00	4.74	4.86	4.75	4.92	4.95	5.39	4.59	4.63	4.82	4.75	4.58	4.95	4.16
Bryn Mawr	1,629	8.36	8.39	8.93	8.93	7.18	6.97	6.66	7.29	7.04	6.61	6.34	7.38	5.21	5.95	6.75	7.84	5.51
Carleton	1,889	5.99	5.65	5.37	3.78	5.73	5.34	5.23	5.13	4.07	4.68	4.90	4.69	4.63	4.48	4.64	5.28	3.92
Davidson	1,391	6.03	6.00	6.05	6.13	6.00	5.67	5.31	5.57	5.39	5.25	4.64	4.91	4.49	4.12	5.04	5.85	4.11
Grinnell	1,293	4.59	4.53	4.59	4.59	5.10	5.09	4.88	4.99	4.74	4.80	4.26	5.30	4.86	4.99	4.49	4.79	4.14
Haverford	1,103	8.62	7.46	6.65	6.94	6.37	6.01	6.42	6.29	5.88	3.93	4.21	3.97	4.37	6.48	5.57	6.85	4.12
Middlebury	2,050	5.22	4.99	5.48	5.27	5.09	4.76	4.72	4.64	4.61	4.68	4.57	4.66	4.22	3.98	4.46	5.02	3.82
Mount Holyoke	1,976	5.58	5.27	5.12	5.07	4.97	4.92	4.78	4.64	4.35	4.20	4.13	4.03	5.23	5.37	4.51	5.04	3.90
Oberlin	2,797	5.26	5.91	6.17	5.75	5.79	5.80	5.94	6.20	6.23	5.90	5.44	6.46	6.25	6.60	5.58	5.85	5.27
Pomona	1,421	4.43	4.65	4.31	4.14	4.24	3.82	4.32	4.27	4.35	3.96	3.51	2.37	3.63	3.13	3.68	4.27	3.00
Reed	1,234	4.65	4.93	4.79	4.09	4.28	3.87	4.37	4.13	3.62	3.61	1.93	3.21	3.72	4.49	3.71	4.39	2.94
Smith	2,928	6.69	6.69	6.73	6.07	5.81	5.76	5.72	5.60	5.51	6.72	5.26	5.01	4.75	4.59	5.39	6.13	4.55
Swarthmore	1,355	8.42	8.18	8.45	7.66	7.20	6.76	6.05	6.01	5.67	5.47	5.01	5.20	5.25	5.80	6.08	7.34	4.63
Trinity	1,844	5.83	5.46	5.46	5.96	5.89	5.91	5.94	6.06	5.67	6.00	5.79	5.52	5.77	5.57	5.39	5.82	4.90
Vassar	2,312	6.69	6.67	6.84	6.84	3.44	6.96	6.82	6.77	6.41	6.55	5.13	5.03	5.13	5.41	5.65	6.38	4.81
Average	1,776	6.10	5.98	6.01	5.75	5.46	5.50	5.46	5.50	5.23	5.18	4.65	4.83	4.82	5.05	5.03	5.72	4.25

Notes: For "Total Library Expenditures," Swarthmore (1988) and Trinity (1987) were calculated as the average of the neighboring years.
Reed (1977), Oberlin (1989, 1990), Smith (1989), Mount Holyoke (1990), Grinnell (1990), and Bowdoin (1990) were imputed so as to reflect rate of change of other component institutions between missing and subsequent (in the case of Reed) or previous (in the case of Oberlin, Smith, Mount Holyoke, Grinnell, and Bowdoin) years.
For "Total Educational & General Expenditures," Grinnell (1990) and Mount Holyoke (1990) were imputed so as to reflect rate of change of other component institutions between missing and previous year.

Appendix Table 3.5
Total Library Expenditures as a Percent of Instruction and Departmental Research Expenditures

	1989 FTE Enroll	1977	1978	1979	1980	1981	1982	1983	1984	1985	1986	1987	1988	1989	1990	Average (1977–90)	Average (1977–84)	Average (1985–90)
Bowdoin	1,418	20.40	19.78	21.56	20.89	21.19	22.24	21.74	17.24	18.01	19.87	19.02	18.59	16.28	17.43	18.28	20.63	15.60
Bryn Mawr	1,629	21.79	21.55	23.31	23.31	22.70	20.51	19.31	21.79	20.90	20.80	19.63	22.82	16.64	19.38	19.63	21.78	17.17
Carleton	1,889	15.04	14.18	13.71	9.41	14.61	13.48	13.85	13.40	10.79	12.37	13.20	12.90	13.01	12.55	12.17	13.46	10.69
Davidson	1,391	15.17	15.44	15.85	15.90	15.79	15.40	15.14	15.49	15.30	14.77	15.77	17.28	15.93	15.27	14.57	15.52	13.47
Grinnell	1,293	11.34	11.37	13.05	13.33	15.13	15.88	15.33	16.71	17.57	16.65	17.41	16.96	15.97	16.83	14.24	14.02	14.49
Haverford	1,103	25.86	21.85	19.55	2–	19.87	19.38	20.60	19.39	17.44	12.49	13.29	12.67	13.96	20.71	17.14	20.81	12.94
Middlebury	2,050	15.58	15.15	16.00	14.80	18.71	14.87	15.29	14.55	14.06	13.94	13.44	13.67	12.32	12.07	13.63	15.62	11.36
Mount Holyoke	1,976	13.25	12.34	12.49	12.90	13.54	13.76	13.31	12.56	12.48	12.74	14.80	14.07	14.08	14.84	12.48	13.02	11.86
Oberlin	2,797	14.48	14.98	15.31	17.23	17.15	17.76	18.43	18.24	18.35	17.62	17.23	19.87	19.46	20.90	16.47	16.70	16.20
Pomona	1,421	12.38	13.66	13.00	12.72	13.24	12.13	14.37	14.14	14.21	13.50	13.65	13.60	13.20	13.65	12.50	13.21	11.69
Reed	1,234	12.45	12.70	12.45	12.08	12.91	11.47	12.83	11.70	11.16	11.74	11.15	11.74	12.65	12.26	11.29	12.32	10.10
Smith	2,928	17.52	16.95	17.47	16.21	15.85	16.03	15.59	15.63	15.80	19.61	15.56	15.44	15.06	15.07	15.19	16.41	13.79
Swarthmore	1,355	21.20	20.20	21.63	19.81	20.10	18.21	17.57	19.18	17.54	17.16	16.42	16.59	16.25	17.34	17.28	19.74	14.47
Trinity	1,844	13.72	12.79	13.81	14.48	14.52	14.48	14.41	14.65	13.85	13.94	13.27	12.81	13.39	12.92	12.87	14.11	14.47
Vassar	2,312	15.88	15.97	16.75	16.64	8.85	17.23	17.12	17.08	16.12	16.80	15.26	14.82	15.01	16.67	14.68	15.69	11.45
Average	1,776	16.40	15.93	16.40	15.98	16.28	16.19	16.32	16.12	15.57	15.60	15.27	15.59	14.88	15.86	14.83	16.20	13.25

Notes: For "Total Library Expenditures," Swarthmore (1988) and Trinity (1987) were calculated as the average of the neighboring years. Reed (1977), Oberlin (1989, 1990), Smith (1989), Mount Holyoke (1990), Grinnell (1990), and Bowdoin (1990)were imputed so as to reflect rate of change of other component institutions between missing and subsequent (in the case of Reed) or previous (in the case of Oberlin, Smith, Mount Holyoke, Grinnell, and Bowdoin) years.
For "Total Instruction & Departmental Research Expenditures," Grinnell (1990) and Mount Holyoke (1990) were imputed so as to reflect rate of change of other component institutions between missing and previous year.

Appendix Table 5.1
UNESCO Counts of Numbers of Titles Published in Selected Countries

YEAR	France	West Germany	Italy	Netherl.	Switzer.	U.K.	U.S.A.	All Total	W. Europe Total
1937			10715	5896	2119	17286	10912		59893
1938	8124		10351	6172	2162	16091	11067		62625
1939	6762		10465	6554	1802	14913	10640		62716
1940	5400		9798	4885	1705	10732	11328		63620
1941	3888		10282	4943	2510	7581	11112		65902
1942	6008		9062	3320	2875	7241	9525		66091
1943	7918		7173	2836	3358	6705	8325		64600
1944	8680		2268	1847	3831	6781	6970		65282
1945	6987		4159	2436	3949	6747	6548		73149
1946	8892		5654	6593	4001	11411	7735		69897
1947	13419		5770	7086	3810	13046	9182		77661
1948	14143		7841	8047	4691	14686	9897		80956
1949	9908		10513	6722	3562	17034	10892		83946
1950	9993	13860	8904	6537	3527	17072	11022	70915	85291
1951	10298	14094	10035	6531	3601	18066	11255	73880	89887
1952	10410	13913	9679	6728	3245	18741	11840	74556	96391
1953	10017	15738	8972	7045	3591	18257	12050	75670	
1954	10622	16240	9158	7019	3675	19188	11901	77803	
1955	11793	16660	6494	7353	3829	19962	12589	78680	
1956	11079	16185	5653	7319	4023	20341	12866	77466	
1957	10364	15710	6989	7284	4216	20719	13142	78424	
1958	11725	19618	7297	7817	4549	22143	13462	86611	
1959	12032	16532	7684	8588	4371	20690	14876	84773	
1960	11872	21103	8111	7893	4899	23783	15012	92673	
1961	12705	21877	7401	9010	5070	24893	18060	99016	
1962	13282	21481	8797	9674	5633	25079	21901	105847	
1963	11478	24216	8785	9448	5341	26023	25784	111075	
1964	13479	25204	9585	10026	5470	26123	28451	118338	
1965	17138	25994	10385	10193	6367	26314	54378	105769	

Notes: See footnote 18 in text for sources of data and various qualifications concerning interpretation.

Appendix Table 5.1 (continued)
UNESCO Counts of Numbers of Titles Published in Selected Countries

YEAR	France	West Germany	Italy	Netherl.	Switzer.	U.K.	U.S.A.	All Total	W. Europe Total
1966	19289	22720	10593	10582	6232	28789	58517	156722	98205
1967	19021	29524	8215	11262	6041	29564	58877	162504	103627
1968	18646	30223	8868	11174	6228	31372	59247	165758	106511
1969	21958	33454	8440	11204	7505	32321	62083	176965	114882
1970	22935	45369	8615	11159	8321	33441	79530	209370	129840
1971	22372	40354	8283	10827	7205	33275	80569	202885	122316
1972	24497	42914	8381	11800	8449	33109	82405	211555	129150
1973	27186	45474	8122	11640	7942	35177	83724	219265	135541
1974	28245	48034	9443	11440	9310	32133	81023	219628	138605
1975	28808	40616	9187	12028	9928	35526	85287	221380	136093
1976	29371	44477	9463	12557	9989	34340	84542	224739	140197
1977	31673	48736	10016	13111	9894	36196	87780	237506	149726
1978	21225	50950	10679	13393	9453	38641	85126	229467	144341
1979	25019	59666	11162	13429	10765	41864	88721	250626	161905
1980	32318	64761	12029	14591	10362	48069	86377	268507	182130
1981	37308	56568	13457	13939	10544	42972	91517	266305	174788
1982	42186	58592	12926	13324	11405	48029	95649	282111	186462
1983	37576	58489	13718	13267	11355	50981	108783	294169	185386
1984	37189	48836	14312	13209	11806	51411	104051	280814	176763
1985	37860	54442	15545	12629	11822	52994	102038	287330	185292
1986	38701	63724	16297	13368	11626	57845	107269	308830	201561
1987	43505	65670	17109	13329	12410	59837	114178	326038	211860
1988	39026	68611	19620	13845	12698	62051	113069	328920	215851

Notes: See footnote 18 in text for sources of data and various qualifications concerning interpretation.

Appendix Table 6.1
Average Price for Hardbound Books in Various Fields

YEAR	Agric.	Art	Biogr.	Bus.	Educ.	Hist.	Law	Lit.	Med.	Music	Psych.	Drama	Relig.	Sci.	Econ.	Techn.	AVG
1963	7.60	10.32	6.56	9.47	5.71	6.75	9.09	5.31	10.98	7.79		5.38	4.48	11.22	8.70	10.69	8.00
1964	7.69	10.68	6.65	9.74	5.50	7.73	9.96	5.16	11.22	6.98		5.01	4.63	10.99	7.63	11.02	8.04
1965	8.04	10.60	7.65	9.68	5.78	8.83	10.64	6.90	11.88	8.04		4.70	6.72	12.13	8.43	12.30	8.82
1966	8.37	14.73	7.57	9.47	5.61	8.56	10.95	6.67	12.37	8.15		5.71	5.38	11.72	9.08	12.51	9.12
1967	8.50	12.32	8.52	9.77	5.61	8.21	12.52	6.84	12.78	8.69		5.99	5.66	12.15	8.65	12.86	9.27
1968	10.23	12.00	9.03	10.00	6.22	9.03	12.79	7.83	12.55	8.65		7.06	6.02	11.90	9.68	12.93	9.73
1969	8.97	12.65	10.63	10.47	6.99	10.64	13.39	8.67	13.89	9.03		8.20	6.75	11.96	9.65	13.37	10.35
1970	10.42	16.16	11.49	12.45	10.75	14.75	16.41	11.05	18.05	11.44	10.72	9.35	8.51	14.95	12.38	14.91	12.87
1971	13.64	16.41	11.64	12.60	7.81	12.97	18.37	11.43	17.58	11.73	10.77	9.15	8.48	15.94	17.47	15.28	13.37
1972	10.94	14.94	12.80	12.45	10.26	14.92	17.15	12.03	16.19	13.53	10.44	10.62	9.80	16.05	16.93	16.11	13.65
1973	11.79	15.42	12.70	13.23	9.67	15.56	16.78	11.48	15.92	12.68	10.89	10.50	9.35	17.34	12.22	15.38	13.33
1974	13.21	14.46	12.64	14.97	10.33	15.69	18.24	12.63	18.92	14.43	11.57	9.93	9.70	20.83	17.47	17.74	14.75
1975	13.72	17.90	14.09	16.54	10.81	15.85	23.22	14.89	22.15	14.83	12.75	10.76	11.16	22.81	21.65	19.66	16.67
1976	15.40	20.29	15.05	17.18	12.91	16.74	20.65	15.07	24.04	16.38	14.27	12.66	12.44	24.42	22.79	21.19	17.81
1977	16.24	21.24	15.34	18.00	12.95	17.12	25.04	15.78	24.00	20.13	14.43	13.63	12.26	24.88	29.88	23.61	19.34
1978	17.24	21.11	15.76	19.27	13.86	17.20	24.26	17.98	25.01	24.68	14.75	14.86	13.04	26.20	29.66	22.64	20.18
1979	20.94	21.95	17.52	23.11	15.10	19.79	29.44	17.64	29.27	18.93	17.98	15.83	14.83	30.59	43.57	27.82	23.09
1980	27.55	27.70	19.77	22.45	17.01	22.78	33.25	18.70	34.28	21.79	21.70	17.85	17.61	37.45	31.76	33.64	25.57
1981	31.88	31.87	21.85	23.09	18.77	23.15	36.30	19.79	36.47	25.82	22.41	19.34	18.54	40.63	29.28	36.76	27.57
1982	33.54	31.68	22.27	25.58	20.74	26.25	35.61	21.40	38.88	26.42	23.28	19.96	17.89	44.44	45.12	40.65	30.03
1983	33.39	33.79	22.40	27.72	21.56	24.96	39.09	23.63	39.84	25.77	25.72	22.42	16.74	47.04	43.34	41.14	30.86
1984	34.92	33.03	22.53	26.01	24.47	27.53	43.88	23.57	40.65	27.79	29.70	26.75	17.76	46.57	33.35	45.80	31.64
1985	36.77	35.15	22.20	28.84	27.28	27.02	41.70	24.53	44.36	28.79	28.11	22.14	19.31	51.19	33.33	50.37	32.87
1986	39.26	35.41	22.96	30.72	26.11	28.44	49.20	25.73	49.99	32.59	29.65	25.11	21.60	55.65	30.34	55.00	35.21
1987	46.24	37.71	25.04	33.31	31.58	31.74	49.65	28.70	57.68	35.82	33.32	28.46	24.51	62.16	34.38	60.24	39.15
1988	49.36	39.96	25.99	37.51	33.55	33.44	50.85	30.85	66.59	36.95	34.75	28.02	31.10	66.91	37.25	65.26	42.24
1989	51.05	50.30	27.34	37.94	37.62	37.95	58.62	32.74	69.87	41.73	36.55	31.12	28.12	68.90	41.26	71.04	45.71
1990	55.4	41.74	28.95	45.17	37.8	36.48	56.81	35.81	71.87	41.53	40.3	32.27	31.24	75.2	41.97	76.61	47.26

Notes: Price data are taken from various issues of the *Publishers Weekly.* "AVG" is an unweighted average of all fields except "Phil/Psych."

Appendix Table 6.2
Average Price for Periodicals in Various Fields

	Agric.	Bus./ Econ.	Chem./ Phys.	Educ.	Engin.	Fine/ App. Arts	Hist.	Jrnlsm. Comm.	Labor/ Industr. Rel.	Law	Libr. Sci.	Lit./ Lang.	Math., Botany, Geol., Gn'l Sci.	Med.	Phil., Rel.	Pol. Sci.	Psych.	Soc., Anthr.	Zool.	AVG
1960	2.84	5.34	11.30	4.19	5.86	4.94	4.60	4.08	2.26	5.81	3.71	4.05	7.27	10.28	4.05	4.77	9.57	4.52	8.90	5.70
1961	3.03	5.48	12.28	4.34	6.14	5.13	4.84	4.14	2.35	6.28	3.83	4.22	7.70	11.19	4.20	4.95	10.65	4.59	8.95	6.02
1962	3.34	5.68	13.95	4.62	6.48	5.65	5.08	4.37	2.44	6.82	4.20	4.47	8.28	11.49	4.26	4.98	11.34	4.89	9.05	6.39
1963	3.49	6.06	16.07	4.90	6.69	5.89	5.29	4.67	2.51	6.93	4.43	4.56	9.58	12.22	4.39	5.23	11.45	4.91	9.51	6.78
1964	3.71	6.26	16.50	5.00	7.32	5.92	5.31	4.90	2.66	7.27	5.01	4.66	10.70	13.25	4.40	5.33	11.82	5.07	9.83	7.10
1965	3.83	6.39	18.42	5.14	7.70	5.92	5.30	5.32	2.66	7.49	5.15	4.65	10.96	14.02	4.64	5.57	11.85	5.26	10.31	7.40
1966	4.11	6.89	19.73	5.58	8.19	6.25	5.53	5.41	2.75	7.68	5.51	4.78	12.29	15.53	4.76	5.84	12.67	5.48	10.96	7.89
1967	4.34	7.09	22.35	5.97	9.04	6.52	5.74	5.55	2.85	8.00	5.64	5.08	13.75	17.97	5.01	5.86	13.82	5.86	12.53	8.58
1968	4.74	7.45	24.26	6.26	10.02	6.61	6.03	5.63	3.04	8.77	6.26	5.30	15.42	19.42	5.30	6.14	14.33	6.09	13.49	9.19
1969	4.97	8.07	26.60	6.79	10.98	6.97	6.34	6.00	3.16	9.31	6.85	5.74	16.71	20.77	5.49	6.53	15.40	6.38	14.18	9.85
1970	5.17	9.03	33.45	7.09	12.07	7.50	6.90	6.36	3.59	9.84	7.88	6.15	18.11	23.44	5.84	6.72	17.12	7.31	16.86	11.08
1971	5.74	9.72	38.31	8.25	13.28	8.17	7.40	6.91	3.88	10.19	8.65	6.88	20.06	27.00	6.71	7.23	18.70	7.92	19.29	12.33
1972	6.35	9.95	45.46	9.51	16.04	8.42	8.25	8.68	3.92	11.15	9.40	7.45	22.63	29.59	7.16	8.47	20.98	9.12	22.39	13.94
1973	7.21	12.25	56.61	11.34	23.37	9.16	8.95	13.05	6.02	13.19	10.48	8.14	26.99	33.60	8.12	9.69	23.17	11.28	24.07	16.67
1974	8.12	13.90	65.47	12.64	24.38	9.84	9.57	13.13	6.71	14.56	12.53	9.16	30.27	36.31	8.84	10.79	25.79	13.03	24.78	18.41
1975	9.70	15.26	76.84	14.72	26.64	11.09	11.14	14.70	7.40	15.00	14.18	10.41	35.95	42.38	9.05	12.79	27.51	14.85	27.37	20.89
1976	10.75	16.98	86.72	16.00	31.87	12.42	11.94	15.90	10.33	16.21	15.96	11.60	42.51	47.47	9.94	13.09	29.39	17.11	31.34	23.55
1977	11.58	18.62	93.76	17.54	35.77	13.72	12.64	16.97	11.24	17.36	16.97	11.82	47.13	51.31	10.89	14.83	31.74	19.68	33.69	25.65
1978	12.48	21.09	108.22	19.49	39.77	14.82	13.71	19.95	13.24	18.74	19.34	12.84	54.16	57.06	11.66	15.62	34.21	21.58	37.05	28.69
1979	14.16	22.97	118.33	21.61	42.95	17.42	14.67	23.86	15.74	20.98	20.82	13.84	58.84	63.31	13.25	17.47	38.10	23.70	40.15	31.69
1980	15.24	25.42	137.45	23.45	49.15	18.67	15.77	27.34	18.84	23.00	23.25	15.30	67.54	73.37	14.73	19.30	41.95	27.56	44.58	35.89
1981	17.24	28.88	156.30	25.18	54.55	20.51	17.96	29.80	21.68	24.80	28.47	17.30	75.62	86.38	15.40	22.69	47.27	31.37	48.32	40.51
1982	19.76	32.67	177.94	28.18	61.54	23.35	20.37	33.91	24.72	27.53	33.52	19.39	87.99	102.87	17.92	25.89	54.21	36.38	61.07	46.80
1983	21.27	35.67	207.94	31.36	73.18	25.17	22.43	37.39	29.22	29.66	36.72	21.19	97.26	112.72	20.21	28.97	59.31	40.54	70.74	52.68
1984	24.06	38.87	228.90	34.01	78.70	26.90	23.68	39.25	29.87	31.31	38.85	23.02	106.56	125.57	21.94	32.43	69.74	43.87	78.35	57.68
1985	26.05	44.41	238.43	37.81	84.38	27.03	25.55	46.08	34.75	35.13	40.66	24.18	116.93	137.92	24.30	32.72	76.34	50.87	90.75	62.86
1986	28.71	47.15	264.05	40.47	92.66	28.28	26.04	47.54	37.14	36.44	42.82	25.21	129.95	151.77	24.85	35.19	83.71	56.31	102.83	68.48
1987	31.14	50.39	294.05	43.30	103.49	30.58	27.64	50.66	38.65	39.82	48.42	26.21	146.08	169.36	25.60	39.95	92.05	60.29	112.91	75.29
1988	33.56	53.89	329.99	47.95	114.83	32.43	30.16	53.39	44.06	43.33	51.61	28.04	159.33	180.67	27.09	41.55	100.57	64.27	127.33	82.32
1989	36.62	57.93	367.99	51.43	128.37	35.07	32.27	58.13	50.65	46.01	54.45	29.41	173.21	199.22	28.62	45.03	114.52	66.73	142.13	90.41
1990	42.43	63.25	412.7	56.3	138.8	36.89	35.51	60.85	52.74	50.32	57.34	30.63	188.2	217.9	30.76	49.67	125.31	77.61	153.78	99.0

Notes: Price data are taken from various issues of the *Library Journal.* "AVG" is an unweighted average of all fields.

Glossary

Association of Research Libraries (ARL) Representing the 120 principal research libraries that serve major North American (Canada and the U.S.) research institutions and based in Washington, DC, ARL's mission is to identify and influence forces affecting the future of research libraries in the process of scholarly communication. ARL articulates the concerns of research libraries and their institutions and promotes equitable access to recorded knowledge in support of teaching, research, and scholarship through coalitions for action, information policy development, and innovation in research library programs.

ASCII (American Standard Code for Information Interchange) A standard code designed by the American National Standards Institute (ANSI) to facilitate information interchange between unstandardized data processing and communications equipment. The code, consisting of eight bits including a parity bit, can represent a character set of 128 alphabetic, numeric, and special symbols.

Coalition for Networked Information (CNI) Formed by ARL, CAUSE, and EDUCOM in March 1990 to "advance scholarship and intellectual productivity" by promoting the provision of information resources on existing and future telecommunications networks and the linkage of research libraries to these networks and their respective constituencies.

Council on Library Resources (CLR) A private operating foundation based in Washington, DC, which aims to assist libraries, especially academic and research libraries, to take advantage of emerging technologies to improve operational efficiencies and services for library users.

Commission on Preservation and Access (CPA) A non-profit organization incorporated in 1988 for the purpose of fostering development and supporting systematic and purposeful collaboration in order to ensure the preservation of the public and documentary universe in all formats and to provide equitable access to that information.

Educational and General Expenditures (E&G) The sum of total institutional expenditures for instruction, research, public service, academic support, student services, institutional support, operation and maintenance of plant, scholarships and fellowships, mandatory transfers, and (in recent years) non-mandatory transfers.

EDUCOM A non-profit consortium, based in Washington, DC, of colleges and universities concerned with computing and communications issues. It focuses extensively on networking and integrating computing into the curriculum.

GNP Deflator An updated version of the general price index used to adjust the U.S. gross national product (GNP) for inflation.

Higher Education General Information Survey (HEGIS) The predecessor of the IPEDS surveys of post-secondary education institutions by the National Center for Education Statistics, U.S. Department of Education.

Integrated Postsecondary Education Data System (IPEDS) This system surveys all postsecondary institutions, including universities and colleges, as well as institutions offering technical and vocational education beyond the high school level. Administered by the National Center for Education Statistics (NCES), U.S. Department of Education, IPEDS began in 1986, replacing and supplementing HEGIS.

Instruction and Departmental Research (I&DR) Expenditures of colleges, schools, departments, and other instructional divisions of the institution. Expenditures for departmental research and public service that are not separately budgeted are included in this classification. The instruction category includes general academic instruction, occupational and vocational instruction, special session instruction, community education, preparatory and adult basic education, and remedial and tutorial instruction conducted by teaching faculty for the institution's students.

Materials and Binding Materials are expenditures for items purchased in a given time period, usually a fiscal year, to be added to a library's collections, including books (monographs), periodicals and other serials, microforms, audiovisual materials, and other library materials; also sometimes includes expenditures for electronic searching and other modes of access to information that is not added to library collections in traditional ways. Binding is expenditures for contract binding, usually by commercial binders.

MARC Derived from "machine-readable cataloging," U.S. MARC is a standard for representation and communication of bibliographical and related information in machine-readable form.

Online Computer Library Center (OCLC) A not-for-profit organization serving over 15,000 member libraries worldwide, OCLC provides services such as cataloging copy, interlibrary loan transactions, and retrospective conversion of bibliographic records. It has a bibliographic database currently in excess of 24 million unique bibliographic titles and 500 million items. It has expanded its services into reference, public services, and publishing.

Other Operating Expenditures Any expenditures other than those for materials, binding, and salaries and wages, from a library's budget during a given time period.

Research Libraries Group (RLG) A not-for-profit membership corporation of over 120 libraries, archives, historical societies, museums and other institutions devoted to improving access to information that supports research and learning.

Research Libraries Information Network (RLIN) Owned and operated by RLG, RLIN serves the information access and management needs of its member institutions as well as individuals worldwide. It contains over 55 million bibliographic records.

Retrospective Conversion The process of converting bibliographic records from print to a machine-readable format.

Salaries and Wages All monies paid in salaries and wages from the library's budget during a given period of time before deductions for all staff paid.

Total Library Expenditures (TLE) The sum of expenditures for materials, binding, salaries and wages, and other operating expenditures during a given period of time.

Volume A physical unit of any printed, typewritten, handwritten, mimeographed, or processed work, contained in one binding or portfolio, hardbound or paper-bound, which has been cataloged, classified, and made ready for use. (The study follows the definition used by ARL.)

Volumes Added Gross The volumes cataloged by a library during a given period, usually a fiscal year. Not to be confused with acquisitions, although sometimes considered a surrogate for them.